About the

A *USA Today* bestselling author of one hundred novels in twenty languages, **Tara Taylor Quinn** has sold more than seven million copies. Known for her intense emotional fiction, Ms Quinn's novels have received critical acclaim in the UK and most recently from Harvard. She is the recipient of the Reader's Choice Award, and has appeared often on local and national TV, including *CBS Sunday Morning*. For TTQ offers, news, and competitions, visit tarataylorquinn.com

Andrea Laurence is an award-winning contemporary author who has been a lover of books and writing stories since she learned to read. A dedicated West Coast girl transplanted into the Deep South, she's constantly trying to develop a taste for sweet tea and grits while caring for her husband and two spoiled golden retrievers. You can contact Andrea at her website: andrealaurence.com

Elizabeth Bevarly is the award-winning, nationally number one bestselling author of more than seventy novels and novellas. Her books have been translated into two dozen languages and published in three dozen countries. An honours graduate of the University of Louisville, she has called home places as diverse as San Juan, Puerto Rico and Haddonfield, New Jersey, but now resides back in her native Kentucky with her husband, her son, and two neurotic cats (as if there were any other kind).

A CEO for Christmas

TARA TAYLOR QUINN

ANDREA LAURENCE

ELIZABETH BEVARLY

MILLS & BOON

First Published in Great Britain 2023
By Mills & Boon, an imprint of HarperCollins*Publishers* Ltd,
1 London Bridge Street, London, SE1 9GF

www.harpercollins.co.uk

HarperCollins*Publishers*
Macken House, 39/40 Mayor Street Upper,
Dublin 1, D01 C9W8, Ireland

ISBN: 978-0-263-32118-0

MIX
Paper | Supporting
responsible forestry
FSC™ C007454

FSC
www.fsc.org

This book is produced from independently certified FSC™ paper to ensure responsible forest management.

For more information visit: www.harpercollins.co.uk/green

Printed and Bound in the UK using 100% Renewable Electricity at CPI Group (UK) Ltd, Croydon, CR0 4YY

AN UNEXPECTED CHRISTMAS BABY

TARA TAYLOR QUINN

For my mom, Penny Gumser, who is still showing me the meaning of the word *mother*.

And who still reads every word I publish. I love you!

Chapter One

"Dearly Beloved, we are gathered here today—"

The ceremony had been a dumb idea.

"—Alana Gold Collins to rest. The Father tells us—"

Hands together at his belt buckle, Flint Collins stared down past the crease in his black pants to the tips of his shiny black shoes. *Alana Gold.* Such a lofty name. Like a movie star or something.

Alana Gold. Not much about his mother's life had been golden. Except her hair, he supposed. Back when she'd been young and pretty. Before the hard life, the drugs and prison had had their way with her.

"—all will be changed at the last sounding of the bell..."

The Father might have imparted that message. The Bible surely did, according to the preacher he'd hired to give his mother a funeral. *Dearly Beloved,* he'd said. That would be Flint. The dearly beloved. All one of him.

He'd never known any other family. Didn't even know who his father was.

Footsteps sounded behind him and he stiffened. He'd asked her to come—the caseworker he'd only met two days before. To do the…exchange.

Dearly Beloved. In her own way Alana had loved Flint deeply. Just as, he was absolutely certain, she'd loved the "inheritance" she'd left him. One he hadn't known about. One he hadn't yet seen. One that had arrived behind him.

"So take comfort…" That was the preacher again. For the life of him, Flint drew a blank on his name as he glanced up and met the older man's compassionate gaze.

He almost burst out with a humorless chuckle. *Comfort?* Was the man serious? Flint's whole life had imploded in the space of a week. Would never, ever, be the same or be what he'd planned it to be. Comfort was a pipe dream at best.

As the footsteps in the grass behind him slowed, as he felt the warmth of a body close to him, Flint stood still. Respectful.

He'd lost his business before it had even opened. He'd lost the woman he'd expected to marry, to grow old beside.

Alana Gold had lost her life.

And in her death had taken part of his.

The preacher spoke about angels of mercy. The woman half a step behind him rocked slightly, not announcing herself in any way other than her quiet presence. Flint fought to contain his grief. And his anger.

His entire life he'd had to work longer, fight harder. At first to avoid getting beaten up. And then to make a place for himself in the various families with whom he'd been temporarily settled. He'd had a paper route at twelve and delivered weekly grocery ads to neighborhoods for pennies, just to keep food on the table during the times he'd been with Alana.

The preacher spoke of heaven.

Flint remembered when he'd been a junior in high school, studying for finals, and had had to spend the night before his test getting his mother out of jail. She'd been prostituting that time. Those were the charges. She'd claimed differently.

But then, Alana's troubles had always been someone else's fault.

In the beginning they probably had been. She'd once claimed that she'd gotten on the wrong track because she'd been looking for a way to escape an abusive father. That was the one part of her story Flint fully believed. He'd met the guy once. Had opted, when given the chance in court, to never have to see him again. Sometimes it worked in a guy's favor to have a caseworker.

After Alana's prostitution arrest during his finals week, he'd expected to be seeing his caseworker again, to have her come to pick him up and take him back to foster care. Instead his mother had been sitting in the living room when he'd gotten home from school the next day, completely sober, her fingernails bitten to the quick, with a plate of homemade chocolate-chip cookies on her lap, worried sick that she'd made him fail his exam.

Tears had dripped down her face as he'd told her of course not, he'd aced it. Because he'd skipped lunch to cram. She'd apologized. Again and again. She'd always said he was the only good thing about her. That he was going to grow up to be something great, for both of them. She'd waited on him hand and foot for a few weeks. Had stayed sober and made it to work at the hair salon—where she'd qualified for men's basic cuts only—for most of that summer.

Until one of her clients had talked her into going out for a good time...

"Let us pray."

Flint's head was already bowed. The brief ceremony was almost over. The closed casket holding his mother's body would remain on the stand, waiting over the hole in the ground until after Flint was gone and the groundskeeper came to lower her to her final rest.

Moisture pricked the backs of his eyelids. For a second, he started to panic like he had the first day he'd gone out to catch the bus for school—a puny five-year-old in a trailer park filled with older kids—and been shoved to the back of the line by every one of them. He could have turned and run home. No one would have stopped him. Alana hadn't been sober enough to know, or care, whether he'd made it to his first day of school. But he hadn't run. He'd faced that open bus door, climbed those steps that had seemed like mountains to him and walked halfway to the back of the bus before sitting.

He was Alana Gold's precious baby boy and he was going to *be* someone.

"Amen." The preacher laid a Bible on top of the coffin.

Amen to that. He was Alana's son and he was going to be someone all right.

"Mr. Collins?"

The voice, a woman's voice, was close to him.

"Mr. Collins? I've got her things in the car, as you asked."

Her things. Things for the inheritance Alana had left him. More scared than he could ever remember being, Flint raised his head and turned it to see the brunette standing behind him, a concerned look on her face. A pink bundle in her arms.

Staring at that bundle, he swallowed the lump in his throat. He wasn't prepared. No way could he pass *this* test. In her death, Alana had finally set him up for failure.

She'd unintentionally done it in the past but had never succeeded. This time, though...

He reminded himself that he had to *be* someone.

Brother? Father? Neither fit. He'd never had either.

A breeze blew across the San Diego cemetery. The cemetery close to where he'd grown up, where he'd once seen his mother score dope. And now he was putting her here permanently. Nothing about this day was right.

"Prison records show that your mother had already chosen a name for her. But as I told you, since she died giving birth, no official name has been given. You're free to name her whatever you'd like..."

Prison records and legal documents showed that his forty-five-year-old mother had appointed him, her thirty-year-old son, as guardian of her unborn child. A child Alana had conceived while serving year eight of her ten-year sentence for cooking and dealing methamphetamine in the trailer Flint had purchased for her.

The child's father was listed as "unknown."

He and the inherited baby had that in common. And the fact that their mother had stayed clean the entire time she'd carried them. Birthing them without addiction.

"What did she call her?" he asked, unable to lift his gaze from the pink bundle or to peer further, to seek out the little human inside it.

He'd been bequeathed a little human.

After thirty years of having his mother as his only family, he had a sister.

"Diamond Rose," the caseworker said.

Flint didn't hear any derogatory tone in the voice.

Alana had been gold. A softer metal. He was Flint, a hard rock. And this new member of the family was diamond. Strong enough to cut glass. Valuable and cherished. And Rose... Expensive, beautiful, sweet.

He got Alana's message, even if the world wouldn't. "Then Diamond Rose it is," he said, turning more fully to face the caseworker.

The woman was on the job, had other duties to tend to. She'd already done a preliminary background check but, as family, he had a right to the child even if the woman didn't want to give her to him. Unless the caseworker had found some reason that suggested the baby might be unsafe with him.

Like the fact that he knew nothing whatsoever about infants? Had never changed a diaper in his life? At least not on a real baby. He'd put about thirty of them on a doll he'd purchased the day before—immediately after watching a load of new parenting videos.

He reached for the bundle. Diamond Rose. She'd weighed six pounds, one ounce at birth, he'd been told. He'd put a pound of butter on a five-pound bag of flour the night before, wrapped it in one of the new blankets he'd purchased and walked around the house with it while going about his routine. Figured he could do pretty much anything he might want or need to do while holding it.

Or wearing it. The body-pack sling thing had been a real find. Not that different from the backpacks he'd used all through school, although this one was meant to be worn in front. Put the baby in that, he'd be hands free.

The caseworker, Ms. Bailey, rather than handing him Diamond Rose, took a step back. "Do you have the car seat?"

"I have two," he told her. "In case she has a babysitter and there's an emergency and she needs to be transported when I'm not there." He also had a crib set up in a room that used to be designated as a spare bedroom. Stella, his ex-fiancée, had eyed the unfurnished room as her temporary office until they purchased a home more in line with her wants and needs.

In an even more upscale neighborhood, in other words.

Ms. Bailey held the bundle against her. Flint didn't take offense. Didn't really blame the woman at all. If he were her, he wouldn't want to hand a two-day-old baby over to him, either. But during her two days in the hospital the baby had been fully tested, examined and then released that morning. Released to him. Her family. Via Ms. Bailey. At his request, because he had a funeral to attend. And had wanted Alana's daughter there, too.

"As I said earlier, I strongly recommend a Pack 'n Play. They're less expensive than cribs, double as playpens with a changing table attachment and are easily portable."

Already had that, too. Although he hadn't set it up in his bedroom as the videos he'd watched had recommended. No way was he having a baby sleep with him. Didn't seem… He didn't know what.

He had the monitors. If she woke, he'd have to get up anyway. Walking across the hall only took a few more steps.

"And the bottles and formula?"

"Three scoops of the powder per six ounces of water, slightly warm." He'd done a dozen run-throughs on that. And was opting for boiling all nipples in water just to be safe in his method of cleansing.

He noticed the preacher hovering in the distance. The man of God probably needed to get on to other matters, as well. Flint nodded his thanks and received the older man's nod in return. As he watched him walk away, he couldn't help wondering if Alana Gold would be more than a momentary blip in his memory.

She would be far more than that to her daughter.

Ms. Bailey interrupted his thoughts. "What about child

care? Have you made arrangements for when you go back to work?"

Go back to work? As in, an hour from now? Taking Monday morning off had been difficult enough. With the market closed over the weekend, Mondays were always busy.

And he had some serious backtracking to do at the firm.

In the financial world, things had to be done discreetly and he'd been taking action—confidentially until he knew for sure it was a go—to move out on his own. Somehow his plans had become known and rumors had begun to spread with a bad spin. In the past week there'd been talk that he'd contacted his clients, trying to steal their business away from the firm. A person he trusted had heard something and confided that to him. And then he'd had an oddly formal exchange about the weather with Howard Owens, CEO and, prior to the past week, a man who'd seemed proud to have him around. A man who'd never wasted weather words on Flint. They talked business. All the time. Until the past week.

There was no way he could afford to take time off work now.

"I'm taking her with me." He faced Ms. Bailey, feet apart and firmly grounded. He had to work. Period. "I have a Pack 'n Play already set up in the office."

The woman frowned. "They'll let you have a baby with you at work?"

"My office is private. I'll keep the door closed if it's a problem." The plan was short-term. Eventually he'd have to make other arrangements. He'd only had a weekend to prepare. Had gotten himself trained and the house set up. He figured he'd done a damned impressive job.

Besides, that time Campbell's dog had had surgery, the guy had brought it to the office every day for a week. Kept it in his office. As long as you were a money-maker and didn't get in the way of others making money, you were pretty much untouched at Owens Investments. They were like independent businesses under one roof.

Or so he'd been telling himself repeatedly in the couple of days since he'd realized he couldn't open his own business as planned. Not and have sole responsibility for a newborn. Running a business took a lot more than simply making smart investments. Especially when it was just getting off the ground.

He'd already shut down the entire process. Withdrawn his applications for the licenses required to be an investment adviser to more than five clients and regulated by the SEC in the State of California. Lost his deposit for a proposed suite in a new office building.

If she thought she was going to keep his sister from him now...

Another breeze blew across his face, riffling the edge of the blanket long enough that he caught a flash of skin. A tiny cheek? A forehead?

Panic flared. And then dissipated. That bundle was his sister. His family. Only he could give her that. Only he could tell her about her mother. The good stuff.

Like the times she'd look in on him late at night, thinking he was asleep. Whisper her apologies. And tell him how very, very much she loved him. How much he mattered. How he was the one thing she'd done right. How he was going to make his mark on the world for both of them.

The way she'd throw herself a thousand percent into his school projects, encouraging him, making suggestions, applauding him. How talented she was at crafty things. How she loved to watch sappy movies and made the best popcorn. How she'd want to watch scary movies with him and he'd catch her looking away during the best parts. How she'd never made a big deal out of his mistakes. From spills to a broken window, she'd let him know it was okay. How she'd played cards with him, taught him to cook. How she'd laugh until tears ran down her face. How pretty she used to be when she smiled.

The images flying swiftly through his mind halted abruptly as Ms. Bailey began to close in on him, her arms outstretched.

Hoping to God she didn't notice his sudden trembling, he moved instinctively, settled the weight at the tip of the blanket in the crook of his elbow and took the rest of it on his arm, just as he'd practiced with the flour-and-butter wrap the night before. She was warm. And she squirmed. Shock rippled through him. Ms. Bailey adjusted the blanket, fully exposing the tiniest face he'd ever seen up close. Doll-like nose and chin. Eyelids tightly closed. Puckered little lips. A hint of a frown on a forehead that was smaller than the palm of his hand.

"From what I've seen in pictures, she has your mother's eyes," Ms. Bailey said, a catch in her voice. Because she could hear the tears threatening in his? A grown man who hadn't cried since the first time they'd carted his mother off to prison. He'd been six then.

She has your mother's eyes.

He had his mother's eyes. Deep, dark brown. It was fitting that this baby did, too. "We'll be getting on with it, then," he said, holding his inheritance securely against him as he moved toward his SUV, all but dismissing Ms. Bailey from their lives.

Having a caseworker was a part of his legacy that he wasn't going to pass on to his sister.

Reaching the new blue Lincoln Navigator he'd purchased five months before and hadn't visited the prison in even once, he felt a sharp pang of guilt as he realized once again that he'd let almost half a year pass since seeing his mother.

Before he'd met Stella Wainwright—a lawyer in her father's high-powered firm, whose advice he'd come to rely on as he'd made preparations to open his own investment firm—he'd seen Alana at least twice a month. But once he and Stella had hooked up on a personal level, he'd been distracted. Incredibly busy. And...

He'd been loath to lie to Stella about where he'd been— in the event he'd visited the prison—but had been equally unsure about telling her about his convict mother.

As it turned out, his reticence hadn't been off the mark. As soon as he'd told Stella about his mother's death, and the child who'd been bequeathed to him, she'd balked. She'd assumed he'd give the baby up for adoption. And had made it clear that if he didn't, she was moving on. She'd said from the beginning that she didn't want children, at least not for a while, but he'd also seen the extreme distaste in her expression when he'd mentioned where his mother had been when she died, and why he'd never introduced them.

Her reaction hadn't surprised him.

Eight years had passed since he'd been under investigation and nearly lost his career, but the effects were long-lasting. He'd done nothing more than provide his destitute mother with a place to live, but when his name came up as owner of a drug factory, the truth hadn't mattered.

Stella had done a little research and he'd been cooked.

Opening the back passenger door of the vehicle, he gently laid his sleeping bundle in the car seat, unprepared when the bundle slumped forward. Repositioning her, he pulled her slightly forward, allowing her body weight to lean back—and slouch over to the side of the seat.

Who the hell had thought the design of that seat appropriate?

"This might help."

Straightening, he saw the caseworker holding out a brightly covered, U-shaped piece of foam. He took it from her and arranged it at the top of the car seat as instructed. He was pleased with the result. Until he realized he'd placed the sleeping bundle on top of the straps that were supposed to hold the baby in place.

Expecting Ms. Bailey to interrupt, to push him aside to show him how it was done—half hoping she would so she wasn't standing there watching his big fumbling fingers—he set to righting his mistake. The caseworker must be thinking he was incapable of handling the responsibility. However, she didn't butt in and he managed, after a long minute, to get the baby harnessed. He'd practiced that, too. The hooking and unhooking of those straps. Plastic pieces that slid over metal for the shoulder part, metal into metal over the bottom half.

He stood. Waited for a critique of his first task as a... guardian.

Handing him her card, reminding him of legalities he'd have to complete, Ms. Bailey took one last look at the baby and told him to call her if he had any questions or problems.

He took the card, assuring her he'd call if the need arose. Pretty certain he wouldn't. He'd be like any normal...guardian; he'd call the pediatrician. As soon as he had one. Another item he had to add to the list of immediate things to do.

"And for what it's worth..." Ms. Bailey stood there, looking between him and the little sister he was suddenly starting to feel quite proprietary about. "I think she's a very lucky little girl."

Wow. He hadn't seen that coming. Wasn't sure the words were true. But they rang loudly in his ears as the woman walked away.

Standing in the open space of the back passenger door, he glanced down at the sleeping baby, only her face visible to him, and didn't want to shut the door. Didn't want to leave her in the big back seat all alone.

Which was ridiculous.

He had to get to work. And hope to God he could mend whatever damage had been done by his previous plans to leave. He had some ideas there—a way to redeem himself, to rebuild trust. But he had to be at the office to present them.

Closing the door as softly as he could, he hurried to the driver's seat, adjusted the rearview mirror so he could see enough of the baby to know she was there and started the engine. Not ready to go anywhere. To begin this new life.

He glanced in the mirror again. Sitting forward so he could see the child more clearly. Other than the little chest rising and falling with each breath, she hadn't moved.

But was moving him to the point of panic. And tears, too. He wasn't alone anymore.

"Welcome home, Diamond Rose," he whispered.

And put the car in Drive.

Chapter Two

"Dad, seriously, tell me what's going on." Tamara Owens faced her father, not the least bit intimidated by the massive cherry desk separating him from her. Or the elegantly imposing décor throughout her father's office.

She'd seen him at home, unshaved, walking around their equally elegant five-thousand-square-foot home in boxers and a T-shirt. In a bathrobe, sick with the flu. And, also in a bathrobe, holding her hair while she'd thrown up, sick with the same flu. Her mom, the doctor in the family, had been at the hospital that night.

"You didn't put pressure on me to move home just because you and Mom are getting older and I'm your only child." It was the story they'd given her when they'd bombarded her with their "do what you need to do, but at least think about it" requests. Then her father, in a conversation alone with her, had given Tamara a second choice, an "at least take a month off and stay for a real visit" that had made the final decision for her. She'd gotten the feeling that he needed her home. She'd already been contemplating leaving the East Coast, where she'd fled two years earlier after having lived in San Diego her entire life. Her reputation as an efficiency consultant was solid enough to allow her to branch out independently, rather than work through a firm without fear of going backward. Truth be told, in those two years, she'd missed her folks as much as they'd missed her, in spite of their frequent trips across the country to see each other.

She'd lived by the ocean in Boston, but she missed Southern California. The sunshine and year-round warmth. The two-year lease renting out her place by the beach, not far from the home she'd grown up in, had ended and the time seemed right to make the move back home.

"And you didn't ask me down here to have lunch with you just to catch up, either," she told him. Though his thick hair was mostly gray, her father, at six-two, with football shoulders that had absolutely no slump to them, was a commanding figure. She respected him. But he'd never, ever, made her feel afraid of him.

Or afraid to speak up to him, either.

Her parents, both remarkably successful, independent career people, had raised her to be just as independent.

"I wanted to check in—you know, just the two of us— to see how you're really doing."

Watching him, she tried to decide whether she could take him at face value. There'd been times, during her growing-up years, when she'd asked him for private conversations because her mother's ability to jump too completely into her skin had bothered her. And times when he'd wanted the same. This didn't feel like one of those times.

But...

"I'm totally over Steve, if that's what you want to know,"

she told him. "We've been talking for about six months now. Ever since he called to tell me he was getting married. I spoke with him a couple of weeks ago to tell him I was moving home. I care about him as a friend, but there are truly no regrets about our decision to divorce."

The passion between them had died long before the marriage had.

"I was wondering more about the…other areas of your life."

Some of those were permanently broken. She had an "inhospitable" uterus. Nothing anyone could do about that.

"I've come to terms with never having a baby, if that's what you mean." After she'd lost the fourth one, she'd known she couldn't let herself try again. What she'd felt for those babies, even when they'd been little more than blips in an ultrasound, had been the most incredible thing ever. But the devastation when she'd lost them…that had almost killed her. Every single time.

She couldn't do that again.

"There are other ways, Tam."

She shook her head.

"Adoption, for instance."

Another vigorous shake of her head was meant to stop his words.

"Down the road, I mean. When you meet someone, want to have a family…"

She was still shaking her head.

"Just give it some time."

She'd given it two years. Her feelings hadn't changed. Not in the slightest. "Knowing how badly it hurts to lose a child… It's not something I'm going to risk again. Not just because I'm afraid I'd miscarry if I got pregnant again, although it's pretty much assured that I would. But even without that, I can't have children. Whether I lost a child through miscarriage or some other way, just knowing it could happen… I can't take that chance. The last time, I hit a wall. I just don't— I've made my peace with life and I'm happy."

A lot of days she was getting there. Had moments when she *was* there. And felt fully confident she'd be completely there. Soon.

"But you aren't dating."

Leaning forward, she said, "I just got back to town a week ago! Give me time!"

He didn't even blink. "What about Boston? Didn't you meet anyone there?"

"I was hardly ever home long enough to meet anyone," she reminded him. "Traveling all over the country, making a name for myself, took practically every second I had."

The move to Boston had been prompted by an offer she'd had to join a nationally reputed efficiency company. She'd been given the opportunity to build a reputation for herself. To collect an impressive database of statistical proof from more than two dozen assignments that showed she could save a company far more money per year, in many departments, than they'd pay for her one-time services. Her father had seen the results. He'd been keeping his own running tally of her successes.

"You did an incredible job, Tam, I'm not disputing that. I'm impressed. And proud of you, too."

The warmth in those blue eyes comforted her as much now as when she'd been a little kid and fallen off her bike the first time he'd taken off the training wheels. She hadn't even skinned her knee, but she'd been scared and he'd scooped her up, made her look him in the eye and see that she was just fine.

"I guess it's a little hard for me to believe that emotionally you're really doing as well as you say, because I don't see *how* you do it. I can't imagine ever losing you... I don't know how I'd have survived losing four."

"But you *did* lose four, Daddy. You were as excited as anyone when you found out I was pregnant. Heck, you'd already bought Ryan his first fishing rod..."

She still had it, in the back of the shed on her small property. She'd carried Ryan the longest. Almost five months. They'd just found out he was a boy. Everything had looked good. And then...

Through sheer force of will, she stopped the shudder before it rippled through her. Remembering the sharp stabs of debilitating physical pain was nothing compared to the morose emptiness she'd been left with afterward.

"I'm not as strong as you are." Howard Owens's voice sounded...different. She hardly recognized it. Tamara stared at him, truly frightened. Was her father sick? Did her mother know? Was that why they'd needed her home?

Frustrated, she wanted to demand that he tell her what was going on, but knew better. The Owens and their damned independence. Asking for help was like an admission of defeat.

"Of course you are," she told him, ready to hold him up, support him, for whatever length of time it took to get him healthy again. If, indeed, he was sick. She slowed herself down. She'd just been thinking how healthy, robust, strong he looked. His skin as tanned as always, that tiny hint of a belly at his waist... Everything was as it should be. He'd been talking about his golf scores at dinner the night before—until her mother had changed the subject in the charming manner she had that let him know he was going on and on.

Tamara had been warmed by the way her mother had smiled at her father as the words left her mouth—and the way, as usual, he'd smiled back at her.

She and Steve had never had that; they'd never been able to communicate as much or more with a look as they had with words. In the final couple of years, not even words had worked for them…

"Anyway," she continued, pulling her mind out of the abyss, "you're the one who taught me *how* to do it," she said, mimicking him. "It's all about focus, exactly like you taught me. If I wanted to get good grades, I had to focus and study. If I wanted to have a good life, I had to focus on what I wanted. If I wanted to overcome the fear, I had to keep my thoughts on things other than being afraid. And if I want to be a success, I just have to focus on doing the best job I can do. Focus, Dad. That's what you've always taught me and what I've always done. In everything I do."

It was almost like she was telling him how to make it through whatever was bothering him.

He'd always been her greatest example.

Howard's eyes closed for longer than a blink. When he opened them again, he didn't meet her gaze. And for the second time fear struck a cold blow inside her. *Focus on the problem*, she told herself. Not on how she was feeling.

To do that, she had to know the problem.

"What's going on, Dad?" There was no doubt that his call to her asking her to come home had to do with more than missing her. How much more, she had to find out.

"Owens Investments was audited this past spring."

Her relief was so heady she almost saw stars. It was business. Not health. "You've got some misplaced files?" she asked him. "You need me to do a paper trail to satisfy them?" Her Master's in Business Administration had been a formal acknowledgment of her ability, but Tamara's true skills, organization and thoroughness, were what had catapulted her to success in her field. If a paper trail existed, she'd find it. And then know how to better organize the process by which documents were collated so nothing got lost again.

Her father's chin jutted out as he shook his head. "I wish it was missing files. Turns out that someone's been siphoning money from the company for over a year. And I'm not sure it's stopped. If it continues, I could lose everything."

Okay. So, not good news. Also not imminent death. Anything that wasn't death was fixable.

"I need your help, Tam," Howard said, folding his hands on the desk as he faced her. "Money is a vulnerable business. A lucrative one, but vulnerable. If our investors hear there's money missing, they'll get nervous. There could be a massive move out…"

She could see that. Was more or less a novice about the ins and outs of what he did, but she knew how companies worked. And the importance of consumer trust.

"I was hoping I'd be able to figure out what's going on myself, no need to alarm you or bring you home, but I haven't been able to find the leak. I need you to come in and do what you do. To give us a once-over, presumably to see if you can save us money. In reality, I'm hoping that you can give everything more of a thorough study without raising suspicions the way it would if I was taking a deeper look."

She nodded, recognizing how hard it was for her father to have to ask for help. Thinking ahead. Focusing on the job.

"People are going to know I'm your daughter. They might be less comfortable speaking with me."

He shook his head again. "I've thought of that. A few will know, of course. Roger. Emily. And Bill. For the rest, it works in our favor that you kept your married name because it was the name you became known under in the business world. People will have no reason to suspect."

Roger Standish, Emily Porter and Bill Coniff. CFO, VP and Director of Operations, respectively. Her father's very first employees when he'd first started out. She'd met them all but it wasn't as if he'd been close friends with his business associates. He was closer to his clients. Many of those she knew better than her own aunts and uncle. Still, none of his top three people would rat her out to the employees. Unless…

"What if the problem rests with one of those three?"

"I guess we'll find that out," he said, raising a hand and then running it over his face. Clearly he'd been dealing with the problem for a while. Longer than he should have without saying anything. She was thirty-two, not thirteen.

"Does Mom know?"

"Of course. She wanted me to call you home immediately."

"You should have."

"Your happiness and emotional health mean more to me than going bankrupt."

Feeling her skin go cold again, she stared at him. Was it that bad?

"Your well-being is one of the top factors that affects my emotional health," she couldn't help pointing out to him.

With a nod, he conceded that.

He was asking for her help. Nothing else mattered.

"How soon can I start?" she asked.

"That was going to be my question."

"When you finally got around to telling me you needed something…" The slight dig didn't escape him.

"I was going to tell you today. I was just having a bit of trouble getting to it. You've been through so much and I don't like putting more on you…"

"I make my living by having companies put more on

me. It's what I do, what I strive for." She grinned at him. He grinned back.

Her world felt right again.

"So...is now too soon?"

"Now would be great. But...there's one other thing."

The knot was back in her stomach. *Please, not his health.* Had he waited until the stress had taken a physical toll before calling her? "What?"

"I don't want to prejudice or influence your findings, but there's one employee in particular who I think could be the one we're after. Although I wasn't able to find anything concrete that says it's him."

Pulling the tablet she always kept in her bag onto her lap, she turned it on. Opened a new file. "Who is he? And why do you suspect him?"

"His name's Flint Collins. I took him on eight years ago when he was let go by his firm and no one else would hire him. He'd only been in the business a year, but had good instincts. He was up-front about the issues facing him and looked me straight in the eye as we talked. He was... He kind of reminded me of myself. I liked him."

Enough to have been blinded by him? "Have I ever met him? Flint Collins?"

"No." Her father didn't have office parties at home. And rarely ever attended the ones he financed at the office.

"So what were his issues eight years ago?"

Not really an efficiency matter, she knew, unless, of course, he was wasteful to the point of being a detriment to the company. But then, this wasn't just an efficiency case.

This was her father. And she was out for more than saving his firm a few dollars.

"His mother was indicted on multiple drug charges. She'd been running a fairly sophisticated meth lab from her home and was dealing on a large enough scale to get her ten years in prison."

Had to be tough. But… "What did that have to do with him, specifically?"

"The trailer she lived in was in his name. As were all the utilities. Paid by him every month. He had regular contact with his mother. He'd already begun to make decent money and was investing it, so he was worth far more than average for a twenty-two-year-old just out of college. Investigators assumed that part of his wealth came from his cut of his mother's business and named him as a suspect. They froze his assets. Any investors he had at the firm where he worked got scared and moved their accounts. It was a bad deal all the way around."

"Was he ever formally charged?" She figured she knew the answer to that. He wouldn't be working for her father as an investment broker if he had been. But she had to ask.

"No. He says he had no idea what his mother had been doing. Seemed to be in shock about the whole thing, to tell you the truth. A warrant for all his accounts and assets turned up no proof at all that he'd ever taken a dime from anyone for anything. All deposits were easily corroborated with legitimate earnings."

"How'd he do for you?"

"Phenomenal. As well as I thought he might. He's one of our top producers. Until recently, I never suspected him of anything but being one of the best business decisions I'd ever made."

"What happened recently?"

"He hooked up with a fancy lawyer. His spending habits changed. He bought a luxury SUV, started taking exotic vacations, generally living high. I'm not saying he couldn't afford it, just that a guy who's always appeared to be conservative with his own spending was suddenly flashing his wealth."

As in…he'd come into new wealth? Or felt like he'd tapped into a bottomless well? Or was running with a faster crowd and needed more than he was making?

"There's more," her father said. "Last week Bill told me he'd heard from Jane in Accounting that she'd heard from a friend of hers in the office of the Commissioner of Business Oversight that Collins was planning to leave. That he was filing paperwork to open his own firm. Bill says he heard that Collins was planning to take his book of business with him."

She disliked the guy. Thoroughly.

"He can't do that, can he? Solicit his clients away from you?"

"No, but that doesn't mean he won't drop a word in an ear here and there." Howard slowly tapped a finger on the edge of his desk, seeming to concentrate on the movement. "As I said, money is a vulnerable business. His clients trust him. They'll follow him of their own accord."

"So he's going to be direct competition to the man who took a chance on him?" *Hate* was such a strong word. She didn't want it in her vocabulary. Anger, on the other hand…

"I left another firm to start Owens Investments." Her father's words calmed her for the immediate moment. "He was doing what I did. Following in my footsteps, so to speak. I just didn't see it coming from him. I thought he was happy here."

"Unless he's leaving because he knows someone is on to the fact that money is being misplaced."

"That's occurred to me, too. About a hundred times over the past week. A guy who's opening his own business doesn't usually start spending lavishly. And if he was the decent guy I thought he was, he would at least have let me know his plans to leave. Which is what I did when I was branching out.

"And, like I said, he's the only one here who's made any obvious changes in routine or lifestyle over the past year. I did some checking into health-care claims and asked around as much as I could, and no one seems to be going through any medical crisis that would require extra funding. I'm not aware of any rancorous divorces, either."

"So… I start now and my first visit is to Mr. Flint Collins."

Howard nodded. "We need to get a look at every file he has while everything is still here."

Which might take some time. "Do you know how soon he's planning to leave?"

"Technically, I don't actually know that he's going. Like I said, this is all still rumor. He's given me no indication or made any official announcement about his plans."

"But it could be soon?"

Howard shrugged. "Could be any day. I just hope to God it's not. Even if he's not the one who's been stealing from me, he's going to do it indirectly unless I can get to his clients first. I've already started reaching out—making sure everyone's happy, letting them know that if there's any question or discomfort at all, to contact me. I'll take on more accounts myself rather than lose them."

Even then, her dad would have to be careful. He couldn't appear to be stabbing a fellow broker in the back just to keep more profits for himself. She did know *some* things about his business. She also remembered a time when she'd been in high school and another broker had left the firm. Her dad had talked to her mother about a party for the investors who'd be affected, which they'd had and then he'd acted on her advice as to how to deliver his news. She just couldn't remember what that advice had been. What stuck in her mind was that her father had taken it.

Which had given a teenage Tamara respect for, and faith in, both of them.

Standing, she asked her dad for a private space with a locking door that she could use as an office. Told him she'd need passwords and security clearance to access all files. And suggested he send out a memo, or however they normally did such things within the company, to let everyone know, from janitorial on up, that she'd be around and why, giving him wording suggestions. Everything that came with her introductory speech on every new job she took. She had a lot of work to do.

But first she was going to introduce herself to Flint Collins.

While her heart hurt for the young man who, from the sound of things, had a much more difficult upbringing than many—certainly far more difficult than she'd had—that didn't give him the right to screw over her family. Karma didn't work that way.

Chapter Three

Flint took the back way into his office. Leaving the base of the car seat strapped into the back of his SUV, he unlatched the baby carrier, carefully laid a blanket over the top and hightailed it to his private space.

Lunchtime at Owens Investments meant that almost everyone in Flint's wing would be out wining and dining clients, or holed up in his or her office getting work done. His door was the second from the end by the private entrance—because he'd requested the space when it became available. He wasn't big on socializing at work and hadn't liked being close to the door on the opposite end of the hall, which led to reception.

He'd never expected to be thankful that he could sneak something inside without being seen. That Monday he was.

Everyone was going to know. He just needed time to see Bill. His boss, Bill Coniff, was Director of Operations and, he was pretty sure, the person who'd ratted him out before he was ready to go to Howard Owens with his plan to open his own firm. Jane in Accounting had told him about the rumor going around, and said she'd interrupted Bill telling Howard. According to Jane, Bill had twisted the news to make it sound like Flint had been soliciting his current clients to jump ship with him.

Flint would get out of the business altogether before he'd do that.

Business was business. Howard had taught him that. Flint was good at what he did and could earn a lot more money over the course of his career by having his own firm. Could make choices he wasn't currently permitted to make regarding certain investments because Howard wasn't willing to take the same risks.

He felt that to live up to his full potential, he had to go, but he'd been planning to do it ethically. With Howard fully involved in the process—once there was a solid process in which to involve him.

But in less than a week his life had irrevocably changed. Forever. His focus now had to be on making enough money to support a child, not taking risks. To provide a safe, loving home. And to have time to be in that home with the child as much as possible.

How the hell he was supposed to go about that, he had no real idea. First step had been watching all the videos. Buying out the baby store.

And the next was to humble himself, visit Bill Coniff and ensure his current job security. To beg if it came to that.

He spent a few minutes setting up the monitor system he'd purchased for his office, putting the remote receiver in his pocket and taking one last glance at the baby carrier he'd placed on the work table opposite his desk. The floor was too drafty, the couch too narrow. What if she cried and moved her arms and legs a lot and the carrier fell off?

Ms. Bailey had said that the infant had been fed before she'd brought her to the gravesite. Apparently she ate every two hours and slept most of the rest of the time. By his math, that gave him half an hour to get his situation resolved before she'd need him.

Testing the monitor by talking into it and making sure he heard his own voice coming out of his pocket, he left the room, closing the door behind him. Should he lock it? Somehow, locking a baby in a place alone seemed dangerous. Neglectful. But he couldn't leave the door unlocked. Anyone could walk down that hallway and steal her away.

Was he wrong to vacate the room at all?

People left babies in nurseries at home and even went downstairs. Bill's office was two doors away from his. He'd see anyone who walked by. Unless whoever it was came in through the private door. Only employees had access to that hall.

There were security cameras at either end.

If there was a fire and he was hurt, a locked door would prevent firefighters from getting to Diamond Rose.

Decision made, he left the door unlocked.

"Please, Bill, I'm asking you to support me here. I'm prepared to plead my case to Howard. Just back me up on it. I don't know who started spreading the rumors or how far they've reached, but I'm fairly certain they made it to Howard's office..."

On her way to knock on the door of one Flint Collins, Tamara stopped in her tracks. Standing in a deserted private hallway in two-and-a-half-inch heels and her short black skirt with its matching short jacket, plus the lacy camisole her mother had bought to go with the ensemble, she felt conspicuous. But something told her not to move. She'd dressed for a "professional" lunch with her father, not for real business. But business was at hand.

"You're telling me you didn't file paperwork to open your own investment firm?"

She recognized Bill's voice coming from the office with his name on the door. Based on what her father had told her, she figured Bill had to be speaking with Flint Collins. Did her father know Bill was intending to handle the matter?

"No. I'm not saying that. I'm telling you I no longer have plans to do that and would like to do whatever I need to, to ensure my job security here."

"Your plans to hurt this company by soliciting our customers didn't work out, so now I should trust that you're here to stay?"

Bill was in the process of firing the guy? He couldn't! Not yet! She needed time to investigate him while his files were all still in his office at the company. While he didn't know he was being watched.

"I did not, nor did I intend, to solicit anyone. I intended to have a meeting with Howard and do things the right way."

"And now you don't plan to leave anymore."

"Now, in light of the rumors that went around last week, I'd like to guarantee that I have job security here and I was hoping for your cooperation. You know the money I make for this firm, Bill."

"*You* know how important trust is to this firm."

Tamara took a step forward. She couldn't let Bill fire the man, but wasn't sure how to prevent that from happening without exposing more than she could if she was going to be effective in her task.

"I'm willing to sign a noncompete clause to prove my trustworthiness."

"Wow, I like the sound of that!" Tamara burst into the room with a smile that she hoped Bill would accept at face value. She and her father had decided that even his top people shouldn't be told her true reason for being there. At the moment, they could only trust each other.

But he'd called all three of them before she'd left his office, telling them she was going to be doing an efficiency study and that he'd like their cooperation in keeping her relationship to him quiet. Howard wanted to make sure that as she moved about the company, she'd have their full support. She was working under her married name of Frost. Howard had explained that he'd thought people would be less nervous around her if they didn't know she was his daughter.

"Tamara? So good to see you!" Bill turned to her, an odd combination of welcoming smile and bewildered frown warring on his face.

"As you know, Bill, I'm here to study operations on all levels and find ways for Owens Investments to show a higher profit by running more efficiently," she said, holding out her hand to shake his.

Luckily she had her professional spiel down pat. Normally, though, the words weren't accompanied by a pounding heart. Or the sudden flash of heat that had surfaced as she'd looked from Bill to his conversation mate and met the brown-eyed gaze of the compelling blond man she'd been predisposed to dislike on sight.

At first Flint had absolutely no idea who the beautiful, auburn-haired woman with the gold-rimmed green eyes was as she interrupted the meeting upon which his future security could very well rest.

Bill quickly filled him in as he introduced the efficiency expert Howard Owens had hired. Apparently a memo had been sent to Flint and all Owens employees in the past hour. He, of course, had been busy burying his mother and becoming a guardian/father/brother and hadn't gotten to the morning's email yet.

Thinking of the baby girl he'd left sleeping in his office, he reached for the monitor in his pocket, thumb moving along the side to check that the volume was all the way up. He'd been gone almost five minutes. Didn't feel good about that.

"It seems to me, Bill, that if we have a broker on staff who's willing to sign a noncompete clause, then we should give him that opportunity. If he doesn't produce, we can still let him go. If he does, our bottom line has more security. We don't lose either way. Efficient. I like it."

Flint wasn't sure he liked *her.* But he liked what she was saying, since it meant Diamond Rose would have security.

"Unless you know of some reason we shouldn't keep him on?" she asked. "Other than what I just overheard, that he'd been thinking about opening his own firm?"

She looked at him. He didn't deny the charge. But he wasn't going to elaborate. Other than Bill, Howard Owens was the only one to whom Flint would report.

It seemed odd that this outside expert happened to be in the hall just as he'd been speaking with Bill. As though some kind of fate had put her there.

Or a mother in heaven looking out for her children?

The idea was so fanciful, Flint had a second's very serious concern regarding his state of mind. But another completely real concern cut that one short. His pocket made a tiny coughing sound.

All three adults in the room froze. Staring at each other.

And Flint's brand-new little girl made another, half-crying sound. In a pitch without weight. Or strength.

The woman—Tamara Frost, as Bill had introduced her—stared at his pocket. For a second there she looked... horrified. Or maybe sick.

"Not that it's any of my business but...do you have a newborn baby cry as your ringtone?" Her voice, as she looked up at him, sounded professionally nonjudgmental—although definitely taken aback.

Probably didn't happen often... Guys with the sound of crying babies in their pockets during business meetings.

Diamond Rose released another small outburst. Twenty minutes ahead of schedule. He had to get back to her. His first real duty and he was already letting her down. He'd had no time to prepare the bottle, as he'd expected to.

"I'm sorry," he said, looking from Bill to their expert and then heading to the door. "I have to get this."

Let them think it was his phone. And that the call was more important at that moment than they were.

Just until he had things under control.

Chapter Four

She was coming down with something. Wouldn't you know it? First day of the most important job of her life to date—because it was for her father, her family—and she was experiencing hot flashes followed by cold shivers.

That could only mean the flu.

Crap.

"So…you're good with keeping him on?" She looked at Bill and then back to the doorway they'd both been staring at. She'd been listening for Mr. Collins's "hello" as he took the call that was important enough for him to leave a meeting during which he'd been begging for his job. She'd wanted to hear his tone of his voice as he addressed such an important caller.

Business or pleasure?

"Your father said you're the boss." Bill's words didn't seem to have any edge to them.

"Well, he's wrong, of course." She was smiling, glad

to know she didn't have to worry about stepping on at least one director's toes. "But it makes sense, from an efficiency standpoint, to keep on a broker who's willing to sign a noncompete clause. Unless you know of some reason he should go? I heard him say he makes the company money. Is that true?"

"He's one of our top producers."

She knew that already, but there was no reason, as an efficiency expert who hadn't yet seen her first file, that she should.

"You have some hesitation about him?"

She'd asked Bill twice if there was a reason Flint Collins shouldn't stay on. Bill hadn't replied.

He gave a half shrug as he looked at her and crossed to his desk, straightening his tie. "None tops the offer he made a few minutes ago. Still, I don't like having guys around that I can't trust."

He had her total focus. "He's given you reason to mistrust him?"

Bill shook his head. "Just the whole 'opening his own shop' thing."

"It's what my dad did—left a firm to start Owens Investments. And you helped him do it."

"We did it the right way," Bill said. "The first person your father told, before taking any action, was his boss. None of this finding out from a friend in the recorder's office. Makes me wonder what else he isn't telling us…"

Made her wonder, too.

"I'm going over all the company files. He'll know that as soon as he reads his email. Seems like if he's untrustworthy, he'll have a problem with that."

"If he's got anything to hide, you aren't going to find it."

Maybe not.

Ostensibly her job was to come up with ways for Owens

to make more money. "He's a top producer and wants to sign a noncompete agreement."

"Right when he was getting ready to go into business for himself," Bill said, frowning. "Like I said, kind of makes you wonder why, doesn't it?"

"Is it possible that any of his applications for the various licenses were turned down for some reason?"

"From what I heard, he'd been fully approved."

"Could you have heard wrong?"

Bill shrugged again. "Anything's possible."

She nodded. She needed to get hold of Flint Collins's files.

"He came to you knowing he had to contend with trust issues and was armed with a plan that benefits Owens Investments," she said. She wasn't sure how to interpret that yet. Had he seen that he could make more siphoning off money from her father than he would on his own?

"He's a smart businessman."

"So, are you okay with keeping him on or will you be letting him go?" She couldn't allow him to think it really mattered to her. Or that she intended to push her weight around, beyond efficiency expertise.

If Bill planned to fire Collins right away, she'd go to her father, have him handle the situation. She hoped it didn't come to that.

"Of course I'm keeping him on," Bill said. "He's making us a boatload of money. But I don't trust him and I'll be watching him closely."

Her father had a good man in his Director of Operations. Smiling, Tamara told him so, thanked him and promised to do all she could to stay out of his way.

Shouldn't be hard. She had a feeling Flint Collins would be taking up most of her time.

Maybe an efficiency expert wouldn't be able to find

whatever he might be hiding, or anything he might be doing to rip off her family, but a daughter out to protect her father would.

By whatever means it took.

Tamara was certain of that.

For a man who liked to plan his life down to the number of squeezes left in his toothpaste tube, Flint figured he was doing pretty well to be at his desk, with his computer on, twenty minutes after leaving Bill Coniff's office.

His "inheritance," the tiny being who was now his responsibility for life, lay fed, dry and fast asleep in the car seat–carrier combination, her head securely cushioned by that last little gift from the caseworker. He'd placed her on the table across the room, but sitting at his desk, he wasn't satisfied. The carrier was turned sideways. He couldn't see her full face to know at a glance that her blanket hadn't somehow interfered with her breathing, say if she happened to move in her sleep.

Clicking to open his client list, he crossed the room and adjusted the carrier, turning it to face his desk. Looked at the baby. Noticed her steady breathing.

She had the tiniest little nose. Probably the cutest thing he'd ever seen.

She was going to be a beauty.

Like their mother…

He planned to keep her under lock and key. Away from anyone who could attempt to hurt her…

Taken aback by the intensity of that thought, telling himself he wasn't really losing his mind, he returned to work. Found the client file he wanted. Opened it.

On Friday, before his world had completely crumbled, he'd made an investment that was meant to be short-term. A weekend news announcement had caused the stock to plummet, but it would rise again, for a few days at least, before it either plummeted long-term or—as he hoped—held steady. He figured he'd have five days max. Preferably three. The risk was greater than Howard would want, but the potential return should be remarkable enough to secure his job, at least for now.

As long as the risk paid off.

Flint clicked on certain files, clicked some more. Looked at numbers. Studied market movement. It occurred to him that he should be nervous. If he'd invested at a loss, it could potentially mean his job. He knew Bill had been about to fire him when fate had sent in the consultant Howard had hired.

He wasn't nervous. Flint took risks with the market. But only when his gut was at peace with them. His financial gift was about the only thing he trusted.

Glancing up, he checked his new responsibility. He could see movement as she breathed. Stared as a fist pushed its way out of the blanket. Who'd have thought hands came that small? Or that people did?

She looked far too insecure on that big table made for powerful business deals between grown men and women.

Market numbers scrolled on his screen. They were still going up. But they could take a second rapid dive; his guess was they would. And soon. They'd already climbed higher than he'd conservatively predicted, but not as high as he'd optimistically hoped.

Pushing back from his desk, he crossed the room again, lifted the carrier gently, loath to risk waking his charge. With his free hand, he pulled a chair back to his desk, positioning it next to his seat, along the wall to his left. Away from the door and any unseen drafts. Satisfied, he settled the carrier there, glanced at his computer screen and pushed the button to sell.

At a price higher than he'd hoped.

Five minutes later, the stock started to drop.

He still had his touch. And a fairly good chance of securing his job. Even Bill couldn't argue with the kind of money he'd just made.

As was her way, Tamara studied before she went into action. She didn't take the time she would later spend going over individual accounts, one by one, account by account, figure by figure. But when she approached Flint Collins's office late Monday afternoon, she not only knew every piece of information in his employee file, but she was familiar with every account he'd handled in the nearly eight years he'd been working for her father.

Aside from the part about suspecting that he was stealing from them, she was impressed. And more convinced than ever that if anyone could succeed in taking money from Howard without his knowing, it could be Collins. The man was clearly brilliant.

He'd been a suspect in the drug production and distribution that had put his mother in prison; he'd also grown up with her criminal history. According to a pretty thorough background check, the only consistent influence in his life had been his mother—in between her various stints in jail.

The first of which had come when he was only six. She'd been sentenced to three months. Tamara had seen a list of his mother's public criminal record in his file. Probably there because of Flint's ties to her latest arrest. She'd also seen that the woman was only fifteen years older than her son. A child raising a child.

Funny how life worked. A young girl who, judging by the facts, had been ill-equipped to have the responsibility of a child and yet she'd had one. While Tamara…

No. She wasn't going backward.

Passing Bill's open door, she waved at the director who was on the phone but waved back. Smiled at her. And her heart lifted a notch. She'd managed to get her way and not make an enemy. It was always good to have a "friend" among the people she was studying.

A couple of steps from Flint Collins's closed door, she stopped. That damned baby cry was going off again. She didn't want to interrupt his call. Nor did she want to wait around while he talked on the phone.

And really, what kind of guy had a crying newborn as his ringtone?

Not one she'd ever want to associate with, that was for sure.

However she didn't want to get on the guy's bad side. Not yet, anyway. She needed him to like her. To trust her.

She might even need to learn about his life if she hoped to help her father. According to Bill, anyway. The director was pretty certain that Collins wouldn't have hidden anything he was doing in files to which she'd have access.

The crying had stopped. She didn't hear any voices. Had whoever was calling hung up?

Deciding to wait a couple of seconds, just in case he was listening to a caller on the other end, Tamara cringed as the baby cry started back up. Sounding painfully realistic. How could he stand that?

Apparently he'd let the call go to voice mail. And whoever had been at the other end was phoning back. Was Collins ignoring the call? Unless he wasn't there? Had he left his cell in his office?

A man like Flint Collins didn't leave his cell phone behind.

Tamara knocked. And when there was no answer, tried the door. Surprisingly the knob turned. The office was impressive. Neat. Classy. Elegant.

And had nothing on the spread of male shoulders she saw bending over something to the side of his desk. Or the backside beneath them.

"Why aren't you answering your phone?" she blurted. The crying had to stop. It was making her crazy. She had business to do with him and—

The way those shoulders jerked and his glance swung in her direction clearly indicated that he hadn't heard her enter. Making her uncomfortably aware that she should probably have knocked a second time.

How hadn't he heard her first knock?

The thought fled as soon as she realized that the crying was coming from closer to him. There by the window. Not from the cell phone she noticed on his desk as she approached.

And then she saw it...the carrier...on the chair next to him. He'd been rocking it.

"What on earth are you doing to that baby?" she exclaimed, nothing in mind but to rescue the child in obvious distress. To stop the noise that was going to send her spiraling if she wasn't careful.

"Damned if I know," he said loudly enough to be heard over the noise. "I fed her, burped her, changed her. I've done everything they said to do, but she won't stop crying."

Tamara was already unbuckling the strap that held the crying infant in her seat. She was so tiny! Couldn't have been more than a few days old. Her skin was still wrinkled and so, so red. There were no tears on her cheeks.

"There's nothing poking her. I checked," Collins said, not interfering as she lifted the baby from the seat, careful to support the little head.

It wasn't until that warm weight settled against her that Tamara realized what she'd done. She was holding a baby. Something she couldn't do.

She was going to pay. With a hellacious nightmare at the very least.

The baby's cries had stopped as soon as Tamara picked her up.

"What did you do?" Collins was there, practically touching her, he was standing so close.

"Nothing. I picked her up."

"There must've been some problem with the seat, after all…" He'd tossed the infant head support on the desk and was removing the washable cover.

"I'm guessing she just wanted to be held," Tamara said. What the hell was she doing?

Tearless crying generally meant anger, not physical distress.

And why did Flint Collins have a baby in his office?

She had to put the child down. But couldn't until he put the seat back together. The newborn's eyes were closed and she hiccuped and then sighed.

Clenching her lips for a second, Tamara looked away. "Babies need to be held almost as much as they need to be fed," she told him while she tried to understand what was going on. "The skin-to-skin contact, the cuddling, is vitally important not only to their current emotional well-being but to future emotional, developmental and social behavior."

She was quoting books she'd memorized—long ago—in another life. He was checking the foam beneath the seat cover and the straps, too. Her initial analysis indicated that he was fairly distraught himself.

Not what she would've predicted from a hard-core businessman possibly stealing from her father.

"Who is she?" she asked, figuring it was best to start at the bottom and work her way up to exposing him for the thief he probably was.

He straightened. Stared at the baby in her arms, his brown eyes softening and yet giving away a hint of what looked like fear at the same time. In that second she wished like hell that her father was wrong and Collins wouldn't turn out to be the one who was stealing from Owens Investments.

She didn't move. Just stood frozen with her arms holding a baby against her.

"Her name's Diamond Rose." His tone soft, he continued to watch the baby, as though he couldn't look away. But he had to get that seat dealt with. Fast. The lump in her throat grew.

"Whose is she?" She was going to have to put the baby down. Sooner rather than later. Her permanently broken heart couldn't take much more. The tears were already starting to build. Dammit! She'd gone almost two months without them.

"Mine…sort of."

Her head shot up. "Yours?" She glanced at the cell phone on his desk and then noticed the portable baby monitor. "You don't have a baby crying ringtone?"

"No."

"You have a baby?"

There'd been nothing in his file. According to her father, he'd only been dating his current girlfriend—some high-powered attorney—for the past six months. He'd brought her to a dinner Howard had hosted for top producers and their significant others. And had explained where and how they'd met. Which was pertinent because soon after he'd taken the first full vacation he'd had in eight years.

"She's not mine," he said then frowned, glancing at Tamara hesitantly before holding her gaze. "Legally, she is. But I'm not her father."

"Who is?" His personnel records hadn't listed any next of kin other than an incarcerated mother.

He shrugged. "That's the six-million-dollar question. No idea. Biologically she's my sister."

Tamara flooded with emotion. She couldn't swallow. Standing completely still, concentrating on distancing herself from the deluge, focusing on him, she waited for her skin to cool. With a warm baby snuggled against her chest.

She had to get rid of that warmth.

Get away from the baby.

"Your mother had a baby?" she heard herself ask, sounding only a little squeaky.

He nodded.

"I thought she was in prison..." She suddenly realized she might have revealed too much. She was being too invasive for a first business meeting. "Um, Bill told me. He said you'd overcome a...difficult past."

He nodded. "She was. And the fact that she was a convict makes the question about Diamond's father that much harder to answer. Who's going to admit to fathering a child illegally?"

Her nerves were quaking. "She gave birth in prison?"

"Three days ago."

She'd been right. The child was only days old...

Days older than any of hers had lived to be.

"And she gave her to you?" She wasn't going to be able to keep it together much longer.

He'd agreed to take a baby. That said something about him. He needed to take her from Tamara.

He'd taken on a child. But then, his mother, a criminal, had agreed to take him on, too. By birthing him. Keeping him.

"My mother died in childbirth."

Flint's shocking words hit her harder than they would

have if she'd been on the other side of the room. Or in another room. Speaking to him on the phone.

Knees starting to feel weak, she knew she was out of time. "And just like that, you become a father?"

"Just like that."

There were things she should say. More questions to ask. But Tamara simply stood there, staring at him.

Unable to move.

To speak.

She was shaking visibly.

And had to get rid of the bundle she held.

Pronto.

Chapter Five

"Here, you need to take her."

As the pink-wrapped bundle came toward him with more speed than he would've expected, Flint reached out automatically, allowing the baby's head to glide up to his elbow, her body settling on his lower arm. While holding a baby was still foreign to him, he was beginning to notice a rhythm, a sense of having done it before.

"She needs to bond with you." The woman was a stranger to him and yet she was sharing one of the most intimate experiences in his life. His coming to grips with a reality he had little idea how to deal with and a role he was unsure of. Burying his mother. Meeting his sister. Becoming for all intents and purposes, a father. All happening in one day. He'd been about to lose it—and she'd saved him.

Just like she'd saved him from almost certain job loss earlier.

Could she really be, somehow, heaven-sent? By his

mother, not any divine source watching out for him. He'd long ago ceased hoping for that one.

Did he dare even think of his mother making it to an afterlife that would allow her to help her baby girl?

Was he losing his damned mind?

"Until two days ago, I didn't know the first thing about children." He hardly remembered being one. It seemed to him he'd grown up as an adult. "Babies in particular."

"You've had her for two days?" The woman had backed up to the other side of the desk and was halfway to the door. A couple of times she'd rubbed her hands along shapely thighs covered by a deliciously short skirt and was now clasping them together as though, at any second, they might fly apart.

"I just got her today," he said, calming a bit now as the baby settled against him as easily as she had with the efficiency expert. It was the first time he'd actually held the infant.

All he'd done so far was pick her up to lay her on a pad on the table. And to put her back in her carrier to feed her. That was it.

"So, how often does the holding thing need to happen?" How far behind was he?

"All the time." She was nodding, as though following the beat of some song in her head. Rubbed her thighs again, then was wringing her hands. Then reached for the doorknob. "When you're feeding her, certainly, and other times, too. Whenever you can. There are, um, books, classes and, you know, places you can go to learn everything..."

"I spent the weekend crash coursing. I guess I zoned out on the holding part."

"Parents holding their babies is a...biological imperative. They can't get enough of it. The babies, I mean. And..."

She turned away as though she couldn't wait to escape. Which made no sense to him, considering how naturally she'd rescued Diamond Rose from his inept attempts to "parent" her.

"What did you want?" His question was blunt but he wasn't ready for her to go. Not until his baby sister had a few more minutes with him—while he still had the efficiency expert's child-care guidance. To make sure Diamond was satisfied, for now, with what he could do for her.

"Um...oh, it can wait."

She glanced at the baby again, her eyes lingering this time. And then she seemed unusually interested in the wall on the opposite side of the room.

"Seriously. You needed something from me. I'm here to work." He couldn't afford to be a problem, considering how badly he needed this job.

The expert took a step away from the door and he waited for the business discussion to start. Tried not to pay attention to how beautiful she was. Like no woman he'd ever encountered before. A compelling combination of business savvy, sexy, glamorous and natural, too.

He thought her name was Tamara, but wasn't positive he was remembering correctly. He'd been a bit distracted when they'd met earlier.

But if he could get her to put in a good word with Howard on his behalf...

"I'm sorry about your mother." She sounded a little less harassed.

He nodded. Settled his bundle a little more securely against him.

She stared at the crook of his arm, then looked around the office. Seemed to spy the Pack 'n Play still in its box tucked away by the long curtain on the far window. "I guess you haven't had time to make child-care arrangements."

Efficiency expert. Finding a problem with his efficiency?

"I sold three thousand shares at 475 percent of their purchased value today." He'd made an outrageous amount of money for a client who liked to take risks. And a hefty sum for the brokerage, though it wasn't an investment Howard would have approved of because of the risk. He could just as easily have lost the entire sum.

The efficiency expert blinked. Gave her head a little shake. Drawing his attention to the auburn curls falling around her shoulders.

"I...asked about child care?" She sounded as though she was doubting his mental faculties now. She could join the club. If ever a man had lost it, that was him.

"Because if you need help, I know someone..."

Oh.

"I need to find out if I have a job first," he told her. Bill hadn't fired him. But he hadn't said his job was secure, either. Flint hadn't heard from him all afternoon. Or from Howard.

Either of them could have seen the sale he'd made, with their access to the company's portfolios. He assumed they both had. They were that kind of businessmen. Always on top of what mattered.

Which was why he was working there.

"Were you intending to open your own business? I heard Mr. Coniff ask about that as I approached his officer earlier."

Not an efficiency-related question. But it was a human one. He was standing there, holding a baby, and had just told her, before he'd made anyone else in the company aware, that the child was suddenly his.

And that he'd lost his mother.

He'd also told her that he wasn't sure he still had a job.

"Yes, I was in the process of opening my own business." No point in denying the truth. Lying wasn't his way. "I intended to tell Howard as soon as the final paperwork was in order."

"And now you aren't?"

Diamond Rose sighed. He felt that breath as if he'd taken it himself. "Starting a new business, especially in this field, takes an eighteen-hour-a-day commitment and comes with more than average financial risk. I can no longer afford the time or the risk."

"Because of the baby."

Because he had no idea how to be a father. He had to learn. "I'm her only family."

She nodded, looking at him, meeting his gaze. Not glancing, even occasionally, at his baby sister. She wasn't wringing her hands anymore, either, which he considered to be a good thing.

Still…

"Howard doesn't know about her yet. I didn't actually see her myself until this morning. I'd appreciate it if you'd give me a little time to get my act together before you say anything."

"I work for him," she said. And then, "How much time?"

He calculated…between the month he'd probably need and the minute or two she seemed willing to give him. "Twenty-four hours, max."

She watched him.

"I've got sixty times that in vacation days coming to me." From an efficiency standpoint, she wouldn't be risking anything. He could certainly ask for twenty-four hours.

"But you…didn't take today off."

"I rarely take time off. And I had stocks I had to sell or risk a big loss."

He'd had all the losses he could handle. His mother. His fiancée. His business. All at once. In the past couple of days. Astonishing that he was still standing there.

Except that he'd had no choice. Someone had to take care of his mother's brand-new baby.

Tamara—yes, that was definitely her name, Tamara Frost—was silent. A few long seconds later she said, "I see no harm in allowing you the time to go to your boss yourself."

He could have kissed her. He shook off the feeling. He'd just met the woman! Whether or not she was his mother's way of helping him from the great beyond, he had no time— and no mental or emotional capacity—to engage in any kind of liaison.

Yet he clung to the idea of having her on his side.

"Thank you."

"So...you just got her this morning? And came straight here?" She sounded a bit incredulous.

"I had stocks I had to sell," he repeated. A job to save. He couldn't afford a big loss on top of everything else. That much he knew. He needed Howard Owens to need him around; he certainly didn't want to give the older man more reason to fire him.

Her expression changed. Softened, although she hadn't looked at the baby again. Not in a while. "I'd like to give you the name of a friend of mine. She runs a day care not far from here. Most places don't take infants younger than six weeks, but considering your circumstances, I'm pretty sure she'd make an exception. I promise you, you won't be sorry. She treats the children in her care like they're her own. Gets to know them. Loves them. Babies get dedicated holding time. She takes everything that happens to her kids personally."

He wasn't ready to pass off his bundle to a stranger. Not out of his sight, at least.

Ms. Frost had given him twenty-four hours to report to Howard with some kind of baby management plan—well, to report to Howard that he had a child. Having the plan was his own stipulation.

"Does she watch your children?" Tamara wasn't wearing a ring, but she'd been such a natural with Diamond Rose... Seemed to know everything about babies...

A shadow passed over Tamara's face. He pretended not to notice. But when you knew the depth of sorrow yourself, you noticed.

"I don't have children. My work is my life. My job requires a lot of travel. It's not as if companies can come to me! And I don't think it's right to have children and then not be there to raise them. I love what I do, so I made a conscious choice."

Then why the shadow in her eyes?

And what business was that of his?

Particularly since he already owed her so much. She'd interrupted at exactly the right time that morning, preventing him from losing his job, at least temporarily.

Giving him time to close the deal he'd opened at the end of the prior week. To make his company so much money, it would be harder to fire him.

She'd agreed he could have time to come up with a plan to present to Howard regarding his changed life status. A way to convince him that in spite of everything that had happened, he was still a smart business risk.

And she was the expert Howard had just hired— meaning Howard most likely trusted her implicitly. If Flint could stay on her good side...

"I'd appreciate your friend's information," he said. He nodded to a pad and pen on his desk that she could use to write down the woman's name and phone number. All the while, he held the sleeping newborn between his left arm and body.

He could do this. Work. Take care of business. And a baby.

As long as his baby sister didn't cry again. He'd hold her. Feed her. Burp her. Change her. And hold her again. How hard could it be?

"I'll leave you to it, then…"

Momentary panic flared as Tamara Frost walked back to the door of his office. "Wait!"

She turned.

"You… What did you want? Initially?" She couldn't have come to give him her friend's number. She hadn't known he had a baby. "When you knocked at my door?"

"I'm going to be conducting interviews with all department heads, with all top producers and with some randomly chosen office staff throughout the next week or so. I stopped by to set up an appointment to meet with you. But clearly you need to get your ship in order before I climb aboard."

She was smooth. All business. If he hadn't already been attracted to her, he'd have fallen right then. He wasn't going to start anything—or even think about it. But he couldn't help his reaction and was smart enough to acknowledge it to himself. Rather that than have it club him over the head at some point. Now *that*, he couldn't afford.

Reminding himself he'd decided to stay on her good side, to shield his position with Howard, he sent her a smile reserved for his best clients. "Whatever works for you," he told her. "I'll make myself available." Career came first with him.

The bundle in his arms blew a loud fart.

He'd forgotten, for a brief second, that he was no longer the man he'd been.

"Talk to Mallory," Tamara said, referring to the friend whose number she'd written down. "Talk to Howard. And then give me a call."

"I don't have your number."

"It's in the email sent to everyone this morning."

It was late afternoon and he'd yet to read any company-related mail. He'd handled his clients' correspondence, though. Made all his phone calls. Set up a couple of important lunches for later in the week.

Flint would have come up with some charming, pithy response if the expert had waited a little longer. Apparently she was too efficient for that.

Watching the door close behind her, he glanced at the baby in his arms and felt...weak.

The boy who'd been resilient enough to get on a school bus as a runt kindergartener and sit among the bullies wasn't sure how he was going to proceed through the next hour.

Chapter Six

Tamara canceled dinner with her parents two hours after she'd accepted her mother's invitation. Dr. Sheila Owens had reached her after rounds that afternoon, thrilled that Howard had finally spoken with Tamara about his business problems and that she was already at work, trying to find the thief who was stealing from them. Sheila had wanted them to meet as a family and talk about the issue.

Tamara decided her best efforts would be spent poring over files instead. To begin with, eight years' worth of Flint Collins's investments transactions.

First, though, she'd suggested to her father that someone get Collins to sign that noncompete clause and let him know he wasn't on the brink of being fired. Half an hour later she received a call from him, saying that Collins had just come out of Bill Coniff's office and that Coniff had the signed form in his possession. Smiling as she hung up, she was satisfied with her day's work.

And happier than she should be to know that the man she'd so recently met was no longer worrying about being gainfully employed. Flint Collins had enough to deal with at the moment.

She couldn't go soft on him, though. That was how a lot of white-collar criminals succeeded in their fraudulent efforts. By charming those around them, winning the trust of those they were cheating.

At the same time, the guy was human, not yet proved guilty of anything other than wanting to branch out on his own, and deserving of some compassion on the day he'd buried his mother.

She looked away from the computer screen in her compact new office on the third floor of the building her father owned. She had a feeling it had been a big storage closet of some kind prior to being hastily converted for her. Howard knew better than to lay down the red carpet for a paid consultant he supposedly didn't know other than by reputation.

At least the room was private.

She'd had worse in the two years she'd been on the road.

A window would have been nice.

Oh, God… That baby…

Glancing at the time in the corner of her computer screen, she picked up the phone. She'd left one message for Mallory. But it was five o'clock now. Most of the children would have been picked up. And Flint Collins would be calling, if he hadn't already.

She needed to speak with her friend.

"I was about to call you," Mallory said when she answered. "I got your message, and I have one from Mr. Collins, too. He needs to speak with me by tomorrow afternoon, he said."

She'd given him a deadline to talk to her father. Not that

he had to have day care arranged before letting his bosses know that he'd just become a father. Of sorts.

"So you haven't spoken with him?"

"No, your message said I should talk to you first."

Tamara nodded. She thought she'd asked that but couldn't be sure. She'd been a bit off her mark when she'd made the call, having come directly from Flint Collins's office.

Where she'd had a newborn baby snuggled against her chest.

A chill swept through her and her insides started to quake again. Until she focused on the computer screen. The rows of numbers she'd been studying.

It was all about focus.

When she could feel the bands around her chest loosening, she told Mallory about Flint Collins suddenly finding himself the sole caregiver of a newborn baby. She didn't include the personal details. That was for him to share, or not, as he chose. His personal situation wasn't why she was calling.

"I held the baby, Mal," she said in the very next breath. "I was in his office and I didn't know she was there. I heard her cry and saw that he was just standing there, in front of her carrier. Maybe he was rocking it or something, I don't know. But without thinking I went right up and unstrapped her and picked her up."

The silence on the other end of the line wasn't a surprise. Mallory's calm tone when she said, "What happened next?" was different than Tamara had expected.

Only a handful of people knew the true extent of her struggles, how close she'd come to thinking she'd never have another happy moment. Mallory was one of them.

Because Mallory had been there, too, a few years before. They'd met in a small counseling group designed solely for young mothers who'd lost a baby.

"I started to unravel," she admitted. "Not as quickly as I would've expected, but I was working and it took a while for that barrier to break down."

She could feel the bands tightening around her lungs again. Her entire chest. Her ribs. Physical manifestations of the panic she fought, less often now, but still regularly enough that she'd stayed in touch with her support group.

"So, basically, you held it together."

"On the surface."

Their psychiatrist had offered them all medications, individually, of course. She and Mallory had preferred not to depend on drugs and opted to fight the battle on their own. And because neither one of them had ever remotely considered actually taking her own life—on the contrary, they'd both been in possession of enough equilibrium to maintain careers—they'd been left to their decisions without undue pressure.

"And what about now? How do you feel?"

They were supposed to be talking about Flint. And that...needy little child.

"Like I want a glass of wine and a jet to someplace far, far away." She had to be honest. It was the only way to succeed on her personal survival mission. "I've got the jitters, my hands are sweaty on and off."

She'd had hot and cold flashes, too, but didn't mention them. They didn't have anything to do with the infant. Although, come to think of it, both had happened in the presence of Flint Collins. During the first, though, they'd been in Bill Coniff's office and she hadn't known Flint was a new dad. She'd thought she had the flu, but no other symptoms had developed.

She was so busy convincing herself that the hot and

cold flashes, something new in her panic world, had nothing to do with the baby, that she'd walked herself right into another mental trap. Were the flashes because of *Flint*? Because of how incredibly attractive he was? Like, Hollywood ad attractive?

Was she *physically* reacting to him? As in being inordinately turned on?

No. Tamara shook her head. *Don't borrow trouble*, she told herself.

"What's wrong?" she asked when she realized Mallory hadn't responded to her list of symptoms.

"I was hoping..."

She knew what Mallory would've been hoping. They'd had the discussion. Many times.

Now they'd had the experiment Mallory had begged for and Tamara had always point-blank refused.

She'd held a baby. It had been horrible.

"Absolutely not." She made her point quite clear. "Never again."

"Maybe because you were so convinced it was a bad thing..." Mallory, bless her heart, refused to give up.

Tamara had nothing more to say on the subject.

"It works, Tamara, I swear to you. If you'd just try. Give it a chance. I'm living proof, every single day. If you knew how much healthier I am... How much happier... How much stronger..."

She'd only met Mallory after the other woman's infant son had died, yet Tamara knew her well enough now to be certain that Mallory had always had a core of strength.

"I get comfort from them—real, lasting comfort— knowing that little ones are on this earth, healthy and robust and happy and full of love."

"I know you do." And it wasn't that Tamara didn't want

a world filled with healthy, robust, loving babies. She did. Very much. She just couldn't have them in *her* world.

Because her heart knew the pain of four babies who hadn't been healthy enough to make it into the world alive. She knew the pain of losing a baby that everyone had thought was healthy. It happened. Babies died. In the womb and out of it, too. She'd survived losing Ryan. Barely. She couldn't afford the risk of another bout of that kind of pain and the residual depression.

"I'm not you," she said now, aware that it wasn't what Mallory wanted to hear.

Silence hung on the line again. But not as long this time.

"So tell me about this guy you referred. Flint Collins? You said I should speak with you first…" Her voice trailed off in midsentence and then Mallory continued. "Or was that it? It was about how you felt when you held his baby?"

"No." She'd had hot flashes both times she'd been with Flint. Not just because of his looks. He was confident, capable, successful—and had chosen to give up his business dream to care for a sister he hadn't even known he had. He had a baby who desperately needed a mother. He'd be a great match for Mallory.

She shook her head. No, he had a girlfriend. And besides…

"I need your word that what I'm about to tell you stays between you and me. Period. No one else."

"Of course. I assumed everything we told each other was that way. The two of us—our conversations are like an extension of being in session, right?"

The tone of voice… Tamara could picture the vulnerable look that would be shining from Mallory's soft blue eyes.

"Right," she said. "I just… This isn't about us and I needed to make certain…"

"You and me, our friendship—we're sacred," Mallory said, her voice gaining strength.

"Okay, good." Tamara took the first easy breath she'd had since she'd stepped into Flint's office. "I found out today why my mom and dad wanted me home so badly. Dad needs my help at Owens Investments. Someone's stealing from him and he suspects it might be Flint Collins. I'm working as an efficiency expert for him as a cover so I can have access to all the company files and employees, to stick my nose anywhere I want, to see if I can find some kind of proof for Dad to take to the police."

"Why doesn't he hire a detective?"

"Because right now only his accountant knows. If word gets out that there's something untrustworthy going on in the company, his investors will take off like birds flying south for the winter."

"How sure is he that Collins is his guy?"

"The evidence is stacked against him at the moment. But it's all hearsay and circumstantial."

"And he's a new dad?"

"I'll let him fill you in on the details. But, Mal? Whatever he's doing in his business life, this baby… She's only three days old. If ever a baby needed you, it's her. Even more so if it turns out her dad's involved in criminal activity. I felt you had to know, in case something comes down and there's some reflection on your business."

Not too long ago, a woman had showed up at Mallory's day care claiming that one of the kids was the woman's two-year-old son, who'd been kidnapped. Things had been rough going there for several weeks. And then the woman's story turned out to be true. That had all taken place before Tamara had returned from Boston, but she'd heard about it over the phone.

"No one can blame a newborn baby for anything. But I'll be careful not to let him see the books," she said with a chuckle.

Tamara smiled, too. An easy smile. One that felt natural. Her breath came more easily, too. She'd known she could count on Mallory.

And maybe, if Flint wasn't the thief, he and Mallory could make a family for that precious baby—

No, he had a girlfriend. Some powerful lawyer.

Because he was hedging all his bets as a smart investor would? In case he needed a top-notch lawyer?

She couldn't help wondering, as she ended her call with Mallory, what that rich girlfriend, who'd apparently been responsible for a change in Flint's spending habits, or at least his driving and vacation habits, thought of having a convict's baby to raise?

And then berated herself for being so catty.

The other woman was probably perfectly wonderful. She might already be making plans for the baby's care and Flint had just taken Mallory's contact information to give them options.

In any case, it was none of her business.

Yes, she thought again. Flint Collins and his new life were absolutely none of her business. She'd simply been the one to walk in on his intense day.

She looked back at her computer screen.

Focus. That was all it took. Focus.

Chapter Seven

"Bathing your newborn baby with the umbilical cord stump still attached is fine," the pediatrician in the video confirmed. *"There is no great risk that the stump will get infected. Take care to make sure that the area is thoroughly dried."*

Holding his sleeping sister in the crook of one arm, Flint paused his continued scouring of articles and videos on the internet—all from verified, legitimate pediatric sources and nationally recognized clinics and associations. He found this video particularly informative, considering his current dilemma.

"It is not necessary to bathe your baby every day," she continued. *"Up to three times a week, for the first year, is fine. As long as you're quick and thorough with diaper changes and burp cloths, you're cleaning the critical areas often enough. Daily bathing is not recommended, since it can dry out the baby's skin."*

Okay. Good. He didn't have to deal with a bath his first night. Her first night with him.

He could have hired a nurse to help out with this transition stage, but hadn't really even considered doing so. He'd always taken care of himself—and his mother when he could. He'd take care of Diamond, too. The baby wasn't going to be shoved off on strangers anytime that he was available to care for her. As he'd been so many times.

"Dodged a bullet on that one, Diamond Rose," he said, glancing at the sleeping baby. He'd been doing that a lot, all day. Glancing at her. He'd even caught himself staring at her a time or two.

It was just so hard to believe she was there. His flesh and blood.

A rush of love he couldn't have imagined swamped him. He acknowledged it. And moved on. He'd learned a long time ago to move on when it came to those kinds of emotions.

A guy had to cope, to push forward. To accomplish.

"It's best to use a small plastic tub, or a kitchen sink, when bathing a newborn..."

Clicking to open an additional browser window, he shopped for plastic tubs. Found one at the local children's store he'd spent bundles in that weekend. How had he missed the tub aisle? He added it to the shopping list he'd made for the following day.

And thought about Tamara Frost. Wondering what she was doing. If she had a significant other and was with him. She hadn't been wearing a wedding ring, but that didn't necessarily mean anything these days.

He wondered how she'd react if he gave in to the urge that had been nagging at him most of the evening and called her.

Before he'd figured out his immediate plans. Before speaking with Howard as she'd instructed.

He'd spoken with Mallory Harris and had an arrangement to meet with her the following day, time to be determined.

First priority was Howard Owens. He'd sent off an email that afternoon, requesting an in-person meeting as soon as possible. Once he heard back, he'd schedule—or reschedule—everything else.

He checked his email again. No response yet.

Nothing from Stella, either, not that he'd expected anything. She'd made her feelings perfectly clear. The baby or her. His choice was in his arms, breathing against him.

Maybe he should be missing Stella more than he was, or at least be hurting... Maybe he would at some point. There just wasn't room enough right now. His capacity for grief was taken up with Alana Gold.

The woman who'd taught him a long time ago that no matter how much he loved her, it wouldn't be enough to keep her home with him. Not forever.

Having Stella in his life had been wonderful. And yet part of him had always believed it wouldn't last.

Glancing at the clock, Flint figured he had another hour and fifteen minutes before he'd need to measure formula, heat, change, feed and burp again. Adjusting the baby so she was lying against him, propped in the curve of his body, and freeing enough of his left arm to allow him to type, he clicked on the most used site on his browser's favorite bar—the stock exchange.

Twelve-eleven a.m.
One-oh-six a.m.
One fifty-two a.m.
Wiping the tears from her cheeks, Tamara sat up in

bed. Turning on the bedside lamp she'd purchased from an antiques mall before she'd moved east, she pulled her laptop off the nightstand and flipped it open—the third time since she'd gone to bed that she'd done it.

She'd focus. Work until she couldn't keep her eyes open. And then she'd sleep. Until she woke up shaking again.

The nightmares weren't the same. But they all *felt* identical. Sometimes she'd be holding Ryan, feeling so incredibly happy. Complete. And then she'd wake and the devastating loss would be as fresh now as though she was feeling it for the first time.

She didn't completely hate that dream. Those moments holding her baby—they were almost worth waking up for.

That night they were the other kind. The ones where she wasn't even around children at all. She'd be someplace— sometimes she recognized it, sometimes she didn't—and she couldn't get out. It could be a maze. A building. A hole in the ground.

Sometimes she'd be on a path in the dark with so many obstacles she couldn't move.

She'd hear a cry. Someone needing her. And she could never get to whoever it was.

Or she'd reach the end of the path and there'd be a dead baby. Wrapped in a beautiful blanket. Always wrapped in that blanket.

Once there'd been an empty casket.

In the beginning she'd been inside her own womb multiple times. Trapped. Unable to get out.

She'd had that dream again tonight. Before the 1:52 a.m. wakening. Which was why she was sitting up.

She could take a sleeping pill. Knock herself out.

The thought gave her comfort. Knowing she wasn't going to do it gave her determination.

Focus gave her peace.

Damn Flint Collins. Bringing his newborn baby sister to work. She wasn't going to think about him, other than to dissect his dealings with Owens Investments down to the last cent. Every investment. Every sale. Every client. Every expense report. Every report he ever wrote, period.

How his first night with a brand-new baby was going was not her concern.

The vulnerable look in those dark brown eyes didn't mean he wasn't guilty of theft.

The baby resting against that gorgeous, suited torso had no bearing on his business dealings.

Tamara was not going to have a relapse.

She was going to focus.

Setting his phone to wake him every two hours, knowing he was going to be up several times during the night, Flint had considered himself fully prepared for his first night as a brother/father. Or at least his first night as the sole responsible person for his "inheritance."

When at 1:52 a.m. he was up for the fourth time, holding a bottle to a sleeping baby's mouth, he didn't feel capable of anything more. She'd cry. He'd feed her. She'd fall asleep sucking on the nipple. He'd put her back to bed and within half an hour her cry would sound on the monitor again, waking him.

At a little after one, he'd let her cry. She wasn't due for another feeding until two thirty. She was dry. Surely she'd fall back asleep.

She hadn't.

He'd changed her Pack 'n Play sheet.

He'd changed her diaper, even though she'd been completely dry.

He'd checked the stump of her umbilical cord.

And used the axillary thermometer under her arm. It had registered perfectly normal.

So he'd put the bottle back in her mouth and she'd sucked and swallowed for a few minutes before going back to sleep.

He hadn't heard from Howard Owens. Had Tamara put in a good word for him? Or broken her promise and told his CEO that Flint had a crying baby in his office?

Even if he heard from Howard first thing, inviting him up, how sharp was he going to be in the morning on less than two hours' sleep?

He had to get some rest. Parents didn't stop requiring sleep the second they had a kid. His mom had slept.

Not that his mother was the greatest role model but, in this case, the thought made sense.

Settling the baby in her Pack 'n Play, double-checking the monitor, he quietly crossed the hall to his room, slid between the sheets and closed his eyes.

A vision of Tamara Frost was there. Her fiery hair, a cross between brown and red, curling and long, framing the gold-rimmed green eyes…

His eyes open, he stared at the ceiling for a couple of seconds before closing them again. He was supposed to be resting, not getting turned on.

Memories of the gravesite that morning assailed him. And then Bill Coniff's distrusting face when Flint had asked for job security.

The sale he'd made had been a success. He had a client for life on that one. And earned his job security, as it had turned out.

He'd signed the noncompete. Financially he was sound. Careerwise, he'd still be doing what he was good at.

Tamara Frost wanted a sit-down with him—

The monitor beside him blew that thought away.

Diamond Rose was awake again. Desperate now, he picked her up, wasn't even surprised when she quit crying the second he was holding her. With his free hand, he hauled her portable playpen into his room. It wasn't what he'd planned, but it now seemed the only sensible choice.

The playpen went right next to the bed, He placed the baby inside while she was still awake, talking to her the whole time, then lay down beside her, keeping his hand on the netted side of the crib.

"I'm right here, Little One," he said. "Right here. I'm always going to be right here. For as long as I live. That's the one thing you can count on. And I'm going to give it to you straight, too. That's what I do. Mom always said I was going to *be* someone."

He paused, thinking that last statement highly inappropriate. Stupid, even. Diamond Rose's eyes half blinked open.

"We'll get better at this." He started talking again immediately. "We'll figure it out together. No—scratch that. *You're* great. I'll get better. *I'll* figure it out. You go ahead and be a newborn. And then someday you'll be a kid, and I'll still be here, still figuring things out. You won't need to start doing that until you're at least ten. Maybe twenty. Yeah, twenty works. We'll revisit it when you're twenty and see where we're at..."

The baby was zonked. But just for good measure, Flint kept right on telling her how it was going to be until he'd talked himself to sleep.

How could a woman accomplish the tasks before her if the people in her life insisted on pulling her into distractions she could ill afford?

Hating the thought, retracting it immediately, Tamara

picked up the phone when she saw Flint Collins's name pop up.

Yeah, she'd added him to her contacts. Because she'd given him her number and if he was calling, she wanted a warning before she picked up.

"Hello, this is Tamara," she said in her most professional voice.

"I'm available to meet with you at your earliest convenience."

"I'm sorry, who is this?"

"Flint. Collins. You asked me to phone to set up a meeting after I met with Howard Owens. I'm calling to let you know I've done that."

His voice, all masculine confidence, didn't sound like he was reporting anything—and shouldn't be sending chills all the way through her.

"Yes, Mr. Collins. I've got meetings scheduled all day today. Let me see where I can fit you in."

She hadn't scheduled even one yet. She had people waiting to hear on times. She'd been waiting on him. Because, at the moment, her father didn't give a damn about the efficiency of his staff.

"You've met with Mr. Owens already today?" she asked inanely, buying herself a moment to cool down. She knew he had, and not just because he'd told her so. She'd had a call from her father the minute Flint Collins had left his office.

Just as she'd had a call from Mallory earlier that morning, the second she'd had Diamond Rose in her care. For the first time ever Tamara had almost had to ask her friend to stop talking. The way Mallory had gushed over the baby, thanking her for the chance to help care for the motherless infant. And then stating again that she couldn't believe the baby hadn't worked her magic on Tamara.

That had been right about the time Tamara had begun second-guessing the wisdom of her decision in sending Flint to Mallory.

But she'd quickly recovered. She'd made the right choice for Diamond Rose, first. And for Mallory, too.

Flint Collins was still on the line, having told her that not only had he met with her father, but that Howard Owens had been completely decent about everything— about keeping him on and the fact that he suddenly had sole care of an infant.

There it was again. *Sole care*. Her father had told her the same thing, adding that he'd suggested Flint take a few weeks off to get acclimated to this major change in his life. Flint had demurred, saying he already had care plans in effect for the infant. Tamara had wanted to ask about the lawyer girlfriend her father had mentioned the day before—clarifying that "sole care" meant that Flint was the child's only guardian, for now. But she hadn't actually voiced the question.

She still didn't know why she'd hesitated. Just that bringing up Collins's girlfriend to her father had seemed... uncomfortable.

Which made no sense at all.

She looked around her small office. And pictured his, which would undoubtedly still have the baby smell. Or at least her memory of it. "Can you do lunch?" she finished.

Yes, a nice public meeting. Over food. Something to do while she questioned him about...she wasn't sure what. So far, the figures that had put her to sleep the night before were all adding up, and all looked legitimate.

What she needed to see was his personal bank account.

His personal tax records.

She had no access to either.

"Lunch would be fine," Flint said, suggesting a place

that she recognized. Close to the office but more upscale than they needed. A third-floor place down by the pier, overlooking the ocean.

She needed him fully cooperative—willing to give her the goods on himself when she didn't even know where to look—so she graciously accepted. Agreed to meet him in the lobby to walk the short distance between her father's building and the restaurant.

Although it was the first of November, San Diego was San Diego, no matter what season it was. She wouldn't be cold in her navy formfitting dress pants and short navy jacket. And the wedged shoes… Having worn five-inch heels more times than she could count, she figured she could walk in pretty much anything.

She just hoped she wasn't walking *into* something that would turn out to be more than she could handle.

Her father was counting on her.

Chapter Eight

She never should have agreed to walk over to the restaurant with him. While the day was pleasant, and being out in the sun with the blue skies overhead was even better—especially considering the windowless room where she'd spent her morning—Tamara still regretted her choice. The people milling around them, tourists lollygagging and business people bustling, left her and Flint Collins in a world of their own.

At least that was how it felt to her.

While people could probably hear what they said, with everyone moving at a different pace, no one could follow their conversation.

Making their togetherness seem too personal. Too intimate.

To begin with, they just talked about being hungry. About the restaurant. They'd both been there many times.

She liked their grilled chicken salad. He was planning on the grilled chicken and jalapeño ciabatta.

It didn't surprise her that he was a daring eater. Preferred his food hot.

The crowds forced them closer together than she would've liked. At one point he put a hand at her back to lead her ahead of him as they crossed the street.

He didn't touch her, exactly, but she could feel the heat of his presence.

Looking down, she could see the tips of his shining black shoes and the hem of the dark gray business pants he was wearing with a white shirt and red power tie.

New baby or not, he'd been perfectly and professionally put together when he'd greeted her in the lobby earlier. She hadn't asked about Diamond Rose. If she wanted to get closer to him for the sake of her father's investigation, she probably should ask—

"You mentioned that you travel all over the country to the companies you work for, like Owens Investments, yet you seem so familiar with the area. Are you staying nearby?"

"I was born and raised in San Diego." She didn't see any harm in telling him that. "I work locally as much as I can, but I need to be free to go where the jobs take me."

At least that was the plan—to work locally as often as possible. She'd only started to send out her portfolio to companies in the area. She'd always gone where she'd been sent, but she wasn't with a big firm anymore. She was on her own and would be responsible for finding her own work.

As soon as she finished the job she was on.

She'd spoken with her father again, just before leaving for lunch. She'd been through every line item she had on Flint Collins, she'd told him, and had found absolutely nothing that raised a single question mark. Other than that the man pushed the boundaries on risk-taking.

A few of his investments had seemed questionable because of the amounts and the commodities those amounts were spent on—until she'd followed them through to the sale that had grossed impressive amounts.

He'd had a few losses, too, but they were minimal in comparison.

Her father still suspected Collins was behind the thefts. However, he agreed that she should spend equal time on others in the company. She'd already started to do that.

And in the meantime, people who spent time with someone noticed things.

So maybe that was her "in" with Flint. Maybe she had to spend time with him, eyes wide open, and look for whatever could help her father.

While she simultaneously scoured the files of everyone else in the company.

If she failed, her father was going to have to go to the police. Investors would learn that Owens Investments had trouble in the ranks and the client list would dwindle.

Not only would her father's company be at risk of going under, but Flint Collins's job security would be at risk, as well—if he wasn't the thief.

So, in a way, she could be helping him by spying on him.

The thought was a stretch.

Tamara went with it anyway. She was going to help her father. She'd been her parents' only shot at being grandparents and she'd failed them there. She knew it wasn't her fault but...

She wasn't going to fail them here.

Flint had called ahead to make certain they wouldn't have to wait for a table. He'd requested a booth—strictly for the privacy. The fact that they got one by the window facing the ocean was a gift, but one he wasn't surprised to receive. He frequented the restaurant. Almost always with clients who had a lot of money to spend.

"Excuse me a second," he said, pulling out his phone as soon as they'd ordered drinks. Raspberry iced tea for both of them, something the restaurant was known for. Touching the icon for the new app he'd downloaded that morning at the Bouncing Ball Daycare, Flint waited for the portal to open. Mallory Harris had cameras installed in the nursery and with the app he could check in on Diamond Rose whenever he wanted.

Mallory was also keeping a detailed feeding spreadsheet for him—at his request—but, as it turned out, something she normally did anyway.

He'd checked in on his new family member before heading down to the lobby and his meeting with Tamara. But half an hour had passed since then.

That was the longest he'd gone without seeing his baby sister since she'd been placed in his arms the day before. In the office, he'd had his phone propped up on his desk where he could see the screen app at all times.

She'd cried twice to be fed, an hour after he'd dropped her off and then an hour and a half later. He hoped he hadn't missed the next one…

Almost as though on cue, the sound came—a little warning first, more of a cough than a cry. But if they didn't get to her soon, she'd be wailing so hard it would sound like she was going to suffocate or something.

As the second cry followed the warning, a foot hit his shin under the table.

"I'm sorry." Tamara moved in the booth, placing herself more to his left rather than directly across from him.

The accidental touching of their bodies under the table

wasn't attention-worthy. But her hands were clasped so tightly together he could see her knuckles were white.

She was tense.

Because he'd been looking at his phone rather than listening to her questions? He couldn't blame her, really; this was a business lunch. But their food hadn't even been delivered yet.

Still, he set the phone on its stand, pushing it off to his right. He could keep an eye on it and still give her his attention.

"I'm the one who should apologize," he told her in his most affable tone. "Being on my cell—that was rude of me." He couldn't afford to have her thinking that he was wasting business time on personal pursuits. He needed her to know he was in no way a threat to the company's efficiency.

On a hunch, and feeling friendly toward her due to her help the day before—the godsend her friend Mallory was turning out to be—he moved the phone so she could see.

"Mallory has cameras installed, and that means I can keep an eye on Diamond Rose," he explained. And then hastened to add, "This allows me to set my mind at ease where she's concerned so I can focus fully and completely on the job at hand. I'm all yours."

She was staring at his phone, her lips tense now, too.

"I'm glad things worked out with Mallory," she said, her delivery giving no indication that she was upset with him or his activity. On the contrary, she sounded genuine.

Diamond Rose's cries were growing more intense. Tamara looked around them and although his phone's volume was already on its lowest setting, he muted it completely. Mary Beth, the grandmotherly woman Mallory had introduced to him this morning as one of the Bouncing Ball's full-time nursery personnel, appeared on screen, scooping up the baby and holding her close.

Flint relaxed as Diamond Rose snuggled against Mary Beth. He'd made it in time for feeding.

"How'd it go last night?" Tamara was smiling at him now.

He'd thought her heaven-sent before, but that smile... Yeah, she was something.

"With the baby, I mean," she added when he failed to respond in a timely fashion. She was watching him, not his phone. And seeming to care about more than just the business reason for their lunch.

Her look felt...personal.

Of course, he *was* a bit sleep deprived.

"It was rough." He told her the truth, but he grinned, too. "Still, we made it through." He told her about the number of times the baby had cried, shortly after being fed and changed. About going back and forth between his room and hers, and his eventual desperate fix—the Pack 'n Play on the floor right next to his bed.

He was honest with her because he was done living a double life: the convict's kid and the successful businessman. Done lying to himself about who he was.

If he was going to be worthy of that completely innocent little girl taking that bottle on his screen, if he was going to teach her how to come from what they'd come from and still be a success, then he'd have to quit denying to himself that he was different from most of the people in the world he inhabited.

Not that any of this had to do with his first night with a newborn, or was in any way related to the question he'd just been asked. It was simply a reminder of the mode of thinking he was bringing into the meeting ahead. The life ahead.

Emotionally, Stella's leaving hadn't hit him as hard yet as it was bound to, but he knew he wasn't going through that again—a rejection after he was fully committed. A rejection based on something over which he had no control and couldn't change. He was the son of a convict. He'd grown up with her as the constant in his life. Loved her. And the child she'd borne on her prison deathbed. If someone was going to have a problem with the baggage he carried, at least he'd know up front. No more hiding.

He'd had enough disappointment for one lifetime.

"Obviously she didn't like being in a room alone," Tamara was saying while thoughts flew through Flint's brain at Mach speed. "She needed to be close to you, but probably not right up to the bed. I'll bet if you keep her playpen in your room, but along the wall, and put her to bed there, where she can be aware of your presence, you'll both sleep better."

He nodded, finding the concept of a baby in his room with him every night a bit…alarming, but was not completely unfond of the idea. "You seem to know a lot about children."

Her lips tensed again. But then he wasn't sure as she almost immediately smirked and said, "Mallory's my closest friend," as though that explained everything.

And he supposed it did. If Mallory shared the details of her work life on a regular basis.

"How did you two meet?" High school? Grade school, maybe? He knew plenty of people whose friendships went that far back. Whereas he didn't have any from a year ago. Or the year before that.

Other than Stella and Alana Gold, Flint had avoided personal relationships outside one-night stands.

He had clients who went almost as far back as high school, though.

"We were in a women's group together," Tamara said, glancing at his phone and then quickly away. She turned, facing the room, as though looking for their lunch.

"Businesswomen?" He wasn't going to try to explain his curiosity, but Tamara had arrived in his life at a critical time and, as a result, he felt drawn to her.

That was what he believed, anyway. "We were all women who worked, yes," she said. Then added, "Mal's one of the brightest, most successful women I know, on all levels. She's savvy and makes good money. Her day care is always close to maximum capacity, and yet she hasn't become hardened by the shadow sides of business ownership. Like the people who don't pay on time, or at all. The ones who find fault with everything. The hours. Nothing gets to her. She's a nurturer to her core."

He nodded again, not sure why she was selling her friend so hard when he'd already signed a contract with her. The deal was closed. But he liked listening to her talk. Liked how the gold rim around the green of her eyes glistened as she spoke about her friend.

Hell, he liked just sitting across the table from her.

She was there on business.

"You said you had some things to discuss with me?" He'd answer whatever questions she had and was fully confident she'd find nothing wasteful in the way he worked. Then he'd see if maybe she'd have dinner with him sometime. Just dinner. Nothing to do with business.

"Only some clarifications," she explained, taking a sip of her iced tea. Over the next twenty minutes, through the delivery of lunch and eating of same, she talked about several of his dealings during the years. Her questions were strictly from memory, no notes. She asked for justification of certain expenses, mostly making sure that she understood things as the way she thought she did.

He enjoyed talking to her about work even more than talking about her friend. He was good at what he did. One of the best around. And she was a quick and avid learner.

She also seemed genuinely interested. More than Stella had ever been.

He talked about the money saved in throwing one lavish, weekend-long yacht party for a number of investors, rather than many expensive dinners with individuals, mentioning not only the obvious savings on the event costs, but other advantages—like the adrenaline that kicked up when investors talked together about investments.

"Everyone wants to get in on the best deal," he reiterated as the waitress cleared away their plates.

"You drive the market, affect stock prices, by persuading everyone to invest in one thing," she said.

He shook his head. "We discuss the market, in small groups and as a whole, and where we think the trends are headed. Not everyone invests in the same way. They all get excited about investing in whatever they think is the best bet after all conversations are through."

She smiled as she studied him. "In other words, you drive their desire to invest," she summed up.

"Maybe. They have to *want* to invest to get involved in the conversation."

The bill was delivered and he reached for it. He'd suggested the place, but when she took it from him, he didn't try to stop her. This was her lunch, he knew it would be expensed, and he didn't want to insult her. But he hoped there'd be a next time, and that it would be his treat.

As he'd observed earlier, she'd been put in his path at a critical time. And she already knew all about his mother. She'd seen his employee file, so she'd know about his own troubles eight years before. And she'd met Diamond Rose.

She was only with him because she had to be. He didn't miss that point. But if she accepted a personal invitation...

He waited until they were almost back at the office, until they were talking about the weather, clearly not a business discussion, before he asked, "Would you be interested in doing this again sometime? Not as a date, but just having lunch together? If you come up with any more questions about what we do at Owens, I'd be happy to answer them, and you've given me so much insight on raising newborns, I'd just like to say thank you."

Anything later than lunch involved Diamond Rose, and he wasn't ready for that.

"I..." Shaking her head, she let her words trail off.

She was going to turn him down. He was more disappointed than he'd expected to be, but waited for what would no doubt be a polite brush-off.

Or, God help him, was she going to report him to Howard for sexual harassment? He hadn't touched her. Or indicated that he wanted to. He'd just invited her to lunch.

He started to sweat anyway. In his experience, based on who he was, his background, people were more apt to assume he was guilty than the guy next door. Even if he *was* the guy next door.

That mess eight years ago had nearly stolen any hope he'd had of making a decent life for himself.

His mother's death three days ago had stolen even more...

"I'd actually like that, thank you. I'm pretty sure that between now and then I'll come up with more questions and the way you explain things, enough but not too much..." Tamara said after a noticeable time had passed.

Flint had no idea why she'd changed her mind, but he was certain she had. And he was glad of it, too—enough so that he wasn't going to question his luck.

He'd press it, though. "Sometime this week?" he asked. He had a business lunch scheduled for the next day. "Thursday?"

"Thursday would be good."

Okay, then. That was set. He'd been off-line from Diamond Rose for at least twenty minutes and from commodities reports for almost two hours. Holding the door open for Tamara, he thanked her for lunch, told her to contact him if she had any other questions, then wished her a good rest of the day and hightailed it to his office.

Keeping to his priorities was paramount. That was a promise to Alana. And to Diamond Rose.

Chapter Nine

Tamara was too busy Tuesday afternoon to think about the complexities of her lunch meeting. But they were there, a steady presence in the background of her day. She'd visited the head of every department. Had looked at their bottom lines.

Finding very little, even as an efficiency expert, to offer her father, she started to feel overwhelmed. She had some ideas on making the mail room run more smoothly. Thought maybe a delivery service would work better than the current system of having a driver on-site, ready to go if the need arose. Yes, the driver handled other menial tasks when he wasn't driving, but they were tasks that could easily be incorporated into the daily routines of several different employees.

None of which was going to make a damn bit of difference if she couldn't find something really out of place.

Granted, she'd only gone over one broker's files in

depth—Flint's. There was at least a week's worth of information to weed through, already downloaded on her computer that morning, pertaining to all accounts and monies. Everything from commissioned earnings to an annual fund-raiser to benefit underprivileged children that her father had been running around Christmastime every year since Tamara's first miscarriage.

Next, she'd be looking at supply purchases and expense reports.

And figured she could study numbers, tally up columns, run down bids and purchase orders for months and still not find what she needed.

At the end of the day, she went to her father. She needed to know more about the specifics of what his accountant had found.

"I don't think it's Flint Collins," she said the second she sat with him on the solid leather couch at the far end of his office. He'd poured her a glass of tea with ice. And had a shot of whiskey for himself.

One shot. That was what he had every day before leaving the office. His way of unwinding, he'd always said, of leaving the stresses of his business day right where they belonged.

"He's worked too hard to get where he is to jeopardize it over money," she said. That was her gut instinct. At least, that was what she called whatever it was that was driving her to want to help him.

"I went through every single client transaction, Dad. Every expense report. Granted, I didn't study every line item, or look up every purchase order, or check actual filed expense reports against his reimbursements. But I did look at a lot of them, and at overall figures. I couldn't find ten cents that had been misappropriated. Now, if he's claiming expenses he shouldn't be, that's something I can check, but I need more concrete information or I'm wasting valuable time spinning my wheels."

Naïve of her to think she'd just open up a ton of files and come across some glaring discrepancy. Or even a slightly buried one. She was used to comparing figures others didn't look at—like expenses and supplies for each person compared to others working the same or similar job. Looking for waste.

Not looking for a crime.

"I found a couple of people 'stealing' from the company I was at a couple of months ago," she continued, half afraid he was going to be disappointed in her. Which made no sense, considering her parents had been her biggest champions her entire life.

So why the feelings of guilt? As if there was something going on she didn't want him to know about?

"They worked different shifts and were taking turns clocking out for each other so they'd both get overtime pay when they weren't even working their forty-hour shifts."

"And, of course, expense reports not gelling with actual receipts and time stamps has come up more than once, since clamping down on misuse of those perks, or cutting back on some of the more extravagant ones, are the easiest ways to save a company money."

Howard sipped his whiskey. He was frowning as he studied her.

"I didn't want to prejudice you," he said when she fell silent. "And I don't want to hang Collins without giving him a fair shake," he added. "I like the guy. He's always done what he said he'd do. Every single time. Truthfully, I'm not even sure I'll press charges if it turns out to be him, as long as he makes full restitution and agrees to get out of the business permanently. Only a couple of people know about the fraud at this point. My accountant, and you. For the overall health of the business, I'd like to keep it that way."

Sitting forward, he put his glass on the table, elbows on his knees, and faced her. "Who knows? You could've found something as simple as two expense account reports coming out of one business lunch."

"Two different people claiming the same lunch?" If it was done all the time, the money would add up. She got that her father didn't want anyone in the company to know he was checking up on them, but something like that would've been easy for him to discover without her help and without raising too many alarms in his ranks.

"More like two expense reports, each claiming half of one lunch when only one employee was there."

She frowned. She could see duplicity in that but... "If they each claimed only part, then the company wouldn't be out any money."

Unless...

"You think someone, say Flint Collins, has somehow managed to secure *two* expense accounts—both in his name? And is using one to reimburse himself and the other to treat himself to a more expensive lifestyle at the company's expense?"

He supposedly had that rich girlfriend he was keeping up with, although, to date, she'd seen no indication of another woman in his life.

He'd asked her to have lunch with him. Partially, as a thank-you for helping him out with his sister. Not that she'd done anything. But would a man who was in a relationship do that?

Immediate reasons came to mind why he might. Not least of which might be that he was unethical.

"How much do you know about trading?" her father asked.

She knew there were a lot of legal guidelines; that a lot of people had used a lot of different ways to cheat while doing it. And she knew that the world's economic security revolved around the stock market.

"Not enough."

"I thought not knowing too much would make it easier for you to find what we're looking for, because obviously it's designed to be missed by those of us closely involved. I also wanted to find out if it appeared that I was doing anything shady. If you were able to discover records that put you in doubt as to my culpability. I needed to know what someone looking from the outside would find, where a trail might lead, in case it led back to me. I'm not completely sure I'm not being framed. Luckily you haven't found anything." He stood, went across the room to a row of built-in file drawers and started thumbing through folders.

She hoped that was true—that her father wasn't being framed. Because she'd held that baby and it was messing her up. She was off her game, going to fail her father, if she didn't get some help with this assignment. Maybe whatever he was looking for over there in the cabinet would make the difference, would give her a chance to deal with the way she felt and the effect it was having on her ability to do what she needed to do.

This was why Tamara didn't hold babies. Couldn't hold them.

Unlike Mallory, who'd held her son every day for almost five months before he'd died and took comfort from the feeling of a baby in her arms, Tamara had never been able to hold her own child. Not even Ryan, who'd been fully viable when he'd been born four months early.

And while, for the most part, Tamara had recovered, the one thing she could not do was hold a child. It wasn't as if a woman couldn't live a full, productive, happy life without ever holding a baby. Particularly a woman who knew she was never going to have children of her own.

Howard was back, handing her some files. "These are the basic rules of trading," he told her. "You can find the same kind of thing on the internet, but this is something I put together for a college career day I was doing a few months ago. You won't need to know any more than that."

She took the files.

He emptied his glass. "You ready to go meet your mother for dinner?" he asked. She'd taken a rain check the night before. Her mother had already cashed it in.

They stopped by her place to drop off her car and then, in the front seat of her father's Lincoln, she leafed through the material he'd given her—thinking of Flint Collins as she did.

Getting glimpses of him in his world.

Which was also her father's world, she reminded herself.

"Basically, what we're looking at here is a pattern day trader. Someone who makes a certain number of day trades over a set period of time. Four or more in five days, for example. Day traders can trade with a large enough margin to buy and sell with less in the account than is actually being spent. But a pattern day trader has real advantages in that, for him, the margin is larger. He can trade for up to four times the cash value in the account, which about doubles the normal margin. That gives him what's called 'day trader buying power' and is a measurable leverage."

She got enough of what he was saying to nod with some confidence.

"Someone in Owens Investments is using my broker license, basically signing in as me, to make trades that rose to pattern day trader status. The log-ins were from various computers in the building—any of which I could have accessed, and all in secure areas out of view of surveillance cameras. They were made at various times throughout the day.

"The trader was using monies from an account I set up for charitable donations," he explained, "without ever really withdrawing money.

"Whoever it was would make four day trades in a four-day period, meaning they bought and sold in one day, all small trades that lost nothing, but gained little, so no withdrawals were made. Then, on the fifth day, he'd use the day trader buying power to buy and sell for enormous profit."

Howard paused to take a breath as they approached the turn into the upscale neighborhood where she'd grown up.

"At the beginning and the end of every day, the account looked just as it always did, with no visible withdrawals or deposits. One of the things about pattern day trading is that accounts can't be held overnight, so there was a guarantee of ending the day the same way it began." He took another deep breath before adding, "We presume the daily profits went into an offshore account. But we've been unable to trace it due to a complicated computer trail and legalities being different from country to country."

"What happened when he—or she—made a losing trade? Was the money put back?"

"That didn't happen."

"This person traded every day without a single loss?" It meant this trader—or traitor, she thought wryly—had to be damned good.

Signaling the turn, Howard shook his head. "There were only a handful of weeks this was done. Money was made with the use of Owens Investments' funds, but there's no accounting for that cash. It looks like I made a considerable amount of money I didn't report."

Her heart was thudding in her chest. "Can you go to jail for that?"

When he shook his head a second time, Tamara almost cried with relief. "We've already submitted corrected tax returns," he said, "claiming an oversight and paying all appropriate taxes and fees."

"On money you never had."

"That's right. There's a lot more to it, of course. I'm giving you a vastly simplified version. But you've got the gist. The only other thing we found were those expense reports, splitting bills. They were always split between various brokers and me. Basically, someone was tagging me onto various expense reports, from every broker in the house, over the past year."

"Someone was turning in expense reports in your name?" she asked, incredulous.

"That's right."

"What happened with the money?"

"I have all my expense-report checks deposited directly into the charitable donation account."

They'd turned into the long circular drive, pulling up to the fountain in front of her parents' home. That fountain had been the site of family photos commemorating just about every meaningful event in her life—including each time she'd come home to tell her parents she was pregnant.

They'd taken one when she'd left to move to Boston, too. She'd been sick to her stomach that day. And felt like throwing up now, too.

"Who in the company knows you don't keep expense monies reimbursed to you? Who knows you deposit them?"

"Any number of people. My top management, of course. It's a tax write-off. I offer the option to all my managers. But others know, too."

"Which traders know?"

He shrugged but his glance was filled with sadness as he said, "Any of them could, depending on whether or not the people I've told have talked about it."

"Have you ever told any of your traders directly?"

Her stomach in knots, she knew what was coming. She knew why her father suspected Flint Collins.

"One," he said. "Because he mentioned at the Christmas Charity Fund Auction a couple of years ago that he wanted to give back to the company by way of charitable donation. So I told Flint Collins and offered to have his monies deposited into the account."

And Flint Collins, she knew, as a top producer, was inarguably good enough to have made the trades in question without a loss.

He was also a risk-taker. The day she'd met him, he'd made the company an incredible amount of money on a deal that could easily have lost a bundle.

Her heart felt as though it had been pumped full of lead.

"Did he take you up on the offer?"

"Yeah. Until he started dating Stella Wainwright. That was when he bought the Lincoln SUV. I heard of at least two weekend trips he took to exotic locations using a private jet. And he quit donating to the charitable account."

The rich girlfriend had a name.

Tamara didn't want to care anymore whether she existed or not.

She cared about her lunch date on Thursday, though. She might not be making any real progress within the company, but she had an in, just the same. A way to help her father.

She was going to get to know Flint Collins. To infiltrate his life as much as he'd let her and find out everything she could about him.

Just as a supposed friend, of course. She wasn't going

to prostitute herself. Besides, she'd already made up her mind that if by some chance the man turned out to be innocent, she still wouldn't pursue any attraction she might feel for him. But maybe she'd try to set him up with Mallory. If he was half as good a guy as he led one to believe, they'd be perfect for each other.

If he wasn't a crook.

Mallory and Diamond Rose would be perfect for each other. That was what she was really thinking.

As she followed her father into the house, she thought about Stella Wainwright. Wondered about her. Planned to look up her father's firm when she got home. Only for Mallory's sake. Or Diamond's.

In the event that Flint Collins was on the up-and-up.

Yeah, she was bothered about the woman—for Mallory's sake. Which meant she was getting ahead of herself.

Wait until the man's name was cleared first.

Or not cleared.

Then try to find out more about his girlfriend.

Like, why the woman wasn't helping the poor guy, leaving him to sleep with a Pack 'n Play next to his bed so he could get a few minutes' rest.

Again, not her problem.

Or concern.

So why, as she put on a bright face for her parents and focused on giving them no cause for worry on her behalf, was she still thinking about Flint Collins and how he seemed to deserve more than he was getting from Stella Wainwright?

Chapter Ten

Flint had slept better on Tuesday night. Taking Mallory's advice, he'd laid down as soon as Diamond Rose did after dinner and then alternated dozing and lounging for the rest of the night whenever she slept. He hadn't gotten anything else done, but he'd woken on Wednesday morning feeling a hell of a lot better than he had since the call from the prison warden telling him his mother had passed away.

Wednesday evening wasn't as good. He'd set it up to be—had had a great lunch with one of his most lucrative clients and a successful afternoon of trading because of it.

And Diamond Rose seemed to be getting into a schedule of eating every two hours and sleeping well in between. He'd watched her on and off all day, and Mallory's report had been positive.

He'd even dared a stop at the grocery story on the way home from the day care, disconnecting the carrier from the car seat as if he'd been doing it all his life, looping the handle over his forearm and setting it into the grocery cart as soon as he got inside.

If he'd been on the lookout for a woman, he would've been amused by the attention he was getting from the few after-work shoppers—obviously so based on their business attire—who were, like him, he imagined, buying something for a quick dinner.

Two of them met his gaze and smiled. A third stopped and reached down, as though to pull back the blanket looped over the handle of the carrier, effectively building a tent around Diamond Rose. But his quick turn forestalled that move. The woman apologized, said she was a single mom of two little ones, then handed him her card and said to give her a call if he had any questions or needed help or advice.

How she'd known he wasn't married, he had no idea. And then, upon further reflection as he walked the aisles, he wondered if she hadn't cared one way or the other.

Which led him back to the place he'd landed, on and off, all day. Tamara Frost. She'd accepted his invitation to lunch. He'd casually mentioned her to Mallory when he'd received his personal report on Diamond Rose's day, but had gleaned nothing, other than that she worked hard and excelled at her job.

Things he already knew.

He paused at the deli, considering premade pork barbecue and coleslaw. Both looked one step away from congealed.

In his other life he'd have treated himself—and Stella—to an expensive dinner. As it was, he settled for frozen lasagna that could do what it needed to do in the oven without his supervision.

He made it home without mishap. He'd timed it so that Diamond Rose slept through the entire outing. He put his food in the oven and, when she woke up, was ready with a diaper and a warm bottle. He had her back to sleep in record time and was considering a beer—the hardest he liked his alcohol most days—when there was a knock on his door.

He wasn't expecting anyone and didn't ever have drop-in visitors. His thoughts immediately flew to the police, coming to bring yet another bout of bad news about his mother. He was halfway to the door before he realized it wouldn't be the police. At least not about his mother.

He was never going to have another of those visits. The awareness settled on him—with relief, since he was free from that dread now, and with sadness, too. His mother was gone. Any hope he'd held of her ever turning herself around was gone with her.

To his shock, a uniformed officer stood outside his door.

"Are you Flint Collins?" the woman asked.

"Yes."

"You've been served, sir," she said, handing him an envelope.

By the time he glanced from it to her, all he could see was her back.

Tense from the inside out, Flint glanced at the baby sleeping in her carrier on his kitchen table, with the idiotic idea that he didn't want to open the envelope in front of her. Whatever it was, he was going to shield her from it.

Shield her from a life in which officers appeared at your door—for any reason at all.

Was he being sued?

Or, God forbid, was someone after Diamond Rose? Challenging his right to her?

Turning around, he tore open the envelope. No one was taking the baby from him. He had money. He'd fight...

What the hell?

He'd been issued a restraining order. By Stella. Reading it, he could hardly believe what he was seeing. Stella was afraid he was going to hurt her. That he was going to retaliate for her breaking up with him. He was not to distribute any pictures of her that might be in his possession. He was to gather up any of her belongings still in his home—she'd provided a list—and leave them outside his front door, at which point the woman who'd delivered the order would take them and would leave a box of his things in return.

The next sheet was a legal agreement whereby he agreed not to attach to any Wainwright holdings, not to mention them, or say he'd ever been associated with them, not to claim anything of theirs as his, for any reason. Stella agreed to the same, regarding him and his family. It was further understood that any child he had in his custody had no relation to, or bearing on, her.

When he got through the last sheet, he started back at the first. She'd gone to court and requested a restraining order. There was a legal document filed with his name on it. A court date would be set within the next three weeks to allow him to dispute the claims therein, and the order would either be dropped for lack of cause or put into effect for up to three years.

It was the paragraph on the second page that got to him.

Defendant. Him. He was a defendant. His whole life, even eight years before, he'd managed to keep himself clean, no charges filed against him ever. And now...he was a defendant?

Flint's entire being slumped with fatigue. The weight on his shoulders seemed about to push him to the floor as he read the claim.

Defendant has a history of criminal influence and, upon victim asking to end relationship, wouldn't take

no for an answer to the point of victim being fright-
ened for her and her family's safety and well-being.

When Stella had said she was breaking up with him,
he'd given her a chance to calm down, to get used to the
idea of the secret he'd kept about his mother's identity. Because Stella had known the man he'd become. Collins was
a common enough name. There'd been no reason for her
to remember a court case from eight years before when
it had had nothing whatsoever to do with her area of law.
Small-time drug dealers didn't touch corporate lawyers.

But she'd looked up the case. And when, after a few
hours, he'd stopped by her office to see her, thinking they
could talk, she'd been pissed off. He'd waited outside and
she'd warned him not to stalk her.

Stalk her?

That had been that. He'd left. And hadn't tried to contact her since.

He was no threat. Had never been a threat.

But the Wainwright name was apparently too pristine
to be linked, in any way, with his.

Or Diamond Rose's.

In the end, that was what stuck in his throat. The fact
that she'd mentioned his newborn baby in her dirty court
papers.

Glancing at the sleeping baby, he grabbed a garbage bag,
collected the things on Stella's list, down to the toothbrush
he'd meant to throw away, thankful he'd been too distracted
to do that yet—could he be sued for a toothbrush?—and
left the bag out on the porch, looking over at the waiting
unmarked car at his curb. He'd sign her document in the
morning, with a notary present.

And he'd call an attorney, too. One who was good
enough at his or her job to go head-to-head with the Wainwrights. He wanted the whole mess gone before anyone

was the wiser. Wanted no evidence it had ever existed. There was no way in hell he was going to live under the threat of a restraining order for the next three years. Anytime Stella wanted to, she could "run into" him somewhere and claim he'd violated the order. He could end up in jail.

The idea gave him the cold sweats. His whole life, everything he'd worked for...

He was going to "be someone," his mother had told him so many times. What he'd taken her words to mean was that he'd never see the inside of a jail cell.

He'd barely escaped the nightmare eight years before. And had been hell-bent ever since on making sure he never came remotely close again.

He wasn't a defendant. Wasn't ever going to be a defendant. That order had to go away.

When the baby awoke, he was bothered enough by Stella's bombshell that he forgot to be nervous about giving his little one her first bath. Mallory had offered him some pointers and he'd watched several internet videos, too.

He talked to Diamond Rose the whole time, taking care to keep his voice soft, reassuring. He'd turned up the heat in the house first, kept the water tepid and a towel close so she wouldn't get cold, and he worked as rapidly as he could with big hands on such a small, slippery body. In the end, the two of them got through the process without any major upsets.

Something else came out of the evening. Any feelings he might still have had for Stella were washed down the drain with the dirty bathwater.

Too bad about his frozen dinner, though. It dried out in the oven.

Tamara had expected Flint to take her to an establishment not unlike the one they'd visited for lunch on Tuesday.

Instead they'd gone to Balboa Park, sitting in the sun on a cement bench, having a wrap from a nearby food truck—possibly one of the best-tasting meals she'd ever had.

With a man she found more attractive than any other man she'd ever shared lunch with. Business or otherwise.

What was it about Flint Collins that did this to her? It wasn't like he was drop-dead model material, not that she went for that type. Yeah, he was fine-looking—enough that she'd noticed several other women checking him out during the time they'd been in the park. But the blond hair and brown eyes, the more than six-foot-tall lean frame, even the expensive clothes, could've been matched by any number of other "California blond" men. The state was flooded with them.

"I saw a brochure at the Bouncing Ball this morning," he told her. "The founder of this food truck is a lawyer in Mission Viejo and a former client of Mallory's."

"You're talking about Angel's food truck! I didn't know it had been renamed!" she said, glad to have something other than his sexuality to think about. It's a Wrap fit the menu better. It wasn't fancy, but she liked it so much more. It was as though he'd known she'd prefer sitting in the park during her lunch hour to being trapped at a table in a fancy restaurant. She spent a lot of the day trapped in a seat at a desk.

"I never met the couple because I was in Boston," she continued, "but Mallory called me about the case from the first day she met them. The woman wanted Mal's help in identifying her abducted son, without alerting his father, the abductor, to the fact that he'd been found out."

"Why not just call the police?"

"Not enough evidence for them to do anything. The woman was acting on instinct, based on a picture she'd seen at the day care."

"What did Mallory do?"

"She helped her! Without giving up any confidential information, or putting the child or his father at risk, in case the man wasn't guilty. Anyway, it all turned out well."

He was staring at her as though he couldn't get enough. Of her story, she had to remind herself, not of her.

"So...it was the woman's son?"

"Yeah. And Mal was the one who got the proof."

Flint Collins's full attention was a heady thing. Wiping everything else from her mind. And—

This wasn't going to help her father.

He'd pulled out his phone. Had it on his thigh. She couldn't hear any sounds coming from it, but realized, if she glanced at the screen, she'd see the newborn child he'd taken on that week.

Busy avoiding that choice, she wanted to ask if he knew anything about offshore accounts, but couldn't figure out a legitimate reason for wanting to know.

And wondered why he'd asked her out to lunch.

"How's everything going at home?" she asked instead. Not a Stella question. Unless he happened to mention her in the course of his answer.

He told her about Diamond Rose's first bath, complete with turning up the heat in the house. And her heart gave another little flip.

Because of the baby, she told herself.

What kind of fate was forcing her to spend time with a man who had an infant? And be attracted to him to...

"I've been trying to work up to asking if you'd like to join us for an evening," he said as they finished their wraps and threw away the trash, walking side by side as they made their way through the park to where they'd catch a cab back to the office. They'd spent all of twenty minutes together.

"Us?" she asked, concentrating on her step, keeping it steady. She had to do this. To pretend to be friends with him. And it wasn't like she freaked out anytime she was around an infant. She flew on planes with them. Ate in restaurants with them. She just kept her distance.

"Diamond Rose and me." He'd put his phone in his shirt pocket, his hands in the pockets of his dress pants.

She suddenly felt hot and waited for the chill that would sweep over her when the flash ended.

Maybe she really was getting the flu.

Could she at least hope so?

"I'd like that," she told him while hoping the thrill she felt was because she was one step closer to helping her father.

For the next couple of steps she warred with herself over whether or not she should say more—perhaps tell him she had baby issues.

But she didn't tell anyone that except the people to whom she was closest.

Besides, this wasn't a real friendship.

"When?" she asked as their arms touched.

"Tomorrow night? I can make lasagna tonight so we'd just have to heat it up. We could watch a movie."

What about Stella? She had to ask.

"I might be out of line here, but…are you seeing anyone? I…like to know what I'm walking into." No. Wrong. All wrong.

Now it sounded as if she was interested in starting a "seeing each other" relationship. Which she wasn't. She couldn't.

Could she?

In any case, she'd had no business asking.

"Not anymore I'm not," he said. "I was until recently."

"How recently?"

"Last week."

Oh. So, she was…some kind of rebound?

Strangely, that felt okay. Was actually growing on her. A friendship—maybe even a real one?—while he adjusted his life. Because even if he turned out to be her father's thief, Howard wasn't planning to press charges. Yes. This could all work. She could help her father, and maybe be friends for real. Someday. When this was all over.

They just had to make sure those erroneous trades never occurred again.

"Stella wasn't ready to take on a child," Flint said into the silence that had fallen, as though he thought she'd been waiting for more explanation.

She didn't mind knowing what had happened.

"She might come around," she offered, feeling inane.

He shook his head, his hair glinting like gold in the midday sun.

Another few weeks and the park would be decorated for Christmas.

What if their friendship was real? *Became* real? Would they still be friends by Christmastime?

If so, they could bring the baby down here to see the lights.

Her step faltered. If she kept her distance from the child—no physical contact—she'd probably be okay. Knowing from the outset that the friendship was, at most, only temporary.

And even if she wasn't okay, she'd do what had to be done. For her father. Her parents. She was all they had. Or ever would have, as far as blood family went.

"She gave me an ultimatum," he said after waiting for a crowd of schoolchildren to cross their path. "The baby or her."

She knew which he'd chosen. And felt she had to say something.

"Some women just aren't meant to be mothers." Wow. Hadn't meant for her own mantra to slip out.

But maybe it was best that he know, going in, that there could never be more than friendship between them. That she, like Stella, wasn't meant to be a mother.

Even if he turned out not to be guilty, even if they developed a genuine friendship, she was planning to set him up with Mallory. Mallory was perfectly suited to be everything he and Diamond Rose could ever want.

"She wants children," he said. "Just not the bastard child of an incarcerated convict."

The way he said the words—she looked at him—was he the one Stella hadn't wanted? The bastard child of a convict? Or had it really been because he'd wanted to bring his sister into their family?

"You don't sound all that bitter about it." Which surprised her. He had every right to be.

"I'm not. I'm thankful I discovered her lack of mutual respect before we got married and had children, rather than afterward. And to be fair to her, I'd failed to tell her that my mother was in prison."

They'd reached the curb.

He hailed a cab.

Chapter Eleven

By Friday afternoon Flint was feeling pretty good about himself. He'd met with Michael Armstrong, an attorney who'd come highly recommended by one of the clients who'd been with him the longest.

They could be as little as a phone call away from having the order dropped. Michael was certain he could negotiate a mutual agreement between him and the Wainwrights that would prevent either party from bad-mouthing the other, and that he could do it without a court order. Flint was willing to sign anything to that effect as long as they dropped the order.

Otherwise he was going to fight it. He had to. For Diamond Rose's sake. To let it stand unanswered meant it would be put into full effect. It would make him look guilty.

Michael was fairly confident, as was Flint, that the Wainwrights wouldn't want the matter to go to court.

While Flint was comfortable enough with the situation still open, after talking to Michael he felt one hell of a lot better going into the weekend.

The lasagna was already in the oven and Diamond Rose fed and asleep when Tamara pulled into his drive. He'd offered to send a cab for her. She'd preferred her own transportation.

He was pleased with the fact that she'd agreed to come to his house at all. She knew about his past. And had accepted his invitation anyway.

"Wow, this place is nice," she said as he opened the front door into a large entryway with a step-down living room to one side and a great room on the other. It had a wall of windows that opened up to a tiled patio and swimming pool beyond. The outdoor lighting was on and showed the pool, with the waterfall, at its best. He couldn't afford to be right on the ocean, but the pool had been a nice compromise. She turned toward the great room.

"I've got someone coming to put a wrought-iron gate around the pool," he said as he followed her through the room he'd furnished with a complete home theater arrangement, including big leather furniture with charging plug-ins. Stella had thought the room too big for intimate conversation. Too "masculine."

Diamond Rose, in her Pack 'n Play on the floor in the living room, was out of sight, but her monitor rested securely in the back pocket of his jeans.

He stood back as Tamara moved through an archway into the kitchen, which ran almost half the length of the house. One end held an informal eating area with bay windows and the other housed a more formal dining room set. A set his mother would have loved and had never seen.

He'd purchased the high-top suite for eight soon after meeting Stella.

"Dinner smells wonderful," she said, stopping to look at the pool out the kitchen window.

He wanted to tell her she *looked* wonderful. In leggings and a white shirt, gathered at the waist in back, that fell just past the tops of her thighs, with her amber hair loose and falling around her shoulders... He was sure he'd never seen anyone so beautiful.

And was getting way ahead of himself.

She'd turned. Was leaning against the counter, the window at her back with the landscape lighting a soft glow around her.

Maybe he'd pushed things too far, too fast. Having her over for dinner. It wasn't his normal approach.

But nothing about his life was normal anymore.

Nor was anything about this woman. The way she'd showed up in his life at the exact moment she had, preventing him from being fired long enough for him to make the trade that had, he was certain, ensured him his job. And then, when he'd been frantic about Diamond Rose, finding it impossible to calm her, in walked Tamara, who'd calmed her almost instantly.

He might not believe in karma and all the woo-woo stuff his mother used to spout, but he couldn't resist wondering, once again, if Alana Gold, in her death, was sending him her own version of karma. Proving that good was rewarded. That there was help beyond self-reliance.

That miracles really could happen...

"I, um, have to talk to you."

Little good ever came of those words.

He'd been about to get a bottle of wine. Stopped before he'd actually opened the refrigerator door.

His weekend took a nosedive. "What's up?"

"You told me about your ex and...I need to tell you something."

"You know Stella?" It was the first thought that sprang to mind. Was his ex-fiancée having him watched? He wouldn't put it past her. She was going to hang him out to dry for deceiving her by not telling her he wasn't from a nice, clean, *rich* family like hers. For daring to think she'd be willing to raise his dirty mother's orphaned child.

"No!" Tamara frowned, cocking her head to look at him. "Of course not. I just...need to be honest with you about something."

"Wine first," he said, grabbing the bottle of California Chardonnay. He opened it and poured two glasses, handing one to her without asking if she wanted it.

She took a sip, nodded.

Taking that as a win, he scooped up the platter of grapes and cheese he'd prepared and carried it into the dining area. Pulling out one of the chairs for her before seating himself perpendicular to her—where he could also glance across the L-shaped entryway and into the living room.

Tamara had said she needed to be honest with him. He had to listen.

And hope that whatever she had to say wouldn't be as bad as he was imagining. It would be a shame to have a second lasagna dinner drying out in the oven that week. Especially since he'd spent an hour the night before talking to a sleeping Diamond Rose while he'd prepared it.

"I—" Tamara looked at him, her expression...odd. He couldn't figure out why.

Glancing away, she took a grape, put it in her mouth, and he had an instant vision of a movie he'd seen once at a bachelor party. Tamara had a way of making a grape look even sexier than that, and she was fully dressed.

"I don't normally... I haven't ever...talked about this with anyone but my closest friends, so bear with me here."

He wanted to let her off the hook, to tell her that honesty was overrated. But after the week he'd had, the life he'd had, he couldn't do it.

No more stabs in the back, bonks over the head or officers at his door. He had Diamond Rose to protect.

He considered telling her that whatever she was struggling to say could wait. After all, they were just getting to know each other.

But he sensed that they weren't. She'd been more than a casual business introduction since the second she'd walked into Bill Coniff's office at the beginning of the week. Clearly she'd sensed something, too, or she wouldn't be about to share a confidence that only those closest to her had the privilege of knowing.

"I'm not ever going to have children." For all her struggle, she almost blurted out the words.

Did she somehow think he wanted her to? He then remembered the day before, when he'd told her that Stella had said it was either the baby or him.

"That's not really how I meant it to come out." She smiled but her lips were trembling. Flint had to consciously resist an urge to take her hand in his. To have some sort of contact between them.

"Before your… Before she wakes up—and before… Well, so you know going in… I can't do babies." Her face reddened and she was clasping her hands again, the way she'd done that day in his office.

"You were great with her," he said, assuming she needed reassurance for some reason. "The moment you picked he up, she stopped crying."

She shook her head, pushed her wineglass farther away. He had yet to take a second sip from his.

"You don't understand."

He was pretty sure of that.

"I—I can't have children."

"Okay. It's not a problem, Tamara. You figure I'm going to think less of you or something? We all have our crosses to bear." Thinking he sounded like an idiot, he continued. "I mean, I'm sorry for you, if it was something you wanted. I don't mean to trivialize that, but…"

Pulling her wineglass toward her, she took another sip. Her glass shook as she raised it to her lips and he just wanted to do whatever it took to put her at ease.

"I don't know what to say," he murmured.

She nodded. "No one does. Look, I wouldn't have brought it up, but…I've been through some…hard times. Not that I need to unload all of that on you when you've been nice enough to make me homemade lasagna, which I love. But the end result is…I keep my distance from babies. And I don't hold them. Ever."

But she had. Just three days ago.

He remembered her odd behavior then. The way she'd clasped her hands so tightly. Wringing them. Had gone for the door. And when she'd turned back, hadn't looked at Diamond Rose again. She'd been in some deep emotional pain and had done a remarkable job of covering it.

"In Bill's office, when the monitor went off, you heard that cry…" He let his words fade away, wishing he could do something to ease her pain.

She nodded. Took a piece of cheese. Bit off a small corner and played with the rest.

"Can you tell me what happened?"

With the cheese between the fingers of both hands, she shook her head, then let go with one hand to grab her wineglass. "You don't have to do this."

For some reason he did. Covering her cheese hand with his own, Flint said, "I want you to tell me."

How could he get to know her better without finding out? How could he help her if he didn't know?

How else could he understand?

Because, God knew, he wasn't just going to walk away. She'd been sent into that office on Monday for a reason.

She seemed to be weighing the decision. As though fighting a battle. Whether or not to trust him?

Then she glanced up and met his gaze. He felt like he'd won.

"I've been pregnant four times."

Flint's jaw dropped. Whatever he'd been expecting, it hadn't been that. She didn't wear a ring and had asked if he was involved with anyone. He hadn't even thought to ask if she was. He'd been a little preoccupied.

He wasn't generally a person who only considered himself. Alana Gold had taught him that through her own bad example.

He didn't regret asking Tamara to confide in him, but he was ill-prepared.

Questions bounced through his mind. All he came out with was, "What happened?"

"I lost them all."

Four small words. So stark. And carrying such an incredible depth of pain. He admired her for being able to sit there relatively composed.

He'd asked for this. He owed it to her to see it through. "Why?"

Her smirk, and accompanying shrug, held grief he was pretty sure he couldn't even begin to imagine.

"There was no obvious explanation," she said. "My husband and I both went through a battery of tests. Sometimes genetics aren't compatible. There're myriad physical causes. But nothing showed up. Which was why they said there was no reason we shouldn't keep trying."

So many questions. Things he wanted to ask. But this wasn't the time.

What did she need him to know?

"And you tried four times."

She nodded. Took a sip of wine. "Yep." She was staring at her glass and he wondered what she saw there. Wished there was some way he could take on some of her pain, help her deal with it.

Alana Gold had taught him well on that count, too. When he'd been able to keep her happy, she'd stayed clean. It was when she'd needed things he couldn't provide that they'd lost everything.

Tamara Frost had helped him. He felt deeply compelled to help her in return.

"Then what?"

Her gaze shot to his. "What do you mean, then what?"

He squeezed her hand, let it go. "Did they eventually discover a reason for what was happening? What was going wrong?"

She shook her head. "No." And when she looked at him again, there was a mixture of determination and vulnerability in her glistening eyes. "I couldn't do it anymore," she said. "I don't even want to be pregnant. I can't bear the thought of all those weeks of fear and hope, the unknown, not being in control. My own frenetic state of mind would create issues even if the fetus was healthy…"

"And your husband?" It seemed the appropriate time to ask that one.

"We're divorced, by mutual agreement. By the time we lost Ryan, we'd already drifted so far apart…"

"Ryan?" She'd named each lost fetus?

"He was viable," she said as though that explained everything. It didn't.

"I don't—"

"The others… I lost them at six, nine and eleven weeks. Still within the first trimester. But Ryan… He made it far enough to have a chance of survival. I could feel him moving inside me. I was showing. And I was sure that with him—"

She'd lost her last hope with the loss of her fourth child. Understanding came softly, but clearly. Because she was talking to someone who knew exactly when he'd lost his last hope.

Eight years before, when his mother had used the home he'd bought her to run a drug lab, implicating him in her criminal acts.

After that he couldn't help Alana anymore. Couldn't have anything to do with a future that involved her being out of prison and the two of them together. He'd visited her, because he loved her. Because she'd given him life. But he'd kept an emotional distance that had been necessary for his own mental health.

"There comes a time when you have to let go," he said aloud. Whatever the cause of the emotional pain, there came a time when you knew you'd reached the end of your ability to cope. You had to turn away. Say *no more.* "Ryan was your time."

Her gaze locked with his, those green eyes large, their gold rims more pronounced. "You get it."

He did.

And while he had no idea where it left them, with Diamond Rose sleeping in the next room, he knew for certain that their meeting had been no mistake.

She'd helped him.

He was supposed to help her.

Chapter Twelve

The baby cried.

Tamara sipped her wine, telling herself that whatever spell had bound her and Flint Collins had been broken.

He was still watching her.

"You need to go get her," she said.

He nodded. "She has to be changed and then fed," he agreed. "It'll take me about twenty minutes. You want to set the table in the meantime? The lasagna is due to come out in about thirty."

Could she do this? A flash of her father's worried face assured her she could.

"I can do that," she told him. She'd see if he had lettuce. She could make a salad. Salad went well with Italian food. And wine.

She had another sip.

Focus. That was all it took.

That and topping off the glass of wine Flint had poured

for her. Two was her limit. Or she'd have to hang around an extra hour before she drove. She found dishes. Set the kitchen table because of the gorgeous view of the pool from the bay windows.

No. Because there'd be no view at all of the baby sleeping in the living room.

She hadn't known that was where the playpen was until Diamond Rose started to cry. Then she'd had to fight to avoid looking at the room.

But...Flint needed to see the child. For his own sake and the baby's.

Gathering up the dishes and silverware, Tamara moved them to the dining room, placing them so he could see the living room and her back was to it.

Yes, that worked fine.

And she made salad. Cutting the carrots, peeling a cucumber, chopping onion, tearing lettuce. She did it all with precise focus. When Flint's voice broke through her concentration, soft and from a distance, she chopped with more force. The newborn cried once. Tamara replayed in her head the conversation she'd had with her father the day before.

Diamond Rose was a precious little baby who had nothing to do with her. Tamara wanted the best for her. Hoped to God that everything worked out so Flint could continue to care for his sister. If that was what was best.

And it seemed to be.

Flint was different from any other man she'd ever met. He had an emotional awareness she'd never seen in a male before—yet he was masculine and sexy and exuded strength at the same time.

In one conversation, and a sketchy one at best, he'd understood more about her emotional struggle than Steve had in all their years of marriage.

For the first time since she'd lost Ryan, she felt understood.

By a man who might be a thief.

And since her father wasn't planning to press charges, because of the hit his reputation— and then the company— would take if investors knew he'd been frauded, Flint should be free to raise Diamond Rose.

"She's back to sleep."

A piece of lettuce flew out of her hand and onto the floor when she heard his voice behind her. Focus could do that to a girl—take her right out of her surroundings.

"That's impressive." He was smiling as he pointed to her neat piles of chopped vegetables.

"You make your own dressing?" She'd found four jars, with varying labels, lined up in the door of the refrigerator. She'd chosen the creamy Italian to mix in before serving their salads.

"I've been putting meals together pretty much since I could walk, it seems," he said. "By the time I was about eight, I couldn't stand the sight of peanut butter sandwiches anymore, so I asked my mom to teach me to cook."

"She was a good cook?"

"Yes, she was."

There was hesitation in his tone. And she wondered if there was more to the story. Like, when she was sober she was a good cook. Or, when she wasn't in jail she was a good cook. Tamara didn't know many of the details of his growing up, but she knew enough to fill in some of the blanks with at least a modicum of accuracy.

Within minutes they had dinner on the table and were sitting down to eat. He didn't mention the baby at all. She didn't ask, either. But it felt…unfair, somehow, doing that to him. Making him keep such a momentous change in his life all to himself.

A friend wouldn't do that. And posing or not, she had to be a good friend if she was going to find out more about him.

"It doesn't send me into a tailspin to hear about babies," she told him, spearing a bit of salad on her fork. "You can talk about her."

"I just want to make sure I know the boundaries first," he said. "I need to know what you can and can't handle."

"What I can't do is hold her." The words jumped out. "That's my trigger. The rest, I can manage. I can close my eyes if it starts to get me. Or walk away."

There. She relaxed a bit.

"But the other day…you picked her up so naturally."

"And I've been paying for it ever since." Wow…she was playing her part better than she'd ever suspected she could. She was being more honest with him than she was with anyone, including her parents.

Maybe because she knew he wouldn't be in her life all that long? Or because he was an outsider who wouldn't be hurt by her pain?

Maybe because she wasn't *completely* playing a part?

"Paying for it how?" he asked between bites of his salad.

"The first night I think I was up more than you were." And, based on what he'd later told her about it, that was saying a lot. "I have nightmares. And panic attacks."

She was tempted to say she had hot and then cold flashes, since she was having another series right now. But she'd had the first one before she'd known about Diamond Rose.

Speaking of which…

"Did you name her? Diamond Rose—it's such an unusual name."

"No." He finished his salad. "My mother did."

As he started in on his lasagna, he told her about the

names Gold, Flint, Diamond—and the rose. Expensive, beautiful, sweet.

And fragile, she added silently.

She'd taken her first bite of lasagna and was too busy savoring the taste to talk. She loved to cook. Considered herself good at it. He was better.

"It was the first time," she said out of the blue. She'd just swallowed that bite. Wanted to think about the second. Another sip of wine. Or the way Flint's shoulders filled out the black polo shirt he was wearing with his jeans. But she wasn't. She was still thinking about that baby.

"The first time you'd held a baby?" Leave it to him to catch right on. Did the man never miss a beat?

She nodded.

"In how long?"

"Since I lost Ryan, if you don't count the few times we tried in my therapy sessions, which I don't count because I never managed to hold the infant by myself."

Fork hovering over his lasagna, he paused before skewering another bite. "How long has it been?"

"Three years." Hard to believe it had been that long. That brought on another surge of panic. Her life was passing by so quickly.

"And how long since your divorce?"

"Two and a half years. He's remarried." And could be expecting a child any day or week or month.

"Are you two on friendly terms?"

"We talk." She didn't consider Steve a friend. He'd robbed her of her one chance to hold her son, having the baby swept away the second he'd been delivered, and asking the doctor to give Tamara something to calm her down, which had knocked her out. But their split had been amicable. Mutual. They remained…acquaintances.

She drank a little more of her wine. Had to wait a minute before sending anything more solid down her throat. Floundering, losing focus, she stared at her plate. Reminded herself what she was doing here.

"What about you and Stella? You think you'll remain friends?"

She heard the stupidity of that question even as she asked it—since the woman had ditched him because he was taking in his mother's child to raise. But desperation drove many things. Including stupid questions to fill the silence.

"I have no desire to. So, no."

Okay, then. That was clear.

But her father had said that Flint's spending habits had changed when the rich girlfriend came into his life. She had to get around to that somehow.

Or segue into offshore accounts.

She was drawing a blank.

Because she wasn't focused.

Maybe over dessert.

He knew how he could help her. Not the details, not yet. But Flint had a goal now. Find a way to repay Tamara, or the fates, for helping him out on one of the worst days of his life.

Not quite the worst. Because in another way, it might have been the absolute best. He wasn't alone anymore. He had a sister. A brand-new human being to raise.

He had family.

And it now seemed obvious to him that his payback was in helping Tamara heal enough to have a family of her own, too. To someday have a baby of her own to raise. There were other options if she couldn't give birth herself.

His and Diamond Rose's payback, really. They both owed her.

That infant sister of his already had a job to do. Because that was what you did when you planned to amount to something in life. You used the gifts you were given. You worked as hard as you could. You helped others.

The things he'd taught himself somehow. Or a message given to him subliminally in his crib.

His little sister's talents might not be clear yet, but for now, being an infant was all it was going to take.

The connection seemed unmistakable to him. Diamond Rose, who'd been screaming her lungs out, had instantly calmed when Tamara had picked her up.

Sign one.

Sign two. Tamara, who hadn't held a baby in years, who considered herself unable to hold one, had picked up Diamond Rose.

Still piecing things together, he had no idea how it was all going to work. What he should or shouldn't do. But he felt confident, as Tamara helped him with the dishes, that the answers would come to him.

He had the basics down anyway.

"I should be going," she said as soon as the dishes were done and the counters wiped. He'd put some of the leftover lasagna in a container for her. One serving was all she'd take, suggesting he put the rest in serving-size portions in the freezer, so that on nights when the baby wasn't co-operating, he could still eat a good dinner.

He'd been freezing portions for years, but didn't tell her that. He was too busy enjoying the fact that she was look-ing out for him, too. Stella had been mostly about what he could do for her, and he'd been all right with that. Even comfortable with it. And usually insisted on it.

"You want to do this again? Sunday maybe?" He felt confident asking. Some things you just knew.

"What time?"

"You name it. I'll be working at home all day."

She preferred afternoon to evening. He was fine with that, too.

Following her to the door, he moved closer, intending to kiss her good-night. Her expression stopped him before he'd made his intention obvious. She was worried about getting out the door without seeing the baby, not thinking about kisses.

He watched her walk to her car and only after she'd pulled out of his driveway and was out of sight did he close the door.

He really would've liked that kiss. To know her taste on his lips...

Probably just as well, though. He needed to get settled back into his career at Owens Investments and to learn how to be a dad before he took on any other committed relationship.

Friends was nice, though. Friends who helped each other...

Chapter Thirteen

Funny how things worked themselves out. Tamara hadn't had a chance to learn anything on Friday night that could benefit her father. Then, on Saturday, while having lunch with the office manager at Owens Investments—a woman ten years older than her whom she'd never met before the previous week, but instinctively liked—the way in was handed to her.

Maria had been telling her about the system they used to keep up with the fast pace their traders required of them, and in so doing had explained quite a bit more than her father had done about his business. Maria had given her a pretty clear glimpse into the life of a stockbroker. As her father had said, the risks were great, mostly because laws were commonly broken, although it could be hard to prove. Insider trading being one of the most difficult.

She'd asked if Tamara had seen a movie from the late '80s called *Wall Street*. She hadn't. Maria had highly recommended that she watch it.

That night she found it on her streaming app and on Sunday showed up at Flint's door in black-and-white leggings, a comfy oversize white top and zebra-striped flip-flops, with the movie rented and ready. All they had to do was type her account information into his smart TV and they'd be set.

"You've never seen *Wall Street*?" he asked as he brought glasses of iced tea and a bag of microwaved popcorn for them to share.

"No. It was out before I was born," she told him. And then thought to ask, "Have you?"

Of course he would have. He was a stockbroker. And Flint seemed to study everything about anything that involved him. Like the baby, for instance. Yeah, there'd been a couple of common sense things he'd missed during his research before he'd brought his baby home, but in just those three days, he'd become better prepared than most expectant parents she'd known.

"Only about a dozen times," he told her, taking a seat on the opposite end of the couch.

Relieved that he wasn't closer, that she wasn't going to have to let him know they were "just friends," she turned to smile at him, suddenly catching sight of the Pack 'n Play in the sunken living room behind them.

Suspecting that the portable bed was there because Tamara was where she was—in the living room—she felt a crushing weight come down on her. Disappointment, yes, but far more.

A baby was being ostracized because of her.

No, that wasn't quite true. A lot of parents kept their young children separate from the family's activities while the child slept. That was why there were nurseries.

But it wasn't what she would've done if she'd had a child. It wasn't what she'd planned to do.

"Do you keep her in there when you're in here watching TV at night?"

"I'm not usually in here watching TV. I spend any free time I have on the computer. Checking stocks. My job is pretty much a 24/7 affair when I don't specifically schedule time for other things."

Like watching an old movie with her?

He'd turned on the TV. Clicked on the streaming app.

"Where's your computer?"

He nodded toward a hallway off the great-room side of the kitchen. "Down there."

"And does she stay in the living room when you're 'down there'?" She mimicked him with a grin.

No response, which she'd expected. The question had been rhetorical. Of course he didn't keep his baby in other rooms when he was there alone.

With a fancy remote that had a small phone-size keyboard on the back, he was searching for the movie. On his account.

Stood to reason that he already owned it and she'd wasted the three dollars she'd spent. Oh, well.

"You can bring her in here, Flint." She wasn't going to be the cause of any child being on the outside of any gathering ever. "I'm not so fragile that I can't be in the same room as a baby. I fly on a regular basis, and you don't get to choose who you're seated by on a plane. I'll be fine."

She wasn't convinced she would be. But at least she knew how to keep up appearances. As long as she didn't pay attention to the baby, didn't let Diamond's presence pull at her. As long as she didn't even think about picking her up.

Or doing any nurturing in a hands-on way.

"If you're sure, I'll bring her in. But only if you're completely sure that's what you want. It's not like she's going to know the difference. She's out for at least another hour."

"Like she didn't know the difference the night you tried to get her to sleep in the nursery?"

"She's used to me now. We're doing much better." His grin did things to her in inappropriate places. Probably because she was so tense about getting information for her father. And being around a newborn.

She was challenging herself personally and professionally. So it made sense that her emotions would be off-kilter.

And she might've been fighting off a flu bug the previous week, too. Her system could be in recuperation mode. Busy rebuilding antibodies.

That thought was total bunk and she knew it. She didn't have the flu. Hadn't had it the week before, either. The man was attractive. She noticed. Not a big deal.

"I want you to go get her, please," she said as he cued up the movie. "Please."

She wouldn't be able to focus on her real reason for being there if she was busy feeling bad about being the reason that baby was in the other room all alone. She was a grown woman who could take accountability for her issues, her problems. Diamond Rose was a helpless newborn who had to rely on everyone around her to fill every single one of her needs.

Besides, Tamara needed Flint relaxed if she hoped to get information that could help her father one way or the other. She'd spent most of Saturday going through files and meeting with employees who'd come in on their own time to see her, in addition to the hours with Maria in and out of the office. Her father had told her someone was trading on various computers. He knew which ones, so now she did, too. She'd wanted to find out when they were in use most often, as part of her efficiency check, so she could give her father an idea of when or why they might have been freed up for other uses. She had dates now. Other specifics.

And she was slowly making her way through expense reports and comparing them to the provided receipts, examining dates, times, employee credit card numbers, clients. Looking for…anything in the past year. Flint's records had come first. She'd finished them very late Friday night.

He'd had a lot of fancy dinners, gone to shows, on cruises, to games, with a lot of important and wealthy people. And every single dime he'd claimed checked out to the penny.

She'd told herself not to let hope grow. She'd learned the hard way that hoping led to greater heartache. Still, she'd wished she could call and tell her father that things were looking good. So far.

But, of course, she couldn't.

Just when Tamara was hooked to the point of forgetting almost everything else, a little cough jarred her. Then a tiny wail, followed by another.

She looked at Flint, who was already headed over to the playpen. "She's got another hour and a half," he said as though babies watched the clock and knew they were supposed to be hungry at certain times. Focusing on the movie, which he'd paused on the screen—about the young man learning the Wall Street ropes from someone who was at the top of his game, but had gotten there by unethical means—she waited.

"What's the matter, Little One?" Flint crooned softly. The wails grew louder. He rubbed her arm. Felt her cheek. Continued to talk. Tried to get her to take a pacifier. She continued to cry.

Pick her up. Pick her up.

After a few more tries with the pacifier, he picked her up.

The crying didn't stop.

For another ten minutes.

He walked with her. Talked to her about her eating schedule, explaining that it wasn't time yet. He changed her, which only made her angrier.

He left the room, taking her somewhere in another part of the house. Probably to give Tamara space. She could still hear the crying.

She couldn't just sit there, doing nothing. Poor Flint had to be getting tense. Frustrated. Especially with her there. Maybe she should leave and watch the movie another day. It wasn't as if her father had to have his answers within the next few hours.

Or that she was going to find them there that day.

The crying went on. She paced the room. Looking at bookshelves. Reading titles of DVDs. Noticing the lack of any family photos. Or personal mementoes.

Diamond Rose finally stopped crying and Tamara's entire torso seemed to settle. Until then she hadn't realized that her breathing was becoming shallow, the way it did at the onset of a panic attack. Hadn't felt herself tense.

And almost immediately the crying started again. She grabbed her purse. Had her keys and was at the door before she remembered she had to tell Flint she'd take a rain check on the movie. She couldn't just him let come out and find her gone.

Following the sounds of the baby in distress, she traveled a hallway he hadn't showed her yet, passing two rooms—a bathroom, the master suite—and eventually found him in a small back bedroom with a Jack and Jill bathroom leading into one of the rooms she'd passed.

Opening her mouth to tell him she was leaving, she

caught sight of his face. He looked scared. Honest-to-goodness scared.

"I'm sorry," he told her. "Nothing's working. She doesn't feel feverish, but maybe I should take her in."

His gaze moving from the purse on her shoulder to the keys in her hand, he nodded. "I'm sorry," he said, giving her a smile that seemed all for her, in spite of his crying infant, and went back to trying to comfort the child in his arms.

"Put her up on your shoulder," she said. "Pat her back. She might have gas."

He tried. It didn't work.

Tamara felt like crying herself. "Try rubbing her back."

That didn't work, either. Tamara had to get out of there. But she couldn't just leave him. His problems weren't hers, but he was trying so hard and she couldn't simply walk out.

"Do you have a rocking chair?"

He nodded, left the room, and she followed him. Into another room filled with baby furniture and paraphernalia. There was a mobile over the crib, but nothing on the walls. No color. No stimulation. Just…stuff.

A massive amount of stuff to have collected in less than a week.

Sitting in the rocker, he held the baby to his chest and rocked. Cradled her in his arms and rocked. She'd settle for a second or two and then start right back up again.

"Lay her on your lap," Tamara said. "On her stomach." Her purse was still on her shoulder. Her hand hurt, and looking down, she saw imprints of her keys in the flesh of her palm.

Flint pulled a blanket off the arm of the chair and did as Tamara said, settling Diamond Rose across his lap, continuing to rock gently.

"Rub her back," she suggested again.

The crying calmed for a second. Then another second. The baby burped, formula pooled on the blanket, and all was quiet.

Shaking, Tamara started to cry.

She had to get out of there.

In spite of the warmth seeping through the right leg of his jeans, Flint rocked gently, rubbing Diamond's back, while he wiped her mouth and pulled the soiled part of the blanket away from her. Her eyes closed, she sighed deeply and his entire being changed.

Irrevocably.

Almost weak with the infusion of love that swamped him, he knew he was never going to be the same. She was his.

He was hers.

Watching her breathe, he loved her more fiercely than he'd known it was possible to love.

And somehow Tamara Frost was connected to it all.

Tamara was gone when he finally made it back out to the great room. He'd known she would be. Putting Diamond in her Pack 'n Play, he flipped off the television still paused on a close-up of Michael Douglas with his mouth open, caught in midword. Then he gathered up the glasses of leftover iced tea, the half-eaten bag of popcorn and took them to the kitchen. Upon his return, he grabbed his laptop.

Settling back on the sofa, wanting to stay close to the baby, he did a search on medical degrees. They took an average of eight years to earn and then an average of four years of residency before a graduate could begin practice. A list of medical schools came next. He wanted the best. Decided on three and searched tuitions. Then he researched the average cost of living for a medical resident, did a calculation based on average cost of living increase each year, multiplying that by twenty-six, because, based on schooling, she'd be at least that before beginning a residency, and added the figure to his list.

His eventual total was about what he'd estimated when he'd been rocking his baby sister. But it was good to have solid facts.

He knew how much extra money he had to earn to fund Diamond's college account. She could be whatever she wanted. He was prepared for the most expensive, which was why he'd looked into medical schools. He checked the market next—something he did all day every day, using his cell phone when he didn't have access to his computer. Searching now for his own personal investments. There was always more money to be made.

And finding it was his talent.

He had all of half an hour before Diamond was crying again. Deciding it was about time, he tried to feed her. She drank for a couple of minutes and then turned her head. And kept turning it away whenever he tried to guide the nipple into her mouth.

So he rocked her. Laid her on her belly and rubbed her back. Walked with her out by the pool. Talked to her. Loved her.

And thought about Tamara. She'd fought her own demons that afternoon to help Diamond Rose. He couldn't remember a time other people had put themselves out on his behalf.

Except Howard Owens. He'd risked his own reputation to take Flint on eight years before. Flint hated that the man thought he'd been planning to stab him in the back.

Hated it, but wasn't surprised. That was the way his life worked. With his background, he was always suspect.

It was something he'd always known, even as a little kid.

And something he swore Diamond would never face.

Tamara had fought her own demons to hang around.

As he finally set Diamond down in a clean sleeper and with a full feeding of warm formula in her belly sometime after seven that evening, he pulled his cell phone out of his pocket. He'd changed into sweats and a long sleeved T-shirt and was sitting by the pool with a bottle of beer.

Tamara picked up on the second ring.

"I just wanted to apologize for this afternoon," he said as soon as she said hello.

"No apology necessary," she told him. "Seriously. I think what you're doing... Anyway, don't apologize."

There was no missing the wealth of emotion in her tone. He'd had a tough day with a cranky newborn, but he had a feeling Tamara's day had been immeasurably worse.

He did need to apologize. He'd been so certain he could help her—that somehow Diamond Rose would be the baby who'd help her heal from her loss, ease her pain—and with no real knowledge of the subject, he'd invited her into a hellhole.

He should just let her go.

He'd thought about it on and off all afternoon. And as he'd eaten his single serving of reheated lasagna for dinner.

He'd argued with himself and called her anyway.

There had to be *something* he and Diamond Rose could do for her.

"Maybe we should stick to having lunch for now," he offered, still at a loss.

If she even wanted to see him again. He wouldn't blame her if she thought he was too much trouble. He'd probably think so, too, if he were in her shoes.

Except he was beginning to understand that he had no idea how it felt to be in her shoes. Having children was a natural progression in life. Something most people took for granted. To be married and ready to start a family, to know you were pregnant, to be buying things for a nursery, making plans, and then to lose that child—he had no idea how any of that would feel.

And times four.

"Lunch would be good," she said, sounding a little less tense. "But dinner on Friday was good, too."

"Today wasn't."

"No."

"What did you do when you left?" Had she called a friend? How did she cope?

"I went to work." That he could completely relate to.

"Owens is closed on weekends."

"I have temporary clearance with security."

"Are you at the office now?"

"Yes."

He pictured her there. The building was quiet after hours. Peaceful. He did some of his best work when he was the only one on the floor.

Pictured himself there with her and actually got hard.

Either he was heading into the rest of his life or screwing up. At the moment, he wasn't sure which.

"You didn't get to finish your movie," he told her.

"You could tell me about it."

He heard invitation in her response and, settling back in his chair, beer in hand, he gave her a fairly detailed rundown of a movie he'd seen for the first time in junior high. He'd been in foster care, a six-month stint, and the family he'd been staying with had been watching old Charlie Sheen movies. The actor had just been hospitalized after having a stroke from a cocaine overdose. Flint's mother had been in jail at the time for possession of crack. The movie had a profound effect on him—establishing for him, very clearly, that ethics were more important than money.

But that money came a very close second. It had also given him his lifelong fascination with the unending opportunities provided by the stock market.

Not that he told Tamara all of that. With her, he stuck to the plot.

Until she asked him what it was that attracted him to the movie to the point of having watched it so many times. Then he told her about seeing it for the first time.

"Wow, that seems a bit callous to me," she said. "They knew why your mother was in jail, right?"

"I was certainly under that impression." He'd never asked.

"Did you say anything to them?"

"Nope." He'd known from experience that any questions from him would just lead to more lectures that he'd neither needed nor wanted. Or, worse, more scorn.

He was the bastard son of a drug user. Assumed to be like her, because how could he not be? He'd never experienced anything different. Not many good people were drawn to him.

"Did you know from the first time you saw the movie that you wanted to be a stockbroker?"

He sipped from his bottle. Chuckled. Pictured her in the converted closet they'd given her as an office and wished a glass of wine on her.

"I wasn't prone to lofty dreams," he told her. "I was curious about the market, but it didn't really occur to me that I'd have the opportunity to live in that world." She was easy to talk to. He couldn't remember the last time someone had been interested in him as a person.

Maybe some of that was his fault. He hadn't been all that open to sharing his life. Even with Stella. He'd shared his time. His plans. His future. But not himself.

He'd only just realized that...

"So when did you start believing in the opportunity?"

It took him a second to realize they were still talking about the stock market. He picked up the baby monitor on the table. Made sure the volume was all the way up. Diamond, who was just inside the door in her carrier on the table, had been asleep for more than half an hour.

"I had a minimum-wage job in high school, but I'd been earning extra money by going through trash, finding broken things, fixing them and then selling them. I'd made enough to buy a beater car and was saving for college. And I got to thinking I should look for things that were for sale cheap—you know, at garage sales—and then fix them up and resell them.

"I had quite a gig going until my junior year, when my mother got arrested again. I had almost enough saved to pay the minimum bail and went to a bondsman for the rest. I gave him an accounting of the books I'd been keeping with my little enterprise as a way of proving that I was good for the money. It's not like I had any real asset to use as collateral..."

He rattled on, as if he shared his story on a regular basis. Flint hardly recognized himself but didn't want to stop.

Talking to Tamara felt good.

"The guy was pretty decent. He paid the bond, without collateral, but told me he wanted me to check in with him every week, regarding my business intake. He helped me do my tax reporting, too. Supposedly it was just until Mom showed up in court and he got his money back, but I kept stopping in now and then, even after she was sentenced to community service and in the clear. He's actually the one who suggested I think about the stock market. He said I had a knack for making money. Turned out he was right."

He didn't hesitate to tell her the whole truth about this

aspect of his background, in spite of the fact he never did that. He guarded his private life so acutely.

"Did you ever go back and see him? After you made it?"

He hadn't made it yet. He wasn't even sure what "making it" consisted of these days. He'd thought that opening his own firm, having other brokers working for him, earning good money, would be making it.

"He retired and moved to Florida when I was a freshman in college."

And although Flint had given the guy his email address, had emailed him a few times, he'd never heard from him again.

"It was because of him that, years later, I started looking into offshore accounts," he told her. "He fronted money, which meant that he had to make money. He used to do a bit of foreign investing. He'd tell me about foreign currencies and exchanges and the money he'd make. He also talked about security.

"'Diversification equals security,' he'd say. If you keep all your assets in one place, and the place burns down, you're left with nothing. We like to think that our banks, at least the federally insured ones, are completely safe, and I feel that generally they are. But it doesn't hurt to have assets elsewhere, just in case of some major catastrophe— there can always be another crash like we had in 2008. It's not like it hadn't happened before that, too."

Okay, now he was reminding himself of Ross in an old *Friends* episode, going on and on about his field of paleontology and boring his friends to death.

"Sorry," he said, reining himself in. It felt as though a dam had burst inside him, which made him feel a bit awkward. But not sorry.

"Actually, this is the kind of thing I was after," Tamara

said. "Greater understanding of how the investment world works. But...I thought offshore accounts were illegal."

"Not at all. A lot of people use them illegally, because it's relatively easy to do. But they're not only completely legal, they're a financially smart decision. Especially for someone like me who invests internationally. You just have to report any earnings over ten thousand on your taxes."

"Do you do all your own taxes?"

"Yes." He did everything on his own, for the most part. He didn't like giving others the chance to make a mistake for which he'd be held accountable. "I meet with an accountant before I submit them, though," he added, "because the laws change every year."

Such a bizarre conversation. In a lot of ways, more intimate to him than sex.

And he'd started it.

"I'm sitting at the pool having a beer." He felt bad about that, considering his baby girl had sent Tamara running to work. "I wish you were here, enjoying it with me."

"I don't like beer."

"I have wine." It wasn't quite an invitation—he wouldn't do that to her, since there were no guarantees he could avoid a replay of this afternoon—but he had to open the door.

"Will it keep a few days?"

"Absolutely."

He asked her if she was free for lunch early in the week. They settled on Tuesday and Flint was grinning as he hung up the phone.

Chapter Fourteen

Sunday was about as bad a day as she'd had in a while. First with the aborted visit at Flint's in the afternoon and then with the confirmation that he not only had an off-shore account but that he did his own taxes. Things that someone with something to hide might do.

Neither fact made him a thief. But the circumstantial evidence pointing in his direction, along with a lack of anything pointing in anyone else's, was certainly enough to lead her father to that conclusion.

Over the next week and a half, she worked like a fiend as an efficiency expert, finding several ways her father's company could save money. She also searched for any discrepancy that could place doubt or lay suspicion on anyone other than Flint. She found a few. She always did. But nothing that wasn't easily explainable or a product of human error or laziness. Someone cutting corners, but not for nefarious reasons.

She lunched with Flint twice that week. Spoke on the phone with him several times. Getting to know the boy he'd been, who'd grown to become the man he was. Sharing more of herself than she had in a long while. She talked about how—although she now loved her job—when she'd been younger, she'd really wanted to be a stay-at-home wife and mother. Old-fashioned though that might be, she'd thought that, having grown up with a wonderfully successful career mother and an equally successful businessman father, the ideal would be a home with someone always there. Protecting everything they all worked for. She wanted to add the personal touches to her own home that her parents' place had gained at the hands of hired help. But then, she worked a job that could largely be done from home, if she wanted it to be, so maybe that's why staying home seemed doable. All of the records scouring, the line by line accounts she studied, she could do that while the baby slept...

And she told him about her job, too. How she'd entered the efficiency field due to years of learning to live a focused life. How the career fit her, fulfilled her. How great she felt when she found bottom-line savings for her clients.

He'd asked, once, if she'd ever thought about trying one more time to have a family of her own. Her answer had been an unequivocal no.

She didn't see that changing.

Her heart had closed up at his question.

As the days passed, her father was getting more worried. He'd talked about calling Flint in, confronting him. But he knew that could be professional suicide. If the meeting backfired and Flint set out to prove he was innocent before Howard could prove he wasn't, any actions her father might take would expose the fraud at Owens.

He'd risk having everyone in the company finding out

they had a thief among them. He'd not only tip the thief's hand, but he'd jeopardize the company's overall security. Once word reached the investment world that Owens had an unsolved fraudulent situation in-house, it could be the end of everything her father had spent a lifetime working toward.

Howard needed the matter solved quietly. And quickly.

Tamara went to Flint's for dinner the following Saturday night, more intent than ever on learning whatever she could to help her father. But she got so distracted worrying about the baby waking up—and then, when she did, Tamara made herself sit out by the pool for the twenty minutes it took Flint to change and feed her—that she was of little use to Owens Investments that night.

Flint had been pleased for her, though, saying she'd done well, staying put instead of running out. She'd wanted so badly to be in there with him. Changing that baby. Watching him feed her.

And that unexpected desire had scared her to death.

She'd warmed under his emotionally intimate look.

And run out. Sort of. She'd had one more glass of wine—her second—and left before anything truly intimate could happen between them.

She dreamed about him that night. It was a change from her usual dreams about crowds of people holding babies, with only her arms empty. Or the vacant house she'd walk into to find every room a nursery that had been abandoned. Or the one where she'd gotten to hold Ryan for a few minutes and then he'd had to leave.

Dreaming about Flint was a welcome reprieve. And yet a problem, too.

One she figured she knew how to solve.

Calling Mallory Harris, she arranged to meet her friend for dinner the Monday night before Thanksgiving. They had a favorite spot not far from the Bouncing Ball—one that Mallory's ex-husband, who owned and worked in the office complex that housed the Bouncing Ball, didn't like. The food was all organic and salad-based. According to Mallory, Braden preferred full plates of food that stuck to his ribs.

Tamara had never met him. She was part of the life Mallory didn't share with her ex-husband.

"What's up?" Mallory asked as soon as they had glasses of Chardonnay in front of them.

"It's been a while since we hung out and—"

Mallory was shaking her head. With her dark hair trimmed to fall stylishly around her face and over her shoulders, Mallory was softly beautiful, even in clothes as plain as the Bouncing Ball jacket and jeans she'd worn to work that day. "I could tell when you called that something was up. Now, out with it. Did you run into Steve?"

"No." Mallory knew about Howard Owens's suspicions regarding Flint. Tamara had told her when she'd asked her friend to take on Diamond Rose. But there was so much more her friend *didn't* know, that she needed to know.

Mallory was just right for Flint. And he was right for her, too. Tamara really needed them to get together.

She'd almost kissed him the other night. Had been thinking about him sexually more and more over the past several days.

In spite of the baby who was part of his life.

He was making it too easy for her to be involved with him. The way he'd taken on full responsibility for Diamond impressed her. Plus the fact that he expected nothing from Tamara but distance where the baby was concerned.

She was getting in too deep. And, because of her father, she couldn't get out. Or not yet, anyway.

She was even starting to think she might not want to

get out at all. Which wasn't fair to anyone. That baby girl of his deserved—and needed—a full-time mother. Not one who stayed in other parts of the house or in doorways when Diamond was around.

She had to admit that Flint hadn't, in any way, intimated that he saw Tamara as anything more than a friend. Perhaps one with momentary fringe benefits.

He wanted her, too.

That was part of her problem. He was going to be asking. She'd managed to put him off without actually saying anything so far, but things were escalating between them. At some point he'd ask.

She didn't trust herself to say no.

Unless she thought her friend wanted him...

"It's Flint," she said. "He's such a great guy and I'm worried about him," she said, looking straight into Mallory's pretty blue eyes. "He's in that big house all alone, keeping up an eighteen-hour-a-day workload, being mother and father to that baby girl and—"

"You've been to his house?"

Yeah, she'd forgotten she hadn't mentioned that.

She nodded, but continued. "His girlfriend ditched him when he refused to give Diamond Rose up for adoption."

"Why were you at his house?"

Was Mallory jealous? That would be a good thing, right?

"I just... My father told me he's not going to press charges if it turns out that Flint's the one who's been stealing from him. And while I'm not excusing theft or fraud, I've seen another side to the man and—"

"When were you at his house?"

"I think you should ask him out, Mal."

Mallory sat back. "Me? Why? I thought you were going to tell me you were falling for him."

"He's got a baby."

"Yeah."

"You think I'm kidding about not going down that road again?" Tamara quipped.

"I think sometimes love is stronger than the things we believe."

"I can't even be in the same room with her for more than a few minutes without getting a cramped feeling."

"Exactly how many times have you been at his house?" Malory asked.

"You need to go out with him, Mal. You'll see what I mean. He's perfect for you."

"You really want me to ask him out?"

"I really do."

Mallory nodded. "He and I—we've talked some."

"And he's gorgeous."

Neither one of them was the type who fell for looks first, but looks didn't hurt.

"But I can't seem to draw him into any kind of conversation beyond caring for his daughter," Mallory said.

Sister. Technically, she was his sister.

Who'd grow up as his daughter.

And she assumed he'd told Mallory that. Probably had to present guardianship papers. None of which changed the fact that, for practical purposes, Flint was Diamond's father.

"He mentioned that he's planning to attend your Thanksgiving dinner at the Bouncing Ball. Said he's always gone out for dinner on Thanksgiving, usually invited clients, but with the baby... He doesn't want Diamond Rose to spend any holidays without family."

Tamara would be at her parents'. She'd told him that when he'd invited her to accompany him to Mallory's dinner—since she and Mallory were friends and all.

Things were just getting too complicated. She couldn't not go to her parents. And she absolutely could not take Flint there with her, Diamond Rose aside, even if she wanted to.

"You're thirty-three, Mal. You want a family of your own. And there's no reason you can't have ten children if you want them. But you need to get started."

"You seriously want me to ask him out?" Mallory asked again.

"At least try to spend some time with him at dinner on Thanksgiving. Ask him to help. He's a great cook."

"He's cooked for you?"

Tamara ignored that. "I think the two of you are perfect for each other."

"Seriously?" Mallory repeated, leaning forward, looking her in the eye.

"Yes." She didn't hesitate. This was the right thing to do. "Unless... I mean, depending on... My dad is still afraid that he's the one who stole from him."

"What do *you* think?"

Shrugging, Tamara took a sip of her wine. "The whole way he is with the baby and all, which has nothing to do with this, but... I don't see it," she said. "At the same time, there's absolutely nothing popping up on anyone else."

"So what do you do now? Hire a detective?"

"I tried to get my dad to do that. He's adamantly against bringing in anyone else. The thief, whoever it is, hasn't done anything in over a month. Dad had some special notification put on one of his passwords, and the second anyone signs in as him, he'll know. But he's hoping it doesn't come to that."

"How much longer are you going to be at the company?"

"I'm about done there." Which was another reason she had to get Flint and Mallory together.

"So you won't be seeing Flint anymore."

"I don't see him much at the office anyway. We're on different floors."

"Do you see him outside the office?"

"Only as a kind of informant," she said, confessing what bothered her the most. "I ask him questions about the business, in my efficiency expert role."

"But he thinks it's more than that."

"Just friends." Tamara sat back and drank some of her wine. Thought maybe they should look at their menus so their waitress would realize they'd be ready to order soon. They'd sent her off the first time she'd asked. "I swear. Nothing's happened between us. I'm not kidding. I've been thinking all along that you and he belong together. You'd love him if you got to know him. And you already love his little girl."

Which Tamara could never do.

Even if she wanted to try, she knew she'd go into emotional shutdown.

"You're falling for him."

"I am not! How could I? I only met him a few weeks ago."

"I knew I was in love with Braden the first night I met him."

A love that had been blown apart, for both of them, by the death of their five-month-old son. They'd been divorced for three years and had found a way to build a good, solid friendship between them.

"And now it's time for you to find someone else to love," Tamara said. "To share your life with."

"Maybe the one it's time for is you."

Mallory just wasn't getting it. "Are you not listening to me?"

"Actually I think that's exactly what I'm doing."

"You want me to open myself to possible feelings for a man who might be stealing from my father? And who has a newborn?" How could Mallory suggest such a thing?

"I want you to be honest with yourself." Mallory's words fell gently between them.

"I am," she insisted. "It's not like I can bring him home to dinner with the folks, Mal. And even if I could, I can't take on his baby. He already had a woman leave him because of Diamond Rose and he just doesn't deserve another kick in the teeth."

She started to tear up, took a deep breath and then said, "His whole life, Flint has done nothing but try, and give, and work hard. And his whole life, people have done nothing but desert him. It's not even like he lets that get to him. He's the least victimized person I've ever met. He'd doesn't get bitter. Or lay blame. He just picks up the pieces and keeps trying. Giving one hundred percent to whatever he does."

"It sounds to me like you know him pretty well."

"I've been…investigating him." At work. At lunch. In his home. On the phone. She'd spent more time with him than any other person since she'd been home.

"Really? Is that all?"

It *had* to be all.

For so many reasons.

But there was one that could convince Mallory…

"How do you suppose he's going to feel when he finds out that I'm Howard Owens's daughter? And that I've been spying on him because my father, his one-time mentor and current boss, thinks he's a thief?"

"You're in love with him, aren't you?"

"I've never even kissed the man!"

"You want to."

"I imagine half the women he meets want to."

"Maybe two-thirds." Mallory smiled. And then immediately sobered.

"I wish I knew what to tell you, Tamara. I just know that you don't get to choose love. It chooses you."

"It chose you and you're alone."

Tamara realized how cruel that sounded but Mallory didn't seem offended.

"I am," Mallory said. "Because human beings are fallible. Love gave Braden and me a chance. We failed it. But you're right. More than anything, I want to be married again, to have a family. And yes, I'm thirty-three. If I'm going to have a houseful of kids, I have to get moving on that. And here I sit. You know why? Because I can't *choose* to fall in love. I have to keep my heart open and wait for it to find me."

"You could go out more."

"I've been dating."

"Ask Flint out. Like I said, maybe love will choose the two of you."

If it was half as powerful as Mallory believed, it would choose her and Flint. It should! The match was obvious.

"I'm not doing anything with Flint Collins with you feeling the way you do about him."

"I don't feel any way about him except for horrible. I'm deceiving him, and he's such a great guy."

"Aside from possibly stealing from your father."

"Aside from that," she said. In spite of the number of times she kept reminding herself of the facts, such as they were, she just couldn't believe Flint was a thief.

Not considering everything he'd told her. Everything she'd seen in him over the past few weeks.

And as far as Stella went, Flint had seemed fully over her a week after they'd parted. He'd chosen Diamond Rose rather than her without looking back.

He'd changed his entire life for that baby. Because that was the kind of man he was.

And because it had been his mother's dying wish.

Because the baby was his only flesh and blood.

But what about before that? Maybe the Flint she'd gotten to know over the past weeks wasn't the man he'd been a month ago.

He'd had no idea his mother was pregnant, so clearly he hadn't seen her in a while.

He'd been hell-bent on starting his own business behind her father's back.

And what about those foreign investments he'd made on his own behalf, the risks he'd taken?

Maybe she just hadn't been looking in the right place for information. Maybe it wasn't information she needed.

Maybe what she needed here was a motive. Did it have something to do with Stella?

Was she the reason Flint Collins needed to steal money? Had she made him that desperate? And if not, had something else? If Tamara could find the answer to that question, she might be able to end this whole episode in her life.

Problem was, after her conversation with Mallory, Tamara wasn't sure she wanted it to end.

Chapter Fifteen

Stella wasn't going away. Whether she was truly frightened of him now that she knew about his past or—more likely—just incredibly pissed off, she wanted a restraining order against him. No mutual agreement, nothing that could ever come back looking negative on her. All she wanted was him signing her damned paper, agreeing to release her family from any wrongdoing in perpetuity. And an order to stay away from her.

After almost two weeks of back and forth, trying to come to an amicable agreement, Flint's attorney called him the Friday after Thanksgiving and told him the only way to be free of the family was to fight them. In court. A date had been set for a hearing on the order for Thursday of the following week—on Diamond Rose's first-month birthday. Standing at the window in his office, watching the bustle of Black Friday shoppers on the streets below, he listened as his attorney highly recommended that he show up.

If he didn't, the order would automatically be put in place. Would become a matter of permanent record. In other words, if he didn't show up, he looked guilty.

Which meant that if he hoped to have any kind of long-term relationship with Tamara, even as just the close friends that was all she seemed capable of considering at the moment, he was going to have to tell her about the order.

It might be enough to push her out of his life.

He'd have to take that chance. He was done living with lies, hiding things because he was ashamed of them.

He was tired of being ashamed of his past.

The truth hit him so hard, he had to sit down. He was *ashamed* of who he was.

Almost as quickly as he sat, he stood again. The second he let life knock him to the ground, he gave it a chance to keep him there.

His much younger self had had the guts to stand up to the bullies on the bus and he sure as hell wasn't going to allow a selfish woman and her wealthy, powerful family to make him cower.

He had no reason to feel ashamed about anything. It was time to quit acting as if he did. Time to quit hiding the facts of his life.

Finishing with his attorney, agreeing to make the court date and authorizing him to go full-force ahead to have the order dismissed without cause, Flint hung up and called Tamara. She was working upstairs in her office, but she'd told him the night before, when she'd called after Thanksgiving with her folks, that she wouldn't be at the investment firm much longer. Her work there was almost finished.

She'd had a couple of offers. One local, one out of state. The out-of-state company was larger, but she hadn't yet confirmed either one. Hoped to be able to schedule both.

He hoped she'd be scheduling time for him, too.

"I hear there's an old-fashioned country Christmas-tree lighting at Pioneer Park in Julian tomorrow," he told her. "I've never been to a lighting, so I don't know what we'd be in for, but I was thinking it would be good for Diamond's first outing. Bright lights for her to focus on, and if she cries, we're outside in a noisy atmosphere. You want to come along?" He was taking a huge chance, maybe pushing her too fast. He went with his gut and did it anyway.

"I've actually been to that celebration before," she said. "Several times. It's nice. They have a lot going on. Santa. And other Christmas things. And…have you checked the weather? Do you know if it's going to be too cold to take her out?"

"The stroller has zip-up plastic walls and I've got a hat that completely covers her ears. And blankets."

He also had to tell her about the restraining order.

If they were going to move forward after her work at Owens Investments was done.

"So you hardly had a chance to talk to Mallory yesterday at the dinner, huh?" she asked out of the blue.

"There was another single father there, one she's apparently gone out with a time or two. While I like your friend, I had absolutely no interest in butting in where I clearly didn't belong."

"Would you have wanted to butt in if the other guy hadn't been there?"

Was she jealous?

Was it wrong of him to be smiling at that thought?

"If he hadn't, there wouldn't have been anything to butt into."

"Would you have asked her to the tree lighting if he hadn't been there? And the two of you had spent more time talking?"

"I just learned about it this morning," he told her. "I happened to see a sign on the way to work. If you don't want to go, you don't have to, Tamara. I'm not pressuring you. I'm just asking."

"It's not that I don't want to go..."

The problem was Diamond. He understood. So much more than she thought.

"She'll be in her stroller the whole time," he said. "And if there's an issue, I'll take her back to the car and handle it."

"Don't you think this seems more like a date?"

"It's whatever you and I decide it is. Just like our lunches. And dinners. Do *you* think it's too much like a date?" Maybe he was putting on some pressure, after all.

Maybe it was time.

"No. You're right, Flint. I'm making excuses."

"You don't have to go."

"I want to..." She sighed, hesitating.

"Then come with us."

"I'm scared."

"I know." He could support her. He couldn't take away her battle. Or fight it for her.

"Okay."

"You'll come?"

"What time?"

"It's about an hour's drive, so I'm guessing around five, being flexible in that I want to have Diamond freshly changed and fed right before I swing by to get you." He knew she owned a bungalow by the beach. He'd yet to be invited there. And he didn't even have the address.

"I'll meet you at your house," she said. "It's easier that way."

He'd prefer to deliver her safely to her door when they

got back, but let it go. She needed to be in control of her destiny. He was good with that.

And good with life in general, too. There would always be roadblocks. It was how he handled them that defined him.

Tamara had no idea what she was doing. Not really. Not deep down where it mattered. She'd told her parents, over a quiet Thanksgiving dinner the day before, that she'd befriended Flint for the purpose of spying on him for her father.

Neither of them had been thrilled with the news.

When she'd added that she liked him, and was struggling because of it, they'd looked at each other and frowned.

Her father had asked if that was how she'd known about the offshore bank account and, when she'd affirmed it, he'd asked her not to use a friendship to get any more information on his behalf.

He hadn't asked her not to be friends with Flint, although she figured from the concern on his face, and the hesitation in his tone, that he wanted to.

Instead, when she left, her parents had both implored her to be careful. They'd hugged her tight and she could almost physically feel their worry palpitating through them.

At no point during the day, not in a single conversation, had any of them mentioned a baby. Any baby.

And now here she was, sitting in Flint's car on the way to a holiday celebration, dressed in black leggings with black boots and a festive long black sweater with Christmas-tree embroidery. She wore Santa Claus earrings. Flint in his black pants and red sweater looked equally festive and she caught a glimpse of the baby's red knit hat when he'd loaded her carrier into the back seat. They resembled the stereotypical American family out to enjoy the season.

So not what they were.

It wasn't supposed to drop below forty degrees, but she'd dressed warmly.

At the moment she was sweating.

She hadn't turned around in the front seat, but she knew the baby was right behind her. Kept waiting for her to wake up. To need attention while Flint was driving...

"I have something to tell you." Flint's words brought her back to sanity fast. Was he going to confess that he'd siphoned money from his boss?

If he had, she needed to know. Needed all of this to be over.

And yet she didn't want it to end.

She felt trapped, with no way out. Or no way that would let her be happy when she got out.

For someone who had something to say, Flint was far too quiet. Maybe he wasn't ready?

"I have to be in court next Thursday to defend myself."

Everything stopped. It was far worse than she'd expected. He hadn't just stolen from her father? Someone else had pressed charges?

Where were her feelings of validation for her dad? Her rage?

All she could find was cold fear.

Disbelief.

"I told you about Stella—how I didn't tell her about my background..." He was continuing in the same calm tone. It took Tamara a second or two to catch up. There was an innocent baby right behind her. One who'd never have her own mom or dad, since her mother died without naming him, but had a brother who loved her as much as any parent could have.

"...she's taken out a restraining order against me. My attorney's been trying for two weeks to get her to sign a mutual stay away agreement, but she's more of a barracuda than I realized."

Focusing on the traffic along the freeway, taking herself outside something she wasn't handling well, Tamara juggled her thoughts.

"Stella claims you hurt her? That she fears for her safety?" She knew what restraining orders were for. Steve's sister'd had to get one against an ex-boyfriend.

Heaven help her, but there was no way she could believe Flint had threatened anyone, let alone a woman. He didn't deal with anger by attacking. He sucked it up.

She didn't have to see how livid he was to know that. She just had to listen to him, to see his tenderness, his unending patience with a crying child. And to know he'd given the mother who'd made his life hell a funeral, even though—as she'd later found out when she'd asked—he'd been the only one in attendance.

"The order actually reads that due to the fact that I hid from her who I really was, she fears for her and her family's safety."

"I thought you had to have proof of harm, or threat of harm, in order to get a restraining order."

"You only have to say you fear harm to get the initial order. The accused then has a chance to rebut the charge before the court and then the order's either granted or dismissed. If I don't go to court, it'll be automatically granted and become a permanent part of my record. Anytime someone did a background check, it would show up and I'd look like I'm an abuser."

"What a bitch." The words were out before she could stop them. She wasn't proud of them.

Flint's grin surprised her. "Thank you."

He didn't say any more about the situation and she didn't ask. He'd been honest with her, but she was lying to him every single second she was with him, by not telling him who she was. And she'd be breaking her word to her father if she did.

She felt like crap. She could blame Stella What's-Her-Name for wronging Flint, but she'd have to shoot recrimination at herself, too. Even after these weeks of getting to know him, she'd doubted him. The second he'd told her he was going to court, she'd assumed he'd done something wrong.

It could've been a simple traffic ticket he'd had to defend. That had never entered her mind.

And yet...she was drawn to him. To be with him.

So much it hurt.

Chapter Sixteen

Public restrooms. Something else Flint had failed to consider in his new life. He was a man with a baby girl and he had to pee.

They'd been at the festival for an hour, had a couple of chai lattes and, together with the coffee he'd had before they'd left home, his situation was becoming critical.

He could take Diamond with him. Just wheel her right in. It wasn't like she'd know the difference.

But he would.

He didn't want her in a men's restroom, sleeping there close to the urinals or…in there at all.

His only other option was to leave her with Tamara. Which wasn't fair.

Urgency won out over fairness. "Can you just hold on to this while I pop in here?" he asked as they approached the cement building that housed the facilities. Not giving her much choice, he pushed the handle of the stroller in her direction and made his break.

Three minutes later, when he rushed back out again, his hands still wet from a brisk wash, they were exactly as he'd left them. Tamara hadn't moved. Taken a step. She was standing there, her hand on the stroller, staring at the men's restroom door.

And when he got close, he saw the tears in her eyes.

"I'm so sorry." He took the stroller, wheeled them out of the crowd and off to a bench not far from the festivities but far enough to give them privacy. With darkness having fallen, a chill had entered the air, although it wasn't cold enough to warrant the shiver he felt running through her as they sat.

"I should've thought ahead," he said, not sure what he could have done differently. Even without the latte, he'd have had to go at some point. It was what people did.

And what he'd need to do again before the evening was over.

"This isn't going to work, is it?" he asked her, not ready to give up but not willing to hurt her any more, either. "This is too hard for you."

She shook her head and, in a season filled with hope, he felt his dwindling once again. No matter how many times that happened, he never got used to it. It never got easier.

He wasn't going to try to convince her, though. He cared about her too much to watch her suffer.

"I'm the one who needs to apologize," she told him, turning so that she was looking him in the eye. "I need to try harder, Flint."

She'd lost four babies. Heartache wasn't something that could be brushed off or ignored. On the contrary, broken heart syndrome was a medically proved reality, as he'd discovered when doing some research on her situation.

"You're doing great, sweetie. I just…" What? He just what? He'd called her "sweetie." As if they were a couple.

She was still looking at him, all wide-eyed and filled with emotion. So close. He leaned in. She did, too. And their lips touched.

Maybe he'd meant it to be a light touch. A sweet good-bye to go with the endearment.

Maybe he hadn't been thinking at all.

What Flint knew was that he couldn't let go. Her lips on his... His world changed again and he moved his lips over hers. Exploring. Discovering. Exploding.

He felt for her tongue. Lifted his hand to the back of her head, guiding them more closely together. Felt her hand on his thigh.

Laughter sounded and it was a little too close. An intrusion, shattering the moment. He pulled back.

"I'm not going to apologize for that," he said, breathing hard. He glanced at Diamond, her stroller right there in front of them, the wheels lodged against his feet. The baby had been asleep for almost two hours. She'd be awake soon. Needing attention.

And Tamara...

She was looking at the stroller, too.

"I'm not going to run," she said. Maybe that made more sense to her than it did to him.

"Okay."

"There are a lot of things against us," she continued. "And chances are they'll win out eventually, but I'm not going to run away."

If the park staff had chosen that exact second to light the huge tree across the way from them, Flint's world wouldn't have been any brighter. He could hear "A Country Christmas" coming from the live band onstage in the distance and, for the first time, understood what people meant when they talked about the magic of Christmas.

"I'm very glad you aren't running away," he said aloud.

* * *

"I want to hold her so badly it hurts."

They were in the car on the way home. Tamara had tried to keep her mouth shut. There was no future for them; she had to let him go.

And couldn't bear the thought of it. Of deserting him. Of him being deserted again.

"I'll help you try to hold her..."

She shook her head, arms wrapped tightly around her.

"We could start out easy," he said. "Just fix a bottle for her. Nothing else. See where that leads us."

Fix a bottle. She could do that. Maybe even do it without undue stress as long as she focused on something else while she completed the task. That wasn't how she usually did things; she typically focused on whatever needed doing immediately. But that wasn't what she needed here. She'd think about...what?

At the same time, she'd be paying attention to the amount of water to powder, of course.

"My dad bought Ryan a plastic baby fishing pole," she said, when fighting the inevitable didn't work. Babies always brought her to this place. "It's blue plastic with a red reel, and it has a big plastic handle that really turns and makes noise."

He glanced at her and then back at the highway.

Diamond had woken shortly after their kiss. He'd fed and changed her in the SUV while Tamara had wandered into a couple of nearby shops. After that, they decided to head out rather than wait for the big tree lighting.

"It's in the back of my shed." *Still in its plastic wrapping.*

"You never talk much about your parents."

Understandably, given the situation.

He didn't *know* the situation.

Guilt assailed her. She'd kissed him.

And she'd liked it.

Far more than she'd ever liked Steve's kisses.

What did that mean?

"Mom's a doctor." The darkness in the SUV made her feel safe. Secure.

Or maybe it was being with him.

"A cardiologist." Fitting. She was dying of heartache.

"And your dad?"

"He's into a lot of different things." He had investments in just about every field out there. "Computers, mostly," she said. She couldn't tell him the truth. But she wouldn't out-and-out lie any more than she had to.

She'd already told him she was an only child in one of their earlier phone conversations. They'd both been "onlys." She knew, from that same converation, that he didn't want Diamond to be.

"Have you told them about me?" he asked.

Oh, God, don't strike me down in my sleep. "Yes."

"And?"

"They're worried about my…well-being." She could be completely honest with that one.

"Surely they don't think you're better off alone."

"No, of course not. It's just been so hard…on them, too."

"Are they afraid of the possibility that you might get talked into trying again?"

Trying again.

Her chest tightened. The cords in her neck were taut. Her throat. What if she wanted that someday? Not simply to try again but…to try with Flint?

She shook her head.

She couldn't stretch the truth that far.

"I don't know," she finally said when she could.

"Do you think they want you to? Or hope you might?"

Looking out the car window, she thought about her mom and dad. "They've never said," she told him, but figured if they had, the answer would be no.

Just the thought of living through the months of waiting and worrying that would be involved—

Enough was enough.

And the three of them...they'd had enough.

The week following their trip to Julian was inarguably the best week of Flint's life so far. The only shadow at all was Stella's restraining order hearing and, in the end, it had been postponed. She'd asked for more time to prepare.

Not surprisingly, the judge had granted her request. Flint had had no say in the matter and only heard about the changed date when his attorney called to tell him he had to be in court the week before Christmas.

On the surface, not a lot had changed with Tamara. He still hadn't been to her home. She hadn't said why, but he could understand that it would be near impossible for her to have an infant in her most private space.

He would've been open to considering a lunchtime visit, but when she didn't suggest it, neither did he.

She'd wrapped up her work at Owens and while he'd liked knowing she was in the building, they hadn't crossed paths often enough for there to be a real difference in their time together. She'd taken the job in town, only a few miles from Owens, tentatively scheduling it for after the New Year. And on her last day in the office, he'd grabbed her out of view of all security cameras, telling her that knowing where the cameras were was a perk of spending so much time in the building—and then he kissed her. Soundly. So he could have that memory with him every single day he went to work.

She'd kissed him back fiercely. Telling him she wanted the memory to last.

They'd met for lunch four times that week. Twice they'd ended up in his Lincoln, making out. While it had been years since he'd even thought about kissing in a car, Flint was enjoying the slow pace of their relationship.

Tamara needed time.

He wanted her to have it.

If they went to her place, or his, they'd end up having sex and, as acutely as he needed that with her, he wanted it to be fantastic for both of them.

It wasn't going to be for her until she had some things worked out.

She'd been over for dinner twice and on Saturday afternoon to watch a movie. *ET* not *Wall Street*. One day at lunch they'd been talking about their favorite movies growing up and had decided to watch them all with each other. Her top three were *Mary Poppins*, *Annie* and *ET*. Other than *Wall Street*, his were *The Goose That Laid the Golden Egg*, *Rocky* and *Heaven Can Wait*.

Things were vastly different between them when they were around Diamond. The baby wasn't sleeping quite as much anymore. She'd happily spend time in her swing. Liked to be held for a while after she ate and before she went to sleep. She was also happy on a blanket on the floor for short periods, maybe ten minutes or so.

Tamara had mastered the art of bottle preparation. She'd taken over the sterilizing process, too, whenever she was there. She sat in a chair instead of on the couch with him when he was holding Diamond. And avoided looking in her direction at all other times.

Still, Flint took the week as a huge win.

She was trying.

And there was no doubt now that they equally craved their time together.

She came back on Sunday, bringing sushi for them to share while they watched a second movie. And then a third. They'd just finished *Heaven Can Wait*, a story about a young football player who'd left this world too soon, and she asked Flint about his mom. Not the bad stuff, she'd said, the good. She wanted to know all the things he'd loved about Alana Gold.

The things he wanted to pass on to Diamond.

If he was a guy who cried, he could have wept.

Over sushi, he asked her what she loved most about her parents. She'd liked that her mom never seemed like a doctor at home. She was just Mom.

Someone who worried too much. And was her greatest champion in the world.

"Dr. Frost," he said, anxious for the time to come when he could meet them. He'd been hoping by Christmas, but Tamara hadn't said anything.

"Her name's not Frost." The change in her tone was odd. Off. She looked like she had the day she'd picked up Diamond in his office.

Only different. Maybe worse.

"Your parents aren't married?"

"Yes. They are."

Sitting at the dining room table, with Diamond in her baby swing behind her, she dropped her California roll on the paper plate she'd brought.

He wasn't getting the problem. His baby girl hadn't made a sound. And Tamara couldn't see her to know she'd just smiled at him.

She'd been doing that a lot lately, this girl of his, smiling when she saw him.

"So your mother kept her maiden name?" he asked,

waiting to pick up another roll. He drank from the glass of wine she'd poured him.

She shook her head. "Frost's my married name." You'd have thought she'd admitted to some horrible crime, the way she'd said that. As if she expected him to be upset that she'd kept her ex's name.

A lot of women did that. For various reasons.

It was just a name.

"Okay."

Watching him for a second, she seemed to relax. She picked up her roll. And then another. Back to normal.

"So what *is* your maiden name?" he asked. He was planning to meet her parents at some point. He should know what to call them. Maybe even have their number in case of an emergency. They knew about him, so there was no reason he shouldn't have that information. "And do I call them Dr. and Mr. or—"

She'd gone completely white. Looked like she might be sick.

"Tamara? What's wrong, hon?" He stood, thinking he'd grab a cool cloth.

When she stood, too, he backed away from the table, giving her room to make it to the bathroom. But she wasn't going anywhere. She just stood there, facing him, looking... horrible.

"My parents are Dr. and Mr. Howard Owens."

Chapter Seventeen

She hadn't meant to tell him. Oh, God, she hadn't meant to tell him. They'd been sitting there, eating sushi and having a great day, and she'd been so aware of the baby, needing to help care for her, and the awful lie had been there between them. He'd called her mother Dr. Frost. Dr. Steve's-Last-Name.

The lie had been too horrendous to keep to herself.

"Say something," she said.

He was standing there staring at her, frowning at her, completely confused.

"I… Did you just tell me that Howard Owens, my boss, is your father?"

She'd thought she'd felt every acute stab of pain there was to feel. She'd been wrong. The grip on her heart when she looked at Flint was different than anything she'd ever felt before.

"Yes." And if, judging by the expression on his face,

he was this put out about that part of it, he'd never be able to accept the rest.

She hadn't expected him to.

"You were working for your father."

"Yes."

He nodded. "Bill knew that."

She could almost hear his mind buzzing as he started putting the pieces together. But even Bill didn't know the whole truth.

"And your father told both of you not to say anything to the rest of the staff."

"Something like that." Exactly like that, except that he, in particular, had been singled out not to know.

"So when you interrupted us that first day… You're the real reason I kept my job. You talked to your father—"

"No!" She shook her head. "I mean, I did say something, but he'd already decided to keep you on. He'd met with you by then. You'd already signed the noncompete agreement."

"Which you thought was a good idea."

"I did."

He nodded, his brow clearing a bit. She wished she could feel relief but she knew better. Her lips were trembling. Her hands and knees, too. Tamara slid back onto her chair.

"I can see why your father wanted you to do your work without anyone knowing you were his daughter. People would be more honest with a stranger who had no ties to their boss."

She wanted to nod. He was right—to a point.

She could sense that he was taking hope. Saw him working everything out in his mind.

It was an endeavor doomed to fail before he'd even begun.

The sound of the swing, back and forth, back and forth,

click, click, played a rhythm in her mind. Soothing her. She concentrated on that. Focused on it.

"Did you really tell them you're seeing me?"

"Of course."

There were no longer any creases on his brow.

"And they were okay with it?"

"They didn't tell me not to." That point was key. He had to know they hadn't rejected him—despite believing he might have stolen from them. She'd even go so far as to say, "They're supportive of whatever choice I make where you're concerned."

"But they're worried."

She'd already told him that much. She nodded.

"Your dad knows about my past. And about Diamond Rose."

Of course he knew. Flint had informed Howard about the baby himself.

He frowned again. "When I asked you to give me time to tell him...did you?"

"Yes."

His brow cleared. If she didn't know better, she'd start to take hope herself. As it was, she wanted to throw herself in his arms, beg his forgiveness and have wild, passionate sex.

She wanted to focus on him. On them. All the issues separating them be damned.

At the same time she wanted to run, but didn't trust her knees to carry her away from him.

"So...now that the cat's out of the bag," he began, "how about we pack up the girl here and stop over to see them? I know Howard generally spends his Sunday evenings during football season in front of the seventy-two-inch screen he had installed in your parents' family room."

"You've seen it?" She gulped. Buying time she didn't have.

"Of course not. He doesn't expose his employees to his family—and vice versa. You'd be the first to know that."

She nodded.

"So…give them a call. Let's get this over with." His tone was light. His expression wasn't, but it was filled with the warm light of…caring she'd become addicted to seeing from him over the past weeks.

She shook her head.

Flint sat on the edge of the seat closest to her then leaned forward, taking both of her hands in his. "I know there's a lot we still have to face, sweetie. Just as I understand why they're so concerned for you. Let me assure them that I know what's going on. That I have no intention of asking you to do anything if you aren't ready. Even if you're never ready. Let me set their minds at ease."

She couldn't do that. But how to tell this wonderful man—the man she seemed to have fallen in love with—that nothing was as it seemed.

She loved him? Nothing like going for the bottom line when everything was falling apart.

Mallory had been right. She'd known how Tamara felt before Tamara knew it herself.

She wasn't surprised by that.

"You owe it to me," he said next, his tone still light, grinning as she looked up at him. "I have to see him at work tomorrow, knowing that he knows but that he doesn't know I do." He rolled his eyes. "Whew. This is complicated."

He made her smile.

Which made her cry.

She loved him.

And she was about to hurt him so badly.

She loved him.

And she was about to lose him.

* * *

Getting over the initial shock, Flint was filled with undeniable energy. Ready to forge into the future. Taking Tamara in his arms, understanding her emotions as she finally told him a secret he'd had no idea she'd been keeping, wanting her to know that he understood and held no hard feelings. He rubbed her back. Buried his face in that glorious auburn hair. Inhaled her soft, flowery scent.

If ever he could have scripted a life for himself, it would be this one.

He'd known Howard Owens had a daughter, but he hadn't heard much about her. She'd gone to college. Gotten married. He'd never heard anything else.

He certainly hadn't known that Howard had lost four grandchildren before they were born. The man he'd thought unemotional to the point of impassive had gone out and bought his unborn grandson a fishing rod. Hard to accept that one—and yet he'd always admired Howard, had wanted to be like him. Other than the older man's penchant for playing it safer than Flint's gut told him to do.

And now...here he was, in an incredible relationship with the man's daughter. Howard knew, and hadn't told his daughter to run in the opposite direction.

"Flint..."

Sniffling, Tamara pulled away from him. Wiped her eyes. She wasn't smiling.

He stilled. "What's wrong?"

Tears welled in her eyes again as she looked up at him.

He didn't start to sink back to reality, though, until she took another step back. Bracing himself, he waited.

No point in reacting until you knew what you were reacting to.

"There's more. And I want you to know, right up front, that I don't care anymore."

Now he was confused. "Care about what?"

Was she telling him she had no feelings for him? He found that hard to believe. She had to be running scared because of Diamond.

A problem, to be sure. But they could work on it.

There had to be a way...

"Whether or not there's any truth to my father's suspicions. I *should* care. But I don't. I told him that on Thanksgiving Day." She stopped. Took another couple of steps backward, toward the great room where she'd left her purse.

He was watching her leave him.

He didn't get it.

"I told him I wasn't sure how much longer I could go without telling you..."

What, that she was Howard's daughter?

And what were Howard's suspicions? Flint had already admitted he'd been in the process of opening his own business. That had all been before Diamond. Before Tamara.

"What did he say to that?" he asked because he couldn't come up with anything else.

"He understood that I had to do what I had to do."

"But he didn't want me to know?"

She shook her head.

Okay, so all was not as he would've scripted it.

"He wanted proof, first."

Proof? Flint needed her back in her chair, across from him, eating sushi. He had no idea how to make that happen.

"He's not going to press charges," she said. "He told me so. Especially not if it's you. You need to know that..."

Press charges? What the hell?

No.

Grabbing the back of the chair with both hands, he

stood calmly. His life was what it was. Always had been. Maybe it always would be.

And he'd deal with it.

"Why don't you leave out all the preliminaries and tell me what your father thinks I've done."

"Someone's been siphoning money from the company."

"And he thinks it's me."

She nodded.

Her tears didn't faze him. The stricken look on her face didn't, either. He noted both, but was somewhere else entirely now. He was in his own world, where there was just him. Knowing that he had what it took to deal with whatever was in front of him.

First was finding out the facts. All of them.

"And you've known this how long?"

"It's why I was working at Owens," she said, exposing more and more of a nightmare he'd thought he'd already seen in its entirety. "As an efficiency expert, I'd have access to everyone and everything in the company. He wanted me to see what I could find out."

"You were his spy." His mind was working. The rest of him was dead to the world. Shock, maybe.

Survival, certainly.

"Yes." He respected the fact that she didn't spare herself. Didn't lie to him.

Ha! Irony to the hilt. She'd been lying to him since the moment they'd met.

A flash of that day in Bill's office came to him, along with a stab hard enough to stop his airflow. "Bill knew."

She shook her head. "Well, he knew who I was, but he doesn't know why I was really there. No one does, except my mom and dad and me."

She hadn't been sent to him by Alana Gold. Or for any

good reason. Her presence hadn't been a coincidence; he'd been right about that. But her purpose...

"He wanted you to look into me in particular," he said aloud. "Your interest in me—it wasn't real..."

Thinking of her there, in his home, with Diamond Rose, he wanted to puke up the sushi he'd just consumed.

He wanted her gone.

"I wish that was true!" Her words came out on a wail. "I wish to God my interest was nothing more than a way to ease my father's worry. Instead, I fell in love with you. When he told me he wasn't going to press charges, it was as though this huge flood of relief opened up inside me and I've been a mess ever since."

She fell in love with him.

Right. She expected him to believe that?

"I'm guessing you didn't find anything to convict me?" he asked almost dryly, although he was starting to sweat in earnest.

If he'd made a mistake along the way, and they were going to make it look like he'd purposely cheated the firm...

Who'd believe him?

"Obviously, I'm not a criminal investigator, but I couldn't find anything on anyone," she said. "But circumstantially, you're the most suspect."

Criminal investigator.

Sweat turned to steel. No way was he going to jail!

He would not lose Diamond.

His mind took over. "Circumstances meaning my past? My background?"

"Your offshore accounts."

The night he'd been talking to her about the *Wall Street* movie. He'd been falling in love. She'd been taking notes to betray him.

He'd think about that another time. If an occasion arose that required it.

"I know of four other brokers in the firm who have them. What else?"

"Your spending habits changed."

"I had a rich girlfriend I was trying to impress, and money I'd saved for a day when I had someone to spend it on."

She didn't deserve any explanations, but he was *not* going to jail.

"You were opening your own firm behind my father's back."

"I intended to do just as he'd done when he opened his firm. Once I knew the legalities were in place and it was actually going to happen, I intended to go to him with my plan. I was about a week away from that when I got word that my mother was dead. I'd planned to give Howard the opportunity to send a letter to all my clients, naming a broker in my stead, and move on. If any of them found me elsewhere and chose to follow me of their own accord, then I'd continue to service them. Instead, I heard from Jane in Accounting, that someone found out—I don't know who or how—and I heard that Bill went to your father with a version of the truth that made me out to be unethical."

And clearly Howard had believed that version.

She hadn't stepped back any farther. He was ready for her to do so. To keep stepping back until she was gone from his home. From his life.

He wanted to forget ever knowing her.

Forget that he'd ever thought her beautiful…

Her eyes flooded again. Like a sucker, he'd fallen for that compassionate look in her eye. And the fear she'd exposed to him.

But no more.

"Jane is the one who started the rumor. She found out what you were doing from a friend of hers who works at the office of the Commissioner of Business Oversight. She knew you worked at Owens, where Jane works. Jane's the one who told Bill. Why Bill spun the news when he told my father, I have no idea. A charity account was used to run the money through." She spoke as though she was giving testimony.

Jane had betrayed him! He'd thought the grandmother of four liked him.

"You were the only broker who knew the account number because, for a time, you donated your expense checks to it as a tax write-off."

"All three of the company directors, and your father, as well as at least one person in Accounting, not Jane, has access to that account."

She could keep throwing things at him. He'd done nothing wrong. Knowingly, at least. But it was clear to him that she was prepared to keep talking. He had to know whatever she knew, to find out what he was defending himself against. He was careful to keep his tone as level as hers. To converse. Not to shut her down.

"The broker who took the money used various office computers at all different hours of the day—always computers that aren't within view of security cameras."

A flash of memory from the past week visited him. The quip he'd made about knowing corners that were out of view of security cameras when he'd kissed her.

"You were spying all along?"

She neither confirmed nor denied that one.

Her list—and her father's—could be convincing. He was seeing the picture she was building.

And yet…

He was *not* going to jail. He would not abandon Diamond Rose as he'd been abandoned. He'd give her up first.

The baby, not three feet from him, slept obliviously. He was thankful for that. She didn't know. And if he had his way, she'd never know.

"Whoever it was signed in under my father's account."

"Then why don't you look at someone who knows his password?"

"He thinks you do."

"I don't. Go talk to Bill Coniff, since you're so fond of him. He has the password. Maybe he gave it to someone."

"How do you know Bill has it?"

"I've seen him use it," he told her. "A couple of times when we needed something critical and your father was out. I'm assuming the other two directors have it, as well."

"You've actually seen Bill sign in to my father's account?"

He saw where this was going. If he'd seen Bill type the password, then it would stand to reason he could retype it himself.

"I was on the other side of the desk. I didn't see him type. I just know he accessed the information we needed."

Tamara stared at him. They were done.

"Look, Bill's the one who told your father that I was starting my own business, spinning it to look like I was planning to contact my clients and steal my book of business. When, instead, upon hearing the rumor from Jane, he could have just come to me. Given me the chance to go to your father. And Howard believed Bill's take on what I was doing, without discussing it with me. And he apparently still believes I'm guilty of stealing from the company. Just as he's going to believe whatever else Bill tells him. Including that he gave me your father's password. Or that I was on his side of the desk and saw him type it."

He could see the evidence piling up. Bill would testify that he'd seen Flint use the password. It would be Bill's word against his, and even a kid could figure out who a judge would believe on that one.

Tamara wiped her eyes. Picked up her purse. "I'm sorry, Flint. I—"

"Just go."

"I'm going to do everything in my power to clear your name," she said. "That's what I've been trying to do—"

"You could've just asked me if I'd stolen money from your father's company."

She nodded. "If you ever need anything…"

He'd know who not to call.

Flint watched her walk out of his life and then calmly locked the door behind her.

Merry Christmas.

He allowed that one bitter thought and then got busy.

He'd do what it took. Just as he always had. He was going to *be* someone.

Not for Alana Gold. Not even for himself.

For Diamond Rose.

Chapter Eighteen

Four days later

Bill Coniff, who, it turned out, had a gambling problem, resigned from Owens Investments and quietly disappeared. After signing a full confession, as well as other documents at the behest of Howard's team of lawyers, making sure he couldn't malign Owens Investments, the Owens family, or ever again work as a trader in the State of California. In exchange Howard didn't press charges because it was best for the company not to have it out there that they'd had a traitor in their midst.

Tamara discovered that Bill hadn't originally planned to frame Flint; at first he'd truly been pissed that the guy was leaving. But not because of Howard. Because of himself.

As Flint's boss, he got a percentage of the money Flint made for the company. But then he'd figured out that Howard knew about the siphoning of money thanks to an extra-long meeting Howard had with his accountant after the company taxes had been done. A meeting that Howard hadn't shared with his top three people, as he usually did. And, after which, Howard had asked the three of them about their use of the charity account.

Bill had known by then that Flint was leaving. He'd known, too, that with Flint's expertise, plus his background, he could easily frame him for his own wrongdoing. He'd seen a way out. And had been desperate enough to take it. And then Flint had changed his mind about leaving. He'd needed Flint gone. His chances of getting Howard to believe him would not only be much stronger that way, but he'd been afraid that, once accused, Flint would figure out for himself who was guilty. Bill had gambled on the fact that Howard would believe him over Flint if it ever came to a "his word against Flint's" situation.

As much as Tamara wished differently, Flint wasn't around to know about any of it, including Bill's leaving, or the agreement between him and Owens Investments.

Sometime after she'd left him that Sunday night, he'd packed up Diamond Rose and gone to Owens Investments, clearing out his office and leaving his key in an envelope under Bill Coniff's door. Howard had told her it had looked almost as though he'd purposely left behind a trail of his actions by staying within security-camera range anytime he could. He'd packed his office in the hallway, carrying things out and loading them into bags he'd brought with him, one by one. Showing the camera everything he was taking.

In tears, Tamara had asked for a copy of the tape. She watched it several times in the days that followed, sometimes staring only at Flint. And at others, finding herself looking at the precious baby she'd once held.

Once.

She started the job she'd accepted early and worked long hours so she'd be finished by Christmas. Focusing on the task and not on herself. She knew how to cope with grief.

And when the nightmares woke her, she lay in bed and replayed her time with Flint over and over—starting with the first meeting between her and her father in Howard's office, to that last horrendous half hour at Flint's house.

Working for her father, virtually undercover, to preserve the integrity of his business had not been wrong. Hanging out with Flint...that didn't feel wrong.

Falling in love, though? Completely inappropriate. And yet if Mallory was right, she didn't get to choose love, love chose her.

So what the hell? She'd been chosen to have a life of misery? Of unrequited love? First for the four children she'd lost? And now for Flint?

And little Diamond.

Even from a distance, that little girl had found her way through Tamara's defenses.

Tamara was crying too much again.

She spent a lot of time with her parents. Going over lawyers' paperwork with them as they moved immediately on getting Bill Coniff out of their lives. From start to finish had taken four days.

And now, here she was, on Saturday, two weeks and two days before Christmas—almost done with the current job and another beginning in the new year, with holiday functions to attend with her parents and shopping to do—walking up to Flint's front door like an idiot.

She knocked, having no idea what she'd say to him. She'd already said it all. She'd explained. She'd taken full responsibility. She'd also told him she didn't give a damn whether or not he was guilty. That she'd known her father wouldn't press charges. That he'd be okay. She'd told him she'd fallen in love with him.

Nothing she'd said had mattered. She understood that, too.

Knocking a second time, she told herself that her behavior was bordering on asinine. But she had to see him. To let him know he was off the hook—they'd found their thief. Just so he didn't worry that, on top of Stella's order, he had another possible court situation to face.

And she needed to know he was okay.

Maybe find out where he was working, so she'd know that he and Diamond were secure.

She'd already called Mallory, knew that Diamond Rose was still coming to day care on her regular schedule. Had been there the day before.

She knocked again.

Flint didn't answer any of her knocks.

With the garage door closed, she couldn't tell if he was home or not.

One thing was clear, though. If he was inside, he'd seen who was on his porch and definitely didn't want anything to do with her.

She had to honor that choice.

She just hadn't expected it to hurt so much and couldn't contain the sobs that broke out as she turned and walked away.

Flint heard from Howard Owens every day that first week after his last meeting with Tamara. He didn't pick up, leaving them with one-way conversations via voice mail. One way—from Howard to him. He didn't return any of the calls. Howard was requesting an in-person sit-down. He wanted Flint to stay on at Owens Investments. He never mentioned the theft, or his suspicions, not even on the first call Monday morning, when it had become known that Flint had cleared out. By midweek, his messages changed only to add that he'd put out the word to Flint's clients that, due to having just become a father, he was taking a week or two off. Howard was personally handling Flint's entire book of business.

Flint might have called him back to tell him to go to hell. If he'd been a bitter man.

Even when Owens implored him, he ignored the summons.

And when he sent his spy daughter to Flint's home to plead his case? Especially then. He was fighting for his very life. Something neither of them would know anything about.

It was possible he would've capitulated after a full week's worth of calls, but on the Tuesday after the truth about Tamara had come out, while Flint was home alone researching his next career path, he'd received another court notice.

Not from Stella this time.

Much worse than Stella.

Lucille Redding, Diamond's paternal grandmother, a woman no older than Diamond's mother, was petitioning for custody of his little girl. No one had told him Diamond's paternity had been discovered, let alone that there was a paternal family.

He'd called Michael Armstrong, his attorney, immediately. Faxed the petition over to him. Asked about the repercussions of taking his baby sister and disappearing from the country. Hadn't liked that answer at all.

Michael had told him to sit tight and let him do some investigating.

Flint had cashed in some of his more lucrative personal investments, moving the money to his offshore account.

He called his attorney again, filling him in on the news Tamara had given him on Sunday, assuring him that he absolutely had not taken any money from anyone in any kind of illegal capacity. Michael told Flint he believed him.

He wouldn't blame the guy for having doubts. But he was paying him to keep them to himself.

Instructed once again to sit tight, Flint packed a couple of emergency suitcases, one for him, one for Diamond Rose, just in case, storing them in the trunk compartment in the back of his Lincoln.

For the rest of that day he'd researched career options and tried not to hear Tamara's voice in the back of his mind. He played music. Turned it up louder. Left the news on in the background, watching the stock channel on cable.

She didn't love him. Truth was, she'd been so hurt, she was probably incapable of truly loving anyone, other than maybe her parents.

He'd put Diamond to bed in her carrier that night, keeping it on the bed with him, a hand on her, on it, at all times. If he hadn't read that it was unsafe to have the baby sleeping right beside him—read about the danger of rolling over in his sleep and suffocating her—he'd have snuggled her little self right up against his heart, where he intended to keep her forever. Safe from a world that would judge her just because of who she'd been born to. And where she'd been born.

As if she'd had a choice about any of that!

Michael called Wednesday morning just as Flint was pulling out of the Bouncing Ball Daycare.

Turned out that Alana Gold had had an affair with a twenty-eight-year-old male nurse, Simon Redding, an army reservist working in the prison infirmary. Simon had fallen in love with her and, according to what he'd told his mother, Alana had loved him, too.

Which was why Alana had refused to name him as her baby's father. She'd been protecting him from prosecution.

At his mother's insistence, Simon had volunteered for deployment shortly after he'd slept with Alana, to get himself as far away from temptation as possible. He'd died in Afghanistan just after Thanksgiving and his mother, honoring the love her son had said he'd felt, and knowing he could no longer be hurt by it, had tried to contact Alana. To visit her.

Only to learn that she'd died in childbirth. That the affair could have resulted in a baby girl.

She was requesting a DNA test to prove that her son was Diamond's father.

And, assuming the test was positive, would be suing for custody. She was married. To a colonel in the air force. Was a schoolteacher. Simon had been their only child.

They had the perfect family unit in which to bring up a little girl.

On Friday he'd received a court order to provide Diamond's DNA.

And as early as Monday or Tuesday, he could be faced with having to set up a time to make her available for a grandparent visit.

He wasn't leaving the house at all that day or the next. He and Diamond were going to lie on her blanket on the floor and watch children's movies. He was going to rock her. Feed her. Bathe her. Take pictures and video of all of it.

And come Monday, in spite of the fact that he had a pending restraining order against him, an ex-boss who suspected him of theft, no job and had been suspected of helping his convict mother finance the drug business that had put her in prison, he was going to fight like hell to keep Diamond and him together.

He could be a good father. And a good brother. Both at once. He knew that now.

No one was going to love her more than he did.

No one but him could raise her to understand the good that came from being Alana Gold's child. Or teach her about the good that had been in Alana herself.

Diamond wasn't just a convict's daughter. She was the daughter of a woman who, though afflicted with the disease of addiction, had loved fiercely. Laughed often. Who'd listened to understand. Who'd always, always, come back.

And who'd taught him how to live with determination, not bitterness. To stand instead of cower. To carry dignity with honor even when others tried to strip it away.

She'd made him the man he was.

It was up to him to teach Diamond all the value to which she'd been born.

Because she wasn't just going to *be* someone.

She *was* someone.

On the Tuesday of that next week, fourteen days before Christmas, Tamara joined Mallory at the Bouncing Ball after work to help her friend put up Christmas decorations. Saying that putting the tree up too early made the little ones anxious, Mallory always decorated for two weeks and two weeks only. If the day after Christmas was a workday, she came in Christmas night to take down the decorations.

Tamara had promised herself that she wasn't going to mention Flint or Diamond Rose. Nor was she going to look for any evidence that either of them had been there.

If Flint wanted her to know anything about them, he'd call her.

He'd have answered his door.

Her spying days were over.

Which made it a bit difficult when, after they'd hauled

the artificial tree out of the back of the storage closet, straightened its branches and were just starting to string lights, Mallory said, "Flint offered to stay and help do this."

Mallory knew Tamara wasn't friends with Flint anymore. Knew he'd quit her father's company. Why on earth was she...?

And then it hit her. Flint and Mallory.

Standing on one side of the tree, she passed the long strand of stay-cool lights over to Tamara, who wrapped the two top branches in front of her and handed them back. Mallory's tree always had lights on every single branch to make up for the lack of ornaments that she said just tempted little ones to reach out and touch.

Tamara had insisted that Mallory and Flint would be perfect for each other.

Had thrown him at Mallory.

Her pain at the thought of them together was no one's fault but her own.

"I figured Braden would be here," she said, bringing up Mallory's ex only because she'd promised herself that she wouldn't talk about Flint behind his back. But lying to herself was really no better than lying to Flint, although the truth was that she couldn't bear to hear Mallory talk about him.

Mallory passed the lights back to her.

She didn't know what she'd do if Flint and Mallory became a couple.

Move back to Boston probably.

Keep in touch with Mallory for a while by phone, wish her well from the bottom of her heart, then slowly fade away from them completely.

It was the right thing to do.

"Braden's always helped you in the past," she continued just because she'd already started the conversation. Taking off the section she'd just wrapped when the lights all fell onto the same branch, she tried to rearrange them.

"He's out on a date tonight."

Oh. She passed the lights back to her friend. "Is she someone new?"

"I have no idea. I didn't ask." Mallory's tone said she didn't care. Tamara wasn't sure she believed that. She'd never completely understood the relationship between Mallory and Braden.

"How about that guy you were seeing at Thanksgiving? What was his name? Colton something? Is that going anywhere?"

"No. My call. Not interested." Mallory returned the lights to her.

So it was Flint, then. Leaning down as they reached their way along the tree, Tamara covered a wider section of branches.

She should be glad to know that Flint and Mallory might find each other. She loved both of them and neither deserved to be alone. And yet…what kind of woman did it make her that she couldn't bear the thought of the two of them together?

"Flint's in a real bind, Tamara."

With the string of lights hung, Mallory plugged it in, making the room glow with the overabundance of multicolored twinkling lights. Tamara barely saw them.

"What's wrong?" she asked. Was it Stella? His court date wasn't until the following week. But the woman could have showed up somewhere he'd been and then called the police to report that he'd been near her.

"Please don't tell him I told you, but if there's anything you or your family can do to help…" Mallory bent to the box of decorations, hauling out plastic wall hangings. Tamara recognized the long faux mantel she was unfolding, on which Mallory would hang stockings for each of the kids, with their names on them.

"What's wrong?" she asked again, more tension in her voice than she'd ever used with Mallory before.

"He just doesn't strike me as a man who'd ever ask anyone for help, at least not that he couldn't pay for and..." Mallory was bent over the box again.

"Mallory!"

Her friend stood, a garland of bells in hand, facing her.

"It goes against everything in me to talk about a client but...he might lose Diamond Rose, and if he at least had a job..."

Heart pounding, Tamara could hardly breathe. Lose Diamond Rose?

She hadn't told Mallory he'd quit Owens Investments. Apparently he'd done that himself.

"My father's been calling him every day for a week, trying to get him to come back," she said. "He doesn't pick up and won't return his calls. What's going on?"

Flint could lose his baby?

Because of Stella's order?

"Her paternal grandparents have come forward, demanding a DNA test, and they're suing for custody."

Tamara fell into the chair closest to her. A tiny, hardbacked one. Mallory told her what Flint had been going through since she'd last seen him, at least the parts he'd shared with her. And only because he'd had to give Mallory's name to the courts, who'd be contacting her as Diamond's caregiver.

"Her father's younger than Flint." Tamara said the only thing she could focus on that didn't make her feel like she was suffocating.

Wow.

Oh, God.

"The grandparents are in their late forties, young enough to participate fully in her activities as they raise her. They've been married for twenty-five years, have professional jobs and not so much as a speeding ticket. Their son was a nurse and in the army reserves. His only apparent mistake in life was falling in love with Alana and having sex with her while he was working in the prison infirmary."

Mind speeding ahead now, Tamara stood as a list of supposed sins against Flint sprang to mind. She knew them well because she and her father had listed them as reasons to suspect him of theft.

She knew how easily that list could convince someone against him. And she and her dad hadn't even had the restraining order to include in the mix.

Add to that, he'd just left his job—walking away from all the people who'd been loyal to him for almost a decade, some more than that, who would've been able to testify on his behalf. Including his client list.

He had no one. No family. No girlfriend. No one to stand up and tell the court what a travesty it would be to take that baby away from him.

"He's a single man without a job," Mallory said. "I was thinking, if your father took him back, at least that issue would be solved... I didn't know he was already trying to do so."

And Flint hadn't returned Howard's calls. Because the one thing Flint had never learned was to rely on others. To allow himself to need anything he couldn't provide for himself. Or pay for.

Because he could never believe that anyone would help him.

He'd probably thought, in spite of Howard's assurances

otherwise, that her father was trying to get him to talk about the missing money. He'd have no way of knowing that Bill had admitted his gambling addiction, confessed everything. Some of it was confidential and couldn't be told, and the rest... Her father wanted to apologize to Flint in person, man to man. Eye to eye.

"I'm sure he won't value his pride over Diamond Rose," she said. "He can't. Especially once he finds out what's been going on." Apologizing to Mallory for abandoning her, she grabbed her bag and ran out.

She had to get to her father. To convince him to do whatever he had to—beg at Flint's front door if it came to that, or camp out in the Bouncing Ball parking lot until he showed up there—to give him his job back, whether he wanted it or not.

That was for starters.

What she could do after that, she hadn't figured out.

She just knew she had to focus. Get to her father.

And figure it out.

Chapter Nineteen

The last thing Flint had expected to see as he was coming out of the Bouncing Ball Wednesday morning was Howard Owens standing beside his Lincoln.

"I have nothing to say to you," he said, getting close enough that the fob in his suit pocket unlocked the door. He rattled off the name of his attorney, telling Howard to say anything he had to say to Michael.

He got in his vehicle and pushed the button to lock the doors behind him.

DNA tests were expected that day or the next. They could've been in as early as Monday. Flint was considering every night he had with Diamond as a gift at this point.

Living from moment to moment.

And planning for a future with his baby girl, too. He had to, if he was going to stay sane.

He had to, to give Michael something to present to the judge. Something that could stand up to practically perfect grandparents.

About to put the SUV in drive, he glanced out the windshield and stopped. Howard was standing there, right in front of the vehicle. Arms crossed.

Challenging him.

The man was in his fifties, graying, but every inch the fit and muscular man he'd been when Flint had first met him.

Flint couldn't be intimidated anymore. He'd had enough. He reached for his phone to call the police and then thought about having that on his record.

It would be his word against Howard's regarding who'd started the confrontation. Howard would bring up the suspicions of theft against Flint...

Leaving the vehicle running, he got out.

Stood face-to-face with the other man, his arms crossed.

"I'm here to help." Howard's gravelly voice didn't sound helpful.

"If she put you up to this, tell her that she can consider her conscience cleared. And while you're at it, tell her to stay off my property."

With a single bow of the head, Howard acknowledged the order. But didn't move. "You're a smart man, Flint."

He refused to let the compliment distract him.

"Too smart to risk losing your daughter without doing all you possibly could do to keep her."

They knew.

Glancing at the door of the day care, he realized he should've known. Michael had said he had to provide Diamond's day-care information. Tamara had recommended Mallory to him.

They were all in it together.

Like hanging with like.

Sticking together.

That was how things worked.

"She's my sister, not my daughter." It was all the fight he had in that second, while he figured out what Howard was after and then did something to circumvent whatever it was.

"She won't know the difference until after you're more father than brother to her."

Point to Howard Owens.

The admission was like a slug to his shoulder. Nothing more.

"Let me help you."

He stared at the older man. There'd been a real plea in his tone. He'd never taken Howard for an actor. Never knew he had that talent.

Stood to reason, though, considering his wealth and the business he was in, convincing people to part with their money.

Flint's business, too. His one real talent.

"Why?" he asked.

"Does it matter? You don't want to lose that baby, you need a job."

"I'll find a job."

"Not with almost a decade's experience, not with a book of business large enough to impress even the most jaded of judges, not one that's going to give you the security you've got at Owens."

"Until you fire me for fraud, you mean."

"We got our man," Howard said, giving him nothing more on that.

He wouldn't have expected anything different. Howard would be bound by a legal agreement not to discuss the matter.

"There'll be a next time."

"Probably not before your custody hearing." Howard didn't even blink.

"I don't accept pity."

"Not even for your little girl?"

He had him there, and Flint made a fast decision.

"Thank you, sir. I appreciate the offer. I'll move back into my office this morning. Would you like to send word to my clients that I'm back from sabbatical or should I do that?" The question was a real one, and issued with sarcasm, too. He wasn't dishing up a load of respect to the man.

"I'll do it. I have a few things I'd like to say to them on your behalf. And then you do what you damned well please. You're the best I have and I need you on board."

Now, that made sense to Flint.

He nodded, got in his car and drove off.

Later that week Flint got a call from Howard Owens. Sitting at his desk, he picked up.

"I misjudged you," the older man said.

"Yes."

"In the numbers business, the money business, we play percentages."

Flint more than Howard, and yet it was true.

"The percentages pointed at you," Howard noted.

"Years' worth of faithful and diligent service, coupled with high returns, don't rate well with you?"

"Most of the traders on staff have that."

Also true. "I'm your top earner."

"You were making plans to leave."

This conversation was going nowhere.

Or it had already arrived there.

He got Howard's point in making the call.

"Thanks for getting in touch," he said, his tone more amenable. He'd just received an explanation from Howard Owens. A collectible to be sure. Because of its rarity.

"I was wrong. I realize now that you were planning to do it right, Flint. I want you to know how much I appreciate that."

Damn. The man must've seen his bottom line drop significantly over the week of Flint's absence.

"Just glad to be back, sir," he said, determined to get busy and earn his future job security.

Which was all Howard had to offer.

He didn't kid himself about that.

A week before Christmas, just after Tamara had arrived at work Tuesday morning, Mallory called.

"He asked me not to say anything, and I haven't, but I think what you said about him is right, Tam. Flint doesn't ask anyone to help him and I'm really afraid he's going to lose Diamond."

"It's because he doesn't trust that anyone *will* help him," she said, having reached that conclusion sometime over the past week of thinking about him. About them. About herself, too. She took for granted that there'd always be people around her who would help her out.

Flint had never known a day in his life where he could take anything good for granted. Least of all the people around him.

"Tell me what's going on," she said. She'd called him a couple of times since he'd been back at Owens Investments, almost grateful to get his voice mail so that she could just say what she had to say.

She'd told him how sorry she was. She said she understood that the issues between them, including her aversion to motherhood, would always keep them apart, but that she wanted him to know she loved him and that if he ever needed anything, she hoped he'd call her.

She'd asked that he let her know about Diamond. Told him how deeply she believed the child belonged with him.

He'd called back the last time. When she'd answered, he'd simply told her to cease calling him and then hung up.

Very clearly she'd been warned.

He could keep her from contacting him, but he couldn't control her heart.

Love chose her. She most assuredly didn't choose it.

"The DNA must've come back positive," Mallory told her, "because Flint has to take the baby to court for a hearing this afternoon."

Tamara was just wrapping up her job with the box-making company she'd been working for since leaving Owens. She expected to be out of there for good by late afternoon.

"It's just a hearing, though, right? Nothing happens today, even if a decision's made?"

"From what I understand—and he's not too chatty with me since he knows I talked to you about him last week—it could go one of three ways. He could be given full custody, with the grandparents getting some kind of visitation rights. They could get joint custody. Or the grandparents could get full custody with him having visitation rights.

"I think he only told me that much because the outcome will affect Diamond's time here, as well as who can pick her up. He said he's going to request that in the event they get joint custody, the Reddings agree to continue bringing her here on a regular basis so her life has as much stability as possible."

Heart pounding, Tamara stood from the temporary desk she'd been clearing off. "You think there's really a chance they'd decide custody today?"

"He sure seems to think so because he said he'd let me know if she'd be here tomorrow. I guess he had an in-home study done over the past week, and I'm assuming the Reddings did, too. It's my understanding that they live somewhere in the area."

"So the case is being heard here in San Diego?" Tamara.

"Yes, I know that because I had to fill out a form, answering questions, and send it in to the court."

The hearing would be at the courthouse. She could find out the room when she got there. "Do you know what time the hearing is?"

"I know it's after lunch because he's picking her up at noon."

That was enough. "Gotta go," she said, thinking furiously. "Thanks, Mal."

"Just help him, Tamara, and then for God's sake, let yourself be happy."

She didn't really get that last part. But couldn't think about it, either. She was one hundred percent focused on devising a plan to change a course of life events and only had until noon.

You're going to be someone.
You're special. The best part of me.
Don't you ever give up.
You're going to be someone.

With the baby carrier on his arm, his tiny girl asleep and completely unaware of where they were, Flint walked into the courtroom just before two that afternoon.

He'd never met the Reddings, but knew instantly who they were when he saw the couple sitting at the table on the right, holding hands.

Her hair was brown, probably dyed based on the evenness of the color, her dress a cheery shade of rose.

Rose for Diamond Rose.

He was in full military dress.

Good move.

Flint didn't have a chance in hell in spite of his hand-tailored shirt and three-hundred-dollar shiny black shoes.

Much smaller than he'd expected, the room had only two benches for spectators behind the two tables facing the judge's bench. He'd been told the hearing was closed, but to expect a caseworker, probably Ms. Bailey, in addition to attorneys for both sides. Michael had also warned him that the Reddings could call witnesses on their behalf if they chose.

He'd been given the same opportunity, but had no one to call.

Certainly not Stella Wainright. He'd be back in court in two days for his hearing with her.

Merry Christmas.

He could feel the older couple staring in his direction as he pulled a chair next to him for the baby carrier and took his seat at the table. He didn't glance over.

It occurred to him that they probably wanted a glimpse of their granddaughter. All they had left of their only child.

He didn't blame them.

He just didn't like them. Or rather, didn't like that they existed.

Michael arrived and the hearing began shortly after. Flint had purposely timed his arrival so Diamond wouldn't be in court any longer than necessary. He'd tried to time her feeding so she'd sleep through the whole thing, too, but she hadn't been interested in lunch at one thirty. He hoped the little bit she got down would tide her over until he got her out of there.

Because he was going to get her out of there.

He had to believe that.

And he did, right up until he heard the voices of Grandma

and Grandpa Redding, heard their tears and the love they had for a child they'd never even met. Their own flesh and blood. The only grandchild they'd ever have.

Maybe Diamond would be better off with them, after all.

He had to get outside himself, his own sorry feelings, and do what was best for her.

Trouble was, he couldn't seem to get far enough outside himself to believe that she was better off without him.

Being the child of a convict... It was tough. Like Howard Owens had said, people went for percentages. And chances were, if you came from a life of crime, you'd be more apt to get involved in a life of crime.

People were always going to judge you accordingly.

Which tipped the scale even further toward a life of crime.

But that didn't mean you had to make that choice.

He *knew*.

And could teach her.

And while she was the Reddings' only grandchild, she was his only family, period.

He'd had his chance to speak. Had said some version of all that. He couldn't remember exactly what he'd said as he sat back down, but he could tell by the worried frown on Michael's face that he had to prepare himself for a best-case scenario of joint custody.

Which meant a life of upheaval for Diamond. She'd never have one place to call home. Or the same place. She'd never be able to come home day after day, week after week, to the same family. Or spend Christmas with the same people every year of her growing up, making memories they all shared.

He hadn't had it, either, not all the time. But he'd sometimes had it. Even when home had been a dingy trailer with a hole in the bathroom floor that looked down onto the dirt below, he'd preferred being with Alana Gold over the nicest of foster homes.

The Reddings had a couple of witnesses. A preacher. And someone else. Flint spaced it.

"If there are no further witnesses, I'm ready to issue my decision."

"Excuse me, Judge." Flint looked over as his attorney stood beside him. "I do have another witness to call—or rather a group of them. They weren't sure they were going to make it, but I just received a text that they're here in the courthouse. If I may ask the court to be patient for just another minute or two..."

The judge, a man of about fifty, not far from the Reddings' age, glanced over his glasses at the couple, at Flint and then at the baby carrier beside him. He seemed like a good guy. Flint didn't blame him for deciding, as he probably had, that the Reddings could give his baby sister so much more than a single man, son of a convict, could. In the obvious ways, at any rate.

"A child's future is at stake," the judge said after a long minute. "Of course I'll wait."

Agitated as hell, Flint scowled at Michael. "What's going on?" he whispered.

Michael leaned over. "You want to learn to trust that someone will actually help you, or just hand her over?"

He didn't like the man's tone. But sat straight, turning when he heard the door behind him open.

If Stella was pulling some prank, trying to play nice only to annihilate him...

Howard Owens walked in with a woman Flint had never met. The way her arm looped through his made him figure he was looking at Dr. Owens. Tamara's mother.

A fact that seemed more obvious when Tamara walked in right behind them.

In a pair of navy dress pants, and a navy-and-white fitted top, with her auburn hair falling around her shoulders, she looked stunning.

Just stunning.

He was stunned.

Because behind her, more people were filing in. Men, women, all in dress clothes. Rich men. Rich women. In rich clothes. A politician. The police commissioner. A college president. He knew, because he knew them all.

He'd talked to most of them that week, assuring them that their portfolios were solidly back in his hands.

"Your Honor, these people all know Flint Collins personally, have known him, and trusted him, for years. Most of them for more than a decade." Michael proceeded to introduce them, one by one, begging the judge's pardon for a few more minutes to allow each of them to relate just one piece of information about Flint's ability to provide Diamond Rose Collins with a secure and healthy home. The home her mother had chosen for her. Because she'd known her son.

Flint could hardly hear for the roaring in his ears. The tightness consuming him. He couldn't take it in. Couldn't comprehend it.

But before anything else could happen, before those around him could speak, his baby girl, maybe distressed by all the people gathering around them, started to cry. He shushed her quietly. Rocked her carrier. But the wails grew louder. He had a bottle, just in case. Was reaching for it, feeling heat rush up his body, when he noticed that someone was beside him. He caught a whiff of flowers. And then feminine fingers were expertly unlatching the carrier straps, Diamond was up, held in Tamara's arms, and the crying had stopped.

Tears in her eyes, Tamara faced the judge.

"I am in love with Flint Collins, Your Honor. These are my parents." She nodded to Dr. and Mr. Owens. "Flint felt he had to fight this on his own, but that's not what family's about. Yes, he had a challenging upbringing, which means he doesn't yet know how extended family works, and that's why we're here to show him. I've had the honor to be in this little girl's life since the day she came home to Flint, and I am fully prepared to be in her life until the day I die, just as any biological mother would."

Her words, a little hard to understand at times through her tears, were no less effective. Not where Flint was concerned.

Diamond lifted her head, throwing it back a bit, but Tamara's hand was right there, steadying her. She looked at Tamara and then laid her head down on Tamara's chest again, closing her eyes.

"If it pleases the court, I've got something to say," Howard said.

The judge shook his head. "I don't need to hear any more."

Just as quickly as Flint's hope had risen, his heart dropped. Until Tamara took his hand. When he looked at her she was grinning, for him only. Holding his gaze. Telling him something important.

He might not know a lot about family, but he wasn't a stupid man. He held on to her hand.

"After giving this matter consideration, I feel it's in the best interests of this particular child to honor her mother's legal wishes by giving sole custody to her brother, Flint Collins…"

The man's voice continued. Flint heard mention of the

Reddings working out visitation times with Flint. He heard some technicalities. And a comment about hoping to see them back in his court again for the young lady to officially adopt Diamond.

He heard it, but couldn't believe it. None of it.

"Court dismissed." A gavel sounded.

It made no sense to him.

He was going to wake up. Find out that he was still in bed, it was Thursday morning and he had to face getting up, knowing he might lose Diamond that day.

Except that Tamara's fingers were digging into his palm. People were gathering around him. Patting him on the shoulders. Dr. Owens came up to his side, opposite her daughter, put her arms around him and gave him a hug.

"Thank you," was all she said. Which made no sense to him, either.

He nodded, though. Because it seemed appropriate.

And as soon as he could, he turned to Tamara, put his arms around her and hugged gently, feeling how hard she was trembling. With an arm still around her, he took his baby girl in his other arm and knew he was never going to let go. Of either of them.

He'd done what he'd had to do.

He'd just become somebody he'd never known he could be.

Chapter Twenty

The tree was lit, Diamond had been fed and was asleep in her swing, steaks were ready to grill, and Flint stood in the kitchen, opening a bottle of wine.

Christmas Eve, and he wasn't working.

He'd put on the black jeans, the red sweater. He had gifts wrapped and under the first tree he'd had since he'd left for college, and he still couldn't quite believe he was going to have a family Christmas celebration.

The Reddings had been over. Almost every day since their court appearance. They'd agreed that when Diamond got older, if she wanted to spend some weekends with them, she could, but for now, they were content to settle for babysitting. And visits.

When his attorney, Michael, had called Stella's attorney and, with Flint's permission, started dropping names of those on the support team who'd showed up for Flint in court, the Wainrights had dropped the charge against him. And then, when Flint's attorney had pressed, they'd agreed to sign a settlement to stay away from Flint and any member of his family and never to speak ill of him. Even after he'd refused to sign a similar one for them.

Tamara was on her way over after going to an early service with her parents. And he and Diamond had been invited to Christmas dinner at their place the next day.

Not so sure about that, having dinner at the boss's home, he figured he'd handle it like he did everything else. Standing up. Moving forward.

But for now, he had something more important to do.

As soon as Tamara got there.

He had a plan.

Because she was born to be someone, too.

Life had a funny way of working itself out, Tamara reminded herself as she climbed the steps to Flint's door on Christmas Eve night.

She'd sat through church, hearing about a blessed birth and feeling sorry for herself because she hadn't been blessed with the ability to give birth.

And then, ashamed, she stopped that train of thought. She was truly lucky. She'd been given a second chance with Flint, and she wasn't going to blow it.

Her issues weren't going away. She'd been unable to sleep for two nights after her day in court with Diamond Rose. But she was going to fight. Every moment of her life, if that was what it took. She was going to be in Flint's life. And that meant finding a way to let herself love Diamond Rose without falling apart.

She'd talked to Mallory right before church. Her friend was spending Christmas on a yacht in the harbor with some friends, and sounded like she was having a great time.

As good a time as it was possible to have during the

holidays when you didn't have family of your own. But Mallory wasn't giving up on life. Wasn't letting the past prevent her future.

Tamara needed to do the same.

Flint opened the door before she'd even knocked. He'd obviously been waiting for her and she loved that.

She took the glass of wine he held out to her, but leaned in to kiss him first. Long and slow and deep. He was much more delicious than wine.

They'd yet to consummate their relationship, but she hoped to rectify that situation this evening. The lacy red thong and barely-there bra she'd worn under a festively red-sequined sweater and black pants were there to help.

But when she began to make her move, he stepped back.

"I want to try something," he said, leading her into the living room. "Have a seat."

He seemed nervous, which was saying a lot. No matter what Flint was feeling on the inside, he didn't let weakness show very often.

So she sat. And wondered if he was about to ask her to marry him. It was a little early, considering they hadn't even slept together, and yet...it didn't feel early at all.

Except that she was a woman who might never be able to be a mother to his little girl. And who almost certainly wouldn't be able to have any more children with him.

"Drink your wine," he said, taking a sip of his as he told her about his day. About running out of tape in the middle of wrapping and having to go out and get more, his baby girl right by his side. She listened because he wanted her to. Sipped wine for the same reason.

But she really wanted to know what was going on.

When she'd all but finished her wine, he set down his glass. "I need you to try something with me. If it fails... well, then it does, but I feel strongly that we should try."

"Is this like one of those times when you take a risk on an investment because you're sure it's going to pay out, and then it makes you a load of money?"

"Kind of like that, yes. The feeling is the same. But I'm going to need you to trust me."

Though he prided himself on his knowledge, gleaned from studying everything he could about a particular topic, he'd been gifted with acute instincts. She'd learned that much about him very early on. Believed it was those instincts that had guided him so successfully through a life filled with hardship. Aided by what he'd learned, of course.

Her mind was babbling again. His nervousness was contagious.

She didn't know where he'd gone or what he was doing. Maybe seeing to the baby, although she hadn't heard a peep.

Then she heard his voice, speaking calmly. "Lie back and close your eyes."

An odd request, but he'd asked her to trust him. And she did. Implicitly. She lay back. Closed her eyes.

"Take me back to the day Ryan was born," he said, coming closer. She opened her eyes and he turned away. "No, please, Tamara, close your eyes and tell me about that day. Everything you can remember. Even if it's just about running out of tape."

She didn't like this. At all. But the tape? He'd focused on the mundane for a reason, so she did, too. Because she trusted him.

She was safe with him. Emotionally safe. And so she did as he asked, sharing that day with him in the little things, things that hadn't mattered to anyone else who'd talked to her since her son's death. She remembered that she'd had chocolate for breakfast—in the granola bar she'd eaten. That she'd shaved her legs. She'd had a day off work. Had gone in for a haircut and had wanted to leave the salon. To be home.

Her car had half a tank of gas.

The weather was warm, balmy. The sun shining. She'd thought about picking a cucumber from her garden to have with cheese and crackers for lunch. Wanted to remember to call her mom.

He asked her what she was wearing that day, his voice so soft she almost didn't hear him. So soft, he didn't break her spell. And she told him about the pregnancy pants. Not leggings, but real pregnancy pants with the panel. Her friends had teased her, but she'd wanted them because she was actually showing enough to need them.

The maternity top had been blue with little white, red and light blue flowers.

She talked and talked. Remembering so much. Relaxed from the wine. And the goodness of the feelings that had welled up in her that day. The hope.

But it didn't stop there. In the same soft voice, closer, right next to her on the couch, Flint asked her to talk about the first labor pain she'd felt. What she was doing. What she was thinking.

One second at a time, through the little things, the thoughts she could remember, she went through that horrific afternoon with him, including every moment she remembered in the hospital, talking about the sounds, the voices she heard, other people's conversations.

A conversation about babies who'd been born at her gestational time period surviving and eventually thriving.

She took him with her through the pain of the birth, the silence when she'd expected to hear a baby's cry. The look on the doctor's face. On Steve's face. She'd known. They hadn't had to tell her, she'd known. Her precious baby boy hadn't survived the birth. Tears streamed down her face as she felt the hysteria building inside her. Steve told the doctor to give her something and—

Just before the darkness came… "Stop." Flint's voice was still soft. The command was not to be denied. She lay there, eyes closed, and waited.

"Do you want to hold him, Tamara? Just once? To say goodbye?" His voice. She started to sob. To sit up. To lash out and—

Gentle hands against her face. "Keep your eyes closed, Tamara. Stay with me. Trust me. It's okay to cry, sweetie. Just tell me if you want to hold him."

She was back in that hospital room, right before the darkness.

"Yes," she said. "Yes, I want to hold my baby."

"Here." Flint's arm slid behind her back, supporting her weight as he lifted her, straightening her a little. Something touched her chest and she reached up automatically, cradling it.

The weight was slight. He was only four pounds.

"He's in a blanket, Tamara, wrapped up and warm. He looks so peaceful. Don't be afraid to hold him tight. You can't hurt him."

Of their own volition, her arms closed around that bundle. She didn't think to question, to wonder what it was. She just held on for all she was worth. Crushing it to her. Aware that it had more give when she squeezed than a human body would, but she was holding him. Eyes closed, lying there against Flint, she was holding her baby boy.

She cried. Hard. And Flint held her. She lay there until Diamond's cries broke the spell. And then, when Flint didn't move, she opened her eyes, told him she was okay and urged him to go care for the baby.

He didn't bring Diamond in to her. She'd thought he might, but knew he'd made the right choice.

She was still sitting there, holding what she now knew was a teddy bear, weighted and stuffed with a gel-like pillow pad.

Her trials weren't over. She was well aware of that, and Flint was, too. His gift to her hadn't been a cure, hadn't been meant as one. Flint was too much of a realist for that. And it was clear he'd done a lot of reading she hadn't known about. Studying her situation. Giving her the gift she needed most of all. He'd given her what no one else had even tried. A chance to hold her own baby boy.

Mostly, Flint had just sat with her in her pain. Taking some of the weight of it from her.

Flint grilled the steaks. He picked at his dinner just like Tamara did. And when she said something about maybe heading home, he asked her to spend the night.

Not to have sex. Just to lie in his arms and sleep.

Diamond was old enough to spend a night in her nursery. He'd keep the monitor beside him.

He'd had it all worked out and was still surprised when she agreed.

Leaving a T-shirt and boxer shorts on the end of his bed, with a cellophane-wrapped toothbrush—compliments of the dentist—on top, he told her he'd get the baby fed and down and would be back.

"Just get in whatever side you'd like," he said, growing hard as he pictured her in his bed, and yet, not achingly so. Some things were more important than sex. "The remote is on the stand there. Find whatever you'd like to watch."

By the time he got back, she was asleep.

Tamara woke with something warm against her back. She couldn't figure it out at first and then memory came crashing back.

Flint. He was spooning her. In his bed.

She had no idea what time it was, but felt like she'd been sleeping for days. Deeply. It was still dark outside.

Diamond Rose. Had he fed the baby?

Listening, she heard a little sigh and then even breathing coming through the monitor.

It was a good sound.

A very good sound.

There were other good things, too. Like the arm looped over her side, holding her close. The...ohhh...pressed up against her.

It was growing.

In his sleep, or had she woken him?

She wanted him awake.

Turning her head slowly, she kissed his chin. Or what she thought was his chin. He moved and caught her lips with his.

He must've said something because she was back in a trance again. Letting him take her away, to a different place this time.

A much happier place.

With an incredible ending.

But when they lay together, exhausted and complete, she didn't feel as though anything was over.

"Marry me," he whispered in her ear.

"I want to, Flint, so badly, but I can't do that to you or Diamond. That little girl deserves to have a mother who can hug her all the time and let her know how much she's loved. Kids need to be hugged."

"She needs *you*," he said. And when she shook her head, he asked, "You want me to tell you how I know?"

She nodded.

"When it comes to Diamond, you've got a mother's instinct. That's what makes mothers special. It's not something you buy. Or even learn. It's something you have that makes a kid feel okay even when things aren't okay. It's what my mother had."

"I don't have that." He was romanticizing now. So not like him.

"When you came into my office that day, I couldn't do it for her. I didn't know what she needed. You did and you didn't hesitate. She quieted immediately. That was no mistake, Tamara. Surely you've been around crying babies in the past few years, but you've never walked over to pick one up and quiet him or her."

Yeah, but…

"Anytime I talked about Diamond, you seemed to know instantly what she needed. What I needed to do."

Well, that had just been common sense.

"And in court, I was going to lose her…we were going to lose her. And you swooped in and saved us. Not just by being there, but when she started to cry…she needed a mother to seal the deal and you became one. You are one. She looked at you, laid her head down and closed her eyes."

"I—"

He put a finger to her lips. "I don't have all the answers yet," he told her. "I don't have any more at all right now. I might not ever have them. But I know that you're meant for us, Tamara, and we're meant for you. It's all up to you now."

He knew what he was getting into and wanted to take it on. Take *her* on. Maybe even needed to. He'd never even told her he loved her. She imagined that didn't come easily to a man like Flint. But he'd showed her. In a million different ways.

Mallory had told her to let herself be happy.

No one could do it for her.

"Yes."

"Yes, it's up to you now?"

"Yes, I'll marry you."

She was done with letting her past prevent her future.

They made love a second time and still didn't fall asleep afterward.

Maybe he was waiting for Diamond's next feeding. A couple of hours had passed. She had too much on her mind to let sleep take over.

"I want to try again," she said, feeling sick to her stomach even as she said the words. "Not right now. Not anytime soon, but I want to have your baby. Our baby."

"We have our baby, Tamara," he told her, sitting up and pulling her against him. "Biologically she has two other parents, but she's all ours. And if at some point, we're sure you're ready, then we'll face whatever happens together."

Whatever happens. Because you couldn't control life. You could only control what you did with what you were given.

Which was why Flint had grown out of an environment of crime into a remarkable man.

Diamond's whimpers came over the baby monitor. Slipping into a pair of shorts, Flint went in to change her.

"I'll get her bottle." Tamara, wearing an oversize T-shirt of Flint's, was already on her way to the kitchen. She was the bottle-getter when she was in the house.

But when she went to the door of the nursery to drop it off, she didn't let it go.

She wanted to hold the baby. To sit in the rocker and know she could be a mom.

She started to shake.

"Bring her in with us," she said. "Just while she eats. I'll sit up to make sure we don't fall asleep."

Without saying a word, Flint did as she asked, setting the baby down in the middle of the bed, half lying beside her and reaching for the bottle. Tamara still didn't give it to him. Kneeling on the mattress, keeping her distance, she leaned over. Diamond Rose looked at her—that little chin dimpled, lower lip jutting out—and started to cry. With the baby watching her, needing what she had, expecting Tamara to give it to her, there was no thought. From her distance, Tamara guided the nipple to that tiny birdlike mouth as though it was the most natural thing in the world.

Because it was.

For a mom.

* * * * *

THE BABY PROPOSAL

ANDREA LAURENCE

To My Dancing Queens

Theresa, Jaime, Lucretia, and Amanda

Thanks for all the girls' nights, the Soul Train dance
parties, beach time and laughs. I'm not going to
thank you for the tequila. Tequila is the devil.
Even the good stuff.

One

Showtime.

The rhythmic sound of the drums pounded in the distance. On cue, one spotlight, then another, lit up the stage at the center of the open courtyard. With loud whoops and cries, the Mau Loa Maui dancing troupe took the stage.

Kalani Bishop watched the show begin from the dark corner of the courtyard. Spread out across the lawn of his resort were hundreds of hotel guests. They were mesmerized, as was Kal, by the beautiful movements of the traditional Hawaiian dancers onstage. He had no doubt that he had the finest traditional dancers on the entire island of Maui. He could have nothing less at his hotel.

The Mau Loa Maui had been the brainchild of Kal and his younger brother, Mano. Their family hotel, the original Mau Loa, was located on Waikiki Beach on Oahu. Growing up, they had dreamed of one day not only taking over the Oahu location but expanding the resort chain to other islands. First—Ka'anapali Beach in Maui. Kal had fallen in love with the island the moment he arrived. It was so different from Oahu— so lush and serenely beautiful. Even the women were more sensual, in his opinion, like ripe fruits waiting for him to pick them.

It was without question the most beautiful hotel on the island. The look on his grandparents' faces when they arrived at the resort the first time was proof enough that they approved of his work. The tourists certainly did. Since they opened, the resort had remained at capacity and had reservations booked solid a year in advance. They made vacation fantasies come true.

Part of the Hawaiian fantasy included attending an authentic luau with the kind of dancing seen in movies. At the Mau Loa Maui, the luau took place three nights a week and included a full dinner of kalua pork, poi, fresh pineapple, mango rice and other traditional Hawaiian foods. The guests sat on pillows around low tables that surrounded the stage.

Kal had worked hard to craft the perfect atmosphere for this hotel. Flames leaped from torches stationed around the wide lawn, lighting the area now that the sun had finally set into the sea beyond the stage. The fire cast shadows that flickered across the faces of the dancers and the musicians who beat drums and chanted along with them.

One of the female dancers took center stage. Kal smiled as his best friend, Lanakila Hale, commanded the attention of every person in the courtyard. Before she even began her solo dance performance, she had captivated the audience with her traditional Hawaiian beauty. She had long, wavy black hair that flowed over her golden brown skin. A crown of Plumeria flowers sat atop her head and circled her wrists and ankles. She was wearing a skirt made of long, green ti leaves that showed the occasional flash of her upper thighs and a bright yellow fabric top that bound her full breasts, leaving her stomach bare to highlight her toned core.

He couldn't help admiring her figure. They were friends, but it was impossible to ignore that Lana had an amazing dancer's body. It was hard, sculpted and lean after years and years of professional dance training. While she specialized in traditional Hawaiian dance, she had studied dance at the University of Hawaii and was well versed in almost every style including ballet, modern dance and hip-hop.

As the drums continued to beat faster, Lana kicked her movements into high gear. Her hips gyrated and swayed to the rhythm as her arms moved gracefully to tell the story of that particular hula dance. The hula wasn't just entertainment for tourists; it was his culture's ancient storytelling method. She was amazing, even better than she had been the night he first saw her dance in nearby Lahaina and knew he wanted her at his new hotel as the head choreographer.

Lana was the human embodiment of contradiction. She was both an athlete and a lady: strong and feminine, hard and yet with womanly curves in abundance. He couldn't imagine a more physically perfect specimen of a woman. She was an amazing person, too.

Smart, quick-witted, talented and not afraid to call him on his crap, which he needed from time to time.

He turned away to focus on the crowd as he felt his body start to react to her physical display. He didn't know why he tortured himself by watching the show when he knew what it would lead to. With each beat of the drum and thrust of her hips, his muscles tensed and his pulse sped up.

Kal reached up to loosen his tie and take a deep breath to wish away his attraction to Lana. It happened more often than he'd like where she was concerned, but who could blame him?

She might be his best friend, but she was undeniably his type. She was every red-blooded male's type, but she specifically checked every one of his boxes. *If* he had a list, and he didn't, because Kal didn't do relationships. Even if it wouldn't damage their friendship—and it would—there were other issues at play. Namely that he wasn't interested in the family and the white picket fence, and of course, Lana wanted the whole shebang more than anything. He couldn't risk sampling the forbidden fruit because she'd want him to buy the whole fruit basket. Giving in to his attraction for her could be a disaster, because if she wanted more and he didn't, where did that leave them?

Former best friends.

That wasn't an option, so they were to be friends and nothing more. He just wished he could convince his erection of that. They'd been friends for over three years now and he'd been unsuccessful so far. That meant the occasional cold shower to keep things in check, but he was managing.

The other female dancers joined Lana after her solo

to complete the routine. That was a helpful distraction. When they were finished, the male dancers took the stage and the ladies made a quick exit to change into their next dance costume. At the Mau Loa, the show went through the whole history of hula, covering years of styles and dress as it evolved. Kal didn't just want some cheesy performance to entertain the hotel guests; he wanted them to learn and appreciate his people and their culture.

"Do we meet with your approval, boss man?" a woman's voice asked from beside him.

Kal didn't have to turn to recognize Lana's low, sultry voice. He glanced to his left and found her standing beside him. As the choreographer, she did some dancing and filled in for ill or absent performers, but she didn't participate in the majority of the numbers herself.

"Some of you do," he noted, turning away from the show to focus all his attention on her. To be honest, the only dancer who could truly hold his interest was standing right beside him. "Alek is looking a little off tonight."

Lana's head snapped around to the stage and she narrowed her gaze at the performers. She watched the male dancer with her ever-critical eye. "I think he's a little hungover. I heard him talking to one of the other dancers about some wild night in Paia during practice this afternoon. I'll talk to him in the morning. He knows better than to mess around the night before a performance."

That was one of the reasons that Kal and Lana were such good friends. They both had a drive for perfection in all they did, Lana even more so than Kal. Kal liked everything to be just so, and he enjoyed his success, but he also enjoyed his play time. Lana was superfocused all the time, and really, she had to be to get to where she had in life. Not everyone could pull themselves up from poverty and turn their life into exactly what they'd wanted. It took drive and she had it in spades.

Sometimes he liked to point out faults just to watch her head spin like a top. Her cheeks would flush red, her nostrils would flare and her breasts would heave against her tight little tops in anger. It didn't help lessen his attraction to her, but it certainly made things more interesting.

"Everyone else looks great, though," he added to soothe her. "Good job tonight."

Lana crossed her arms over her chest and bumped her shoulder into his. She wasn't the most physically affectionate kind of person, never one to hang on other people. A bounce off the shoulder or a fist bump was about all she was comfortable with unless she was upset. When something was bothering her, all she wanted was a hug from Kal. He'd happily hold her until she felt better, enjoying what little affection she was willing to share.

The rest of the time, Lana was a no-nonsense kind of woman. He was actually kind of glad he wasn't one of her dancers. He'd seen her drill them in rehearsals, accepting nothing less than the perfection she herself was willing to give.

He was pretty sure that friends or no, if he ever got fresh he'd earn a stinging slap across the face. He liked that about her. Most of the local women he encountered on Maui knew exactly who he was. That meant they also knew exactly what he was worth. Like flies to honey, they'd do whatever he wanted to get close to him. He liked Lana with her tart vinegar to break up the sweetness from time to time.

The stage went dark and silent for a moment, catching both their attention. When the lights came back on, the men were gone and the ladies were returning to the stage in their long grass skirts, coconut bras and large headdresses. Kal lovingly referred to this routine as "the bootie shaker." He had no idea how the women moved as quickly as they did.

"There's a good crowd tonight," Lana noted.

"We always sell out on Sunday nights. Everyone knows this is the best luau in Maui."

Lana's dark gaze flicked over him and returned to the stage. Kal was bored with the dancing and instead focused on her. A light breeze carried the fragrance of her Plumeria flowers along with the sweet smell of her cocoa butter lotion to his nose. He drew it into his lungs, enjoying the scent that reminded him so much of nights laughing on the couch and sharing platters of sushi.

They spent a lot of their free time together. Kal dated periodically, as did Lana, but it never went anywhere. Him, by choice. Lana, because she had horrible taste in men. He loved her, but she was a loser magnet. She'd never get the husband and family she wanted with the kind of men she spent her time dating. That meant they spent a lot of time together. Kal's family was all on Oahu. Lana's family just wasn't worth the effort. Occasionally she would go visit her sister, Mele, and baby niece, Akela, but she always came back to the resort in a surly mood.

Thinking of family and free time jogged his memory. "Do you have plans for Christmas?" he asked. It was less than a month away, but the time would go by quickly.

"Not really," Lana answered. "You know it's so busy around here at Christmas. I've got the musicians working on some Christmas songs to do caroling, and we're adding a new holiday dance medley to the luau next week, which means extra rehearsals. I wouldn't ever presume to ask for time off around the holidays. What about you?"

Kal chuckled. "I'll be here, of course, helping guests celebrate Christmas at their tropical home away from home. Shall we carry on our annual holiday tradition of Christmas Eve sushi by my new fireplace while we exchange gifts?"

Lana nodded. "Sounds like a plan."

Kal was relieved. He didn't know what he would do if Lana ever found the man of her dreams. If she were to fall in love, start a family and build a life outside the Mau Loa, he would be all by himself. She'd been at his side since they broke ground on the hotel and he'd gotten used to her always being there.

Finding out his brother was engaged and expecting a baby with his fiancée made the worry crop up in his mind lately. His brother, Mano, had been fairly dedicated to not getting seriously involved with a woman, and yet Paige had gotten under his skin. Before he knew what hit him, he was in love. Kal didn't expect anything like that to ever happen to him—he was too stubborn to let anyone get that close.

But Lana…she deserved more than sushi with him on Christmas Eve. She deserved the life and family she wanted. He knew her childhood sucked. She wouldn't say as much, but he knew that having a family of her own was her way of building what she'd never had. He'd just have to find an outlet for his loneliness and jealousy when she was gone.

He glanced over and noticed Lana was leaning against the wall. She looked tired. "Are you okay?" he asked.

"Yeah," she said as she stared intently at the stage. "It's just been a long day. I'm going to go back to my room and change. Are you up for a late dinner after the show?"

"I am." Kal nodded in agreement. He actually couldn't remember when he'd eaten last. He could lose himself in work so easily.

"I'll meet you at the bar in half an hour. Let me know how the show goes."

"You've got it."

Lanakila made her way upstairs to her suite in the farthest corner of the hotel. It was, for all intents and purposes, her home. Kal had recently completed the construction of his private residence on the other side of the Mau Loa golf course. The sprawling home had taken quite a while to complete with its four bedrooms, large gourmet kitchen, three-car garage and tropical pool oasis in the backyard. Prior to that, he'd been living in a suite in the hotel so he could oversee every detail of operations.

Once he moved out into his new home, he'd opted to let Lana stay in his suite instead of remodeling it for a hotel room. She used to keep a small studio apartment up the coast in Kahakuloa, but she gave it up and sold all her furniture when she moved into the hotel. She stayed late most nights at the resort and was usually too exhausted to bother with the long drive home, so it was perfect.

It was actually bigger than her studio apartment had been anyway, and had a view of the ocean. She opened the door with her key card and slipped inside. Lana turned on the light in the tiny kitchenette before continuing through the living room into the bedroom. There, she slipped out of her costume and put her regular clothes back on.

She didn't like wandering around the hotel in her dance clothes. It made her feel like a character in a Hawaiian theme park or something. Besides that, she could tell it made Kal uncomfortable when she wasn't fully dressed. He averted his eyes and shifted nervously, something he never did when she was in street clothes.

Lana supposed that if Kal walked around in the men's dance costume all the time, it would make her uncomfortable, too, although for different reasons. The men danced in little more than a skirt of ti leaves. She had a hard enough time focusing on Kal's words when he was fully dressed in one of his designer suits. They covered every inch of his tanned skin, but they fit him like a glove and left little to the imagination.

Kalani Bishop was the most amazing specimen of male she'd ever laid her eyes on, and she'd gone to dance school, so that was saying something. And yet that was all she'd say on the subject. Longing for Kal was like longing for a pet tiger. It was beautiful and, if handled properly, could be a loving companion. But it was always wild. No matter what, you could never domesticate it. As much as she liked to live dangerously from time to time, she knew Kal was a beast well out of her league.

Clad in a pair of jeans and a tank top, she returned to the living room and picked up her phone where she'd left it during the performance. She noticed a message on her screen showing a missed call and a voice mail message from the Maui Police Department. Her stomach sank. Not again.

With her evermore violent father and her older sister, Mele, always getting into trouble, a call from the police station was not as rare as she'd like it to be.

Her mother had died when Lana was still a toddler. Their father, at least so she was told, had been a good man before that, but lost it when she died. He struggled after that, both in caring for his two young daughters and in coping with the loss. He turned to the bottle, a habit that released his temper. He'd never hit Lana or Mele, but he would shout the house down. He was also prone to getting in fights at the bar and getting arrested.

Lana had done everything right in an attempt to keep her father happy. That was how she got into dancing. Despite everything, her father was a proud Hawaiian man who believed they should honor their culture. Lana started taking hula as a child and continued into high school. Her father had never looked at her with as much pride as he did when he watched her dance.

Mele hadn't been as concerned. In her mind, she was going to be in trouble no matter what, so she might as well have some fun. That included dating every boy she could find except for the native Hawaiian ones whom their father would've approved of. When she finally did start dating a Hawaiian, he was nothing to get excited about. Tua Keawe was a criminal in the making. Mele met him while he was hustling tourists, and he only escalated his illegal activities from there. Lana stopped visiting her sister when she was home from college because Mele was always high or drunk.

Last year, Mele had found out she was pregnant and she really seemed to clean up her act. Lana's niece, Akela, was born free of addiction or side effects from fetal alcohol syndrome. She was a perfect, beautiful bundle that Lana adored more than anything. She'd always wanted a daughter of her own. Sometimes she wished the little girl was hers and not Mele's, if just for Akela's sake. Mele's model behavior hadn't lasted long past her delivery. She slipped back into her old habits, but there wasn't much Lana could do about it without risking Child Services taking the baby away.

One thing Lana had never confided in Kal about was her sister and her criminal lifestyle. He knew about her father, and that her sister was prone to get in trouble, but she tried to keep Mele's arrests under wraps. It was embarrassing, for one thing, to tell him. She knew he would understand and not judge her for their actions, but he was part of such an important and well-respected family. She was…not. Lana tried to pretend that she wasn't from poor trash most of the time, but her family always saw fit to remind her.

Lana also avoided the topic because she was always hoping that Mele would grow up and start acting like the older, responsible sister she was supposed to be. So far her hopes for a big sister she could rely on instead of keep an eye on hadn't materialized. Instead she leaned on Kal to be her responsible older sibling. She could go to him for advice and he would help her in any way he could.

Glancing at the screen, Lana worried that this time would be the one that her family had gotten into a mess that even Kal couldn't help her clean up. It was coming sooner or later. She finally worked up the nerve to hit the button on her phone and listen to the message.

"Lana, this is Mele. Tua and I got arrested. I need you to come get us out of here. This whole thing is just a load of crap. It was entrapment!" she shouted. "Entrapment!" she repeated, most likely to the officer nearby.

The line went dead and Lana sighed. It sounded like she was going to spend another night waiting to pay her sister's bail. Before she drove over there in the middle of the night, however, she was going to call the station. It had been a couple hours since her sister's message and she wanted to make sure she was still there.

She pressed the key to call back the police station. The switchboard operator answered.

"Yes, this is Lana Hale. I received a call from my sister, Mele Hale, about bail."

There was a moment of silence as the woman looked something up in the computer. "Yes, ma'am, please hold while I transfer you to the officer at the holding desk."

"This is Officer Wood," a man answered after a few moments.

"This is Lana Hale," she repeated. "I got a call from my sister about coming to bail her out. I wanted to check before I came down there so late."

The officer made a thoughtful noise before he answered. "Yes, your sister and her boyfriend were arrested today for possession of narcotics with intent to distribute. Apparently they attempted to sell heroin to an undercover police officer."

Lana bit back a groan. This was worse than she thought. She hadn't realized her sister had moved up from pot and LSD to a higher class of drug felony. "How much is her bail?" she asked.

"Actually your sister was misinformed when she called. There's no bail set for either of them. They're being held until tomorrow. Miss Hale will be meeting with a court-appointed attorney Monday morning prior to going before the judge."

That wasn't good. It sounded like their constant run-ins with the police were catching up with them. "Which judge?"

"I believe they're scheduled to see Judge Kona."

This time, the groan escaped Lana's lips before she could stop it. Judge Kona was known for being a hard nut. He was superconservative, supertraditional and he didn't tolerate any kind of crap in his courtroom. It wouldn't be Mele's first time before Judge Kona, and that wasn't good news. He didn't take kindly to repeat offenders.

A sudden thought popped into Lana's mind, making her heart stop in her throat. "What about their daughter?" Her niece, Akela, was only six months old. Hopefully they hadn't left her sleeping in her crib while they ran out to make a few bucks. It certainly wouldn't surprise Lana if they had.

"The baby was in the car, asleep in her car seat,

when the drug deal went down. She's been taken by Child Protective Services."

Panic made Lana's chest tight even though she knew her niece was technically safe. "No!" she insisted. "What can I do? I'll take her. She doesn't need to go to be with strangers."

"I understand how you feel," Officer Wood said, "but I'm afraid you'll have to wait and petition the judge for temporary guardianship while the legal guardians are incarcerated. In the meantime, the child will be placed in foster care. I assure you the baby will be well looked after. Perhaps more so than she was with her own parents."

Lana's knees gave out from under her and she sank down onto the couch. The rest of the call went quickly and before she knew it, the officer had hung up and she was staring blankly at her black phone screen.

She turned it back on to look at the time. It was late on a Sunday night. She'd have to wait to contact an attorney. Akela would be in foster care overnight no matter what, but if Lana had anything to say about it, she'd be with her by Monday afternoon.

It was a scary thought to leap unexpectedly into motherhood—she was completely unprepared—and yet she would do it gladly. Mele could be going to jail for months or years. Lana wouldn't be watching Akela overnight or for a weekend this time. She would be her guardian for however long it took for Mele to serve her debt to society.

She would need help to pull this off. Lana didn't want to do it, but she knew she had to tell Kal about what happened. Maybe he knew an attorney who would be better for Mele than the public defender or at the very least help her get guardianship of Akela.

Getting up from the couch, she slipped her phone into her back pocket and headed out to the bar to meet Kal. If anyone could help her out of this mess, it was him.

Two

Kal sat back in the chair at his lawyer's office the next day trying to keep quiet. They weren't here about him. They were here for Lana and Akela. Still, it was difficult to keep his mouth shut about the whole thing.

Lana had met him at the bar late last night, her eyes wild with panic. He'd never seen her like that. He'd forced a shot down her throat, sat her in a chair and made her tell him everything. Until that moment, he hadn't realized exactly how much Lana had kept from him about her family. He knew her father was a mess, but it seemed her sister was even worse. The thought of Lana's little niece being with strangers had made his blood boil. He'd only met her once, when Lana had her for an afternoon, but she was adorable, with chubby cheeks, long eyelashes and a toothless grin. Lana had been a fool for that baby, and now the baby was in trouble.

He'd called his attorney right then. When you had a six-figure retainer with Dexter Lyon, you got his personal number and permission to call him whenever you needed him. While Kal had never personally had a reason to summon his attorney from bed in the middle of the night, Lana did, and that was what mattered. He agreed to see them first thing Monday morning.

"It doesn't look good to be honest," Dexter said.

"What do you mean?" Lana said. Her face was flushed red and had been since the night before. She seemed to be on the verge of tears every second.

"I mean Judge Kona is a hard-ass. Yes, it absolutely makes sense for you to get custody of your niece. But let me tell you why he'd turn your petition down." Dexter looked at his notepad. "You're a dancer. You live out of a hotel room. You keep crazy hours. You're single. While none of those make you legally unfit to have children, adding them all together makes you a hard sell to the judge."

Lana frowned. "Well, for one thing, I'm a choreographer. I do stay in the hotel for convenience, but I can get an apartment if that's what it takes. I am single, but I can afford day care while I'm at work."

"And at night?" Dexter's brow went up curiously. "I'm just playing devil's advocate here. Judge Kona will ask these questions, so it's best you be prepared for them."

"I just don't understand how Lana can be considered unfit when the baby's actual parents are drug dealers. Even if she was an exotic dancer that lived in a van down by the river, she'd be more fit than Mele and Tua." Kal was getting mad. He wasn't used to being told no, especially when he called Dexter. Dexter was supposed to fix things. His reluctance to handle this made Kal more irritated by the second.

The attorney held up his hands in surrender. "I get it. I do. And I've gone ahead and filed for temporary guardianship. We're on the judge's docket for Wednesday."

"Wednesday!" Lana looked heartbroken. Kal imagined that if his niece was with strangers, he wouldn't want an hour to go by, much less a few days.

"There is no such thing as 'hurry' in the court system. We're lucky we got in Wednesday. Look at this time as the opportunity it is."

"Opportunity?" Lana repeated, skeptically.

"Yes. You've got two days to make yourself more fit. Find a place to live. Arrange for a nanny. Buy a crib. If you've got a serious boyfriend, marry him. All of that will help the cause."

Marry him? "Now, wait just a second," Kal said. He couldn't be quiet about this any longer. "You're recommending she just run out and marry someone so she can get custody?"

"Not just anyone. But if she's with someone serious, it's a great time to make the leap."

Lana sat back in her chair and dropped her head into her hands. "Just the way I'd always pictured it."

Kal didn't like seeing her like this. She looked totally defeated. He wasn't about to let her feel that way. "That's a nice idea, Dexter, but not everyone is in a relationship that can go to the next level on a day's notice."

Dexter shrugged. "Well, I figured it was a long shot, but it certainly wouldn't hurt. Focus your energies on an apartment and a caregiver, then. A nice place too. A studio isn't any better than a suite at a hotel." He stood and walked around his desk to lean against it. "I know that it seems like a lot of changes just for a temporary guardianship, but your sister and her boyfriend are in a lot of trouble. It might not be as temporary as you expect it to be.

"Life will get really complicated in a cramped apartment with a small baby after the first few weeks. My house is three thousand square feet, and when we brought our son home from the hospital, it felt like a tiny cardboard box. Baby crap everywhere. Everything is complicated by a factor of ten at least. It takes twenty minutes just to load up the car to run to the grocery store."

Lana groaned aloud. "Are you trying to talk me out of doing this?"

Dexter's eyes widened. "No, of course not. Kids are great. We have four now. My point is that I need you to do whatever you can to make it an easier transition. I have every intention of winning the motion Wednesday. I just need your help to make it impossible for the judge to say no. Every little thing you do can help."

A soft knock came at the door.

"Yes?" Dexter asked loudly.

His assistant poked her head inside. "I'm sorry, Mr. Lyon, but Mr. Patterson is on line two and he's very upset. He refuses to speak to anyone but you."

Dexter looked at Lana, then at Kal. "Do you mind if I take this call in the other room? It should only take a minute."

Kal nodded and Dexter slipped out the door with his assistant. He couldn't shake the irritation that furrowed his brow. He didn't like any of this and he certainly didn't like this judge. Who was he to impose his value system on others? Lana shouldn't have to rearrange her whole life for this. There was nothing wrong with the way she lived. She wasn't a drug dealer or a heroin addict, so she was a step above her sister as a fit guardian, easily.

He wanted to say something, but Lana's pensive expression gave him pause. He didn't want to interrupt her. She got the same look on her face when she was working out a dance routine. The whole thing would play out in her mind like a film as she thought it through. If you spoke to her, she'd have to start over from the beginning.

Finally her brown eyes came into focus and she turned to look at him. Her dark hair was pulled into a ponytail today that swung over her shoulder as she moved. While her long, thick hair was beautiful and he often fantasized about running his fingers through it, he knew it annoyed the hell out of her. She kept it long for the show, but if she wasn't performing, it was usually pulled back from her face. Thankfully that relieved the temptation. Most of the time.

"So I've got an idea," she said. "It's a little out there, so do me a favor and just go with it for a second."

He didn't know that he liked the sound of that. It usually meant trouble where she was concerned. "Okay."

She held out her hands to count her points on her fingers. "So, obviously my job isn't going to change and there's no reason that it should."

"Agreed."

"I can find a day care for the days I work with the dancers and a babysitter for the nights of the luau."

"That's true. I can also give you some time off, you know. I think you have about two hundred hours' worth of vacation you've never used."

Lana frowned at him. She seemed to be doing a lot of that lately, and he didn't like it. He wanted to reach out and rub away the crease between her eyebrows and kiss the pout of her lips until she smiled again. Or hit him. As long as she stopped looking so upset. Instead he kept his hands and mouth to himself.

"While that's a nice idea, it's Christmas. We're super busy. There's no way I'm taking off the whole month. Besides, if what your lawyer says is true and I have Akela longer than a month or two, I'm going to need my leave for when she's sick or has doctor's appointments. No one I know with kids under the age of three has any personal leave accrued, especially if the child goes to day care. They catch all the bugs there."

Kal hadn't really thought about that. If this did turn into a long-term arrangement, Akela would take up a huge portion of her time. He felt a pang of jealousy at the idea that he might be losing his best friend for a while. He totally understood, but he wondered what he would do while she was consumed by caring for her niece. "Okay. I just wanted to let it be known that your boss says it's all right if you have to do it."

Lana nodded. "Thanks. He's usually a jerk, so I'm glad he can be reasonable about this." She grinned for the first time since she'd gotten the call from her sister, and he felt a sense of relief wash over him at last. That smile gave him a little hope, even if it was at his expense.

"A bigger apartment in Maui…now, that's a hard one. I can't afford anything like that on the west side of the island. And if I move any farther east, the commute will be awful."

Real estate in Maui really was ridiculous. He tried not to think about how much he'd paid for the land his hotel sat on. There were so many zeroes in that check that he had a hard time signing it and he *had* the money. He couldn't imagine trying to live here on an average income. Lana made good money, but she didn't make beachfront condo money.

He'd forgotten her old apartment was so small. She'd noted how big the hotel suite was when she moved in, so he should've considered that. It felt tiny to him now that he was living in such a huge house. *Huge house…* that was a thought.

"What about moving in with me?" He spat the words out before really thinking them through.

Lana looked at him, narrowing her almond-shaped eyes. "That would help a lot, actually. Are you sure, though? It's going to be a major cramp on your bachelorhood to have me and a baby in the house."

Kal shrugged that off. He rarely had time for anything aside from work this time of year. Plus, if Lana was in the house with the baby, he wouldn't miss out on his time with her. He'd never admit to his selfish motivations, however. "I've got three extra bedrooms just sitting empty. If it will help, I'm happy to do what I can."

Lana beamed at him. "I'm actually really glad you said that, because I was just about to get to the crazy part of my plan."

Kal swallowed hard. She had something in mind that was crazier than moving in together with a baby?

Just then Lana slid off of her chair and onto one

knee in front of him. She took his hand and held it as he frowned down at her. "What are you doing?" he asked as his chest grew tight and he struggled to breathe. His hand was suddenly burning up where she held him in hers, the contact lighting his every nerve on fire. He wanted to pull away and regain control of himself, but he knew he couldn't. This was just the calm before the storm.

Lana took a deep breath and looked up at him with a hopeful smile. "I'm asking you to marry me."

Lana looked up at Kal and anxiously waited for his answer. The idea had just come to her and she acted on it before she lost her nerve. It was crazy, she knew that, but she was willing to do whatever it took to get guardianship of Akela. So now here she was, on one knee, proposing marriage to her best friend, who had no interest in ever marrying.

Judging by the panic-stricken expression on Kal's face, this wasn't what he was expecting and he didn't want to say yes. She clutched his hand tighter in hers, noting that his touch strengthened her even when he'd much rather pull away. He was her support, her ideal, her everything. This could work. It had to.

"I'm sorry I don't have a diamond ring for you," she started rambling in the hopes of breaking the tension in the room. "I wasn't planning on getting engaged today."

Kal didn't laugh. His eyes just grew wider as he subtly shook his head in disbelief. "Are you serious?" he asked.

"Dead serious. You just said you were happy to do whatever you could to help me get Akela. If we're married and living together in your big house when we go into court on Wednesday, there's no way the judge will turn down the request."

Kal leaned forward and squeezed her hands. "You know I would do anything for you. But married? I never... I mean...that's kind of a big deal."

The fact that Kal hadn't flat-out said no to this whole thing made her love him even more. "It doesn't have to be a big deal," she argued. "Listen, I know how you feel about marriage, and I get it. I'm not asking you to stay with me forever or fall madly in love with me. We're not going to sleep together or anything. That would be crazy talk. I just want this marriage to be for show. We spend so much time together that no one would find it suspect that we've quietly fallen in love and eloped. It's the perfect cover. We get married, stay married as long as we need to to make the judge and Child Services happy. Then we annul it or divorce or whatever when it's all done. At most, you'll have to kiss me a couple times in public. That shouldn't be too horrible, right?"

A flicker of what looked like disappointment crossed Kal's face for a moment. Lana wasn't sure what that was about. It wasn't possible that he might relish the idea of them being man and wife. The thought alone sent a thrill through Lana that she refused to acknowledge, but it was all obligation on his part, she was certain.

After a moment, he took a deep breath and then he nodded. "So we get married, move you into my place and play the happy couple for the general public until Akela can safely return to her parents. That's it?"

Lana nodded. "That's it, I promise. If you so much

as try anything more than that, I'll be sure to give you a good slap to remind you who you're dealing with."

That, finally, brought a smile to Kal's face. She breathed a sigh of relief, knowing that he was going to go along with her harebrained plan even though it involved a major life milestone that he never expected to achieve with the kind of woman he'd never lower himself to love.

"So, Kalani Bishop, would you do me the honor of being my fake husband?" she asked again, since he hadn't truly responded the first time.

He pressed his lips together for a moment, and then he finally nodded. "I guess so."

"Yay!" Lana leaped into his arms and hugged him close. She buried her nose in his neck, drawing in the scent of his cologne. The familiar musk of her best friend drew a decidedly physical response from deep inside her that she wasn't expecting with everything else that was going on. Her heart started racing in her chest as she held his spicy male scent in her lungs and enjoyed his arms wrapped tightly around her. No one held her like he did, and there was no one she wanted to hold her more than Kal.

Then she felt him stiffen awkwardly against her. She pulled herself out of the romantic fog she'd let herself accidentally slip into. This wasn't the reaction of someone who was comfortable with his decision. She drew back and looked at the lines on his face that reflected conflict and shame instead of excitement and confidence. Lana needed to remember that this was all for show. It might be her innermost secret fantasy coming to life, but he was only doing this for her because it was important and they were friends, not for any other reason. She needed to save her physical reactions to him for public consumption or she'd scare him off.

"Are you really okay with this?" she asked.

"No," he said, ever honest, "but I'm going to do it anyway. For you."

His words nearly brought tears to her eyes. She leaned in to hug him again and spoke softly into his ear. "Thank you for being the best friend a girl could ever have. I owe you big-time."

Kal chuckled, a low rumble that vibrated against her chest and made her want to snuggle closer to him. "Oh, you have no idea."

The door of the room opened again and Lana pulled away from Kal to turn to Dexter. "We're getting married," she announced before he could change his mind.

Dexter looked at Lana, then curiously at Kal and his pained expression. "Excellent. Shall I draw up a prenup? I presume that assets won't comingle, and everyone keeps what they have going into the union?"

"Sure," Lana said. Part of her thought that Kal might balk at the idea of a prenuptial agreement, but she wanted him to have that protection. She didn't want any of his stuff and she wanted to make sure he knew it. "I don't want him getting his hands on my old-school hi-fi system."

Kal turned to look at her. "Your what?"

"It has a turntable. Records are cool again."

He just shook his head. "Draw something up and we'll come back to sign it in the morning. We'll get married tomorrow afternoon assuming the wedding pavilion at the hotel isn't booked. That should be good enough for the judge, right?"

"The two of you married and living in that big new

house…oh yeah." Dexter nodded enthusiastically. "Then you'll just have to put on a good show for Child Services when they come for home visits. If you can pull this off, it will make my job ten times easier."

"Okay," Kal said, pushing up from his seat. "We'll see you in the morning, then." He reached out for Lana's hand, something he'd never done before. "Come on, *honey*. We've got a lot of plans to make if we're going to get married tomorrow afternoon."

Lana twisted her lips in amusement. The stiff way he said the words was proof enough that he was really uncomfortable with the situation but was too good of a friend to say no. She didn't say anything, though. Instead she took his hand and they walked out of the attorney's office together.

They were silent until they got back to the car. Kal had parked his F-type Jaguar convertible in the shade on the far side of the parking lot. Lana had always loved Kal's car. It was the kind of vehicle that motorheads fantasized about. Lana drove an old Jeep without doors, so this felt superluxurious. As she climbed in beside him and looked around this time, however, she realized they had an issue.

"Kal?"

"Yeah?" he asked as he started the engine and it roared to life.

"You drive a two-seater convertible and I drive a Jeep Wrangler without doors or a roof."

Kal pulled the car out of the parking lot and onto the main highway. "And?"

"And… I don't think we can put a car seat in either of those."

"Hmm," he said thoughtfully as they went down the

highway. "You're probably right. It's never something that's mattered before. I'll have someone bring a car over. I'll lease one for as long as we have Akela. What do you think is responsible enough? A minivan? An SUV with all the airbags? Or would you rather have a sedan of some kind?"

She hadn't really thought that far ahead, as evidenced by this predicament. "Not a minivan. That's all I ask. Other than that, as long as it has a backseat I can put a car seat in and will protect her from the elements, I think I'm good. Thank you."

"No problem." Kal looked past her toward the shopping center they were coming up on. "Since we're discussing the ways we're completely unprepared for marriage and parenthood, I think we need to make a pit stop."

Lana held on as he whipped the car into the parking lot and came to a stop outside a baby supercenter. She'd only set foot in it once, to buy a baby shower gift for Mele. "I don't know what we need yet. I've got to go by Mele's apartment and see what she has."

Kal shook his head and turned off the car. "No, you don't. We're getting all new stuff. Come on."

Lana leaped out of the car and jogged to catch up with him. "Are you serious? I can't afford to buy all new baby things."

Kal pulled his dark sunglasses down his nose to look at her with an expression that could've melted a woman's panties right off. Lana had learned early on that when he looked at *her* that way, it wasn't smoldering, it was irritation.

"You're not buying it. I am."

She suspected he might say that. "This is too much,

Kal," she complained. He simply ignored her, going into the store ahead of her. "Kal!" she finally shouted with her hands planted on her hips.

He stopped and turned around to look at her. "What is the problem?"

She narrowed her gaze at him. Women she'd had as friends over the years had asked her how she could be friends with a man as hot at Kal and not want more. While she convinced herself she didn't want more, she used this as exhibit number one: he was stubborn as an ox. "It's too much."

"We're already getting married and moving in together to pull this off. What is too much, exactly?"

She knew he was right. "I don't want you to buy a ton of things. We might only have her for a few weeks."

"Or we might have her for years. Either way, she needs a place to sleep, food, clothes, diapers... If it makes you happy, I'll donate everything to charity when we're done. It won't go to waste, okay?"

Lana bit at her bottom lip but knew she'd lost this battle before it started. Kal wasn't about to decorate the baby's nursery with the thrift store finds they collected from Mele's apartment. "Fine."

Inside the store, Kal waved his finger at the manager standing behind the customer service desk. "We're going to need some assistance."

The woman came forward, polite, but curious about his forwardness. "What can I help you with, sir?"

"With everything. We're buying it all, so I need someone to jot down what we choose as we go through the store and have it delivered to my home."

The manager seemed flustered but grabbed a clipboard and the registry scanner and went straight to leading him up and down the aisles. Lana tried not to roll her eyes. Why Kal couldn't just get a cart and shop like a normal person, she didn't know.

She figured it out soon, however. There wasn't a cart big enough. He hadn't been exaggerating when he said he was going to buy everything. It took about two hours to go through the entire store. They bought a complete bedroom suite with a crib, changing table, dresser, lamp and rocking chair. They got bedding, a mobile, a car seat, a high chair, a stroller and a swing. Diaper bags, bottles, cases of baby food and diapers, medicine, shampoo…you name it. They even bought about twenty outfits and pajamas.

It was exhausting, but Lana had to admit Kal had good taste. Everything he selected was beautiful. The furniture for the nursery was a soft gray color that complemented the star and moon bedding set. It was enchanting for a baby's room. Hopefully Akela would love all her new things as much as Lana did. She was so young, she probably couldn't appreciate most of it, but the toys Kal purchased last would be a big hit with the baby at least.

As they finished selecting the last few things, Lana took a step back and counted her blessings. There was no way she could make any of this happen without Kal. He was an amazing friend and person. Not just for agreeing to marry her, but for all of it.

She really didn't understand why Kal was determined to stay single. He insisted he was too busy for that sort of thing, but she didn't believe it. He was the kind of man who could make any dream into reality. If he wanted a family, all he had to do was snap his fingers and women would line up to volunteer for the job. He was tall and muscular with a build they would clamor to run their hands over. His hair was dark and wavy, and his skin was golden brown. His smile could melt her defenses. Honestly, when he was wearing one of his expensive suits and marching around the hotel like a man on a mission, she had a hard time figuring out why she didn't just throw herself at him.

She joked about what a pain he could be, how stubborn he was, what a playboy he was to go through women the way he did. The truth was far different. She loved Kal. He was the best thing in her life, where she didn't have much outside of her job and her friendship with him to rave about. If she really let herself think about it, she probably would want him. It was just a ridiculous thought, so she never let herself have it.

Kal was simply too good for her. He was educated, rich, cultured and from an important family. Yes, they could be friends and even fake husband and wife, but a real relationship with a woman like her? Even if he was open to marriage, he wouldn't choose her. She was really surprised he agreed to fake marry her considering her sister was in jail and her family was such a mess. Their friendship made it possible and she would cling to that for dear life. It was better than any romantic relationship, anyway.

It sure made dating hard, though. Where would she find a man to measure up to Kal? It was impossible, and she'd certainly tried. Over the last few years, she'd gone through a steady stream of losers. None even came close to Kal. Not only was he handsome and ridiculously rich, but he was funny, kind, thoughtful… She couldn't have chosen a better best friend. And come tomorrow, a better husband, even if just for show.

All she'd expected him to do was sign on the dotted line, hold her hand in court and act like a loving husband in public. Instead he was paying a small fortune, fully committing to making this work. All to make Lana happy.

Lana didn't know why Kal was single, but it was easy to see why she couldn't commit to someone else.

Three

Kal straightened the bow tie of his white tuxedo and looked himself over in the mirror. He certainly looked like a groom. He was as nervous as he imagined a groom would be. But that spark of excitement was missing. It just all felt awkward. Backward. Definitely not how he'd intended to spend his Tuesday.

Marriage hadn't always been an alien concept to Kal. When he was younger it was something he knew he would do someday, but reality intruded. When he was twenty, a car accident claimed the lives of his parents and left his brother blind. Kal realized then that no one was invincible, including him. He'd grown up so sheltered and privileged that he almost thought nothing bad could ever happen to him. Then, in an instant, he'd lost the most important people in his life. No warnings, no goodbyes, just gone forever.

Suddenly he had more responsibilities piled on him than most kids his age. His grandparents helped with the hotel while Kal finished college and Mano adjusted to his disability, but Kal eventually stepped up to lead the family when he graduated. That was enough family and responsibility for him. Marriage was not in the cards for Kal. He wasn't sure he could go through something like that again—getting attached to someone else just to lose her...or to leave a family behind to pick up the pieces after his death. It seemed like too much risk for the potential reward.

So why, then, was he pinning an orchid to his lapel and heading out the door to the Mau Loa's wedding pavilion? Well, because he just couldn't say no to Lana.

When she'd looked up at him, her dark brown eyes pleading with him to say yes...there was no question that he would do whatever she asked of him. He just wanted to make sure she was serious and set boundaries for this "marriage."

It wasn't that Lana wasn't beautiful. She was exactly his type. Therein lay the problem. The day they met, Kal knew she could very easily be the one to make him throw caution to the wind and fall in love. Since they had such different priorities for their futures, he knew better than to let that happen. Instead he'd placed her in the friend bucket. It was the smartest thing to do considering how important their friendship was to him and that she was technically his employee.

Knowing that Lana just wanted a wedding for show had been both a relief and a challenge for him. A part of him had always wondered if they would be as great together as a couple as they were as friends. He suspected so. Being this close, having to touch her and kiss her to keep up their public facade, and yet to still have to maintain that friendly distance when they were alone would be difficult. It was like letting himself have a single bite of his favorite dessert—just enough to whet his appetite, but not enough to satisfy him. It was easier to just avoid the dish entirely, especially when the dish was as sensual and tasty as Lana.

Giving himself one last glance in the mirror, Kal stepped out of his house and drove his Jaguar to the hotel. His home was on the far corner of the property, with a sprawling golf course separating it from the rest of the resort. Most days he would walk or take the golf cart, but it seemed wrong to have his new bride hop on a golf cart after their ceremony.

The wedding pavilion was right on the beach. The bright white gazebo had room for a wedding party of ten and seating for up to a hundred guests on the lawn in front of it. It was raised up, overlooking the ocean and surrounded by lush plants to give some privacy from the tourists sunbathing nearby.

Kal had built it because he thought it was good business. They didn't have room for one at the Waikiki location, so he'd been certain to reserve a place for it to be built here. Hawaii was a huge destination wedding locale and they needed to get in on the action. Not once had he ever thought he would use it for himself.

The traditional Hawaiian officiant, the kahuna *pule*, was already there, waiting under the pavilion to start the wedding. The short, round, older man with snow-white hair wore the traditional crown of *haku lei*. A small table in front of him was already set up with everything that was needed for the ceremony— the conch shell, the white orchid and green *maile* leis, and a wooden *Koa* bowl filled with ocean water and *ti* leaves to bless the rings.

Kal felt his breast pocket in a moment of panic and realized that he did remember the rings. Earlier that morning, they'd gotten their marriage license and taken care of all the legal details at Dexter's office. They'd then stopped at a jewelry store to select two simple but attractive wedding bands. Lana had insisted that he'd already spent too much already and flat-out refused a diamond. It felt odd not to buy one, although buying a wedding ring at all was odd enough.

All that was left was for the kahuna *pule* to perform the ceremony and sign the paperwork, and he and Lana were married. The thought sent a momentary surge of panic though him. He'd tried to suppress it the last few days, focusing on details and plans, but things were suddenly getting very real. Every step he took toward the pavilion made it even more so.

His family was going to kill him when they found out about this, especially Mano. His tūtū Ani would likely chew his ear off over the phone. He wished he could just keep it a secret, but since they had to play this relationship as real, he had to tell them. Dexter had warned that Child Services would not only come by the house but could conduct interviews with family and friends. That meant everyone needed to believe that they were husband and wife in every sense of the word. That seemed cruel to do to his family, as they waited anxiously for him to find a wife. Considering he would be divorcing in a short time and this was all a sham, he hated to get their hopes up for nothing. Hopefully he could get away with just telling Mano for now and wait to tell the rest of the family, if necessary, after the New Year.

"Aloha, Mr. Bishop," the Hawaiian holy man greeted him as he stepped up into the pavilion.

"Aloha and *mahalo*. I want to thank you for coming on such short notice."

The older man shook his head. "I always have time in my day to bring together a couple in love. Your hotel is one of my favorite places to perform ceremonies."

Kal felt a pang of guilt, but he knew he'd better get over it. This man was just the first of many they were lying to to get guardianship of Akela. "I appreciate that. I tried to build something our guests would be willing to travel to Maui to have."

"Do you have the rings?"

Kal reached into his breast pocket and pulled out the two wedding bands. "I do. Here they are."

"Very good. I will be ready to start whenever your bride arrives."

Kal looked down at his watch. They'd agreed on four in the afternoon. It was a minute till. He took a deep breath and tried not to be concerned about Lana's punctuality. Kal wasn't in a rush to marry anyway, but he did want this part to be over with quickly.

"Ah, there she is."

Kal turned to look in the direction the kahuna *pule* indicated and felt his heart go stone silent in his chest. It was like he'd hit a brick wall at full speed when he saw her. His whole body tightened when he took in his bride, and his tuxedo chafed at his collar and other unmentionable places as though it had suddenly shrunk two sizes.

Lana looked...amazing.

Traditionally Hawaiian brides wore a flowing white dress that was cut in the style of a muumuu. He was extremely thankful at that moment that Lana had opted for something more modern and formfitting on the top. The white lace gown had a deep V neckline that accentuated her shapely décolletage and plunged all the way to the waist. There, the dress flowed down in soft layers of organza that moved in the breeze. Her hair was loose around her shoulders and she was wearing a traditional ring of haku flowers on her head.

Everything about her was soft, romantic and made him long for a wedding night he wasn't going to have. It was possible that Lana was the most beautiful bride in the history of brides. He couldn't take his eyes off her. Everything around them faded away as though she were all there was in the whole world. In fact, when the kahuna *pule* blew into the conch shell to announce the arrival of the bride and summon the elements to bear witness to the ceremony, Kal nearly leaped off the ground in surprise.

Lana grinned wide with rosy-pink lips as she walked up the path to him. He reached out to take her hand and help her up the stairs. Despite her joyful demeanor, her hands were ice-cold. He was relieved to know he wasn't the only nervous one.

"Are we ready to begin?" the holy man asked.

"Yes."

"Very well." The kahuna *pule* opened up his prayer booklet to the marked page. "The Hawaiian word for love is aloha. Today we've come together to celebrate the special aloha that exists between you, Kalani and Lanakila, and your desire to make your aloha eternal through the commitment of marriage. As you know, the giving of a lei is an expression of aloha. Kal and Lana, you will exchange leis as a symbol of your aloha for each other. When two people promise to share the adventure of life together, it is a beautiful moment that they will always remember.

"Kal, please place the orchid lei around Lana's neck."

Kal reached for the white orchid lei on the table, and Lana tipped her head down for him to place it over her shoulders.

"The unbroken circle of the lei represents your eternal commitment and devotion to each other. The beauty of each individual flower is not lost when it becomes a part of the lei, but is enhanced because of the strength of its bond. Lana, would you place the maile leaf lei around Kal's neck."

Kal watched as she took the long strand of green leaves off the table. Her hands were trembling as she lifted it over his head. He caught her eye and winked to reassure her. They would get through this together because that was what best friends did.

"Kal and Lana, you are entering into marriage because you want to be together. You are marrying because you know you will grow more in happiness and aloha more fully as life mates. You will belong entirely to each other, one in mind, one in heart and in all things. Now please hold hands and look into each other's eyes."

Kal took her hands in his and held them tightly. He didn't know if it was the situation or how beautiful she looked today, but touching her was different than before. He felt an unexpected thrill as he took her hand, and it raced all the way through his nervous system like the burning fuse of a firecracker. He was suddenly very aware of the scent of the flowers in her hair, the subtle sparkle of her lipstick and the silky softness of her skin.

"Do you, Kalani, take Lanakila to be your wife? To have and to hold, from this day forward? For better or for worse, for richer or for poorer, in sickness and in health? To cherish with devoted love and faithfulness till death do you part?"

Kal swallowed hard and found his mouth so dry he could barely part his tongue from the roof of his mouth. He wasn't used to being nervous, but this had certainly done the trick. "I do," he managed at last.

That was the easy part. Now he just had to try to live up to the impossible vow he'd just taken.

The holy man repeated the vows for Lana, but she was hardly listening. How could she hear what he said over the loud pounding of her heart?

She'd been okay until the ceremony started. She'd had butterflies in her stomach, but she'd held it together as long as she focused on each little task—finding a dress, doing her hair, applying her makeup. In the mirror of her suite, she kept repeating to herself that this wasn't about love, this was about Akela. The ceremony itself was the only real part of this entire marriage. Perhaps that was the problem. As she stood here looking into Kal's dark brown eyes and let his warm hands steady her shaky ones, it felt real. Too real.

Lana let a ragged breath escape her lungs, then realized both men were looking expectantly at her. "I do," she said quickly, and hoped that was the correct response.

It was. The kahuna *pule* continued with the ceremony by blessing the wedding rings. He placed the ti leaf in the koa bowl that was filled with seawater. He then sprinkled the water three times over the ring and repeated the blessing before handing the smaller of the two rings to Kal.

Kal repeated the required words, all the while looking into Lana's eyes as though there were no other person on the whole planet. There was a twinkle of mischief there in his dark gaze that she recognized and appreciated. He was trying to calm her nerves by acting as though he wasn't nervous. She knew better. His right eyelid kept twitching. It hadn't done that since opening day of the resort.

"Lana, please place the ring on Kal's finger and repeat after me."

Lana slipped the platinum band onto Kal's finger and pledged to be with him until death. She squeezed her eyes shut for a moment and tried not to let the doubts creep in as the words left her lips. She only had seconds to change her mind and then she would legally be Mrs. Kalani Bishop.

It's not real, she repeated silently to herself as the kahuna *pule* continued to speak. She was not Kal's blushing bride, he wasn't in love with her and there would be no wedding night fantasy come to life tonight. Lana needed to shut down her brain and her libido before it was met with a great deal of disappointment.

"Lana and Kal," the kahuna *pule* continued, "you have pledged your eternal aloha to each other and your commitment to live together faithfully in lawful wedlock. By the authority vested in me by the laws of the state of Hawaii, I pronounce you husband and wife. Kal, you may kiss your bride."

And just like that, it was done.

With that worry aside, Lana suddenly had a new one. Kal was moving closer and the charade was about to get physical for the first time. Repeating vows was one thing, but the line between friend and lover was on the verge of being irrevocably blurred.

Kal's hand rested against her cheek and drew her lips closer to his. Lana's breath caught in her throat as the panic threatened to seize her. She vacillated between wanting this kiss more than she should, dreading it, and hoping they managed to convince the holy man it was authentic. With no other choice but to go through with this, she closed her eyes and tried to relax.

Half a heartbeat later, she felt Kal's lips against her own. They were soft and gentle as they pressed insistently to hers. Lana couldn't suppress the shiver that ran through her body or the prickle of energy that shot down her spine. She hadn't intended to, but she was having a genuine physical reaction to his kiss.

Before she could stop herself, she climbed to her toes to get closer to him. Her palms pressed against the massive wall of his chest. The scent of his cologne mingled with the tropical flowers and the warmth of his skin, and they all combined to draw her in.

Lana had never quite understood why women threw themselves at Kal when they couldn't keep him. Well, she understood he was handsome, charming and rich, but she watched as time after time they fell under his spell and lost all their good sense. She'd always thought that those women were silly. Yes, her best friend was a great catch, but he was also a blanket hog and he always ate the last piece of sushi. There was no reason to make a fool of themselves over him. Especially when he had no intention of taking their relationship much past the bedroom.

The bedroom.

Lana felt a pang of need deep inside her at the thought. No matter how often she reminded herself about how fake this all was, her body clearly ignored her. It had decided that she was married, so she would be getting a little action tonight from the tall, dark piece of man kissing her. Not so.

With her hands still pressed on his chest, she pushed back and ended the kiss. Certainly that was enough to satisfy the holy man and make this official. There was no need to go overboard, right?

When she looked up at Kal, he seemed affected by their kiss, as well. His dark eyes were glassy and dilated. His skin seemed a little more flushed than usual. Good. It wasn't just her. She'd feel like an idiot if she got all worked up over that simple kiss and he treated it like just another day at the races.

She expelled the air and his scent out of her lungs slowly and looked back toward the kahuna *pule* before she tried to kiss Kal again. This had all happened so fast she hadn't truly allowed herself to prepare, mentally, for the change in their friendship.

"*Ho'omaika'i 'ana,*" the kahuna *pule* said with a wide smile across his face. "Congratulations to you both."

"*Mahalo,*" Kal said, thanking him.

The next few minutes were a blur. They all signed the marriage license, making it truly official. Then the kahuna *pule* gathered up his things and was gone, leaving them alone in the pavilion. Man and wife.

Lana looked out at the ocean for a minute, waiting for the surreal feeling to pass. It wasn't going to. No matter how many times she pinched herself, she would still be married.

"That went well, I think."

Lana turned to look at Kal. He was standing with his hands shoved casually into his pockets, as though they hadn't just gotten married a moment before. He had the same smirk on his face as always.

"I suppose. We're married, so that was the most important part."

He sauntered over to where she was standing and eyed her with a curiously raised brow. "That kiss was pretty convincing."

More convincing than she'd anticipated. She didn't want to admit that to him, though. The potential for things to be awkward between them was high enough without that. "We're pretty good actors, aren't we?"

The smirk disappeared. Was he disappointed because he thought that he could nearly melt her knees out from under her? Lana could tell her best friend many things, but that wasn't one of them. She'd promised him this would just be for show and short term at that. If he knew he could turn her on without even trying, she'd never live that down. He still liked to remind her of the time she'd had too much to drink and groped his rear end.

"So, now what?" she asked.

Kal shrugged. "Well, I think normal people would go have some wild sex to make things official."

Lana's entire body clenched at the mere thought of it. What was wrong with her? This was never a problem before, but one little ceremony that wasn't supposed to mean anything had flipped some sort of switch inside her libido where Kal was concerned.

"Since that's off the table," he continued, "I say we change and go out to a celebratory dinner. While we're gone, I'll have your things packed up and moved to my place."

"So soon?" she asked. "I can pack my own stuff."

"I'm sure you can, but why would you? That's what I pay people for. You need to be all moved in and ready to go for tomorrow. If the judge sends some kind of social services worker to the house to check on everything and make sure we have a proper home for Akela, I don't want the place to be a mess of moving boxes."

He was right. Lana knew he was right.

"Come on. I'll give you a ride back to the hotel and you can change and grab a few things. Then someone will pack up the rest."

"You don't want to go out to dinner in our wedding finery?" she teased. She held out her dress and swayed a little to make the flowing fabric swirl around her. Having twenty-four hours to find a dress had made things difficult, but when she saw this one in the window of the bridal shop, she knew it was the one for her. Thankfully the cut didn't require alterations and she was able to buy the sample. She loved it.

And judging by the way Kal looked at her when she was walking up the path to the pavilion, he liked it, too. He'd stared at her so intensely she could almost feel his gaze on her bare skin.

"We could," he said, eyeing the low cut of the dress's bodice and clearing his throat uncomfortably. "I, uh, just thought you would be more comfortable. And I wouldn't want you to spill something on it."

Lana smiled. Finally he seemed as awkward as she did. She wouldn't mind wearing the dress out or changing; she just wanted to see him squirm. "You're right. I'll change. It's pretty, but it isn't very comfortable."

Kal nodded and reached his hand out to her. "Shall we go, then, Mrs. Bishop?"

She froze in her tracks at the sound of her married name. She tried to recover, reaching out to him. Her eyes fell on the shiny wedding band on her ring finger and followed it as it rested on his outstretched palm. *Mrs. Bishop.*

"Are you having second thoughts, Lana?"

She looked up at him with wide eyes. "What?"

Kal pulled her close to him and looked down at her. His eyes were lined with concern as he searched her face. "You look…troubled. I went along with this because it was what you wanted, but if you've changed your mind, we can rip up the license and pretend it never happened."

Part of her wanted to say yes. She felt she was dangling off a cliff and he was the only one who could snatch her back from the precipice. But she knew she couldn't. She had to do this for Akela.

"No," she said as firmly as she could. "This was the right thing to do. A little scary, but the right thing. Thank you for doing this for me."

Kal smiled and pulled her into a comforting hug. "For you, Lana…anything."

Four

They drove up the coast to have a celebratory sushi dinner at their favorite place in Kapalua. When they told their server they were there celebrating their wedding, she ran to the bakery next door and got them a vanilla cupcake to share, since they didn't serve desserts.

Lana felt guilty about the whole thing. Kal insisted they needed to celebrate and share the news with as many people as possible, but it bothered her. She hadn't really thought about the part of the plan where they had to lie to everyone about their relationship. Lying to the judge and the county employees didn't seem as bad as lying to their favorite waitress, their family or their friends.

When they got back to the house, Lana was amazed to find her things there and mostly put away. In Kal's closet, a large section had been dedicated to her clothes and shoes, and in the bathroom the second sink and vanity were peppered with all her toiletries. A couple boxes of miscellaneous things, like a few books and picture frames, were in a box on the kitchen counter for her to place where she liked. She'd hoped to kill some time tonight getting settled in, but Kal's minions had taken care of everything already.

"Would you like to see the new nursery?" he asked as they wandered around the house that was now supposed to be her home.

Lana couldn't help the expression of surprise on her face. "What do you mean?"

"It's all done. The store delivered everything this morning, and I paid the interior decorator that did the house to come over and get it all ready to go." Kal took her hand and led her to the room that had until recently housed all his exercise equipment.

A plush moon hung on the door with the name "Akela" embroidered in golden thread. Kal had a wide, excited grin on his face as he opened the door, as if it were Christmas morning. His enthusiasm was contagious and Lana couldn't help smiling, too, as they went inside.

There, she stopped, frozen in place. It was...amazing. The last time she'd been in this room it was wall-to-wall weights and cardio equipment. A massive mirror had stretched along one whole side. It was all gone now. The walls were painted a soft gray to highlight the new wainscoting that wrapped around the room. The gray crib was against the back wall with the moon-and-stars bedding. The mobile that hung overhead had little plush stars in white and blue, and matching decals were sprinkled across the walls like constellations.

There was a coordinating dresser, an armoire and a comfy-looking rocking chair. A crystal chandelier had replaced the previous lighting. Apparently he'd bought far more than she thought while she wasn't paying attention. It was the classiest, most adorable nursery she'd ever seen, fitting in with the rest of the luxurious décor in Kal's house.

Kal stepped inside and opened up the closet. There was the assembled high chair, stroller, car seat and swing. "It's all ready for tomorrow. I'll have to get the car seat anchor installed in the rental tomorrow morning so hopefully we can take Akela home with us right away."

Looking around at everything, Lana felt the emotions start to overwhelm her. The last few days had been so stressful, but Kal had been there for her through everything. He'd gone over and above, by far, and not just by marrying her. Tears started to well in her eyes no matter how hard she fought them.

Kal turned to look at her and his face morphed into panic at her tears. Lana almost never cried. "What's wrong? You don't like it? I thought a gender-neutral set would be best, since I told you I'd donate it all once this was over."

Lana shook her head vehemently. "It's beautiful. I love it." She launched herself into his arms and clung to his chest. He held her tightly and made no moves to pull away. That was one of her favorite things about Kal. She wasn't very touchy-feely, but every now and then, she needed a good hug. He would hold her for as long as she wanted to be held. He never pulled away first.

This time, however, suddenly felt different. He held her the way he always had, but she could hear his heartbeat speed up in his chest. He seemed a little stiff, a little more tense than usual. Memories of their kiss flashed through her mind, drying her tears and making her own pulse quicken. Had their fake marriage managed to ruin their innocent hugs, as well? It didn't feel as innocent as it used to.

Finally Lana straightened up to look him in the eye. She intended to speak but instead found herself in his arms, their lips only inches from each other. They lingered like that, both of them unsure what to do. Lana could feel the current running between them. It urged her to kiss him. At the same time, her rational brain was screaming at her to step back before this sudden attraction ruined their friendship.

That was the thought that snapped her out of it. She took a cleansing breath and smiled. "Thank you for all this, Kal. It's more than I'd ever hoped for. This is all more than I expected. You're amazing."

Kal smiled, a smaller, almost shy smile that made the tiny flecks of gold in his otherwise dark brown eyes twinkle. His square jaw was still a little tense as though he was struggling to hold back all the feelings that had danced between them a moment ago. "You deserve all this and more."

She didn't, but she appreciated that he thought so. "Akela is going to love it," she said, shifting the conversation off herself. Lana pulled away and took a lap through the room, circling the gray-and-white chevron rug and heading back to the door. "You're just too efficient, Kal. I thought I would spend tonight assembling a crib or putting away my things and now I don't have anything to do."

His brow furrowed as he turned to her and followed her out of the nursery. "I didn't want you to have anything to do. I wanted to make this all as easy as possible. What's wrong with that?"

"Nothing," she sighed. She took a hard right to return to the living room and away from the master suite. Nothing aside from the fact that it was their wedding night, and although she knew nothing was supposed to happen between her and Kal, her nerves were getting the best of her nonetheless. Their lingering touches were becoming increasingly potent. "It's just something to occupy my mind."

"Hopefully tomorrow you'll have an infant to occupy you. Tonight you'll just have to cope with the boredom of being married to me."

He smiled wide and Lana felt her belly tighten in response. Their wedding was supposed to be a piece of paper to make the judge happy, but ever since their kiss this afternoon, things had felt different between them. Every touch, every glance her direction stirred a response in her body when it never had before. She wished it would stop. The situation was complicated enough without a sudden attraction to Kal.

Lana turned away and glanced down at her phone. It was just after nine. Too early to turn in but too late to start a movie or something. She really needed a little time away from Kal. That might help the situation. Of course, now they lived together, so there was only so far she could go.

Then she remembered the giant jetted tub he had installed in the master bathroom. It was probably still unused. "I think I'm going to take a bath and break in your new tub," she said. "It's been a long day."

Kal nodded. "There's fresh towels in the linen closet just beside it."

Lana disappeared into the bathroom and, once she shut the door, let her back fall against it to block Kal and all these new feelings outside. She took a deep breath, happy to find the air in here was not scented with his cologne.

She had to shake this off, she told herself as she went to the tub and started filling it. Kal agreed to a marriage on paper, and she wasn't about to repay his kindness by getting all moony-eyed over him now that they were married.

As Lana slipped out of her clothes and pulled a towel from the cabinet, she realized just how odd it was to think of herself as married. It certainly wasn't where she had expected herself to be a week ago. Things had changed so quickly. Then again, it wasn't a real marriage. And this wasn't a real wedding night. And yet her friendship with Kal didn't feel the same as before. Something had changed, something more than just a piece of legally binding paper.

Lana slipped down into the hot, steamy water and felt her muscles instantly relax. She pressed the button on the side, and the jets came to life. They massaged her neck and back, forcing her to enjoy her time there and not worry about everything that was waiting outside the doors.

Eventually, however, the water started to cool and her fingers started pruning. She couldn't hide in the bathroom forever. She had to face Kal again and determine what their sleeping arrangements would be. Although there was a nicely appointed guest room down the hallway, for appearances they probably needed to share the master bedroom. Everyone from the nanny to the cleaning lady needed to believe they were married, but that huge king-size bed didn't seem nearly large enough for the two of them.

Funny how they'd actually shared that same bed before when they stayed up late watching movies and fell asleep, but it hadn't been such a big deal then.

She pulled the drain on the tub and climbed out, wrapping herself in a fluffy white towel. It felt childish, but she avoided leaving the bathroom for as long as possible. She brushed out and braided her hair, went through the complicated nighttime skin care routine she rarely, if ever, did, brushed and flossed, then rearranged all her things on the counter the way she liked them.

When Lana was out of things to do, she scooped up her clothes and carried them with her toward the bedroom. When she stepped out, she found Kal lying on the bed. He had changed into a pair of pajama pants and was propped up with a bunch of pillows, reading.

She tried not to pay too much attention to the carved muscles of his bare chest or how handsome he looked with his reading glasses on. Instead she pivoted on her heel and marched straight to the closet without making eye contact. There, she tossed her clothes into the hamper and searched through her new space for pajamas of her own.

Ones with full coverage, if she had some.

Kal had a really large closet, but not so large that Lana could get lost in it. True, she had to find out where all her things were stored, but after ten minutes, he started to wonder if she would ever come out.

He could tell that things had changed between them. The minute their lips had touched, it was like a switch had been flipped in their relationship. Despite all their agreements going into this marriage about it being on paper, a part of him wondered if that was even possible. Seeing her in that amazing wedding dress, feeling her surrender to his kiss, noticing how skittish she seemed around him...the attraction wasn't in his imagination.

That kiss had unleashed something that the two of them had worked hard to keep suppressed. He was sure they both had their reasons for ignoring the sexual tension that buzzed between them, but now it was nearly impossible. It was exactly what Kal had been afraid of. Pandora's box was open and there was no way to shove the temptation back inside.

That was probably why Lana was in the closet layering on every piece of clothing she had. Not that it would help. He knew each curve of her body—it was on display three nights a week at the luau. They'd hung out by the pool together. His best friend...wife now... had few secrets from him, physical or otherwise.

He was about to investigate her disappearance when the door opened and she finally stepped out. She was wearing less than he expected—a pair of flannel shorts and a relatively skimpy tank top. The top clung to her curves and left little to the imagination without a bra on beneath it. Lana hovered awkwardly by the closet door, so Kal turned his attention back to his book.

"Find everything okay?" he asked.

"Yes." Lana strode to the bed and pulled back the comforter. She crawled in beside him and tugged the sheets up under her arms. On the nightstand was her iPad, and she picked it up to start playing her game of choice.

"Feel free to move anything around in there if you don't like how they put things away."

"It was fine. I just had trouble trying to decide what I wanted to wear to bed."

Kal put the bookmark between the pages and set his book in his lap before he turned to look at her. "Don't change what you would normally wear on my account. I want you to be comfortable here. I know none of this is normal, but this is your home now, too, for as long as this goes on."

Lana looked at him with a curiously raised brow. "I appreciate that, I really do, but I don't think my normal attire is appropriate."

Kal frowned. "Why?"

"I sleep in the nude."

He was pretty sure he'd never blushed in his whole life, but suddenly he could feel his cheeks start to burn. He should've anticipated that answer. He slept in boxers on the hotter evenings and flannel pants on cooler nights. Lana had lived alone for as long as he'd known her, so why wouldn't she sleep naked?

"W-well…" he stammered, "I say do what you want to. We're both mature adults. If you're more comfortable that way, I'm sure we can deal with it."

Lana twisted her lips into a thoughtful expression. "So if I just stripped all my clothes off right now, you'd be okay with that?"

Kal swallowed hard, grateful for the thick comforter over his lap. "Absolutely."

"And that wouldn't make you uncomfortable?"

He sighed. "You're my best friend, and now you're legally my wife. I think me seeing you naked shouldn't be that big a deal. I'm not going to lose all my self-control and ravish you or anything."

Lana's almond-shaped brown eyes narrowed at him. "Okay. If you really feel that way." She reached for the hem of her tank top to pull it up over her head.

Kal froze, his breath catching in his throat. He knew he should look away, but he couldn't even move enough to do that. Was she really going to just pull her clothes off? She'd been more nervous since their ceremony than he was. It seemed like an awfully bold move on her part.

Lana stopped and flopped back against the pillows in a fit of laughter. "Oh my goodness. You should see your face," she managed to get out between giggles. She flushed bright red and her eyes teared up with amusement. "Abject panic."

She was just messing with him. That wasn't nice of her at all. Kal grabbed a nearby pillow and smacked her in the face with it. It silenced the laughter at last as she looked at him, stunned by the assault. "You're evil," he said.

"Oh yeah?" Lana grabbed a pillow of her own and swung it at him. The movement knocked the book off his lap, and the bookmark fell out onto the floor, losing his place.

Great.

Now it was war. Flinging back the blanket, Kal climbed to his knees and grabbed the pillow tight in his hands. He started wailing on Lana in between taking blows to the head and shoulders from her assault. They battled for several minutes until he managed to knock the pillow from her hands. That was when he moved in for the kill. Lana was extremely ticklish and he was going to get back at her.

He lunged forward and his fingers found her sensitive sides and belly.

"Oh no!" she wailed through laughter and tears. "No tickling!" Lana shrieked, but he wasn't letting up.

She scrambled to try and crawl off the bed, but Kal took advantage of her distraction. He climbed over her legs and pinned her arms down to the bed. "Gotcha!" he shouted triumphantly.

Lana struggled beneath his grip for a moment before she realized she'd lost the battle. Her breathing was labored from the wrestling and the laughter, and her normally golden tan skin was flushed and blotchy red from exertion. It was then that he noticed her breasts as they moved up and down against the thin cotton of her tank top. Her nipples were hard and pressing through. She might as well be naked, really, for all the shirt left to the imagination.

He swallowed hard and tore his gaze away to look her in the eye before she caught him checking her out. The light of amusement was gone as she watched him, and something different was in its place. The same something he'd seen after they shared their first kiss this afternoon—a perplexing mix of attraction, confusion and apprehension.

This playful game had suddenly taken a turn into dangerous territory.

For the first time in his life, Kal wasn't sure what to do. If it were any other woman in his bed looking at him that way, he'd kiss the living daylights out of her, then strip off those clothes and make love to her all night.

But this was Lana. His *wife*, Lana. It made more sense and no sense all at once.

He wanted to kiss her again. That kiss earlier had been sweet and unexpectedly enticing, leaving him wanting more. It was his wedding night. A kiss from his new wife wouldn't be too forward, would it?

Before he could decide, Lana's hand reached up, and she threaded her fingers through the hair at the nape of his neck. She tugged his mouth to hers and they collided with the impact of an atom bomb. She made the move, so he put his reservations aside and went with it.

It was nothing like their earlier kiss. This one was fueled by pent-up desire, a taboo attraction and an overwhelming sense of exhaustion that made it impossible to fight anymore. The kiss was hard and Lana's mouth was demanding. He freed her other arm and she tugged him closer to her. Whatever hesitation she might have been feeling earlier had flown out the window, and she was ready and willing to take what she wanted from him.

He almost couldn't breathe from the intensity of their kiss, but he refused to back away from it. When her tongue glided along his lips and demanded entry, he gave in with a groan of need he couldn't suppress. He drank her in, meeting her toe-to-toe with every move.

Kal couldn't remember the last time he'd been kissed with so much passion. Perhaps he never had. He'd suspected that his best friend was a bit of a firecracker in her relationships, but it wasn't something he'd allowed much thought. Now, as her long, shaped nails dragged across his bare shoulders and her breasts pressed urgently against his chest, that was all he could think about.

Every nerve lit up in his body like a neon sign. This was no slow-burning fire; it was an inferno that swept him up. He was hard and throbbing with need after only a kiss. Kal could feel his self-control slipping away with each flick of her tongue across his.

If he didn't take a step back, right now, they would consummate this marriage. Lana had been very clear that it was not her intention going into their wedding. It was supposed to be on paper only. They were on the verge of breaking that arrangement after only a few hours together.

He finally ripped his mouth away and moved back out of her reach. They both lay still and panting for a few moments as they tried to process what had just happened between them.

"I'm sorry," Lana said after a few minutes. She sat up and covered her flushed face with her hands. "I don't know what got into me just now."

"Don't be sorry," he said. "I wasn't exactly fighting you off." Even as he pulled away, he felt his desire for Lana drawing him back in. They needed some space apart. "I think that maybe tonight, I should sleep in the guest room." Kal backed off the bed and picked his book up from the floor.

"Kal, no. You don't have to do that. This was all my fault just now. I shouldn't have…" Her voice trailed off and she shook her head. "I'll sleep in the guest room," she offered. "I'm not going to drive you out of your own bed. That's silly."

He held out his arm to stop her and took another step toward the door. "It's your bed now too, Lana. Stay. I insist. I think I'm going to be up for a while anyway. I'm going to read for a few hours."

Lana's face was lined with conflicting emotions. She didn't want him to go, but they both knew it was probably for the best. There were too many emotions flying around after the day they'd had and what just happened between them was evidence of it all combusting at once. Tomorrow they needed to focus on meeting with the judge and getting guardianship of Akela. That required a good night's sleep. At least for Lana. Kal doubted he would get that no matter where he slept tonight, but being apart would be better for now.

She didn't argue with him. He turned off the lamp by his bedside and backed away toward the bedroom door.

"Good night, Mrs. Bishop."

Five

Judge Kona eyed Lana and Kal as they stood together in front of the bench. She clutched Kal's hand with all her might to keep from shaking. Her nerves were getting the best of her, even with Kal's reassuring touch to steady her. It didn't help that the judge was a very large and intimidating man with a bald head and heavy, dark eyebrows. His eyes were nearly black and seemed to look right through her.

"Mr. Lyon, your attorney, has filed your motion for temporary guardianship of Akela Hale. It looks as though he has everything in order." The judge's sharp gaze dropped to the paperwork as he flipped through everything Dexter had submitted for them.

"I do have a few questions for you. It says here that you are the owner of the Mau Loa Maui Hotel, Mr. Bishop. Is that correct?"

"Yes, sir."

"You and Mrs. Bishop live on the premises?"

"Yes, sir. I recently completed the construction of our home, which is on the property, but on the far side away from the hotel. It's over three thousand square feet with a decorated nursery ready to bring Akela home."

Judge Kona nodded and looked at the paperwork again. "Mrs. Bishop, you are employed at the hotel as a choreographer. Will you be continuing to work?"

Lana took a deep breath and hoped her answer was the right one. "Yes, sir, I will. However, it is a flexible position. We are interviewing caregivers to watch Akela in the home while we are both working instead of putting her in day care."

The judge made a note. "Very good. Now, my understanding is that you two are newlyweds. Bringing a child into the situation will seriously cramp your honeymoon phase. Have you taken that into consideration before making this decision?"

"We have, Your Honor," Kal answered. "We welcome the opportunity to make Akela part of our lives for as long as may be required."

"Mrs. Bishop," Judge Kona said, the name still sounding foreign to her ears, "your sister agreed to a plea bargain yesterday. In exchange for her testimony against Mr. Keawe and his distributor, she is receiving a reduced sentence of two years' probation and mandatory in-house drug and alcohol dependency treatment. If she completes the twenty-eight-day program successfully, she will be released and I will grant her custody of her daughter again. That means you will be her guardian for a minimum of that time.

"If, however, she leaves the program, fails a mandatory drug test or otherwise breaks her probation requirements, she will go to jail for no less than a year. Are you and Mr. Bishop willing to take on your niece in the event that this arrangement is longer than planned?"

"Absolutely, Your Honor." Lana meant it. Kal might not be thrilled with his whole life being uprooted for a year or more, but she was willing to do whatever was necessary for Akela.

Judge Kona's dark gaze raked over the two of them one last time before he sorted through the paperwork and signed off on one of the pages. "Very well. Mr. and Mrs. Bishop, you hereby receive the temporary guardianship of your niece, Akela Hale. Social services will be making several unannounced visits to the home to ensure the child's welfare and safety, in addition to making calls to your provided references. You may meet with the clerk to pick up Akela."

The sound of the gavel smacking the wooden desk echoed through the courtroom and Lana took her first deep breath in half an hour. In relief, she turned and wrapped her arms around Kal's neck. "Thank you for this."

"You're welcome. I knew everything would work out. Now let's go get her."

Dexter escorted them out of the courtroom and they followed him down the hallway to the clerk's office. She thought they might have to go pick Akela up wherever her foster family was living, but she found an older dark-haired woman sitting on a bench in the hallway holding her infant niece.

"Akela!" she shouted, pulling away from Kal to run down the tile corridor to her niece.

The baby was oblivious of what was happening around her, but the woman holding her looked up as Lana came closer and smiled. She stood, shifting the baby on her hip and swinging a diaper bag on her shoulder. "You must be her aunt," she said.

Lana nodded. "Yes." She ached to hold her niece but didn't want to tear her out of the woman's arms. From the looks of Akela, the foster mother had taken excellent care of her. Her blue-and-white dress was clean and well fitting, her dark baby curls were combed and she wore a little white headband with a bow. The baby smiled when she saw Lana, her slobbery grin exposing her first bottom tooth.

"I'm Jenny. I've been watching this little ray of sunshine the past few days. She's very lucky to have family willing to jump through the hoops to take her in."

Dexter and Kal finally came up behind them. "Everything went as planned," her lawyer said. "We've just got to sign some paperwork in the clerk's office and you'll be able to take Akela home."

The woman handed Lana the baby. "Your attorney has my number if you need to get in contact with me. I've only had Akela a few days, but I've cared for dozens of foster children over the years. If you have any questions about babies, feel free to call me. She's been napping about two in the afternoon. This one is teething, and it makes her a bit crabby, so good luck with that."

Lana cuddled her niece into her arms. She'd been worried about who had Akela, but the kind, soft-spoken woman put her fears to rest. "I may take you up on that," she admitted. "I honestly know very little about babies, but that's how most moms start out, right?"

Jenny smiled brightly and patted her arm. "Absolutely. You'll do just fine." She placed the diaper bag over Lana's shoulder. "Everything she had with her when social services picked her up is in that bag. There's a bottle made up for her in the side pocket if she gets hungry before you get home."

"Thank you, Mrs. Paynter," Dexter said before opening the clerk's door and ushering Lana, Akela and Kal inside. There were discussions and forms and paperwork, but Lana couldn't really focus on what was going on. Let her lawyer and her husband handle things. All she could think about was the baby in her arms. It hadn't been the simplest process to get to this point, but it was worth it all.

"How are you, baby girl?" she cooed in the voice she reserved for babies and animals.

Akela got excited by the question, grinning and reaching up with her chubby baby fingers to grab a fistful of Lana's hair.

"Oh, ow," Lana said, extracting her hair and brushing the rest of it over her other shoulder. Lesson one— keep the hair away if you want it to remain in your scalp.

The men's voices got louder and Lana knew they were wrapping things up. Lana gave a gummy kiss to Akela's cheek until she squealed in delight and everyone's attention in the room turned to them.

"Well, okay, then," Kal said with a smile. "I think that means it's time to go home. What do you say, Miss Akela?"

They all headed out to the parking lot together. They'd ridden over that morning in the new Lexus SUV he'd rented while they had the baby. Kal opened the door to the backseat, where they'd mounted the car seat.

"Here you go," Lana said, handing the baby over to him.

There was a momentary flash of panic in his eyes as he held Akela and eyed the car seat with suspicion. "O-kay," he said, quickly recovering. "Baby goes here," he muttered aloud. "Snap this thing. Arm through there. Snap that thing. And then..." He looked around. "Done!"

Lana let her gaze flicker over it for just a moment to ensure that he did it right, but it looked good to her. She didn't exactly know how everything was supposed to be, either. She was the youngest child. Kal was the oldest, but just by a couple years. She doubted he did much to take care of Mano when he was an infant.

They climbed into the front seat and started the car. "Well, we did it," Kal said. "In just a few days, we managed to get married, move in together and gain guardianship of a baby." He ran his fingers though his hair and sighed. "Now what?"

That was a good question. To be honest, Lana hadn't entirely thought the plan through to the conclusion. All she knew was that she needed her niece to be with her. Now that that was accomplished... "Now I guess we just start living like every other family in America."

Kal shook his head and pulled the SUV out of the parking lot. "I hope you know what that means, because I sure don't. Do we need to stop at the store? What do six-month-olds eat? I ordered some formula at the baby store. Does she eat baby food yet?"

Lana bit at her lip. "I don't know." She picked up the diaper bag and started sorting through the contents.

She found a box of something called rice cereal, but it didn't look like any kind of cereal she'd ever seen before. There were also a couple of small jars with pureed fruits and vegetables. "There's some baby food in here. Enough to last us today and tomorrow until we figure out what she likes."

Now that the worry of getting guardianship was out of the way, Lana found herself blindsided by the fear that she had no clue what she was doing. "You didn't happen to buy a baby book at the store, did you?"

"No." Kal turned to her with a wry smile. "You mean they don't come with instruction manuals?"

"I sincerely doubt that. Thank goodness for the internet." She was Googling everything she could think of the moment they got in the car.

"Well, I don't know much about babies, but I do know one thing," Kal said with a laugh. "We need to interview a nanny as soon as possible."

Day one went better than Kal had expected. Lana hovered nervously over the baby between feedings and frantic readings on the internet. Kal, regrettably, had to leave her to put in a few hours at the hotel, but when he came home, the house wasn't on fire, the baby was alive and Lana wasn't drinking hard liquor, so it was a success in his book.

He played on the floor with Akela for about an hour while Lana passed out on the couch, and then he and the baby did a test-run bath with the fancy baby bathtub he'd bought. He'd never seen anything like it before—it weighed the baby, reported the temperature of the water and had a nice place to lay the baby down where she couldn't slip and slide around. Akela had a great time splashing around in the water. He wasn't sure how clean she actually got, but it had to be worth something to at least sit in soapy water for a while.

When he was done, he wrapped her in a towel, put on a clean diaper, then slipped her into some footie pajamas they'd bought at the store with little sheep on them. He put her into the baby swing in the kitchen with one of the bottles made up in the fridge and ordered dinner from room service to be couriered over for him and Lana. He might not be in the hotel, but he owned it and got what he wanted.

When Akela finally fell asleep that night, Lana was right behind her. Kal grabbed his phone and took it into his office. He knew he needed to call his brother, Mano, and it couldn't be put off any longer. Some of the hotel staff in Maui worked with the Oahu staff, and if word got back to Mano that Kal had married and had a baby girl, things would get blown way out of proportion.

He was content to keep things quiet for now. He'd only listed his brother as a reference, so Mano was the only one who needed to know about the marriage. They'd successfully gotten custody, and if all went well, in a month Akela could return home and he and Lana could quietly divorce. If things stretched on... well, eventually he'd have to tell the rest of his family. Kal would cross that bridge when he got there, however.

Closing his office door, he dialed up his brother and settled into the leather executive chair he'd chosen for the new house. He leaned back and propped his feet up on the corner of the desk. From there, he had a clear view out onto the lanai. The sun had long set on the golf course, but he could see the lights of the resort in the distance and a sailboat on the water with lights up the mast.

"Hello?" his brother answered with a husky, sleepy voice.

"Aloha, Mano. Did I wake you? It's just past eight."

Mano chuckled and cleared his throat. "You know me, living the wild life. Paige and I fell asleep on the couch watching a movie."

"Watching a movie?" Mano was completely blind and had been for a decade.

"Yes, well, she was watching it. I was just listening. Apparently it was boring even if you can see, and we nodded off. To what do we owe a phone call on this random Wednesday evening? I've barely heard from you since Tūtū Ani's birthday party."

Kal snorted into the phone. "You're turning into an old woman, Mano. Complaining I don't call enough. Next you'll be telling me I'm too thin and I need to eat, like Aunt Kini always does."

"That's what domesticity does to you," Mano said. "Paige and I spent all weekend house-hunting. We have an ultrasound next week where we find out if we're having a boy or a girl. All that focus on home and family makes you look at things differently."

Kal certainly understood, although his brother didn't know that yet. "How is Paige doing?" His brother's fiancée was almost halfway through her pregnancy. She'd just moved from her home in San Diego to Oahu. Kal had yet to go to Oahu and meet her, and he felt bad about that. Work had just gotten in the way, like it did with everything else. Now that he had a wife and child to worry about, he imagined it would get even harder to fit in time for things like that.

What a strange thought to cross his mind so easily… a wife and child. The idea didn't bother him as much as he thought it would. Of course, it was a fake marriage and someone else's baby, but still, the words slipped into his vocabulary easier than he expected after years of resisting the idea of it.

"She's good. I think the move and all the excitement has worn her out. Her ankles swell up at night, so I've been rubbing them for her and ordering milk shakes from room service. She's adequately spoiled."

"What are you going to do when you get a house and there is no room service?"

"Takeout and delivery," Mano answered without hesitation. "I do think we've found a house she likes, though. We're going to put an offer in on it in the morning. It had amazing views."

"How would you know?" Kal and Mano had always tried to make light of his brother's disability. He never wanted him to wallow in it, so their humor was dark where that was concerned.

"It was in the listing, so it has to be true. Besides, Paige made a squealy, girlie sound when we walked out onto the deck. I figure it's nice. The price tag definitely falls in the category of nice view, beach accessible."

"Well, let me know what happens. I'll fly over to see it."

"Sounds good." Mano hesitated on the line for a minute. "So what's the call about? You rarely dial me up just to chat, big brother."

Mano was right. They didn't spend a lot of time

catching up on the minutiae of each other's lives. "I'm calling because I have some pretty big news."

"Well, considering this is my brother, Kalani, on the phone, I'll exclude romantic engagements from the list of options. Have you impregnated your tennis instructor?"

Kal bit his lip. This news really would blow Mano out of the water. It was very unlike Kal. He hadn't so much as mentioned a woman he was dating to his brother by name in years, much less talked about one like there was future potential with them. Mano knew how he felt about commitment. And knowing he'd married Lana of all people… "I gave up tennis two years ago. And my tutor was a man."

"You're growing out your beard," Mano guessed.

"How is that big news?"

"You've never had a beard. I don't know. Just tell me. I'm no good at the guessing games."

"Okay, fine," Kal relented. "I'll tell you, but for now I need you to keep this between us. I don't need the whole family going crazy over it."

"Hmm…" Mano said thoughtfully. "This is going to be good. I promise not to share it with anyone but Paige."

"I said not to share it with anyone," Kal pointed out.

Mano sighed. "When you're a couple, telling me is like telling her by default. If Paige can't know, just don't tell me. I'm physically incapable of not telling her. She won't spill the story to anyone, I promise. So lay it on me."

"All right. I've gotten married." He spat the words out as fast as he could. "And we have a six-month-old little girl staying with us for a while."

There was a long silence as Mano processed his words. Kal waited for the questions, the confused exclamations, but there was nothing. "You always have to one-up me on everything," Mano complained at last. "I get engaged, you get married. We're expecting a baby, you come up with one already born. You can't let me have anything, can you?"

"I'm not kidding, Mano. Lana and I got married yesterday. We got guardianship of her niece today."

"You and *Lana*?" His voice went up an octave in surprise. Mano had met Lana once when he came to the grand opening of the Maui resort. He knew they were close friends, but married? Even Kal couldn't believe that. "Wow. I mean, you told me she was an amazing person and crazy gorgeous, but I thought you two were just friends."

So did he. Then they got married. And then they kissed and he questioned everything he'd believed about their friendship. "She is amazing and gorgeous and a great friend. It's a long story."

"You also swore up and down that you'd never marry."

Kal's jaw tightened. It was true. And it still was true in terms of a real marriage and family. But he couldn't say that. "I realized that I wanted more and so did she. She changed my mind about the whole thing. We decided to just take the plunge before one of us chickened out."

As much as Kal wanted to tell his brother the truth, he couldn't risk anyone finding out the marriage was a sham. If they lost custody of Akela for lying to the judge, he'd never forgive himself, and neither would Lana. Everyone had to believe the story for it to work.

"And how does the baby come into play?"

"It belongs to her sister. I'd already proposed when we found out that she's in rehab and the father is in jail for selling drugs to a cop. We went ahead and got married sooner than later so we could take the baby."

"Wow. Married with a baby…a sister-in-law in rehab… There's a lot going on over on Maui."

Kal chuckled. "You have no idea. It's a ton of information to process, I know, but I wanted to tell you so you heard it from me and not the staff."

"Thanks for that. You know how they love to spread gossip. I feel like I should say congratulations, and yet I'm not certain. As a man recently in love, I find I don't hear that edge of panic in your voice that's usually associated with love and marriage. Are you sure you're excited about these sudden developments? You've asked me not to tell anyone, which seems weird for a joyous event. No one has blackmailed you into doing this, right?"

Not exactly. A little arm twisting perhaps, but he'd given in easily for Lana. "I married Lana of my own free will, I just don't want the family swarming yet. It was a lovely ceremony."

"That's good to know. I never imagined you getting married, but now that you have, I'm glad it was because you wanted to. I have to say I'm a little disappointed to miss out on the major event. It's less than an hour's flight, you know. Paige and I could've come. Or are we part of the pesky swarm you're avoiding?"

Kal tried to ignore the slight sound of hurt in his brother's voice. They teased each other so much it was hard to tell if he was messing with him or seriously regretted missing the wedding. "Of course not. It was just the two of us. Not a big deal. You didn't miss anything. I'm sure your wedding extravaganza will far outshine ours."

Mano made a grumbling sound under his breath. "I have no doubt of it. Paige keeps meeting with Tūtū Ani, plotting and planning. We want to get it done before she has the baby, but I can feel the ceremony and the budget growing exponentially every time they get together."

"Got a date in mind?"

"Valentine's Day, I think. Probably at the new house. The yard was big enough."

Kal needed to note that on his calendar. It was a busy time in Hawaii, with everyone desperate for a romantic getaway somewhere that wasn't covered in snow and ice. He wondered how he'd explain to his brother when he showed up without a wife or a baby. Or how would he explain it to everyone else if he did? This relationship had an unstable timeline, and that made it hard for him to plan. It wasn't forever. It was fake. But how long would they fake it? He had no idea.

If Mele screwed up and Lana got the child for months, even years, would she expect them to continue this marriage? He wasn't sure, but it certainly would complicate things. Considering they were two days into their marriage, he opted not to worry too much about it.

"Let me let you go," Kal said at last. He didn't really want Mano pushing for too many details. As soon as Paige got wind of the news, Kal was sure Mano's fiancée would start asking questions neither Mano nor Kal could really answer.

"Enjoy the honeymoon phase," Mano said with a snicker.

"You bet I will," Kal said, trying to sound like an excited new groom. He wasn't sure he pulled it off. As Mano said, he was missing that edge of panic. "Aloha," he added, hanging up.

Now that was done, he had to face another uncomfortable situation—climbing into bed with his wife again.

Six

Lana noticed when Kal finally came to bed that night after eleven, but she was too tired to care. That baby had worn her out completely. She rolled onto her side away from him and snuggled into the blankets, falling back asleep before his head likely hit the pillow.

It seemed like only minutes later that she rolled onto her back and found herself in bed alone. This time, sun was streaming in through the windows. It was morning. She looked at the clock by the bed. It was just after eight. She didn't expect Akela to let her sleep this late.

She sat up and picked up the baby monitor to make sure it was working. It was turned off. The nursery was far enough away that she might not hear the baby crying if she'd accidentally forgotten to turn it on or the battery died. In a panic, she flung back the blankets and moved quickly across the wooden floors of the hall-

way to the nursery. To her surprise the door was open
and there was no baby, crying or otherwise, in the crib.

Then she heard the distant sound of baby giggles.
Lana followed it back down the hallway and through
the living room to the kitchen. There, she found Akela
in Kal's arms and Kal shirtless in those blasted pajama
pants again. This time, putting together a bottle for the
baby with one hand.

"Good morning," she said, rubbing the sleep from
her eyes.

"Good morning," Kal replied. He held up the bottle to her. "It turns out that baby cereal isn't really cereal. I mean, it is. When they're older you can feed it
to them with a spoon, but since we aren't sure if she's
been eating a lot of solids yet, you can add some to the
formula and it gets a little thicker and more satisfying.
Who knew?"

Lana crossed her arms over her chest and eyed Kal
with suspicion. "And who told you that?"

"My grandmother."

Her eyes widened in surprise. "You told your grandmother about Akela? Did you tell her we were married, too?"

"No." Kal tightened the nipple and gave the bottle
to Akela. She reached up for it and helped him hold it
to her mouth. "I told her that I was helping you babysit for your sister. There was some in the diaper bag
the foster mother gave us, so she said this was the best
way to start her off if we aren't sure. She said we could
also try some smooth baby foods and even Cheerios
to see how she does."

Lana just nodded blankly as he spoke and was wondering if she had actually woken up or if this was all

some weird dream. It didn't feel like a dream. And yet the events of the past week had culminated in a moment that didn't seem real. This moment felt so domestic, so unlike the life she was used to living. She was married, living in a home with Kal and they were caring for a baby. It was everything and nothing she'd wanted all at once. All she could do was stand dumbstruck in the kitchen while he fed Akela.

After their first awkward night together in the house, they hadn't had a moment like this. They'd quickly gotten it together in the morning and gone straight to court. Now everything was settled into a domestic bliss that she didn't entirely mind. It was certainly better than living alone in that hotel suite. But she wouldn't let herself become too comfortable. All of this was temporary. The minute she started liking the idea of being married to Kal and having this little family, it would all fall apart. She couldn't get wrapped up in the fantasy they'd crafted for Judge Kona.

"Would you like some coffee? I just brewed a pot."

"Sure." Lana found a mug in the cabinet and poured herself a mug of black coffee. Normally she put cream in it, but she needed a straight shot of caffeine to face another day of motherhood without any help. She wasn't sure how people did it. Generation after generation had managed, so she could, too, but working at the same time would make things complicated.

Kal leaned back against the countertop and watched the baby happily suck down her formula. "So, I called the employment agency today to ask about getting a nanny."

Perfect. It was as though he'd read her mind. "When can they send someone over?" She hated to sound anxious, but she'd missed a lot of work. Given she hadn't taken a sick day in all the years she'd worked at the Mau Loa, she hated missing performances now.

"They're sending over a couple candidates for us to interview tomorrow."

"Tomorrow? That means they probably won't start until the next day at the earliest. I've got a show tonight and rehearsals the next day. We were working on a new *South Pacific* routine before all this came up. Are you going to watch Akela while I work?"

"I could. Or we could get someone to watch her tonight. But I don't think it's a big deal for you to stay home with her if you want to. It might be the best thing to help her adjust to a new situation."

"Kal, I missed the show on Tuesday as it is. I can't miss another night."

"I know your boss," he said with a sly grin. "He's not going to fire you."

"Very funny."

"Okay," he relented. "I'll get someone to watch her this evening during the show, okay? I'm sure I can get a volunteer on staff who would much rather babysit than clean hotel rooms or bus tables."

She felt better. A little. She didn't know why it was bothering her so much. She was the one who insisted on getting custody of Akela. Did she think she could put the baby in the cabinet when she was too busy to deal with her? Kal had signed up to marry her, not to take on caring for an infant. He was already going above and beyond for her.

"Thank you." She reached out her arms. "Here, give her to me. I know you need to get in the shower."

Kal nodded and handed the baby over to her. "I'll

text you when I get someone pinned down for tonight. What time do you need to leave to get ready?"

"No later than six-thirty."

Kal turned to head toward the master suite when the doorbell rang. He frowned and looked at her. "Are you expecting anyone?"

Lana shook her head. "No one I know realizes I'm living here."

He went to the door and looked through the peep hole before shrugging and opening the door. "Hello. Can I help you?"

When it opened all the way, Lana could see a petite woman in a frumpy black suit standing on the doorstep. "Hello, I'm Darlene Andrews with Honolulu Child Services. I'm here to conduct a random review of Akela's home environment."

They hadn't waited long. Kal took a step back to allow her inside. "Please come in, Ms. Andrews. I was just about to get in the shower."

"Please, go ahead," the woman insisted. She pointed to Lana where she was standing with Akela in her arms. "I can speak with Mrs. Bishop while you're getting ready."

Kal looked at her, obviously not wanting to leave Lana alone with the woman, but she shrugged him away. The bigger deal they made out of this, the stranger it would look. "Go on, honey. I don't want you to be late to work."

He reluctantly disappeared and Lana turned to the woman with a smile. "Would you like some coffee? Kal just brewed a pot."

"Yes, thank you."

She followed Lana into the kitchen, where Lana

made her a mug and placed it on the counter. "Is there anything specific you need to see while you're here?"

"Since this is our first visit, I'd like to do a quick walk-through of the house, especially the nursery, to make sure you have adequate facilities for the baby. Then just a few short questions and I'll be out of your way."

"Okay. Follow me and I'll show you Akela's room." They wandered through the living room and down the hallway to the nursery. Lana opened the door and stepped inside so Ms. Andrews could get a good look at it. There was no way she wouldn't be impressed with the room. It was the prettiest nursery in the history of nurseries.

Ms. Andrews didn't react, however. Instead she made notes and checked off items on some form attached to her clipboard. She examined the crib closely and then the stroller and car seat combination that was near the closet. "Very good. And where do you and Mr. Bishop sleep?"

Lana pasted on a smile. "We're on the opposite end of the hallway, here." She checked the bedroom before she pushed the door all the way open, and the bathroom door was shut. She could hear the shower running. "You'll have to excuse the mess, we just got up."

Ms. Andrews paid particular attention to the unmade bed and the two places where Lana and Kal had obviously slept together the night before. She never imagined they would pay that much attention, but she was thankful she hadn't taken to sleeping in the guest room. Then again, maybe Ms. Andrews was looking at the baby monitor and Lana was just paranoid. She couldn't be sure.

When they returned to the living room, they took a seat opposite each other on the sofa. "How are you and Mr. Bishop adjusting to caring for a baby?"

"The last day has been a steep learning curve for both of us, but I think it's going well so far. Kal has a large family on Oahu and they've been just a phone call away for support and questions."

Ms. Andrews nodded and made a note. "My file says that you told the judge you were planning on hiring a caretaker for Akela while you work?"

"Yes. We have interviews scheduled for tomorrow. I'm hopeful we'll find just the right person to take care of her."

"Will she be a live-in or part-time nanny?"

Lana had no idea. "She will be full-time, but as for whether she moves in with us, I guess that depends. I have some late hours at work, so if Kal can be home, it's not an issue. Having someone around the clock would certainly be a help, but I think that will be something we have to discuss with the nanny we end up hiring. We do have a guest suite if we need it."

The woman seemed to take notes for what felt like an eternity. Lana hoped she said and did all the right things, but she couldn't be sure. She kissed Akela on the top of her head, drawing in her sweet baby scent, and tried not to worry about it.

Finally the social worker looked up and smiled. "I think for now that's all I need. Akela seems to be doing well so far and you've set up a nice home for her with the two of you. If I didn't know better, I'd think she was yours." Ms. Andrews organized her paperwork and slid it back into her leather briefcase bag. She stood and shook Lana's hand. "Thank you for your time."

Lana walked her to the door and stood there holding Akela as she stepped out into the morning sunlight. "You'll be hearing from me again," she said with a polite, detached smile.

Lana returned the smile and stepped back inside. She was certain they would.

Tonight was the first night that Kal had watched Lana perform in the luau as his wife. Less than a week ago, he'd stood in the exact same spot and done the exact same thing, but everything was different now.

Before, when Lana had danced sensually onstage, he'd tried hard not to notice. She was his best friend and employee, so the shimmy of her hips and the hard muscles of her exposed core weren't his to admire. But now they were. Sort of.

The pulsating sound of the drums as she moved her body made a bolt of liquid heat surge through his veins. Each flash of thigh from between the large ti leaves of her skirt made him wish it crept just the tiniest bit higher. He wanted to run his hands over the smooth skin of her inner thigh and press a kiss against the belly that was exposed to the crowd.

Just the image in his mind of doing that made every muscle in his body tense up. He was overwhelmed with need, driven by it for the first time in his adult life. He felt like an overstimulated teenage boy, aching almost to the point of pain to reach out and touch her. He had managed to keep his hands to himself the last couple nights, but he couldn't imagine sleeping beside her again without reaching out to her.

Life and dealing with Akela had distracted him from wanting Lana, but now that things were settling down, he couldn't shake these thoughts. The sight of her in her wedding gown with the plunging neckline, the memory of that red-hot kiss on their bed…it haunted him every time he had a free moment to himself. And now, seeing her dance, he was on the verge of losing his tight grip of control.

This was what he'd been afraid of with Lana. What he'd fought so hard to avoid. She was everything he'd ever wanted but knew he couldn't have. Marriage had never been his forte, but a temporary one wasn't so bad. Going into it knowing it would end, without any false expectations of forever, made it much more tolerable. The hardest part so far was not enjoying the benefits. That was their agreement—a sensible one at the time—but now he regretted going along with it. If he was going to have Lana for his wife on paper, he wanted her for his wife in bed, as well.

When her last number finished, Lana met him in the back of the courtyard. She'd changed backstage this time into a short, strapless dress in a bright tropical pattern. That didn't help matters. It clung to her curves and showcased the legs he'd been admiring earlier.

"Are you ready to go? We need to relieve the babysitter."

Lana nodded. "Once we get the nanny position filled, I'll be more comfortable staying all the way to the end and giving notes. Tonight I've got Pam watching for feedback to give them at rehearsal tomorrow. So far, the audience really seems to enjoy the new singing number at the end."

Aware of the people around them and desperate for an excuse to touch her, he reached out and grabbed her hand. "Let's go home, then."

She didn't resist taking his hand and following him to the lot where he parked the Jaguar. Once they arrived home, Kal paid the young woman from housekeeping for watching Akela, and she left quickly.

Akela was asleep. They poked their heads into the nursery to check on her, but all was well. She was in her sheep jammies and contentedly dreaming in her crib. So far, Akela had slept through the night, which was nice. And after that show, he hoped the trend continued tonight.

"I'm exhausted," Lana said as they shut the nursery door and headed toward the master bedroom. "I thought being a dancer was hard work, but being a dancer and having an infant to care for is masochism at its finest."

"Well, if it makes you feel better, you're a beautiful masochist."

Lana dismissed his compliment and stepped out of her sandals. Reaching behind herself, she strained to reach the zipper of the dress.

"Here," Kal said as he tugged off his tie. "Let me get it."

Coming up behind her, he grazed her skin with his fingertips as he reached for the clasp. Lana lifted her hair up, exposing her bare neck and shoulders, and sending a whiff of Plumeria to his nose. His skin tingled as it brushed hers, undoing the clasp and running the zipper down to the small of her back.

When he reached the bottom, the rough lace of her panties peeked out at him, and he could feel the desire he'd suppressed surge through him again. Kal didn't let go the way he should then. Instead he moved closer, until his warm breath brushed over her bare shoulders.

Lana didn't move away, either. She stood very still, drawing in a ragged breath and slowly letting it out. Kal rested his palms on her shoulders, relishing the silky feel of her skin under his hands. He wanted to touch more of her and prayed that she'd let him.

She leaned back against him, finally swooping her hair over one shoulder. As she lowered her arms, Kal felt the fabric of her dress slip away until it pooled at her feet. His gaze ran over her shoulders, finding no strapless bra where he expected it to be. Of course not…they didn't wear anything like that beneath their traditional outfits. It complicated costume changes backstage.

One glance at her full, mocha-tipped breasts was enough to undo him. "Lana…" he said in a pained voice as his fingertips pressed into her shoulders. The single word expressed everything he needed to say to her in that moment. That he wanted her. That he knew he shouldn't. That one more minute together like this and he wouldn't be able to tear himself away.

Lana didn't respond. Instead she reached up for his hands and moved them around her until they cupped her breasts. His own groan muffled her soft sigh of pleasure as the weight of them rested in his hands. He brushed his thumbs over her nipples and they hardened to peaks that pressed insistently into him.

Leaning down, Kal pressed his lips against her shoulder. Her skin was warm against his lips and smelled like cocoa butter and tropical flowers. He traveled up the exposed line of her neck, inhaling her scent into his lungs. He teased at the sensitive hollow beneath her ear, biting gently at her earlobe until she gasped.

"Kal," she whispered, and arched her back to press

her rear into the straining length of his erection. The movement elicited a growl from deep in his throat, a sound he didn't even know he was capable of making until then. Lana was able to rouse something from deep inside him. Something primal that he'd never let out before.

He got the feeling that if he truly let go with Lana, there would be no going back. He didn't just want to make love to her, he wanted to claim her as his own. Kal had no right to do that. She didn't belong to him. But that was what she drew out of him. "Last time I pulled back, Lana. I pulled away when I didn't want to because I thought we'd both regret it. And yet we're here again. I don't think I can walk away from you twice."

Lana turned in his arms to face him. She looked at him with her dark, almond-shaped eyes and there was no hesitation there. No concern. Nothing but a blazing desire for him that he'd never seen from her before. Perhaps something new and primitive had been released in her, as well. "Then don't."

If Lana felt the slightest hesitation about making love to Kal, it was only in that moment when he finally gave in to wanting her and she saw the passion unleash in him. He was a large man, a strong man, but although she wasn't afraid of him, she wondered in that moment if she was enough woman to satisfy the lust that rolled off him in waves.

Then he kissed her and her doubts were put to rest. His powerfully possessive kiss and firm desire against her belly proved that he wanted her and only her. His fingers dove into her hair, pulling her close and refusing to let her go. All she could do was cling to him and go along for the ride. This was something she'd always wanted but had been too afraid to have. Now was her chance and she needed to make the most of every second in case this never happened again.

His tongue invaded her, deepening the kiss and demanding more, which she gladly gave. Then, just as suddenly, he pulled away, ripping his lips from hers.

Lana thought for a moment that he had gathered his senses and was about to walk out, but he just stood there. His breath was ragged and his gaze never left her body as he tugged off his tie and slipped out of his suit coat. She was standing there in nothing but the nude panties they wore under their dance costumes. Lana had never felt more exposed yet more desired in her whole life.

Feeling bolstered by his attraction to her, she hooked her thumbs under her panties and slowly slid them over her hips. Kal watched with his mouth agape and his shirt half unbuttoned as she shimmied them down her legs and kicked them to the side. Then, completely naked, she planted her hands on her hips and waited for him with a sly smile curling her lips.

The rest of his clothing came off much faster, and suddenly she was hit by a wall of hard, male flesh. It pushed her back until she fell onto the mattress. Kal covered her body with his own, hardly allowing her the opportunity to enjoy the view as he had. Instead his mouth was on hers again and his hands were roaming over her exposed flesh.

Lana loved the feel of his weight pressing her against the mattress and the insistent desire against her thigh. She parted her legs, letting Kal nestle between them just as he started moving lower down her body. His lips nibbled and tasted at her throat, her collarbone, her sternum, and then finally he drew one nipple into his mouth. He sucked hard, teasing at her sensitive flesh before soothing it with his tongue. The powerful caress sent a bolt of sensation straight to her core. Her insides grew molten as they began to pulse with the insistent rhythm of need.

As if he could sense her building demand for his touch, Kal reached between her thighs. He brushed over her ever so faintly once, then twice, making her nearly want to scream with pent-up desire, even though she knew she couldn't risk waking the baby. Then his fingertips delved deeper, finding her sensitive center and drawing a silent cry from her throat. Lana couldn't keep her hips from moving against his hand. She needed Kal's touch. She needed Kal.

She wasn't sure how much longer she could wait. Lana appreciated the extended seduction that Kal likely had planned, but she was ready to jump to the main course. "Do you have…" she gasped between strokes "…protection?"

Instead of answering right away, he slipped a finger inside her, making her whole body tense up and a soft whimper pass her lips.

"I do," he answered as he slowly, torturously, moved in and out of her. "Are you sure you want me to go get it so soon? I was just starting to have some fun."

Lana bit her lip as he continued to tease her, verbally and otherwise. Her muscles were tightening with building sparks of pleasure that she wasn't ready to give into yet. "Get it," she managed between clenched teeth. "Now."

Kal grinned wide and pulled his hand away. "Yes, ma'am." He moved to the side of the bed and returned a moment later with a condom in his hand. She took advantage of the view, spying the hard length she'd been longing for. Her eyes widened for a moment as she watched him sheathe himself in latex. Kal was above average in all ways. This would be interesting.

As quickly as he'd left, Kal returned to his place between her thighs. Instead of entering her, he continued to tease at her with his hand. Whether she wanted to or not, she was responding to his touch. He was driving her toward the edge before they'd even begun.

"Not yet," she gasped, reaching one arm out to caress the stubble on his cheek. "With you."

His dark gaze met hers, and then he nodded silently. His body hovered over her on his powerful arms. She drew her knees up, opening to Kal when she felt the press of his desire. "Please," she urged, and finally felt him move into her.

It was slow, but Lana closed her eyes and enjoyed every moment of it. She bit at her lip again to hold in a gasp of pleasure as he sank deeper and deeper. Kal moved one hand to clutch her hip and lift her up to take him all the way. When he was finally buried deep inside her, they both let out a soft groan of pleasure.

Kal dropped onto his left elbow and pressed a softer kiss to her lips. Then he started rocking in and out of her. All the sensations he'd aroused in her earlier returned at once as he retreated, then advanced more forcefully each time. The ratchet inside her moved one notch higher with every thrust. Her soft cries and gasps were a steady chorus in the tropical evening air.

Then Kal let go of her hip and slid his hand down

her leg to the back of her knee. He sat up, hooking her leg over his shoulder, and planted a kiss on the inside of her knee. Looking into her eyes, he thrust again, deepening his reach tenfold. Lana couldn't hold on much longer. She clawed at the sheets as he pounded deep inside her, until at last she couldn't resist it and shattered into an explosive orgasm. Her whole body shuddered with the power of it. She grasped a pillow and used it to smother her cries, gasping Kal's name into the fabric as he continued the pleasurable assault on her body.

He wasn't far behind. Gripping her leg in one hand and her breast in the other, he thrust one last time and came undone with a silent roar. He shook with the force of his release, as though it were sucking out every ounce of energy he had; then he pulled away and collapsed onto the bed beside her.

Lana lay there for what seemed like hours with her mind racing, although it was only minutes that passed. She couldn't quite believe what had just happened. Instead of enjoying the moment and basking in the afterglow, she anxiously awaited Kal's reaction. She didn't regret it, but once the erection faded and reality set in, would he?

She was beginning to think he'd already fallen asleep when he rolled toward her. He wrapped one large, protective arm over her waist and tugged her body against his. Curled against him, she found it harder to worry. With his warm breath on her neck, she snuggled into the pillows and gave in to sleep.

Seven

Things in Kal's world were finally getting back to normal. At least, back to normal in terms of work. He'd returned to the office and Lana was in the dance studio with her team and performing in the luaus with them again. Nanny Sonia had started. She was the fifth nanny they interviewed and came highly recommended. Akela was instantly drawn to the older woman and the choice was easy to make.

So far, she was amazing, working happily with their strange hours. Even though they hadn't originally asked for a live-in caretaker, that was where they'd ended up. Once Kal and Lana were working again at all hours, it was just easier for Sonia to move into the guest room. It was next door to the nursery and had an en suite bathroom so she had plenty of her own space.

At home, things weren't *quite* the same. At least not

since the night they'd given in to their desire for each other. Looking back, he couldn't quite figure out how it happened, but he refused to regret it even though he knew he should. It was a night he'd never forget. How could he? His best friend—the one with the fist bumps and reluctant hugs—had given herself to him in a way he'd never imagined possible. Or maybe he had, which was why he'd kept his distance.

The last thing done for the night, Kal decided to head home. Normally he would put in a few more hours walking the resort and making sure the guests were all happy. Lately he'd just rather go. Even with the situation being different, he found that he looked forward to the end of his day more than he had when he was a bachelor. There was actually someone waiting for him at home. A houseful of someones.

It hadn't taken him long, but he found he missed those chubby cheeks and that toothless grin while he was at the office. That must be why people always put pictures of their family on their desk. He'd never understood that before, but he was considering it now. He found he was also missing Lana. They'd spent more time together than ever before, but it wasn't enough. The more he had with her, it seemed like the more he wanted. It was a dangerously slippery slope, but a part of him was tempted to see where it would lead.

That night, when he walked in the front door of the house, he wasn't sure what he expected to find, but what he got was a hell of a lot more.

Christmas had arrived in Maui.

In the great room, a huge Christmas tree was placed in front of the picture window. It was decked out in a rainbow of ornaments, lights and tinsel. A silver star shone on the top. Between the tree and the pine garland that went across the fireplace mantel, the house was thick with the fresh scent of real, imported Norfolk pine from the mainland.

Four stockings hung beneath the pine garland, one for each of them, including Nanny Sonia. The coffee table had a festive poinsettia runner and bowls of sparkling ornaments and peppermint candies. There were lights and candles all around the room, and festive Christmas music playing in the background.

Kal wasn't entirely sure what to say. He didn't own any Christmas decorations. This was his first Christmas in the house and he hadn't given much thought to the holidays with everything else going on. It was such a busy month at the resort he was more concerned with decorating the hotel and pleasing his guests than worrying about his own place. Who would see it aside from him anyway?

"You're home!" Lana said as she came out of the kitchen and spied him, dumbstruck by the front door.

"I am. Is this our house?" he asked. "It looks a little like our house, but not really. Now it looks more like the North Pole than Hawaii."

Lana beamed at his words. "It does, doesn't it?"

"Where did all this come from?"

"The store. I just realized that this was going to be Akela's first Christmas and I wanted it to be nice. It's also our first Christmas together, so I thought people might think it odd if we didn't decorate at least a little bit. I had some free time this afternoon, so I went crazy at the home store."

"It looks great," Kal said. He listened and heard Akela babbling in the kitchen over the crooning sounds of Bing Crosby on the wireless surround-sound system. "What are you all doing in there?"

"We're baking cookies." Lana reached for his hand and pulled him into the kitchen.

Akela was sitting in her high chair with a bottle of juice and a scattering of Cheerios. Sonia was pulling a tray of just-baked cookies out of the oven.

"Are those chocolate chip?" Kal asked, his mouth starting to water involuntarily as the smell hit him.

"Yes," Sonia said brightly. "It's my grandmother's recipe. We've also baked white chocolate macadamia nut cookies, sugar cookies, coconut snowballs and fudge."

"Wow," Kal said. He reached over and snatched a cooling cookie from one of the wire racks and shoved it in his mouth. It tasted like gooey, melting chocolate butter heaven, if that was even a thing, and it should be. "I love cookies."

The holidays had always been a big deal with his family, but like most things, they were more traditionally Hawaiian than mainland Christmas. There was always kalua pork in the imu, lomi salmon, coconut haupia for dessert, and Santa or *Kanakaloka*, wearing flip-flops and his best Hawaiian shirt.

He did get a taste for more Americanized Christmas from his father, however. His father was born and raised in upstate New York before he joined the navy and ended up stationed in Hawaii. While his father was happy to fall in love with a Hawaiian girl and escape the hellish New York winters once and for all, there were things he still missed. He would go shopping at the PX for things he couldn't normally get here, like gingerbread cookies and peppermint candy canes.

More of it had made its way into stores over the last twenty years, but when Kal was a kid, those special treats had been his favorites. Especially the cookies.

Lana looked at him with a frown. "I never knew you liked cookies."

"Who doesn't like cookies?" he replied, snatching another off the rack.

"Well, I mean, I didn't know you were so fond of them. You've never been big on desserts when we've gone out."

"That's because most restaurants don't offer cookies. Especially warm ones." He reached out for a third, but Lana smacked his hand.

"Pace yourself."

Sonia giggled and continued to scoop another batch of dough onto the cookie sheet.

Lana looked down at her watch. "You know what, Sonia, you were supposed to go off duty half an hour ago. Tonight is your weekday evening off."

Once they decided that Sonia would be a live-in nanny, they arranged for her to have all day Saturday and Wednesday nights off. There weren't luaus on either day, so Lana or Kal could be home with Akela when she was gone.

Sonia turned to the kitchen clock in surprise and dusted her hands off on her apron. "You're right! I have book club tonight. I'd better get cleaned up and get out of here or I'll be late. Do you mind if I take some of the fudge for the ladies?"

"Not at all."

Sonia quickly made up a small plate of fudge squares and hurried to her room to get ready to leave.

Once they were alone, Kal and Lana worked together to clean up the last of the baking stuff and put the cookies and candies in airtight containers.

"Those cookies are great, but I think I need more than that to eat tonight."

"You're right. It's about time for Akela's dinner, too. If you can feed her one of those jars of baby food, I'll see what I can find in the pantry to make for our dinner."

Kal looked at her with unmasked surprise. "You're going to cook?"

Lana crossed her arms over her chest in irritation. He couldn't help noticing the way she cocked her hip and pressed her breasts tight against her shirt with the movement. Even though he'd seen Lana perform in a lot less clothing, this was better. He liked seeing the casual side of her—her womanly curves evident, but hidden away like a treasure he ached to seek out and uncover again. Most of the time at work, she was in performance mode or strict choreographer mode. Neither was much fun to be around, frankly.

"Watch it, mister." Lana smirked and turned her back on him to look in the refrigerator.

He'd be lying to himself if he said he didn't also like her in sassy wife mode. In their home, with her hair up in a messy bun and a clean, fresh face. In their bed, with her cheeks flushed and her eyes glassy with desire. As she bent over to look in the fridge, the clinging yoga pants she wore after finishing dance rehearsal that morning highlighted one of her best assets. Those hips were carved by Mother Nature to be cupped by his palms. He could still feel the silk of her skin against his, making his hands tingle with the memory of touching her.

Things between them had been a little awkward since they had sex. They'd both tried to dance around the issue and deal with everything *but* that. It was easy to ignore the tension and ignore each other when the baby needed to be fed and work beckoned. He didn't want it to be that way. He didn't know how long this situation would last, but he wanted the best of both worlds—the mind-blowing sex and the amazing friendship they'd had before. It made sense that they should enjoy the physical pleasures…they were married, weren't they? It shouldn't cost them the easygoing friendship he enjoyed. He didn't understand why one had to affect the other.

Maybe tonight, after Akela went down for the night and Sonia was out for the evening, they could talk about it. That was one thing they hadn't really had the opportunity to do since it happened.

And maybe, if he was lucky, she'd let him make love to her again.

Lana had to admit that having Sonia around made a world of difference. She felt better being back at work and didn't pass out with exhaustion the minute her head hit the pillow. Akela was another matter. Sonia kept that baby busy. They went on walks, played peekaboo, read books and had plenty of tummy time. After a bath and a quick change into her pajamas, now it was the baby who was out cold when she laid her out on the crib mattress.

"Was she fussy?" Kal asked as she came back into the living room.

"Not at all. She's already asleep. Between Sonia and the lavender bubble bath, she doesn't stand a chance."

Kal nodded and looked at her with the same dark eyes she'd fallen prey to the other night. "Come sit with me."

Lana was considering cleaning up after dinner, but it didn't take much to convince her to put that off. Kal was sitting on the sofa near the gas fireplace. It was rare that you needed one in Hawaii, but with the Christmas lights twinkling and the candles around the room flickering, it added a bit of ambience.

Kal had changed out of his work suit. He was in a pair of jeans and an old surfing T-shirt she'd never seen before. The way it clung to his broad shoulders and large arms, he probably had bought the thing in high school. It looked good on him, though. He was handsome as always in his power suits, but when Kal had jeans on, it meant it was time for fun, not time for work. That was the time she enjoyed the most.

Lana settled onto the couch beside him and accepted the glass of wine he offered. "The house looks beautiful," he said. "I mean it. I spent a fortune having an interior decorator put this place together, and in a single day you made it feel more like a home than it ever has."

She swallowed her sip of wine, surprised by his words. "Thank you. I'm glad you like it. It's just a few things. I didn't want to take over your whole house, but I wanted to make a good Christmas for Akela's first."

"It's your house, too, Lana. If you want to decorate the whole place, I'll give you my credit card and you can go crazy. This is a special occasion."

Lana tried to shrug that off. They both knew this wasn't a real marriage. Sex hadn't changed that any more than their vows had. "I'd hold off on buying a commemorative ornament, since we won't make it to our second Christmas."

Kal sighed. "Other people don't know that, though." He stretched and wrapped an arm around her shoulder. "At the very least you have to admit that this is quite a romantic setup with the lights and the fire."

"It is." She hadn't thought of it that way at the time she put it all up, but she hadn't envisioned snuggling on the couch with him like this, either.

"It's a shame you didn't hang any mistletoe."

Lana stiffened. Apparently they needed to have the discussion they'd avoided since they had sex. If Kal was under the impression that it was going to happen again, he was wrong. She'd let herself get wrapped up in the moment, falling under the spell of the fantasy they'd crafted for appearances, but she couldn't let it continue. She knew her heart and how easily she could fall for Kal. That would only end in heartbreak for her.

He would walk away from this whole thing like it was just another adventure they'd shared without carrying any feelings for her. He might want her physically while they were together, but he didn't want to be with her beyond this arrangement. Lana knew that. Sex just led to thoughts of a future they wouldn't have. She couldn't do that to herself. "I don't think mistletoe is the best idea, Kal."

"Sometimes the worst ideas are the most fun, Lana."

She turned to pull away from the arm that was cradling her to his side. "Kal...that night between us was..."

"Amazing?"

"A mistake," she corrected. "I think we both let this fake relationship get the best of us, but it can't continue. It just clouds our friendship with all these physical complications."

"Physical complications? What's an orgasm or two between friends?"

Lana ignored his smirk. "I'm serious, Kal. You might be the master of sex without strings, but we've got a lot of history together. I don't want things to get complicated. Our friendship is so important to me. I don't want to compromise it."

Kal's face grew uncharacteristically serious as he reached out and caressed her cheek. "The last thing on this earth I'll do is hurt you, Lana. If you're not attracted to me—"

"I didn't say that," she interrupted.

"Then you *are* attracted to me," he said with a mischievous twinkle returning to his eye.

Lana sighed. This conversation was not going the way she'd expected it to. Was Kal truly attracted to her? She couldn't imagine it. "The point is not if we're into each other."

"I think that is the point, Lana. Listen, I know that we're not compatible in the long run. We want different things out of life and relationships. But this is a special opportunity we've been given to enjoy our time together. We're married. We might as well enjoy some of the perks. I think it will carry over out of the bedroom and make our relationship seem more authentic in the eyes of others."

"And when it's over?" Lana asked. Were they just supposed to go back to the way things were before? Was that even possible?

"And when it's over, it's over. You go back to hunting for your soul mate and I regain my crown as the most eligible bachelor on Maui."

Lana shook her head. She knew she couldn't just go back to looking for another guy the way she had done before. Being with Kal might have very well ruined her for every other man. But right now she was more worried about how the two of them moved forward together. "So our friendship just goes back to the way it was before all this? I don't see how that's possible."

Kal sighed and sat forward in his seat, pinning her with his dark gaze. "Lana, the minute you proposed to me, our friendship changed. It will never be exactly the way it was. When we married, when we kissed, when we had sex…all those things changed it. But that's okay. Relationships aren't meant to be static. They evolve. We might as well enjoy where our friendship is right now while it lasts, because it will evolve to something else in the future. It's not better or worse, it's just the way life is.

"And no," he continued, "I'm not offering you that white-picket-fence future you want when this charade is all over. It's what you want and it's what you deserve. One day you'll find it, but you and I both know it won't be with me. You know me better than anyone else, so you know exactly what I'm offering and what I'm not. So why can't we enjoy where our friendship has evolved to right now? Indulge in the physical while it lasts?"

Kal very nearly had her convinced. It all sounded good in theory. Keeping her emotions out of the situation would be hard, but maybe she could do it. He was right—her eyes were wide-open where he was concerned.

"Lana, you can't tell me that in all our years of friendship, you hadn't been the tiniest bit curious about what it would be like to make love to me. I'll be honest and say I thought about it. A lot."

"Kal!" Lana complained.

"We're being honest here," he insisted. "Tell me that you never once fantasized about me."

Lana tried not to squirm under his heated gaze. Of course she'd fantasized about him. She wasn't about to admit to how much, though. "I can't. You know full well I can't say that."

"Okay, then tell me you didn't enjoy the other night."

This time Lana frowned. "You know I can't say that, either." It was incredibly evident she'd had a good time. If she hadn't worried about waking the baby, she would've screamed the house down.

"Okay, then." His hand reached out to stoke her bare arm. The caress sent a shudder through her whole body that would've betrayed any lie she told about not wanting him. "So let's just stop stressing out about the whole thing and just do what feels right for us. If that means making love every night…" He let the words hang in the air between them. "…then so be it."

That was certainly a tempting offer. The idea of spending the upcoming weeks getting to know every inch of Kal's hard body was a benefit of this arrangement that she'd never anticipated. It might not be smart but was definitely tempting. "You're working pretty hard to convince me to sleep with you again, Kal."

A smile curled his lips. "Harder than I normally have to work, I assure you."

"Good. You should have to work for it. All those women falling all over you just inflates your ego."

"You're always there to take me back down a notch. It's a bit of a turn-on, I have to say. Most things about you turn me on." Kal looked at her with desire hooding his eyes as he spoke. She never imagined he'd look at her that way and yet here he was, talking about her as if she were some kind of sex siren. "What do you say we retire to the bedroom for the evening and I help you get on Santa's naughty list?"

Lana leaned in close, considering his offer. If he really did like it when she was sassy, she'd be sure he got a good dose of it. "Hmm…" she said thoughtfully as she ran her hand over the stubble of his cheek and down the tight fabric of his T-shirt to his bulging biceps. "That sounds like a nice offer, but I've got a better one."

"What's that?" he said with eager interest.

"I cooked dinner, so you need to clean the kitchen. That's how marriage works. And when you're done, then maybe," she said seductively, letting her thumb brush over his bottom lip, "I'll let you earn some coal for your stocking."

Kal wrapped his arms around her waist and tugged her into his lap. "How about we earn the coal and then I clean the kitchen? Does the order really matter as long as it all gets done?"

Lana considered his counter offer with a smile. "I suppose not."

In one swift movement, Kal stood up from the couch with Lana in his arms and started carrying her toward the master bedroom. She bit back a yelp of surprise, hoping not to wake the baby. She clung to his neck and buried her face in his soft, worn surfing T-shirt as they went down the hallway. The scent of him permeated the fabric, and once she drew him into her lungs, her whole nervous system seemed to spring to life.

She was instantly ready for him. As much as she had resisted this mentally, her body was on board with getting as much of Kal as she possibly could before all of this was over. Her nipples were tight against her top and her breasts ached for him to touch them. She felt her core turn to warm liquid when he looked down at her and smiled. One time together was all it had taken to train Lana's body. This time she was ready without so much as a kiss.

Kal sat her at the edge of the bed, and she wasted no time pulling off her top. They both quietly and swiftly cast aside their clothes. He pulled away long enough to shut and lock the bedroom door in case Nanny Sonia came home early, and then he crawled onto the bed beside her.

He immediately drew her body against his, and her upper thigh made contact with the firm length of his need. Kal groaned aloud, and then caught himself. He sat still, not even breathing for a moment, to see if he'd awoken Akela. When he realized it was still safe, he pressed his lips to hers, smothering any more sounds.

They came together quickly in a tangle of legs and blankets. Lana gasped silently as he filled her. She clung to him even as he rolled onto his back and brought her with him. She flipped onto her knees, bracing herself with her hands as she found herself astride him. Kal pulled her down against his chest until her face was buried in his neck, and then he started moving slowly beneath her.

It was an agonizing journey to release, with each moment slow and deliberate. They moved silently together in the dim moonlight of the bedroom, the quiet gasps and heavy breathing sounding like a cacophony in each other's ears. Their bodies tensed and flexed together, Lana sensing he was getting close by the rapid beat of his heart and the press of his fingers into her hips.

When her release came, she buried her face in his throat and nearly sobbed as the waves of pleasure rocked through her. Kal bit tentatively into the thick muscle of her shoulder as he held her still and fought to hold himself back, but he was lost. The flutter of her orgasm coaxed one from him, and he poured into her, his mouth agape with unexpressed feelings.

Lana rolled off Kal onto her side of the bed and took a deep breath to recover. Even their quick, frantic lovemaking was amazing.

She was on the verge of closing her eyes and drifting off to sleep when she felt Kal's weight shift on the bed. When she looked up, he had stood and was tugging his clothes back on.

"Where are you going?" she asked.

"A deal is a deal," he insisted. "I'm going to clean the kitchen. And when I'm done, I'm coming back in here with that container of chocolate chip cookies."

Lana wrinkled her nose. "What are you going to do with a whole container?" He was going to make himself sick eating all of them.

"I don't know yet," Kal admitted. "But even if all I do is line your beautiful, naked body with them, lick melted chocolate from your nipples and eat them off you one at a time, it will be the greatest meal I've ever had."

Eight

You need to come home. Now.

Kal frowned at his cell phone and the disconcerting text he'd just gotten from Lana. Is Akela okay? Did social services come back already?

Everyone is fine. But you're going to want to come home and see who's showed up. Note: it's not social services this time.

He was usually in the office for another hour or so, but he knew better than to ignore this message from Lana. He slipped his phone into his pocket and walked out of his office. "I'm heading home," he said to his assistant, Jane, outside the door. "I don't think I'll be back. Something came up."

Jane looked at him with concern lining her face.

He may have stopped staying late, but he still wasn't the type who left in the middle of the day. "Is everything okay, sir?"

"I think so. Just unannounced visitors from the sound of it. Call the night manager on his cell phone if something happens before he arrives."

He slipped out and got into his convertible. It only took a few minutes to drive around the property to his house, but the suspense was killing him. When he arrived, there weren't many clues, either. Only nanny Sonia's car and the rental SUV were parked out front. Whoever had arrived must have come by taxi.

It wasn't until he walked in the door that he realized who had invaded. It all made sense now. His brother had flown over from Oahu.

Mano was sitting on the couch with his Seeing Eye dog, Hōkū, at his side. A thin, yet pregnant woman with long brown hair was holding Akela on her lap and cooing at her. Nanny Sonia stood out of the way as though she didn't want to intrude on the family gathering but didn't want to be thought neglectful of her charge, either. And then there was Lana, who turned to look at him with an expression of pure panic lighting her dark eyes.

"Honey," she said in an overly sweet voice she never ever used when she spoke to him. "Look who's here to spend Christmas with us."

Christmas was three days away. They weren't just visiting. They were unannounced holiday houseguests.

Everyone turned and looked in Kal's direction except his brother, who had on his dark Ray-Ban sunglasses. His attention was focused on the woman beside him, who Kal assumed was Mano's fiancée, Paige.

He tried not to look dismayed by their arrival, pasting an excited smile on his face. He ensured that he matched the tone with his voice so Mano couldn't call him out for it.

"Wow. I didn't know you two were coming here for the holidays. This is such a great surprise. If you'd told me, I would've reserved our best suite for you at the hotel."

Everyone stood up to greet him. Mano made his way over with Hōkū at his side. He hugged his brother and took a step back. "You almost sold me on that," he said, speaking low. "And of course I didn't tell you. I want to be here at your new home, getting to know your bride and niece, not tucked away in that boring old hotel."

The smirk on Kal's face said everything. That phone call announcing his sudden marriage had sent up warning flags that even his busy brother couldn't ignore. Mano was using Christmas as an excuse to come down here and spy on him. Sneaky little weasel.

Well, two could play at that game. "Mano, you've met Lana before, haven't you?"

Mano turned expectantly and Lana quickly stepped forward to take his hand. "It's good to see you again, Mano."

He laughed and pulled her in for a hug. "There's no handshakes in this family. You'd better get used to that now before you meet the rest of them. Congratulations to you and Kal. He didn't let on that you two were serious."

Kal ignored his brother's pointed tone. "Well, you of all people know how quickly love can strike. In two weeks' time, you and Paige went from strangers to lovers to an engaged couple. Are you going to introduce us to the lovely lady whom I presume is your new fiancée?"

"Of course. Everyone, this is Paige Edwards."

Paige handed the baby back to Sonia and stepped forward, smiling uncomfortably at the strangers who were now her family. Kal didn't know what he was expecting of the woman who captured his brother's heart, but it wasn't what he'd gotten. She was tall and thin, pale and nervous-looking. But there was a light in her eyes that Kal immediately recognized as love and affection for his brother, and that was enough for him. He was excited to learn more about her and find out what had drawn the two of them together while she was vacationing in Hawaii.

"It's nice to finally meet Mano's brother, and now, his sister-in-law!" she said. "He talks so much about you."

"Does he, now?"

Mano placed a hand on his fiancée's rounding belly. "And this, we found out for certain yesterday, is our daughter, Eleu Aolani Bishop."

There was another round of cheers and congratulations. Kal was pleased they'd chosen their mother's name for the baby's middle name. She would love that. "There's so much to celebrate," Kal said. "If you'd told me you were coming, I'd have been prepared with champagne and food in the refrigerator." They really didn't have much but some snacks and baby food. Thank goodness he had a second guest room and room service at his fingertips. It wasn't as well appointed as Sonia's room, but it was somewhere for them to sleep with no notice.

"I'm sorry, Kal," Paige said, nudging Mano's shoulder. "I didn't like the idea of dropping in unannounced, but he insisted you two do it all the time."

"All the time, as in never once in all these years," Kal countered with a grin.

"Mano!" Paige chided, and smacked him playfully on the arm. "You tricked me into imposing on your family." Mano just shrugged, refusing to look guilty for what he'd done.

"You're not imposing. Really. The more the merrier at Christmas, right?" Kal looked to Lana for support.

"Absolutely. I was just telling him the other night how excited I was for Akela's first Christmas and our first Christmas as a married couple. It will be so much more memorable with family here to share it with us. This is your first Christmas together, too, right?"

"It is," Paige confirmed with a beaming smile. "We have plenty to celebrate."

"Mano," Kal said, "I'll show you to the guest room and we can carry your bags back there. Ladies, why don't you decide where you'd like to go for dinner tonight? I'll have some food delivered in the meantime so we aren't eating crackers for Christmas Eve."

Mano gripped Hōkū's lead and followed him to where their bags and a stack of unfamiliar gifts were waiting by the door. Kal picked the bags up and started through the house to the spare bedroom. Once they reached it, he set the bags out of the walkway. "The bed is here on the left just when you come into the room. The bathroom is just past the closet on the right."

Mano just nodded passively with Hōkū panting at his side. "Great. Thanks for putting us up on such short notice."

Since they were alone, Kal turned to look at his

brother. "You mean no notice. Are you here just to spy on me?"

"No. I'm not just here to spy on you. I'm here to introduce you to Paige, to meet your new wife and spend the holidays with my brother." He smiled wide. "And to spy on you."

"You haven't told anyone in the family about this, have you?"

"Of course not," Mano said with a frown. "You told me not to. That doesn't mean I'm not going to fly over here and see what the hell is really going on after social services calls me with a lengthy interview to make sure this is all legit."

"And what did you tell them?"

"That you two are madly in love, of course."

Kal narrowed his gaze at his brother, although his annoyed expression drew no reaction, since he couldn't see it. Instead he crouched down to give his brother's service dog—a friendly chocolate-brown Lab—a good scratch behind the ears. "Good, because it's true. You're going to be disappointed, brother. There's nothing scandalous here to find. Just a happy, newly married couple caring for their niece for a few weeks."

Mano stood for a moment, studying his brother's words. He couldn't rely on visual cues, so he was quick to notice tone, word choice and physical response. It made it harder than hell to lie to him, but Kal had gotten better at it over the last ten years. Considering everything going on, Mano was the worst person to crash their fake marriage, but also the only one he'd dare trust with the truth. Hopefully he wouldn't have to spill his guts before the holiday was over.

"Okay, then." Mano seemed satisfied. For now.

Standing back up, Kal said, "Let's go back to the living room and see where the ladies chose to eat tonight."

Mano nodded to him. "Can you believe we both have ladies? Us? The Bishop Bachelors have finally been tamed."

"A great loss to the women of the islands, I must say."

Kal's brother was right. At least where Mano was concerned. Kal wasn't exactly tamed by love, although his wild nights out would cease until he was officially divorced. He might not be in love with Lana for real, but he wasn't about to cheat on her, either. Mano had really tripped and fallen in love, for sure. Kal had never seen or heard his brother as entranced with a woman as he was with Paige. The time they were apart earlier had nearly destroyed Mano. He'd chased Paige all the way to San Diego to propose and ask her to move to Oahu to be with him. That was serious stuff for a man who'd had a sporadic string of affairs over the years but insisted he wouldn't settle down and be a burden on a woman.

Paige didn't seem burdened. She seemed pretty happy. When they came back into the living room and her eyes fell on Mano, her face lit up. Suddenly she was more beautiful than she had been before, and Kal understood more about his brother's love for her. It radiated out of her.

It made Kal wonder, marriage or no, if he'd ever have a woman look at him that way. He'd never wanted that before—it came with a level of commitment he couldn't give—but suddenly he had a longing for it that he'd never expected. Had he made the wrong decision keeping himself emotionally isolated? Mano certainly seemed happier than he had been alone.

"What have we decided for tonight?" Kal asked, trying not to let the thoughts of his parents' death creep in and ruin his mood.

"Well, Paige has never been to Maui," Lana explained, "so I thought we'd go to your rooftop restaurant. It's hard to beat the view or the food."

"Great choice." Unlike Mano, who put a pair of penthouse suites at the top of his resort, Kal had opted for an exclusive restaurant. With wall-to-wall windows, it had a three-hundred-sixty-degree view. To the east, lush green mountains and to the west, the ocean and views of nearby Lanai and Molokai.

"I told her we might even see whales tonight."

Kal nodded. "That's true. This time of year, the humpback whales are just arriving from Alaska. By February, the waters between here and Lanai will have the densest population of humpbacks in the world. It's an amazing sight. Hopefully you'll see at least one while we eat. Why don't you two get settled in and relax, and I'll make a call to the restaurant to hold the best table?"

Paige nodded and joined Mano to head back to their room. Kal noticed the way she clung to him, guiding him gently without dragging him around. He hadn't been sure his brother would ever find a woman who could get through his defenses, but Paige was obviously the love of his life.

Turning to look at Lana and her concerned frown, he wondered if they'd be able to pull off a relationship that convincing over the next few days.

Lana couldn't remember the last time she'd lain on the beach and enjoyed a little sun. It was the kind of indulgent rest and relaxation she rarely allowed herself. Having Kal's brother and Paige visit was the perfect excuse. Tonight she was performing the last luau before Christmas, but she had hours before she had to be ready.

Turning her head to look at Paige, Lana reached for the sunblock. "I think you'd better put more of this on. You don't want to be burned and miserable on Christmas."

Paige sat up on her chaise and accepted the bottle. "My skin just isn't meant for the tropics. I've taken to wearing SPF fifty just to walk from one side of the resort to the other. No major burns yet, though. I wish I had beautiful brown skin like yours."

Lana smiled. "Thank you. I think you have a lovely complexion, though. So creamy and even. I think women always want what they don't have."

"You're right. I've wanted curves all my life and now that I have this baby belly and pregnancy breasts, I'm not so sure. This isn't what I had in mind."

"You'll have a beautiful daughter when it's over. Maybe she'll end up with Mano's coloring."

Paige stiffened and turned to look over her shoulder to where the brothers were playing with Hōkū and Akela in the surf. "I thought Kal would've told you this, but Mano isn't the baby's father. At least not biologically. In every other way, he's convinced the child is his."

Lana perked up in her seat. "Oh. No, he didn't tell me. You're very lucky, then. Mano seems absolutely smitten with you and his baby. I had no idea from the way he talked about his daughter."

Paige nodded. "I am the luckiest woman on the

planet. You must know what that feels like. I can't imagine being so in love that you would just run off one day and elope without telling anyone. That's so romantic, like Romeo and Juliet or something. With a happier ending."

"He's amazing," Lana said. She didn't have to lie to Paige about that, because it was true. Kal was amazing in every way. That was part of the problem of having him for a best friend. No matter how hard she tried, she knew she couldn't find a man like him and wouldn't be able to have him for herself. She wasn't in Kal's league.

There was no sense in letting herself fall for Kal, no matter how he smirked handsomely at her or treated her like a princess. He might be attracted to her, and keen to continue their physical relationship while they were married, but it wouldn't last. He'd said as much. She knew he didn't really want to get married and she wouldn't be the one to change his mind about the convention.

Both women turned back to the brothers. They hadn't opted for swimsuits, but they were both in T-shirts with their pants rolled up to walk barefoot in the water. Kal had Akela in his arms. Occasionally he would dip down and let the cool ocean water tickle her toes until she squealed, and then he'd stand up again and give her kisses on her chubby baby cheeks. Hōkū splashed around happily, his tail wagging so hard his whole rear end wiggled from the force of it.

They were a handsome pair, both brothers tall and lean with thick, dark brown, almost black hair. They both had lazy beards growing in from skipping a day or two of shaving, making them look more alike than ever before. They were a hard duo to resist as they played with a dog and a baby.

Akela had gotten Kal wrapped around her finger in no time. Lana hadn't been so sure how this would go, since he wasn't much of a kid person and never wanted his own, but he was whupped. She noticed that sometimes even when Sonia was around, he'd take the baby and give her a break just to play with her and hear her infectious baby giggle. The big, important hotelier was a huge softie under those expensive suits. All that baby girl had to do was push out her little bottom lip or bat her full, dark eyelashes and Kal was tripping over himself to make her happy. Kind of how he did with Lana.

The difference was that the baby didn't know that she didn't get to keep Kal, and Lana did. She wished she was ignorant enough to enjoy the time with him that way.

"Paige! Lana!" Kal called, and pointed out at the water. "Come quick!"

The women got up and jogged through the sand to where the boys were standing. "What is it?" Paige asked.

"The humpbacks are breaching. Just wait for it."

The two couples gathered on the shore and waited for the whale to make its next appearance. Five seconds later, a great gray mass leaped from the water and came back down with a huge splash.

Paige gasped and clung to Mano's side. "Oh, wow," she whispered. "It's incredible. I wish you could see it," she added softly. There was a sadness in her voice that Lana understood. She wanted the man she loved to enjoy the moment as much as she did. Kal had told her that his brother tried not to dwell too much on losing his vision. People traveled from all over the globe to see the sights that were just out his window, but he was unable to see them. If Mano let himself wallow in those thoughts, he'd probably never get through the day.

"I don't need to see it," he said as he nuzzled her ear with his nose. "I experience it through you, *pelelehua*."

Lana tried not to melt on the spot listening to the two of them. His pet name for her was butterfly. So sweet. To avoid intruding on their moment, she moved to Kal's side and he put his free arm around her shoulder.

"Watch, Akela," he said, as though the infant could follow along with what they were seeing. "See that tail come up out of the ocean? And that little cloud of misty water shoot up? That's the whale breathing."

A few minutes later, one of the whales breached again and Lana felt her chest tighten. She'd seen these whales every season when they returned to Maui to have their calves in the warm waters. It was beautiful and exciting, but she'd never really given it all that much thought, much less stood transfixed on the beach and watched it happen like a tourist.

Somehow it meant more to do it here with Kal and Akela. With her brother-in-law and future sister-in-law. It felt like she was sharing the moment with family, not just her friends. With her family as it was, it was something she'd never really had. As she watched the back of a whale arch up, then slip beneath the waves with a small calf by its side, she felt a similar sinking in her gut.

She was getting too attached to this life they were building just for show. All this time she'd been worried about the sex, but that wasn't the issue. The sex was great. But she also liked having dinner with Kal at the end of the day and listening to him sing old Hawaiian folk songs to Akela while he gave her a bath. She enjoyed waking up to a mug of hot coffee he'd made for her and rolling over in the night to feel the warmth of his body near to hers.

It was like her dream of a family was coming true, and yet it was the simple things that were getting to her. They were the moments that she would miss the most when all this was over. The whole wedding had been her idea, but she was starting to regret it. It was possible that she could've gotten custody of Akela without all this, but now…? How was she supposed to go back to her life the way it was before? Living out of a hotel room, eating out every night and dating one loser after the next held almost no appeal to her now. Not when she compared it to sharing a home with Kal, cooking dinner for both of them and taking time away from her job to have an actual life.

It might not be a *real* life, but it was all she had. And the longer this charade went on, it was all she wanted. Not just a marriage and a family, but *this* marriage and *this* family. She wanted the sweet, tender romance she saw between Mano and Paige. They had come from two different worlds and yet their lives had meshed together so well. Was it possible that she and Kal could have that for themselves?

Lana took a deep breath and dismissed all those thoughts. She'd promised Kal that this would be a simple arrangement for the sole purpose of getting guardianship of her niece. There wasn't supposed to be any kind of entanglements, physical or emotional. Physical entanglements were a problem almost immediately, but she knew she had to hold back when it came to her emotions. Getting attached to Kal was a recipe for heartache.

As she clung to him, Kal leaned in to plant a kiss on Akela's forehead and then one on Lana's lips. He looked down at her with an excited smile and a light in his eyes and Lana knew instantly that it was too late.

She had made the mistake of falling in love with her husband.

Nine

Kal had spent the last three Christmas Eves with Lana. It was their unofficial tradition, although this year would be decidedly different from the previous ones. The twists would be the addition of his family and Akela. The constants would be Lana and sushi. Traditions had to mean something.

He and Mano drove up the coast to pick up the large order of sushi from the same place where he'd celebrated his wedding day with Lana. The big, traditional Hawaiian Christmas meal would be tomorrow, courtesy of the hotel cooks. Lana and Paige had spent part of the morning working on a couple fun desserts that they wouldn't tell the men about. Honestly Kal would be just as happy to find another container of those chocolate chip cookies that he'd missed, but he was curious to see what the ladies would come up with, too.

Paige had more American ideas about the holiday, so maybe there would be a treat he'd never tried before that could rival the cookies.

As they pulled back up at the house, Mano reached for Kal's arm to halt him from getting out of the car. "Hey," he said. "I want to tell you something before we go inside."

Kal killed the engine and sat back in the seat. "Sure. What is it?"

His brother's expression was almost sheepish, a look he almost never—if ever—saw on him. "I wanted to apologize to you. You were right, I came down here just to see what kind of angle you were playing with the marriage bomb you dropped. I thought maybe the whole wedding scheme was just about getting the baby or that maybe Lana was from another country and trying not to get deported or something. I really wasn't sure. But spending the past few days with the two of you has convinced me that I was wrong to doubt you."

Kal stiffened. He needed to stop his brother from apologizing when he was right all along. "Mano—"

"No," Mano insisted. "I need to say it. You two really are amazing together. What's better than marrying your best friend, after all? You're happier than I remember you being since Mom and Dad died. You and Lana seem to really be in love and happy together, and I'm so glad for you."

Kal didn't know what to say. His brother was one of the most perceptive people he knew. He picked up on the little things. He was damn near a human lie detector test. But he was all wrong about him and Lana. That baffled him. Certainly they weren't good enough actors to pull the wool over Mano's eyes, but he truly believed that they were in love. What did his brother sense between them that Kal didn't?

He watched as his brother's expression grew more serious. "You were never the same after our folks died, Kal. It was like you were afraid to let someone get close just to lose her again. I did the same thing, but for different reasons, and now I know it's no way to live your life. You can't let fear rule you. I'm so glad that both of us figured that out before we ended up spending our lives all alone."

Kal couldn't respond to that, because this time it was painfully accurate. His brother had nailed the issue on the head and made him feel foolish for it. "We've got some great things ahead of us," he replied instead.

Mano smiled. "We do. Let's get in there and eat some sushi. That stuff smells amazing. I'm starving."

They went into the house together and laid out platters on the dining room table. There were California rolls, spicy tuna rolls, unagi eel rolls, crunchy tempura and smoked salmon rolls and an assortment of nigari, all artfully arranged by the *itamae*, or head sushi chef, at Sansei. They also had bowls of edamame, fried tofu, a cucumber salad and some teriyaki chicken for Paige.

Looking down at it all, Kal realized he shouldn't order sushi when he was hungry. It was a shame that Nanny Sonia was spending the next two days with her family. The four of them had their work cut out for them.

They gathered at the table with Akela in her high chair. Lana poured warm sake into cups, with a specially requested Sprite for Paige.

"Wow," Paige said as she took in the spread of food

in front of her. "I don't even know what half of this is, but it all looks wonderful. I think sushi for Christmas is a fun tradition, even if I can't eat much of it this year. It's different. I'm excited to try this."

"Do you want to steal it for our own?" Mano asked. "Make it a true Bishop family Christmas Eve tradition?"

"I think so. There's only so much turkey a girl can eat around the holidays."

"Turkey?" Mano frowned at her.

Lana laughed and turned to Paige. "We don't really do turkey for Christmas here," she explained. "It's all about the pork and seafood dishes."

Kal sat back and watched his new family chat while they ate. He'd really begun to like Paige, and the change in his brother was night and day. Lana fit right in, joking and laughing. It was something he never really expected to have, much less to enjoy. He'd always imagined himself and Mano as lone wolves—the Bishop Bachelors. Now there were wives and babies, holidays and gatherings. It was like he imagined things would've been if their parents hadn't died and derailed their lives. They'd almost gotten back on track.

Almost, if his relationship with Lana was more than temporary. Kal presumed he would enjoy time with his brother and Paige even when Lana was no longer his wife, but things would be different. Unbalanced. She would be off living her own life, Akela would be back with her mother, and Kal would be alone again.

For the first time in ten years, Kal balked at the idea of being alone. He was surprised at how quickly he'd gotten used to all this. What did he do with his evenings before he was having dinner with Lana and bathing Akela before bed? He was working all the time. He didn't miss that at all. The hotel was running just fine without him hovering over his staff every moment.

Kal shoved a spicy tuna roll in his mouth and chewed thoughtfully while the others continued to talk and eat. He didn't want to return to being a workaholic. He wasn't sure that the idea of marriage and family really suited him, but *this* marriage and *this* family were perfect in the moment.

That was the problem, he supposed. He liked it too much.

The holidays were drawing them all together in a way he hadn't anticipated, but he'd have to make a bigger effort to keep emotional distance from Lana when they were over. If his brother was picking up on some kind of connection between them, it meant that more was happening than they'd agreed to. That would have to be squashed before it got worse and feelings got hurt. Whether it was his feelings or hers, he wasn't sure.

"So, do we get to open presents tonight or in the morning?" Paige asked after they'd all stuffed themselves.

"We've always exchanged gifts on Christmas Eve," Lana said. "Is that okay with you?"

Paige nodded eagerly. "I don't think I can wait until morning. I'm like a kid when it comes to Christmas."

"Well, let's clean up and I'll get Akela ready for bed," Kal said as he stood up. "Then we can have some of the top-secret dessert you all made today and open a few gifts."

Kal scooped up the baby and took her into the bathroom for her nightly lavender bath. Fed, clean and in a pair of Christmas pajamas Lana had purchased with snowmen on them, he put her down for the night with promises of Santa coming in the morning—not that she really understood, of course.

By the time he returned to the living room, everyone had gathered there. The ladies presented their desserts—a tall red velvet cake with cream cheese icing and homemade peppermint marshmallows dipped in chocolate. Kal opted to put his marshmallow in his coffee, which was heavenly with the cake. He'd never had red velvet before and it was definitely a Christmas indulgence.

Paige went over to the tree first, sorting through the wrapped gifts and picking out a select few for everyone. Kal and Lana had made an emergency run the day after his brother arrived to get gifts for their unexpected guests. They'd shown up with a big bag of wrapped presents even though Kal and Mano rarely exchanged gifts. It had to be Paige's influence on him.

After a few minutes of frantic unwrapping, it was done for the night. Lana had gotten Kal a nice pair of ruby and gold cuff links and a bottle of his favorite scotch. Mano and Paige gave him a set of his favorite action movies on Blu-ray disc, a remote control drone and an ugly Christmas sweater with Santa on it.

Paige squealed so loudly over the emerald and diamond tennis bracelet that Mano bought her that Kal never did find out what she bought him. Eleu's birthstone would be an emerald unless she came early, and each stone in the bracelet was at least a carat. Kal would probably have squealed, too.

When it was all done, Kal turned to where Lana was sitting on the couch, pouting. "What's the matter?" he asked, knowing full well that she was mad he hadn't gotten her anything.

"Nothing," she said, not meeting his gaze.

"Did you think I forgot you?" he asked.

"Maybe. Of course, you've done a lot for me lately, so it's fine."

Kal reached into his back pocket and pulled out a set of car keys. He dangled them in front of her face, giving her a moment to process that they weren't the keys to his Jaguar or the rental Lexus. There was an unmistakable Mercedes logo on it.

Lana frowned at the keys for a moment. Then he watched it all click into place on her face. Her dark brown eyes grew wide; then she looked in panic from him, to the keys and back to him. "Are you messing with me?" she asked.

Kal dropped the keys into her hand. "Why don't you go look in the garage and see?"

Lana leaped up from the couch and dashed through the kitchen and laundry room to the garage door. They normally parked out front, so the garage was reserved for tools and the boat he never took out. But parked in the far bay was a sapphire-blue four-door Mercedes SUV.

"I thought I could return the Lexus to the rental place after Christmas," he said with his hands buried casually in his pockets.

Lana ran to the car, opening the door and sliding inside. The interior smelled of leather and new car, one of the best scents she could imagine. She ran her hands over the steering wheel and caressed the dashboard. "This is really mine?"

"Yes."

"It's not a lease? I don't have to take over payments?"

That would be cruel. "No, it's all yours, free and clear. Now you can drive Akela around in your own car and not get wet when it rains."

She just shook her head in disbelief. Finally she stepped out of the car and looked over Kal's shoulder to the doorway. "Do you two mind watching Akela while I take Kal for a spin?"

Paige grinned. "Not at all. You two have fun. Don't run over any reindeer out there."

Lana's heart was racing a mile a minute as she started the car and opened the garage door. She backed the SUV out of the driveway at a crawl, afraid that somehow she would ruin her new toy almost immediately. She couldn't believe a car this nice could really be hers.

She took her time getting a feel for the Mercedes as they drove around the resort property, and then she turned out onto the highway. They drove south along the western coast of Maui, past Lahaina toward the central part of the island. She finally pulled over at a high overlook where tourists usually stood with cameras and binoculars to watch the humpback whales. No one was out there this late on Christmas Eve, however.

"Do you like it?" Kal asked.

"Do I like it?" Lana repeated as she turned off the car. "Of course I like it. But it's too much, Kal. You've done so much for me lately, I didn't need to get a single thing for Christmas. The wedding, the nursery, the lawyer's fees, the rental car..."

"No more than you deserve."

She shook her head. She didn't feel like she deserved

all this. She felt naughty knowing she had broken the rules of their arrangement and he just didn't know it yet. What would he say when he found out she'd gone and fallen in love with him after he told her not to? Lana didn't need a luxury SUV, she needed a reality check.

Could anyone blame her, though? Whether or not Kal meant to, he was doing everything in his power to make her fall in love with him. She couldn't resist his charms. He'd gone from being her playboy best friend to a thoughtful and caring husband and father. When he was with Akela, her heart swelled with emotions watching them together. He was a skilled and tender lover, and a romantic at heart, even if he didn't know it or admit it to himself.

She was doomed.

Lana wasn't sure how she would ever be able to repay Kal for everything he'd done for her. Somehow the cuff links didn't seem like enough. She wanted to give him more, but she only had a few things to offer— her heart, her body and her soul. She'd gladly give him all three, although she knew he'd rather just have the body part. So she'd give him that, and he just wouldn't know he was getting the whole package.

Putting on the emergency brake, Lana turned to him. "While we're out here alone, I wanted to say thank you." Then she slipped her red cashmere sweater over her head and tossed it in the backseat.

Kal looked around the deserted highway for a moment with concern, then turned back to her. His gaze flickered over her red lace bra and then he licked his lips. "You're very welcome."

Lana tugged her skirt up her thighs, then crawled

over her new console to straddle his lap. The spacious leather seats provided enough room for her to sit there comfortably and wrap her arms around his neck.

Her lips met his without hesitation. She enjoyed kissing him more than almost anything else. He knew just how to kiss her without overwhelming her like some men did. His kisses were erotic and sweet, arousing her and bringing every possible nerve ending to attention. Tonight, the tastes of peppermint and cream cheese icing still lingered on his tongue, as though he were a second helping of their decadent dessert.

She put her everything into the kiss, pouring her disbelief, her gratitude, her love and her need for him into her touch. Kal's fingers gripped her hips, tugging the skirt higher until he had handfuls of bare flesh. He bit at his lip and groaned as she shifted her weight and made contact with the firm heat of his desire for her.

He tore his lips away from hers at last so he could bury his face in her cleavage. Kal licked at her nipples through the lace, teasing them with the rough fabric. Then he tugged the cups down until her breasts spilled out. He drew one nipple, then the other, into his mouth, teasing with his tongue until she gasped aloud. In the small cabin of the car, every noise seemed incredibly loud, but with just the two of them out here, she could make as much noise as she wanted to. No babies would wake up and no nannies or brothers would overhear.

"You are so beautiful," he murmured against her skin before he planted kisses on the inner curves of her breasts. "I don't know how I managed to resist you for the last three years." Kal's hand cupped one breast and squeezed it gently. "How in the hell am I supposed to just stop wanting you when all this is over?"

That was a good question. It was one Lana wasn't able to answer. If she knew how to flip off her emotions like a light switch, she would feel a lot better about her feelings for Kal. It wasn't going to be that easy, though. He might want her, but she was in love with him. That would be far harder to overcome. Like with all his other relationships, he would move on and forget about her in the arms of another woman. She didn't think that would work very well for her. Dating was a far-off prospect once the divorce was final.

"You'll find someone else to warm your bed," she whispered as she reached down and stroked him through his trousers. "Someone prettier or smarter or more interesting will distract you and then you'll wonder why you were attracted to me."

Kal stiffened beneath her touch, eventually reaching for her wrist and pulling her hand away. "Why would you say that?" he asked.

Lana looked at him and sighed. "Because it's true. It might not be the sexiest thing to say in the moment, but you and I both know that you'll move on from this like you always do. Me...this marriage...it will all become a fuzzy memory after a while. I recommend you do your best to study my body while you have the chance." She ground her hips into his lap, making his eyes roll back and a growl form in his throat.

"I might move on, but there's no way I'll forget you, Lana. I already know every curve of your body like the back of my hand. I know how you like to be touched. What makes you squirm. What makes you scream. That's ingrained in my brain for always."

Hearing those words from him was like a dream and a nightmare all at once. How could he say things like that, want her the way he did, but not have any feelings for her? Those were the kinds of things you said to a woman you wanted to be yours for always, but he had no intention of keeping her in his bed forever.

Lana would make herself crazy if she overthought this. She just needed to treasure the moment, treasure tonight, so she would have it in her memory long after he'd moved on without her. "Then make me scream now," she said.

Kal's jaw clenched and he exhaled loudly in response. Reaching down, he hit the button to recline the passenger seat. Lana moved back with him. The incline was just enough to lift her hips. He slipped his hands up under her skirt and felt for her panties. He clenched the fabric in his fist and gave a tug, ripping them from her hips.

Lana gasped in surprise. "In a hurry?" she asked.

"There's not enough room to maneuver. I'll buy you ten new pairs to replace them."

He shifted beneath her, undoing his pants and sliding them out of the way. With all the barriers gone, he sheathed in latex and found his home inside her, and she was ready for him. She shifted her weight back, taking him deeper with a sigh of contentment. Having her body wrapped around him in such an intimate way made her feel like, for that moment, Kal was all hers. With his ring on her finger and his need for her buried deep inside, it truly felt like they belonged to each other.

At the very least, she was his, even if he could never be hers.

Kal pressed his fingertips deep into the flesh of her hips and rocked her body back and forth. They moved together as the tension built and the windows of the Mercedes fogged up. Lana closed her eyes and tried to absorb every sensation of them together. The scents of leather and sex hung heavy in the air, and the sounds he made were like an arrow straight to her core. He was louder tonight, free to moan, free to whisper erotic words of encouragement when she moved just right.

Then he slipped his hand between them. His fingers sought out her moist center and stroked her there. With every thrust, he rubbed her most sensitive spot, urging her closer and closer to reaching her release. Her cries grew louder. His touch became harder. His hips rose off the seat of the car to pound into her body with the fury of need.

When Lana opened her eyes, Kal was watching her. His dark brown and gold gaze was fixed on her face, watching her every expression. He looked at her as though she were the sexiest, most desirable woman he'd ever seen. He didn't look away, even as his own release grew closer. In the moment, he wasn't closing his eyes and thinking of anything but her.

That put her over.

Bracing her hands on the driver's seat and the door, she thrust her hips hard against him and came undone. Her whole body shuddered with the force of her orgasm as it exploded inside her, her loud cries interrupted by her ragged, gasping breaths. "Oh, Kal," she said, nearly groaning his name as the pleasure continued to ripple through her body.

"Lana," he hissed between clenched teeth. He thrust hard into her from below, and then he lost it. His back arched up off the seat, his jaw dropping open. He shouted her name the second time as he poured into her.

He reached for Lana and pulled her down to lie against his chest as they both recovered. Kal wrapped his arms protectively around her and hugged her tight. She was happy to press her ear against the faint, dark curls of his chest hair and listen to the rapid sound of his heartbeat as it slowly returned to normal.

It felt so normal, so right to be in Kal's arms like this. She didn't want to imagine a time where the man she loved was out of her reach. But it was coming. Before she knew it, all of this would be over.

Ten

The phone rang and Lana lunged to answer it before it woke Akela from her nap. She didn't recognize the number. "Hello?"

"Hello. Lana?" a hesitant woman's voice replied. It sounded familiar and yet she couldn't place it either.

"This is she."

"This is Mele."

Lana felt a twinge of guilt at not knowing the sound of her own sister's voice, but it was different. She sounded…sober. Serious. Those were two things Mele rarely was. "Hi," Lana replied, not quite sure what to say to her. They hadn't spoken since before the arrest. At first, Lana had been too angry, then too concerned about Akela to try and contact her. Then, the drug program the judge sent her to had strict rules about communication with the outside, so Mele either couldn't call or hadn't felt the need to before now.

"How's Akela?" Mele asked in a small, quiet voice.

"She's doing great." Lana wasn't about to sugarcoat this. Her sister needed to know that her daughter was thriving outside the environment she'd lived in with Mele and Tua. "She's got a bottom tooth coming in."

"Really? Wow. Her first tooth." Mele sounded sad about missing her daughter's milestones. It was as though she cared. For Akela's sake, Lana hoped she truly did.

"What took you so long to check on her?" Lana asked, unable and unwilling to keep the cold tone from her voice. It had been almost a month. "She could've been in foster care all this time and you wouldn't have known."

"They told me she was with you, so I knew she was in good hands. I needed to focus on getting better for her."

"And how is that going?" Lana tried not to be pessimistic about her sister's recovery, but it wasn't easy to clean up. It took some addicts several rounds of treatment if they were even able to kick it at all. Some didn't.

"Really well," Mele said in a surprisingly upbeat tone. "Today is the last day of treatment. They'll drug-test me this afternoon, and if I pass—and I will—I'll be released tomorrow."

Tomorrow? It seemed like Akela had just come to live with them, but if Mele was getting released, twenty-eight days had gone by. How was that possible?

Lana knew she should be happy for her sister, but she felt her stomach sink as she realized what Mele was really telling her. She'd completed the program and the judge was letting her out. That meant she would be coming for her daughter. That meant that the reason for her marriage to Kal was coming to an end. That meant everything in her life was about to fall apart.

"Good for you," was all she could manage to say.

"You sound doubtful, Lana."

"I'm sorry if I'm not instantly convinced, but you've cleaned up before. How do I know that you'll stay clean this time? I'm not going to just hand Akela over to you to have you go back to using, and neither will the judge."

"I'm glad. She needs as many people in her life as possible that care for her that much. But I'm one of those people, too. If I feel like I'm going to blow it, I'll bring her to you first. I promise. But there's no reason to worry. I'm in a different place now, mentally and emotionally. Tua is in jail and out of my life for good. I'm starting over with new friends that will be better influences. I've cleaned up for good this time, Lana. My probation requires it, and my daughter deserves it. If I fail a random screening, I go to jail and I might lose Akela for good. I'm not going to let that happen. I'm not leaving my baby again."

There was a determination in Mele's voice that Lana had never heard before. She really seemed to be changed. The month of treatment had made a difference. Lana felt hopeful for the first time since Akela was born and Mele relapsed.

"I'll be released in the morning. Do you think you could pick me up? Our car is still in the police impound. It's going to take me a while to be able to pay the fine to get it out."

Lana tried not to flinch. Her sister would ask her for money any second now. She just knew it. "I can pick you up."

"Great. Thank you."

Lana waited, but the request didn't come. "How are you going to get the money to get your car back?" she asked. Her sister hadn't held down a real job in years.

"It's part of the continuing outpatient program. I go to group and individual counseling each week, pass my drug tests and they help me find somewhere to live and work. They partner with local businesses to place us in stable jobs."

That wasn't the answer Lana had expected. Mele sounded like she was going to handle her transition all by herself. Lana was impressed. She was still hesitant to believe this program had worked a miracle, but it was sounding that way.

"Kal's hotel is actually one of the companies. I was going to see about a housekeeping job there, perhaps. Maybe I could work my way up to something better after a while. Do you think you could talk to him about it?"

Lana bit at her lip. She hated to ask him to do anything else after all he'd done. Mele had no idea what lengths Kal had gone to for her daughter. But she knew he'd do it. Getting her in a stable job and away from Tua was the best thing they could do to keep her from relapsing. "I'll talk to him when he gets home tonight."

"Okay. Well, I'd better get off the phone. But before I do, I want to say thank you, Lana."

"Thank you for what?" she asked.

"For everything." There was a moment of silence that lingered between the sisters. "I'll call you tomorrow morning."

The line disconnected and Lana was left staring in astonishment at her phone. She wasn't sure quite what to do. Part of her was still in disbelief that the conversation had actually happened. She'd gone into this situation knowing it could be over in a month when her sister was released, but deep down, not believing it would happen.

And yet it did. The sick feeling of dread in her stomach confirmed it. She looked up from the table into the living room. The Christmas tree was gone along with most of the decorations, but she'd left the lights up for New Year's Eve. Soon everything would come down and be put away, along with the phony life she was living.

This wasn't her husband, her child or her home. It was all a carefully crafted ruse that was coming to an end. Akela would go back to her mother. With the baby gone, there was no reason to continue the marriage or to live together. At least, not any reason based on how they'd gone into this agreement.

Unfortunately she'd been foolish enough to let herself develop feelings for Kal, even knowing this day would come. She would happily continue things the way they were, even with Akela gone, but she had no way of knowing if he felt anything more than physical attraction for her. There were moments when she thought she saw the glimmer of something like love in his eyes, but she couldn't be sure.

He didn't want to marry, so why would he agree to stay married? Especially to someone like her? He deserved better than her.

Lana dreaded having to tell him. She didn't want to let all this go. At the same time, she couldn't just sit around this afternoon and wait for him to come home to find out.

"Sonia, I'm heading over to the hotel," she said.

The nanny just waved her off as she grabbed her bag and jumped into her new Mercedes. She buzzed through the winding streets of the resort, parking in the back area where the employees left their cars.

"You're early for rehearsal today," the security guard noted as she went through the back door.

"You didn't see their miserable performance last night," Lana answered with a smile. She hoped it sounded authentic and that her breaking heart wasn't audible to passersby.

She found Kal in his office, mindlessly typing away at something. He was just going about his day as he always did, with no idea she was about to drop a bomb on him.

He looked up in surprise and smiled when he saw it was her standing there. "Hey. I was just thinking about lunch if you want to join me."

Lana bit at her lip and shook her head. "That's, uh, not why I came over. I just got a call from Mele."

Kal's dark eyebrows drew together in concern. "Is everything okay?"

"Yeah. Great. Amazing, actually. So great she's getting out tomorrow." She barely got the words out before tears started threatening in her eyes.

Kal leaped out of his chair in alarm and wrapped his arms around her. He let her cry for a good minute before he spoke. "Did she say anything about the judge and the guardianship agreement?"

"She said she had to pass one more drug screening tonight and it was done. She intends to pick Akela up as soon as she gets out."

Kal's strong embrace stiffened around her. She understood his reaction. He loved that baby. She had become his everything.

Lana only wished that he loved her that much.

Kal was a ball of nervous energy. Not since his parents died had he felt so helpless. He was used to being in control of every detail of his life, but this was one thing he couldn't change. The judge's decree was official—Mele had met all the terms of her plea deal and custody of her daughter was restored.

Lana had gone to pick up her sister at the rehabilitation center. Kal had remained behind to watch Akela. It was Lana's suggestion so they could have a little more time together. Once they'd delivered the bad news to Sonia, they'd let her off to search for a new position, so it was just the two of them. With no baby, there was no need for a nanny. Or a nursery. Or a marriage.

Kal sat cross-legged on the floor watching Akela play with her taggie bear. He'd dressed her in a cute little white eyelet dress that had ducks on it. She hadn't liked it, but he also put on socks and white Mary Jane shoes. He wanted her to look like the perfect little princess she was when she went home today.

By the door was a bag packed with things for the baby. The rehab center had arranged for Mele to get an apartment at a nearby complex. He'd supplied a room at the resort for a few days while she picked up some furnishings and got settled in. He'd gotten her hired on in the housekeeping department, so being close would allow her to start working.

Once she was settled into her new place, he would have all the nursery furniture sent there. Akela's clothes, supplies and blankets were in the suitcase to leave with her today. He'd damn near gotten teary packing up that bag.

Akela looked up at him with a wide, one-toothed grin and chubby cheeks, and he felt the center of his chest start to contract as though it were a black hole sucking all his feelings into it. He'd never wanted a family or children, but he never imagined it would be this hard to let this little girl go. She was one of the reasons he left work on time every day. She had become his sunshine. And Lana had become his moonlight.

He felt all of it slipping through his fingers.

A sound in the driveway caught his attention. He looked up, listening to the sound of women's voices come nearer. Every muscle in his body tensed. Then the door opened. No monsters stepped inside, just Lana and another woman who looked like a slightly older version of Lana. Her eyes were narrower, like Akela's, and she was almost on the unhealthy side of thin. She didn't look at Kal, though. Her dark eyes sought out her baby the moment she walked in.

"Akela!" she said, dropping to her knees on the floor beside the baby. She scooped her into her arms and held her tight to her chest. Tears flowed down her cheeks, making Kal feel guilty for every thought he'd had about keeping Akela with them instead of her returning to her mother. Akela seemed content in her mother's arms, grabbing a handful of her dark hair and giving a tug.

It was a sweet reunion, but Kal could hardly stomach it. He got up and grabbed his suit coat off the back of the couch. "I'm going to head into the office," he said.

Lana regarded him with concern in her eyes, but she

didn't try to stop him. "Okay. I'm going to take Mele over to the hotel to get her settled," she said.

Fine. Whatever. He just needed to get out of here. He couldn't sit and watch Mele walk out the door with the baby in her arms. He left them, holing himself up in his office for a couple hours. When he finally looked at his watch, it hadn't been a couple hours. It had been seven, and well past the time he normally left.

What reason did he have to go home with Akela gone?

Lana was still there. That was something. But he wouldn't even have that for much longer. He shut down his computer and slipped out. The office area was dark and quiet as he headed out the back door to where he parked. As he pulled up outside his house, it seemed darker than usual.

When he came in the front door, he found Lana sitting at the kitchen counter, holding a glass of wine. She didn't look up when he approached the room.

"Did Mele and Akela get settled in?" he asked.

Lana nodded slowly. "Yes. Thank you for letting her stay there for a few days. Sonia moved out, too. She found another live-in position and they wanted her to start right away."

Kal slumped against the doorway, resting his shoulder on the wall. The emptiness he'd filled with work returned now that he was home and the hollow shell of their house seemed to echo inside him. "It's too quiet in here now," he said.

"I know." Lana rolled the wineglass back and forth between her palms, not drinking it or looking his way. "Quiet is good for thinking, though. I've been doing a lot of thinking today since you left."

That sounded ominous. "About what?" Kal left his spot on the wall and leaned his elbows onto the counter so Lana couldn't avoid him any longer.

"About what happens next. For us."

That was a thought that Kal hadn't really allowed himself to have for more than half a second at a time. It was hard enough to deal with Akela being gone. "I don't think we have to make any decisions right awa—"

"I called Dexter," she said. "He's drawing up the divorce papers. He said we can come by in the morning to sign them and he'll get them filed with the judge. It will take about thirty days to be finalized, but at least the ball will have started rolling."

Even though it was a rational thing to say, Lana's words felt like an emotional sock to the gut. Why was it that he thought he would have to be the one to bring up the inevitable? Why did it bother him that Lana was moving forward to end this? He'd expected that perhaps she would drag her feet. She was the one who wanted to get married after all. And yet here he was, feeling like he was getting dumped for the first time since his freshman year.

"Are you sure we should move so quickly? It's only Mele's first day out of rehab. What if she starts using again in a week? We'll have to get married again. That's a lot of unnecessary hassle. Why don't we wait awhile and see what happens? It's not like either of us needs to run out and marry someone else."

Lana looked at him at last and her delicate brow was furrowed in thought and irritation. "In a week, in a month, in a year…we can't control or anticipate what my sister is going to do and we shouldn't live our lives waiting for the other shoe to drop."

"I'm not saying that. I'm just saying a lot has happened today. Let's not make a knee-jerk decision."

"And do what?" Lana said, perking up in her seat at last. "Stay married? Keep continuing on sleeping together and playing the happy lovers for everyone? We're just torturing ourselves the longer we let this go on."

"I hardly feel tortured being married to you, Lana. It's no hardship on me to continue."

"That's because you're not in l—" She stopped her words short. Her jaw clenched and her nostrils flared with pent up emotions as she seemed to fight to hold them in.

"Not in what?" he pressed.

"In love, Kal. You're not in love with me, so of course this is just some fun game you can play. Play at being married and having a family. It's more fun when you know it will end and things will go back to the way they were before."

In love. Was Lana in love with him? He was stunned nearly speechless by the idea of it. "Hold on. This isn't just a game for me. Why would you think that?"

Lana frowned at him. "Kal, are you in love with me? If you are, say so right now."

Being put on the spot, Kal's lungs seized in his chest. In love? Did he even know what it felt like to be in love with a woman? He didn't know. He knew that he cared for Lana as much as he cared for anyone. Judging by the expression on her face, that wasn't enough for her.

"That says everything," she said, standing up from her barstool.

"Now just wait a minute," Kal argued. "You're not giving me time to think."

Lana just shook her head sadly. "You shouldn't have to think about it, Kal. You either love me or you don't. You either want to stay married or you don't. Since the answer is extremely obvious to me, I say there's no point in dragging this conversation on any longer. It's over. We'll meet with Dexter in the morning."

Kal didn't know what to say. Part of him was relieved to have this all done. He'd been nervous about taking marriage and family on to begin with. The other part of him was screaming inside not to be a fool and ruin the amazing thing they had together. "Lana—"

"Thank you, Kal," Lana interrupted, holding up her hand to silence his argument.

"Thank you for what?"

"For putting your own life on hold for over a month to help me. I'm not sure many friends would've gone to the lengths you went to for me, and I appreciate it."

There was a finality in Lana's voice that he didn't like. As though she were saying goodbye. "I'd do it all over again," he said, and he meant it. He watched as Lana picked up her purse, slung it over her shoulder and walked into the living room. "Where are you going?"

She stopped just short of the front door and reached for the small roller bag he hadn't noticed when he'd come in. Lana was leaving him. She'd spent today thinking while he worked his feelings into submission, and the answer she'd come up with was that they were done. She turned to look at Kal. "I'm going back to my place."

"This is your place," he said firmly.

Lana just shook her head. "Don't worry about having your people pack up my stuff for me yet. I've put a couple things in this bag to last me, but I won't need the rest right away. Today I found a nice studio on the hill in Lahaina that I think I'm going to put an offer on. It would be easier to just have them move my things straight there after I close on it."

She looked down at her hand on the doorknob, then reached for her wedding ring. She pulled it off her finger and set it on the table in the entryway.

Kal had hardly given his wedding ring any notice since the day she'd placed it on his finger. Suddenly the cool metal started to burn his skin. It was like everything was being torn apart and he couldn't stand it. He didn't want to lose all this. He took a few giant steps forward until he was nearly in reach of her. "Ask me again," he demanded.

Lana just looked up at him. "At the moment it hurts. But let's not make that pain out to be more than it really is. You like the idea of what we had, but it won't be the same. This isn't what you wanted for your life, Kal. You did this for me. And if I were to let you stay in the marriage knowing that, I would just be taking advantage of our friendship. I've already done too much of that, so don't ask me to do it again."

Kal's feelings were a jumble inside him. He didn't know how he felt or if she was right. He just knew that he didn't want to lose her. "And what about our friendship?" he asked. It felt like even that was crumbling around him. He feared that more than anything else.

"We're fine," she said, reaching out to give him one of her friendly punches in the shoulder. It felt familiar, like old times, but the faraway look in her eyes as she did it didn't convince him. "I'll just need a little time alone, Kal. I promise."

He was relieved to hear that, and yet the anxiety still kept his chest so tight he could barely breathe.

"Good night, Kal," she said, opening the door and slipping outside.

Kal stood there and watched her pull away in her Jeep, leaving the Mercedes in the garage. He couldn't move, couldn't run after her. She had practically said that she loved him, but she didn't seem like she wanted him to chase her. Had her love for him only made her miserable? Perhaps Kal had been right about relationships all along. They always ended in heartache. Maybe she was right and this was for the best.

Their lives weren't so terrible before. They had fun together. Kids were a big responsibility they didn't need to take on. Marriage was something that other people wanted, not him. If he could adjust to being married with a baby so quickly, he should able to get his life back to normal twice as fast.

Even as he thought that to himself, Kal knew it was a lie.

Eleven

"Do you want me to hang this picture right here?" Lana asked, looking over her shoulder.

Mele came into the living room with Akela on her hip and nodded. "That looks great."

Lana hammered the nail into the wall and hung the painting they'd found at a thrift shop. She took a step back and admired her work with pride. It was really coming along.

Mele's new apartment was nice. It was small, but close to the hotel and therapy. The bedroom was big enough for a full-size bed and Akela's crib. By the time the baby was big enough to need her own room, Mele would hopefully be in better financial shape.

"Thanks for all your help with this," Mele said. She put Akela in her bouncing entertainment center so she could play with all the multicolored trinkets there to amuse her. "I feel like we've spent more time together this week than we have in years."

"That's probably true." Lana hadn't spent much time with her sister after she moved from home. She didn't like being around her friends, and for good reason. Now, with all those influences out of Mele's life, it was like she'd gotten her sister back. When the two of them weren't working, Lana was at her apartment helping her move in. They'd done some thrift store shopping and salvaged a few good items from their old place.

"Do you want some coffee?" Mele asked. She'd used a small portion of her first paycheck to buy an inexpensive coffeemaker at Walmart. It was her new indulgence after setting aside all her other addictions.

"Sure." She joined her sister at the tiny, worn dining room table they'd found at a yard sale for fifty bucks.

They sat quietly sipping their coffee and enjoying each other's company. Lana tried not to think about waking up to a cup from Kal each morning. That just sent her thoughts spiraling down the dark rabbit hole of emotional angst.

Walking away had been the hardest thing she'd ever had to do. But she knew she had to. She loved Kal, but she also loved herself enough to know that she didn't want to settle. If he told her he loved her under pressure like that, she had no reason to think it was how he really felt. Or that he wouldn't recant later when he realized what he'd gotten himself into. She wanted a relationship with a man who knew how he felt and wanted to be with her more than anything else in the world. No question. That just wasn't Kal.

She hadn't seen him since she walked out that night. Lana had opted to go to Dexter's office early the next morning by herself to sign the paperwork and avoid another awkward confrontation. She'd circumvented his normal hunting grounds at the hotel. Somehow it made it easier. She couldn't see him every day and pretend her heart wasn't broken. Perhaps once the divorce was final they could return to being friends again. That was what she'd told him. She just hoped it was true.

"Lana?"

Lana turned to her sister, who had an expectant look on her face. "What?"

"I said your name three times. What planet are you on?"

"I'm sorry. I'm a little distracted today."

Mele nodded. "Is this about Kal?"

Lana sat bolt upright in her chair. "What makes you say that?"

"Because…you haven't mentioned his name all week. When my lawyer told me that my sister and her husband had petitioned for guardianship I kept my mouth shut, but honestly my jaw nearly hit the floor. What is going on with you two?"

Lana twisted her lips in thought as she looked down at her mug. "You don't want to hear my sob story, Mele. We're supposed to be focusing on new starts."

Her sister crossed her arms over her chest and gave her a stern look. "Lanakila, you tell me right now or I'll tug your ear."

Lana looked up with wide eyes at her sister. On more than one occasion when she'd annoyed her older sister, she'd been dragged by the ear into the living room so Mele could tattle to Papa. It usually backfired with both of them being punished. She hadn't tugged on her ear in fifteen years, but Lana could still feel the sharp pinch of her sister's grip. She wasn't looking forward to experiencing that again any time soon. "Okay, fine."

"Start at the beginning. I don't know much about you two and I want every detail."

With a sigh, Lana did as she was told, starting with the day she met Kal and continuing up until the day she walked out. They went through a whole pot of coffee and a breakfast pastry Lana brought from the corner bakery. They even stopped to put Akela down for a nap. The story of Lana and Kal was longer than she had ever expected it to be. They had quite a history together.

"So there you go," she said at last. "I'm in love with my best friend. He doesn't love me. And we're getting divorced in…" She glanced down at her phone. "…twenty-two days."

"Wow," was all Mele could say. She'd asked for the whole story and she'd gotten it. "That's crazy. I got the feeling that you two might be playing some sort of shell game for the judge. I can't believe you two were willing to go to such great lengths for my baby." Her eyes got a little teary as she looked over at the infant who napped in her Pack 'n Play. "You have no idea how much I appreciate everything you two went through for her. I'm worried that you paid too high a price, though."

Lana tried to shrug it off. "It was worth it."

"Was it?"

"Absolutely. I just wish I had known going in that it was going to end like this. I could've protected my heart better. Kept my distance when there wasn't anyone else around. He's just got such a magnetic personality. I'm drawn to him."

"How did you think all this would end?" Mele asked.

"Like this," she had to admit when she really thought about it. She was already half sweet on him going into the situation. Did she really think twenty-four-hour contact, living together, a wedding ring and sex would make him easier to resist? "I can try to blame the heartbreak and the attachment on the sex, which wasn't a part of my plan, but I know that wasn't it. In the end, I would've fallen for him no matter what. I just thought I would handle it better. The sex gave me the illusion that he might fall for me, too, which of course is ridiculous."

Mele flinched at her words. "Why on earth would you think it's ridiculous for him to fall in love with you?"

"Oh, come on, Mele."

"Don't *come on* me. What about you is so repellant that he couldn't fall in love with you? You're beautiful. You're smart. You're talented. You take care of the people you love, and you love more deeply than anyone I've ever known. He should be thrilled that you'd consider falling in love with him, not the other way around."

"You're crazy. Maybe I'm pretty and I'm a good dancer. So what? Kal is from such an important family. I think he mentioned once that he's descended from Hawaiian royalty on his mother's side. He has more money in his bank account on any given day than I'll earn in my whole life. He's from a different kind of people. The kind of people who don't fall in love with people like us."

"You mean people like me," Mele said matter-of-factly.

Lana realized after she said it how it might insult

her sister. "That's not what I meant, I'm sorry, but it certainly doesn't help the situation to have an inebriated, violent father and a sister always on the wrong side of the law."

Mele shook her head with a smile. "No, don't apologize. You're right. At least about our family. We're no great name and we'll be lucky to inherit the tiny plot of useless land where Papa's house sits. We've got issues for sure. But everyone does. Some just have more money to deal with their issues. Our family is lucky, though. You know why? Because we have you. You're our diamond in the rough."

Lana was uncomfortable with her sister's flattery. They'd chosen different paths, but she didn't believe that she was better than her sister. "Oh, quit it. I can dance. That's what got me out of our situation. If I'd had two left feet and buckteeth, who knows what would've happened to me?"

Mele furiously shook her head. "No, you never would've ended up like me. You're too much like Mama for that."

Lana looked at her sister with tears suddenly welling in her eyes. "Really?" She'd only turned two a few weeks before their mother died from the cervical cancer they'd discovered while she was in the hospital having Lana. Instead of being home with her new baby, she'd been in and out of treatment, but they'd caught it too late. Lana had no memories of her, just a few worn photos that showed a resemblance, but not much more. Mele had been five and remembered more about those days.

"Absolutely. Why do you think Papa fell apart when she died? Because Mama was everything to him. He would sit and hold you in his arms and cry because he knew she was slipping away and there was nothing he could do about it. He never let himself fall in love with anyone else because of it. He couldn't stand to have his heart broken again when he knew there wasn't anyone who could replace her."

Lana's words jogged something in her memory. It was something Kal had said once, a long time ago. The night had possibly involved beer, which was the usual catalyst for loosening Kal's tongue about personal matters. He'd said falling in love was too big a risk. That he knew what it was like to lose someone he loved and he didn't understand how she could long for a husband and a family when it could be ripped away at any moment.

"That sounds like Kal," she said aloud.

"What does?"

"What you just said about Papa. Kal lost his parents about ten years ago. He doesn't talk about it very much, but I can tell that it really bothers him, even now. It makes me wonder if that's why…"

"Why he's afraid to admit that he's in love with you?"

Lana shook her head and frowned. "I was going to say that was why he was afraid to be in a serious relationship. Why would you think he's in love with me?" That was quite a stretch, especially for someone who'd only seen him for a handful of minutes and didn't even speak with him. Lana had spent almost every minute of the last month with him and she didn't believe that was true.

Mele stood up and started another pot of coffee. "If everything you've told me about Kal is true, he has to be in love with you."

"Why?"

"Because he's not a fool. He's smart. He's a successful businessman who's used to having everything work out the way he wants it to. But you can't control love the way you control a business empire, and he knows that. He might be scared of admitting the truth to you and getting hurt, but he's not a fool."

Kal was sulking. He wouldn't admit it to anyone else, but he was. At first, he thought he was just missing the baby. And he was. But that wasn't what was haunting him. It was Lana's disappointed face he saw when he closed his eyes to sleep at night. Lana's laughter that he missed when he saw something that they would've had a good time talking about. Lana's lips that he fantasized about kissing.

He missed her. It had been over a week since he'd even seen her. No calls, no texts, no passing in the lobby of the hotel. It was just like she'd vanished from his life entirely, even though she was probably only a couple hundred yards away at any given time.

Kal supposed that if he really wanted to see her, he could watch the luau. But he hadn't been able to bring himself do it. Watching her dance would just torture him even more. Maybe tonight. Or maybe not.

"Mr. Bishop?"

Kal looked up from his desk to see his assistant, Jane, standing in the doorway of his office. "Yes?"

"There's someone here to see you, sir."

"Someone here to see me?"

"Well, not *see* you, per se," a man's voice said as the door flew open the rest of the way, revealing Mano and Hōkū standing behind her. "But we're here to visit."

Kal stood up in surprise. It was weird enough that Mano had shown up for Christmas. This random Monday in January visit was unheard of. He waited to respond until Mano had settled down in a guest chair and Jane had disappeared, closing the door behind her.

"What are you doing here?" he asked. "No bullshit this time."

"Okay, fine. I'm here because your employees are worried about you and they contacted me."

Kal nearly tipped his chair backward in surprise. He surged forward and gripped his desk to stay steady. "You're kidding, right?"

"Nope. Apparently you've been charging up and down the halls like a man on fire, barking orders, criticizing everyone's work and being a general pain in the a—"

"Okay," Kal said, interrupting him. "I get it. I've been unpleasant." He knew he'd been in a bad mood, but he hadn't realized how bad. "Did someone really call you and ask you to come?"

"Actually they asked for permission to slip you a sedative in your morning coffee, so I thought me coming out here was a better solution."

Kal crossed his arms defensively over his chest. "I'll work on it. It's been a bad week."

Mano nodded thoughtfully, then reached out to feel Kal's left hand. "That's what I thought. No ring," he noted.

Kal pulled his hand away and gazed down at the naked ring finger of his left hand. He'd only worn the ring for a month, but he could feel the phantom sensation of it on his finger even with it gone. "No ring," he repeated. "No marriage. No baby. It's all over and done."

"What happened?"

He sighed, not really wanting to admit the truth to his brother but knowing he had to. "You were right about the two of us. None of it was real. We had to let everyone believe it was in case Child Services was sniffing around, but it was all for show. Lana's sister went into rehab and it was the only way we could get guardianship of her niece. Her sister has since completed treatment and has been reunited with her daughter. So it's done. Lana left."

Mano listened, making that infuriatingly thoughtful face that always made Kal nervous. He'd always heard that losing one sense made the others stronger. His brother had picked up some kind of superpower lie detector in the accident that blinded him.

"You mean you let her go," Mano said at last.

"No, I mean she called the lawyer, started the divorce proceedings and moved out." That was all true. Aside from the teeny, tiny detail about her asking if he loved her and him choking.

"It seems strange to me that a woman so obviously in love with her husband would just walk out like that. It sounds to me like self-preservation. What did you do to her?"

"I didn't do anything to her," Kal argued. "I stuck to the agreement. She's the one who broke the rules."

"And what, exactly, were the rules?"

"That it was just for show. That it was just for the baby and nothing more."

"So you didn't sleep with her?"

Kal was starting to feel like he'd woken up in the

Spanish Inquisition. When he found out who had called his brother on him, he was going to show them what a grumpy manager he really could be. "Yes, I slept with her."

"More than once?"

Kal gritted his teeth. "Yes, damn it."

"So you broke the rules, too?"

He supposed that he did. "Yes. We broke that rule. But she wasn't supposed to get attached, and it wasn't supposed to ruin our friendship."

Mano nodded and reached over to pat the top of Hōkū's head. "So you spent a month together playing house, making love and acting like a happy family for everyone, and now you're mad at her because she fell for you in the process."

"Yes."

"Or," Mano postulated, "are you mad at yourself because you fell for her, too?"

Kal closed his eyes and groaned aloud. He did not want to have this conversation with his brother, but he could tell there was no getting out of it. "This is a conversation better suited for the bar," he said. "I need a drink."

Mano smiled cheerfully and stood up. "Lovely. I could use a drink myself."

They made their way to the bar and found a dark corner booth. It was too early for most drinkers, so they had the place to themselves. Once they were settled with beverages and a bowl of Asian snack mix, Mano sat back and waited for the answer Kal had stalled responding to for ten minutes.

"I'm not in love," Kal said at last.

Mano just sighed. "You know, it wasn't that long ago

that I was sitting at Tūtū Ani's birthday party while you talked me into chasing after the woman I loved but had let walk out of my life."

"That was different," Kal insisted. "You *were* in love with her."

"And you can honestly say that you have no feelings for Lana?"

Kal tried to search himself for something he was hiding, but he didn't come up with anything novel. "I feel the same way for Lana that I've always felt. She's my best friend. I enjoy spending time with her, and I miss her when I don't see her often enough. I like sharing things with her, and I can tell her anything. She's great to talk to and always gives good advice."

"If you were in this situation with another woman and you asked Lana for advice, what would she say?"

He knew the answer immediately. He could even hear her say it in his head. "She'd tell me to get my head out of my ass and tell the woman that I love her."

"Considering that you say nothing has changed, is it possible that you're confused about your feelings for her because you've been in love with her all along?"

His brother's words stopped him cold. He gazed silently down into his drink as though the answers to the universe were there among the ice and the scotch. Was it really possible that he'd been in love with her all this time? Was that why he was never interested in anyone else? Why he'd rather spend time with her than go on a date? Why he was terrorizing his employees since she'd walked out on him? The answer washed over him like a tidal wave of emotion that made the hairs stand up on the back of his neck and his chest ache with his foolishness.

His head dropped into his hand and he clutched his skull to keep his mind from being blown. "Oh my God, I've been in love with her the whole time."

"Yep," was all Mano said. He reached a hand out to feel for the snack bowl and grabbed a handful of sesame sticks and peanuts. Kal watched him pop a bit into his mouth as though they were discussing the weather.

"I'm in love with Lana," he said aloud, letting his ears get used to the sound of it. If he ever said it to her, he couldn't have the slightest hesitation or she wouldn't believe him. He certainly hadn't given her any reason to believe him before.

He replayed their last moments together again in his mind, thinking about how she'd looked at him with her heart wide-open and he'd blown it. She'd been right, though. If he'd told her he loved her then, it would've been just lip service to keep her from walking away. Being apart from her this last week had cemented it in his mind. Now he understood the truth of his feelings.

All this time he'd been afraid to get close to anyone and risk losing them, and here he'd gone and pushed away the only person he'd ever loved. The result was the same—he was alone and miserable. The only difference was that he still had a chance to make things right with Lana.

He had to tell her how he felt and stand his ground. He wasn't going to let her walk away this time, or ever again. She was still legally his wife and he wasn't about to let that change.

"Now the question is, what are you going to do about it?"

Twelve

It was Lana's turn to go on. The lights dimmed for a moment and the musicians started chanting an ancient Hawaiian prayer as they beat their drums. She stepped onto the stage, finding her mark in the center before the spotlights focused on her.

Lana had performed this routine three nights a week for three years. She knew it like the back of her hand, and yet she felt sluggish as she started to move. One of her professors in college had told her that she danced with her whole heart and soul. Her heart just wasn't in it lately.

She pasted a smile on her face and fought through it. She'd performed with the flu, she'd performed with a sprained ankle—she could get through this. That was what professionals did.

Instinctively she looked to the far corner of the courtyard as she danced. That was where Kal had watched her every night for as long as she could remember. He wasn't there now and he hadn't been since she moved out. Lana supposed that was her fault. She told him she needed space and he was giving it to her.

Still, it hurt her heart to look up and see nothing but a stone wall where his tall, dark silhouette should be.

Mele had insisted that Kal wasn't a fool and that he would come around. Lana wasn't so sure. Their father had never recovered and moved on; why did she think that Kal would change his ways after all these years? And for her of all people?

She closed her eyes for a moment and forced that negative thought from her mind. If she got nothing else from her time with Mele, it was that she was a valuable person. She needed to stop thinking she wasn't good enough. She was her mother's daughter, and every time she let those negative thoughts creep in, she was tarnishing her mother's memory. She couldn't allow that.

Better to believe that Kal was a fool if he didn't see what a gem he had right in front of him. Lana wasn't going to sit around and wait for him to change his mind, either. She was going to buy that condo, move out of the hotel and start building a life that didn't revolve around him and his resort. She'd actually heard that one of the big luaus in Lahaina was hiring a choreographer. It was a scary thought to leave the place she'd considered home, but maybe it was time.

Her eyes drifted over to the corner even as she considered leaving the Mau Loa. This time, she was startled to see a familiar dark shape. Kal was there. Watching her.

Missing a step, she forced herself to focus back on her performance. When she looked up again, Kal was gone. Her heart ached with disappointment. She couldn't take much more of this. She had to go, she decided. She had to get away from him if she was ever going to be able to move on with her life.

The routine came to an end. The lights went out, allowing her to leave the stage just as the male dancers came rushing out. Turning the corner, she ran face first into Talia, one of her dancers.

"We've got a problem, Lana."

Lana's stomach started aching with dread. "What is it?"

"Callie is puking her guts up in the rehearsal room. There's no way she's going to be able to perform the new *South Pacific* number at the end of the show."

Damn it. That was a really important number, and a relatively new one she performed with one of the male singers from the band. She didn't really have an understudy yet, so that meant that Lana would have to do it. Her worries about Kal faded into the background as she rushed around making last-minute arrangements for the change. "Go over to the band area and let Ryan know that I'm taking Callie's place."

Talia nodded and headed off toward the pit where the musicians sat just to the right of the stage. Lana returned to the dressing room to change out of her current outfit and into Callie's costume. It was a flowing white dress that was paired with a crown of white orchids. It pained Lana to put it on, reminding her too much of her wedding dress. As performance after performance went by, she fidgeted nervously in the dress.

She couldn't wait for the new number to be over with so she could take the costume off.

Finally the last routine of the night was up and she went out to do her job. She stepped out onto the stage first. The setup was a little different from their usual numbers. Ryan would step out behind her and while she danced, sing the song "Some Enchanted Evening" from the musical *South Pacific*. It had been an instant hit with the audience, and gave them the chance to showcase Ryan's singing talents.

Thankfully Lana didn't have to sing. She just had to dance, and in the end, end up in Ryan's arms just before the lights went out. It was a simple dance number, drawing more on her background in contemporary and ballet dance than her hula skills.

The musicians started playing the acoustic guitar version of the song and Lana waited for her cue to begin dancing. She stared out into the crowd, trying not to look for Kal. Then Ryan began singing and her blood went cold. Something was wrong. That wasn't Ryan's voice. It was pleasant enough, and relatively on-key, but it lacked the professional vocal tones of a trained singer like Ryan.

Unfortunately she couldn't turn around. She didn't turn in the performance for a full minute. She danced, listening to him sing about spying her across a crowded room and being enchanted by her.

Then, at last, the routine allowed her to stop and turn to look at her partner. It was Kal, wearing the white linen suit Ryan typically wore.

She froze in place. He was standing there, crooning words of love to her. Lana couldn't make sense of what she was seeing. What was he doing crashing the luau? She hadn't even seen Kal in over a week and now he just appeared in her show without telling her? Lana didn't even know Kal could sing. What was going on?

Either way, she told herself it didn't matter. She would finish this number, then drag him backstage and give him a sound talking-to for putting her on the spot like this. She reached out to him longingly, then turned away and spun across the stage with the dress twirling around her.

She dreaded the final chorus of the song, knowing she would have to look lovingly into Kal's eyes as he serenaded her. If ever there was a time she would blow her professional facade, it would be now.

He started the last verse and she slowly made her way to him. She swallowed hard as she looked into his eyes and saw the serious expression on his face. It was as though he meant every word as he sang to her about finding his true love and flying to her side. She tried not to read too much into it, though. These were Rogers and Hammerstein's words, not Kal's.

As he wrapped his arms around her, he looked down at her as though they weren't onstage surrounded by hundreds of people. He sang the last few lines of the song to her, looking deep into her eyes.

The music faded and the crowd broke into roaring applause. Lana expected him to let go of her, but he didn't. Instead he said, "I don't want to go through my life dreaming alone. I want to go through it with you."

Lana didn't know what to say, and even if she did, she didn't want to speak it aloud. Kal was miked, and everything he said was broadcast to the whole audience. "You don't really mean that, Kal," she whispered, hoping it wouldn't pick up her voice.

"If I didn't mean it, would I be onstage, singing to you and making a fool of myself? Would I have convinced your dancers to fake being sick to make sure you were the one to perform this song?"

It was a setup. Lana turned her head and noticed her entire dance crew, including a quite healthy Callie, watching anxiously from the backstage area. Lana squeezed her eyes closed and tried to wrap her head around what was happening. So was the crowd. The courtyard was so quiet you could hear the waves beyond the stage.

"I went to all this trouble because I wanted to tell you, to tell everyone here tonight, how much I love you, Lana."

She shook her head in disbelief. "You could've just told me this in private."

"You and I both know that wouldn't work. I wanted witnesses. I wanted you to know I mean business. And I didn't want you to be able to run away so you'd have to listen to what I have to say."

Lana was stiff in his arms. He was right to put her on the spot so she couldn't avoid him, but onstage?

"I'm not letting you get rid of me," Kal said. "This last week without you has been pure hell. I don't want to go back to the way things were. I don't want to live in that big house all alone. I want a family. A real one, like my brother has and my parents had. And I want it with you."

"You don't mean that. You're just confusing our friendship for something more."

"You are my friend. You're my best friend. But

you're also the love of my life and I'm not confused about that. I'm not going to settle for anything less than you as my wife for the rest of my life."

Kal's words stole her breath away. With his arms wrapped around her and his eyes pleading with her to love him in return, she didn't know how she could tell him no. But she summoned the strength anyway.

"You've lost your mind. Let go of me," she said angrily, pulling from his arms and running offstage.

The minute Lana turned to Kal while she was dancing and realized it was him singing, he knew he had made a mistake. There was a hardness in her gaze, a stiffness in the set of her jaw. He'd thought that a big, romantic, public gesture would be the way to go. That declaring his love for her in front of everyone would convince her that he meant what he said, but as she ran offstage and the audience audibly gasped at her rebuttal, he knew it was the wrong tactic to take with Lana.

He ran after her, pushing through the crowds of dancers and chasing her down the sandy path that led to the beach. "Lana!" he shouted, hearing his voice echo through the speakers in the distance. He ripped off his microphone and tossed it into the bushes as he chased her down the beach. "Lana, wait!"

She finally came to a stop at the edge of the water. She stood there, with her back to him, as he slowly approached.

"Lana?"

She finally turned to look at him. Her face was flushed and her eyes were glassy with unshed tears. "How dare you!" she shouted.

Kal froze. He wasn't expecting her anger. "What do you mean?"

"How dare you make me look like a fool in front of all those people!"

"You didn't look like a fool! I made myself look like one to try and prove to you how much I love you."

Lana could only shake her head. "In front of my dance team, in front of the hotel guests…"

"Who all thought it was an amazing and romantic gesture. They were all superexcited to help me out. And the audience loved it until you ran away and ruined everything."

"What made you think that putting me on the spot was the right thing to do?" she asked. "Even if I was in love with you, I'm a very private person, Kal. And a professional. I don't like my personal life bleeding into my work like that."

Kal sighed and closed his eyes. "I'm sorry, Lana. I should've known better." He took a few steps closer to her, closing the gap to inches. "I'd just seen them perform that song at the last luau, and it seemed so perfect. The man knows he has to act now if he doesn't want to lose his chance to be with the woman he loves. That was what I was doing. I wanted to sing those words to you so you'd know they were true."

Lana's expression softened. "You've been watching the show? I haven't seen you."

Kal nodded, pleased that Lana had noted his absence. She was annoyed with him, but she *had* been watching for him at each performance. That was something. "I've been sitting in the audience instead so you wouldn't see me."

Lana sighed, her shoulders relaxing along with the

rest of her tense muscles. "I thought you'd stopped coming to watch us dance."

He shook his head. "I did for the first one, but I realized that I couldn't stay away, even though I knew you wanted me to. I'm in love with you, Lana. Whether or not we have an audience, what I have to say to you is the same."

"I don't believe you," she said. "I think you're just lonely and scrambling to keep me in your life. Please don't tell me you love me unless you absolutely mean it. My heart can't take it, Kal, if you change your mind."

"This isn't a new feeling, Lana, it's just a new revelation. Since you've been gone, I realized that my feelings didn't change for you after we married or after we broke up. At first I thought that meant that I didn't have romantic feelings for you. But then I realized that it was because I've been in love with you this whole time."

Lana's lips parted softly in surprise. He wanted to scoop her into his arms and kiss her, but he refrained, since his last romantic gesture had crashed and burned.

"What do you mean, 'this whole time'?"

"I mean I've been in love with you for three years. All this time you were the most important person in my life, my best friend, the one I wanted to share things with, but I was too stubborn to realize that it was more than friendship. I wasn't interested in a relationship with anyone else because it wasn't a relationship with you."

"But you don't want to get married or have a family."

"I was scared to get married and have a family. Scared to lose the one I loved. Then I realized I'd lost you anyway. I couldn't bring my parents back, but I could do something about this. I could tell you how I felt and pray that you believed me."

"You really do love me," Lana said with a touch of disbelief in her voice.

"I do. And I want to stay married to you, as well. I've called Dexter and told him to postpone the divorce proceedings."

Lana just looked at him as though he'd sprouted a second head. She glanced up at his hairline, reaching out to gently brush some of his hair out of his face. "Did you hit your head or something?"

Kal grasped her hand and tugged it to his chest. "Of course not. This isn't a concussion talking, this is me, being honest with myself, and being honest with you, for the first time. Now I want you to be honest with me."

"About what?" she asked.

"I've been pretty clear about my feelings. What about you? Do you love me, Lana?"

She bit nervously at her bottom lip before she nodded. "I do."

Kal broke into a wide grin. He pulled her closer to him. "And do you want to marry me?"

"We're already married, Kal."

He reached into his pocket and fished out the platinum band she'd left behind. "Then I guess you'd better put on your wedding ring."

Lana took a ragged breath and held her fingers outstretched for Kal to slip the ring onto her finger.

"That's not all," he said. Reaching into his pocket again, he pulled out a jewelry box. He opened the lid and held his breath for her response.

"Kal!" she gasped. "I told you I didn't need a diamond ring."

He plucked the ring out of the velvet bed and slipped it onto her finger with the wedding band. The ring was a uniquely Hawaiian design from a local artisan, with an oval diamond set in a band of curling platinum vines and Plumeria flowers. It rested perfectly against her wedding band, as it was designed to do.

"You didn't need a diamond when we were getting married for the judge. Now that you're going to be my wife for real, and for always, you need a diamond ring to prove it."

Lana admired her rings, then placed her hand on his chest and looked up at him. "We don't have to prove our love to anyone anymore. It's just for us."

"Well, there are a few people who would like to know that we're in love and happy and staying married."

"Like who?"

Kal took her hand and started leading her back across the beach toward the stage. As they got closer, the sound of the conch shell being blown echoed through the night. Kal loved the puzzled look on Lana's face that stayed there until they stepped out onto the stage again.

The whole audience was still seated, waiting anxiously for their return. The dancers were sitting in the audience and with the houselights on, Kal could see Mano and Paige sitting up front. He'd wanted them to be here for this, since they'd missed the first ceremony. Right beside them was Mele holding Akela, and Lana's father.

Lana noticed her family sitting there where she

hadn't seen them before. She tugged at his arm, stopping him short. "What is going on?"

Kal stepped to the side and the kahuna *pule* who married them the first time was standing in the middle of the stage. Her eyes grew wide; then she looked back at Kal. "We're renewing our vows," he explained.

"Here? Right now?"

"Why not? You're practically in a wedding dress. Our family is here. The holy man is here. We also have three hundred guests who are anxiously waiting to see us kiss so they can eat the wedding cake at our reception."

"Our reception?"

Kal pointed to the far side of the courtyard where a table was set up to display a beautiful, five-tiered wedding cake covered in purple and white orchids. "We didn't have any of this the first time because it wasn't for real, we were just checking the box. Now that we're staying married, I wanted to have something a little grander to commemorate our vow renewal."

Lana looked around at everyone in the audience. They watched them with silent, expectant faces. "I can't believe you did all this. How did you…? When did you…?"

Kal just shook his head. That was a story for another time. Right now they had a wedding to attend. "So, what do you say we get remarried, Mrs. Bishop?"

Before she could respond, the crowd started to cheer. The roar of applause, whistles and shouts made her cheeks flush bright red. Finally she looked at him and nodded, eliciting another round of cheers.

Kal took her hand and led her to the table where the kahuna *pule* was waiting for them. He opened up his prayer booklet to the marked page and started reciting the words he'd just spoken to them a month before.

"The Hawaiian word for love is aloha. Today we've come together to celebrate the special aloha that exists between you, Kalani and Lanakila, as you renew your vows of marriage. When two people promise to share the adventure of life together, it is a beautiful moment that they will always remember."

They repeated their vows, and this time when they kissed, there was no awkwardness or hesitation. He wrapped his arms around Lana and dipped her backward, drawing a roar of applause from the crowd. They embraced their family members and cut the cake so it could be served to the hotel guests who were, in a way, an extension of their family.

It was late when Kal finally pulled the Jaguar back up to the house. He surprised Lana again by scooping her out of her seat and carrying her across the threshold.

They stood there together in their home with Lana in his arms. "I can't believe any of this is happening," she said. "You are amazing. You put all this together just for me."

"Of course I did. I told you I loved you. I wanted you to have everything you could possibly want. Except for maybe a few surprises so you'd go along with it all. What did you think when you turned around and saw me on the stage?"

Lana arched her brow at him. "Do you really want to know?"

"Of course I do."

"I was thinking that you were a terrible singer."

Kal looked at his wife in mock horror. "You lie!" he

said as he carried her down the hall to the master bedroom. "You're going to pay for that tonight," he said with a wicked grin.

Lana smiled and kissed him with all the passion she could muster. "I hope so."

Epilogue

Lana had to admit she was a little jealous of Mano and Paige's new house. The sprawling house sat atop a cliff overlooking the sea on the eastern side of Oahu. Diamondhead was visible to the right and in front of them was just miles of beautiful blue sea.

It was the perfect backdrop for their wedding. The rain had held out for a lovely Valentine's Day ceremony. Paige had looked beautiful in a pale cream, almost rose colored lace gown. Her hair was swept back in a romantic chignon with pale pink hibiscus woven into it. Her baby bump was on full display and all of Mano's relatives had to keep touching it as though she were a good-luck Buddha statue.

Mano was beaming in his traditional white suit. Hōkū was dressed up, too, with a matching white bow tie, since he was officially the ring bearer for the ceremony.

It all worked out splendidly, which made Lana happy considering how stressed Paige had been over the whole thing. All things considered, Lana was actually happy that her two wedding ceremonies had been virtually spur-of-the-moment with little to no planning on her part. In the end, she'd gotten the dress and the man of her dreams, and that was all she really needed.

"Lana?"

Lana turned to see Kal and Mano's elderly grandmother, Ani, making her way over to her. "Aloha, Tūtū Ani."

The older woman smiled and took her hand. "I had a dream last night that I must tell you about."

Lana looked over at the nearby table. "Let's have a seat and you can tell me all about it." Ani looked like she could use a rest, and frankly so could Lana. It had been a long day and she was pretty tired from all the celebrating.

"Kalani!" Ani called out, waving Kal over to the table. "You should hear this, too. It's important."

Kal came over and took a seat at the table. "What is it, Tūtū?"

"I had an important dream last night."

"About what?" Kal asked.

Ani reached out and placed her palm on Lana's stomach the way everyone else had been touching Paige. "About your son."

Lana stiffened in her seat, looking to Kal in surprise. Their son? "But I'm not pregnant."

Ani laughed and shook her head. "You may not realize it yet, but you are, you are. Your son will be tall and strong, like a Hawaiian god forged from the great fires of Mount Kilauea. Keahilani will be the family successor, the one to lead the family when I am gone, and you are gone."

Kal looked just as startled as Lana was. "Are you certain, Tūtū?"

The old woman narrowed her eyes at them in irritation. "Of course I am. I had the same dreams about you and Mano when your mother was carrying you. That's how your names were chosen—our ancestors spoke to me through dreams and showed me who you would be. You were to be chieftain and your brother arose from the sea and swam with the sharks in my dreams. Your son will be Keahilani—from heaven's fire. I have seen it."

Ani got up from her chair and leaned in to give Lana a kiss on the cheek. "*Ho'omaika'i 'ana* to you both."

Lana and Kal sat dumbfounded at the table as Ani congratulated them and wandered away to talk to someone else. They watched her fade into the crowd. Then they turned to each other and looked down at her still-flat belly.

"Could she be right?" Lana asked.

Kal just grinned and leaned in to give her a kiss. His touch sent a thrill through Lana's whole body, making her wish they were alone together in bed instead of surrounded by family at an event they couldn't escape.

"She always is. Keahi is on his way and our beautiful family has begun."

* * * * *

A CEO IN HER STOCKING

ELIZABETH BEVARLY

For David and Eli,
the people who made Christmas
even better than it already was.

Prologue

Clara Easton was dabbing one final icing berry onto a poinsettia cupcake when the bell over the entrance to Tybee Island's Bread & Buttercream rang for what she hoped was the last time that day. Not that she wasn't grateful for every customer, but with Thanksgiving just over and Christmas barely a month away, the bakery had been getting hammered. Not to mention she had to pick up Hank from his sitter in… She glanced at the clock. Yikes! Thirty minutes! Where had the day gone?

With luck, the customer was someone who'd just remembered she needed a dessert for a weekend party, and *Hey, whatever you have left in the case is fine—I'll take it.* But the visitor was neither a she nor a customer, Tilly, the salesclerk, told Clara when she came back to the kitchen. It was a man asking for her as *Miss Easton.* A man in a suit. Carrying a briefcase.

Which was kind of weird, since no one on the island

called her anything but Clara, and few if any of her customers were business types—or men, for that matter. Moms and brides pretty much kept Bread & Buttercream in business. Clara was intrigued enough that she didn't take time to remove her apron before heading into the shop. She did at least tuck a few raven curls under the white kerchief tied on her head pirate-style.

Though the man might have fit right in on the island with his surfer dude good looks, he clearly wasn't local. His suit was too well cut, his hair too well styled, and he looked completely out of his element amid the white wrought-iron café sets and murals of cartoon cupcakes.

"Hi," Clara greeted him. "Can I help you?"

"Miss Easton?" he asked.

"Clara," she automatically corrected him. *Miss Easton* sounded like a Victorian spinster who ran a boardinghouse for young ladies required to be home by nine o'clock in order to preserve their reputations and their chastity.

"Miss Easton," the man repeated anyway. "My name is August Fiver. I work for Tarrant, Fiver and Twigg. Attorneys."

He extended a business card that bore his name and title—Senior Vice-President and Probate Researcher— and an address in New York City. Clara knew probate had something to do with wills, but she didn't know anyone who had died. She had no family except for her son, and all of her friends were fine.

"Probate researcher?" she asked.

He nodded. "My firm is hired to find heirs who are, for lack of a better term, long-lost relatives of…certain estates."

The explanation did nothing to clear things up. From what Clara knew about the two people who had exchanged enough bodily fluids to produce her, whatever they might have for her to inherit was either stolen or conned. She would just as soon have them stay long lost.

Her confusion must have shown on her face, because August Fiver told her, "It's your son, Henry. I'm here on behalf of his paternal grandmother, Francesca Dunbarton." His lips turned up in just the hint of a smile as he added, "Of the Park Avenue Dunbartons."

Clara's mouth dropped open. She'd spent almost a month with Hank's father four summers ago, when she was working the counter of Bread & Buttercream. Brent had been charming, funny and sweet, with the eyes of a poet, the mouth of a god and a body that could have been roped off in an Italian museum. He'd lived in a tent, played the guitar and read aloud to her by firelight. Then, one morning, he was gone, moving on to whatever came next in his life.

Clara hadn't really minded that much. She hadn't loved him, and she'd had plans for her future that didn't include him. They deliberately hadn't exchanged last names, so certain had both been that whatever they had was temporary. They'd had fun for a few weeks, but like all good things, it had come to an end.

Except it didn't quite come to an end. When Clara discovered she was pregnant, she felt obliged to contact Brent and let him know—she'd still had his number in her phone. But her texts to him about her condition went unanswered, as did her messages when she tried to call. Then the number was disconnected. It hadn't been easy raising a child alone. It still wasn't. But Clara managed. It was her and Hank against the world. And that was just fine with her.

"I didn't realize Brent came from money," she said. "He wasn't... We weren't... That summer was..." She gave up trying to describe what defied description. "I'm surprised he even told his mother about Hank. I'm sorry Mrs. Dunbarton passed away without meeting her grandson."

At this, August Fiver's expression sobered. "Mrs. Dunbarton is alive and well. I'm afraid it's Brent who's passed away."

For the second time in as many minutes, Clara was struck dumb. She tried to identify how she felt about the news of Brent's death and was distressed to discover she had no idea how to feel. It had just been so long since she'd seen him.

"As your son is Brent Dunbarton's sole heir, everything that belonged to him now belongs to Henry. A not insignificant sum."

Not insignificant, Clara echoed to herself. What did that mean?

"One hundred and forty-two million," August Fiver said.

Her stomach dropped. Surely she heard that wrong. He must mean one hundred and forty-two million Legos. Or action figures. Or Thomas the Tank Engines. Those things did seem to multiply quickly. Surely he didn't mean one hundred and forty-two million—

"Dollars," he said, clearing that up. "Mr. Dunbarton's estate—your son's inheritance—is worth in excess of one hundred and forty-two million dollars. And your son's grandmother is looking forward to meeting you both. So is Brent's brother, Grant. I've been charged by them with bringing you and Henry to New York as soon as possible. Can you be ready to leave tomorrow?"

One

Clara had never traveled north of Knoxville, Tennessee. Everything she knew about New York City she'd learned from television and movies, none of which had prepared her for the reality of buildings dissolving into the sky and streets crammed with people and taxis. Even so, as the big town car carrying her, Hank and Gus—as August Fiver had instructed her to call him—turned onto Park Avenue, Clara was beginning to get an inkling about why New York was a town so nice they named it twice.

Ultimately, it had taken four days to leave Tybee Island. Packing for a toddler took a day in itself, and Clara had orders that weekend for a birthday party, a baby shower, a bunco night and a wedding cake. Then there were all the arrangements she needed to make with Hank's preschool and covering shifts at Bread & Buttercream. Thank goodness the week after Thanksgiving was slow enough, barely, to manage that before the Christmas season lurched into gear.

Looking out the window now, she could scarcely believe her eyes. The city was just…awesome. She hated to use such a trite word for such a spectacular place, but she couldn't think of anything more fitting.

"Mama, this is *awesome*!"

Clara smiled at her son. Okay, maybe that was why she couldn't think of another word for it. Because *awesome* was about the only adjective you heard when you had a three-year-old.

Hank strained against the belt of the car seat fastened between her and Gus, struggling to get a glimpse at the passing urban landscape, his fascination as rabid as Clara's. That was where much of their alikeness ended, however. Although he had her black curls and green eyes, too, his face was a copy of Brent's. His disposition was also like his father's. He was easygoing and quick to laugh, endlessly curious about *every*thing and rarely serious.

But Clara was glad Hank was different from her in that respect. She'd been a serious little girl. Things like fun and play had been largely absent from her childhood, and she'd learned early on to never ask questions, because it would only annoy the grown-ups. Such was life for a ward of the state of Georgia, who was shuttled from foster home to children's home to group home and back again. It was why she was determined that her son's life would be as free from turbulence as she could make it, and why he would be well-rooted in one place. She just hoped this inheritance from Brent didn't mess with either of those things.

The car rolled to a halt before a building of a dozen stories whose stone exterior was festooned with gold wreaths for the holidays. Topiaries sparkling with white lights dotted the front walkway leading to beveled lattice windows and French doors, and a red-liveried doorman stood sentry at the front door. It was exactly the kind of place where people would live when they were the owners of an industrial empire that had been in their family for two centuries. The Dunbartons could trace their roots all the way back to England, Gus had told her, where they were distantly related to a duke. Meaning that Hank could potentially become king, if the Black Death returned and took out the several thousand people standing between him and the throne.

The building's lobby was as sumptuous as its exterior, all polished marble and gleaming mahogany bedecked with evergreen boughs and swaths of red velvet ribbon. And when they took the elevator to the top floor, the doors unfolded on more of the same, since the penthouse foyer was decorated with enough poinsettias to germinate a banana republic. Clara curled her arm around Hank's shoulders to hug him close, and Gus seemed to sense her anxiety. He smiled reassuringly as he rang the bell. She glanced at Hank to make sure he was presentable, and, inescapably, had to stoop to tie his sneaker.

"Mr. Fiver," she heard someone greet Gus in a crisp, formal voice.

Butler, she decided as she looped Hank's laces into a serviceable bow. And wow, was the man good at butlering. He totally sounded like someone who was being paid good money to be cool and detached.

"Mr. Dunbarton," Gus replied.

Oh. Okay. Not the butler. Brent's brother. She couldn't remember what Brent's voice had sounded like, but she was sure it hadn't been anywhere near as solemn.

Laces tied, Clara stood to greet their host, and… And took a small step backward, her breath catching in her chest. Because Hank's father had risen from the grave, looking as somber as death itself.

Or maybe not. On closer consideration, Clara saw little of Brent in his brother's blue eyes and close-cropped dark hair. Brent's eyes had laughed with merriment, and his hair had been long enough to dance in the ocean breeze. The salient cheekbones, trenchant jaw and elegant nose were the same, but none were burnished by the caress of salt and sun. And the mouth… Oh, the mouth. Brent's mouth had been perpetually curled into an irreverent smile, full and beautiful, the kind of mouth that incited a woman to commit mayhem. This version was flat and uncompromising, clearly not prone to smiles. And where Brent had worn nothing but T-shirts and baggy shorts, this man was dressed in charcoal trousers, a crisp white Oxford shirt, maroon necktie and black vest.

So it wasn't Zombie Brent. It was Brent's very much alive brother. Brent's very much alive *twin* brother. The mirror image of a man who had, one summer, filled Clara with a happiness unlike any she had ever known, and left her with the gift of a son who would ensure that happiness stayed with her forever.

A mirror image of that man who resembled him not at all.

She wasn't what he'd expected.

Then again, Grant Dunbarton wasn't sure exactly what he had expected the mother of Brent's son to be. His brother had been completely indiscriminate when it came to women. Brent had been indiscriminate about everything. Women, cars, clothes. Friends, family, society. Promises, obligations, responsibilities. You name it, it had held Brent's attention for as long as it interested him—which was rarely more than a few days. Then he'd moved on to something else. He'd been the poster child for Peter Pan Syndrome, no matter how old he was.

Actually, Grant reconsidered, there had been one way his brother discriminated when it came to women. All of them had been jaw-droppingly beautiful. Clara Easton was no exception. Her hair was a riot of black curls, her mouth was as plump and red as a ripe pepper and her eyes were a green so pale and so clear they seemed to go on forever. She was tall, too, probably pushing six feet in her spike-heeled boots.

She might have looked imperious, but she had her arm roped protectively around her son in a way that indicated she was clearly uncomfortable. Grant supposed that shouldn't be surprising. It wasn't every day that a woman who'd been spawned by felons and raised in a string of sketchy environments discovered she'd given birth to the equivalent of American royalty.

Because the Dunbartons of Park Avenue—formerly the Dunbartons of Rittenhouse Square and, before that, the Dunbartons of Beacon Hill—were a family whose name had, since Revolutionary times, been mentioned in the same breath with the Hancocks, Astors, Vanderbilts and Rockefellers. Still, Grant admired her effort to make herself look invulnerable. It was actually kind of cute.

And then there was the boy. He was going to be a problem. Except for his hair and eye color—both a contribution from his mother—he was a replica of his father at that age. Grant hoped his own mother didn't fall apart again when she saw Henry Easton. She'd been a mess since hearing the news of Brent's drowning off the coast of Sri Lanka in the spring. It had only been last month that she'd finally pulled herself together enough to go through his things. Then, when she came across the will none of them knew he'd made and discovered he had a child none of them knew he'd fathered, she'd broken down again.

This time, though, there had been joy tempering the grief. There was a remnant of Brent out there in the world somewhere. In Georgia, of all places. Grant had been worried they'd need a paternity test to ensure Henry Easton really was a Dunbarton before they risked dashing his mother's hopes. But the boy's undeniable resemblance to Brent—and to Grant, for that matter—made that unnecessary.

"Ms. Easton," he said as warmly as he could—though, admittedly, warmth wasn't his strong suit. Brent had pretty much sucked up all the affability genes in the Dunbarton DNA while they were still in the womb. Which was fine, because it left Grant with all the efficiency genes, and those carried a person a lot further in life. "It's nice to finally meet you. You, too," he told Henry.

"It's nice to meet you, too, Mr. Dunbarton," Clara said, her voice low and husky and as bewitching as the rest of her.

A Southern drawl tinted her words, something Grant would have thought he'd find disagreeable, but instead found…well, kind of hot.

She nudged her son lightly. "Right, Hank? Say hello to Mr. Dunbarton."

"Hello, Mr. Dunbarton," the boy echoed dutifully.

Grant did his best to smile. "You don't have to call me Mr. Dunbarton. You can call me…"

He started to say *Uncle Grant*, but the words got

stuck in his throat. *Uncle* wasn't a word that sat well with him. Uncles were affable, easygoing guys who told terrible jokes and pulled nickels from people's ears. Uncles wore argyle sweaters and brought six-packs to Thanksgiving dinner. Uncles taught their nephews the things fathers wouldn't, like where to hide their *Playboy*s and how to get fake IDs. No way was Grant suited to the role of uncle.

So he said, "Call me Grant." When he looked at Clara Easton again, he added, "You, too."

"Thank you…Grant," she said. Awkwardly. In her Southern accent. That was kind of hot.

She glanced at her son. But Henry remained silent, only gazing at Grant with his mother's startlingly green eyes.

"Come in," he said to all of them.

August Fiver did, but Clara hesitated, clearly not confident of their reception, her arm still draped around her son's shoulder.

"Please," Grant tried again, extending his hand toward the interior. "You are welcome here."

Clara still didn't look convinced, but the intrepid Henry took an experimental step forward, his gaze never leaving Grant's. Then he took a second, slightly larger, step. Then a third, something that pulled him free of his mother's grasp. She looked as if she wanted to yank him back, but remained rooted where she stood.

"My mother is looking forward to meeting you," Grant said, hoping the mention of another woman might make her feel better. But mention of his mother only made her look more panicked.

"Is something wrong, Ms. Easton?"

By now, Henry had followed Fiver through the door, so the three of them looked expectantly at Clara. She glanced first at her son, then at Grant. For a moment, he honestly thought she would grab her son and bolt. Then, finally, she strode forward. Again, Grant was impressed by her attempt to seem more confident than she was. This time, though, it didn't seem cute. This time, it seemed kind of…

Hmm. That was weird. For a minute there, he felt toward Clara the way she must have felt when she roped her arm protectively around her son. But why would he feel the need to protect Clara Easton? From what he'd learned about her, she was more than capable of taking care of herself. Not to mention that he barely knew her. And he wouldn't be getting to know her any better than he had to after this first encounter.

Sure, it was inevitable that their paths would cross in the future, since his mother would want to see as much of Henry as possible, and Clara would be included in that. But Grant didn't have the time or inclination to be *Uncle Grant*, even without the *Uncle* part. He and Brent might have been identical in looks, but they'd been totally different in every other way. Brent was always the charming, cheerful twin, while Grant was the sober, silent one. Brent made friends with abandon. Grant's few friends barely knew him. Brent treated life like a party. Grant knew it was a chore. Brent loved everyone he ever met. Grant never—

Clara Easton walked past him, leaving in her wake a faint aroma of something spicy and sweet. Cinnamon, he realized. And ginger. She smelled like Christmas morning. Except not the Christmas mornings he knew now, which were only notable because they were a day off from work. She smelled like the Christmas mornings of his childhood, before his father died, when the Dunbartons were happy.

Wow. He hadn't thought about those Christmas mornings for a long time. Because thinking about mornings like that reminded him of a time and place—reminded him of a person—he would never know again. A time when Grant had been staggeringly contented, and when his future had been filled with the promise of—

Of lots of things that never happened. He didn't usually like being reminded of mornings like that. For some reason, though, he didn't mind having Clara Easton and her cinnamon bun–gingerbread scent remind him today. He just wished he was the kind of person who could reciprocate. The kind of person who could be charming and cheerful and made friends with abandon. The kind who treated life like a party and loved everyone he met.

The kind who could draw the eye of a woman like Clara Easton in a way that didn't make her respond with fear and anxiety.

As Clara followed Grant Dunbarton deeper into the penthouse, she told herself she was silly to feel so intimidated. It was just an apartment. Just a really big, really sumptuous apartment. On one of the most expensive streets in the world. Filled with art and antiques with a value that probably exceeded the gross national product of some sovereign nations. She knew nothing of dates or styles when it came to antiques, but she was going to go out on a limb and say the decor here was Early Conspicuous Consumption.

Inescapably, she compared it to her two-bedroom, one-bath apartment above the bakery. Her furniture was old, too, but her Midcentury Salvage wasn't nearly as chic, and her original artwork had been executed by a preschooler. Add to that the general chaos that came with having said preschooler underfoot—and also rocks, puzzle pieces and Cheerios underfoot—and it was pretty clear who had the better living space. She just hoped Hank didn't notice that, too. But judging by the way he walked with his eyes wide, his neck craned and his mouth open, she was pretty sure he did.

"So…how long have y'all lived here?" she asked Grant. Mostly because no one had said a word since she and Hank and Gus entered, and she was beginning to think none of them would ever speak again.

Grant slowed until she pulled alongside him, which was something of a mixed blessing. On the upside, she could see his face. On the downside, she could see his face. And all she could do was be struck again by how much he resembled Brent. Well, that and also worry about how the resemblance set off little explosions in her midsection that warmed places inside her that really shouldn't be warming in mixed company.

"Brent and I grew up here," he said. "The place has been in the family for three generations."

"Wow," Clara said. Talk about having deep roots somewhere. "I grew up in Macon. But I've been living on Tybee Island since I graduated from college."

"Yes, I know," he told her. "You graduated from Carson High School with a near-perfect GPA and have a business administration degree from the College of Coastal Georgia that you earned in three years. Not bad. Especially considering how you worked three jobs the entire time."

Clara told herself she shouldn't be surprised. Families like the Dunbartons didn't open their door to just anyone. "You had me checked out, I see."

"Yes," he admitted without apology. "I'm sure you understand."

Actually, she did. When it came to family—even if that family only numbered two, like her and Hank—

you did what you had to do to protect it. Had August Fiver not already had a ton of info to give her about the Dunbartons, Clara would have had them checked out, too, before allowing them access to her son.

"Well, the AP classes in high school helped a lot with that three-years thing," she told him.

"So did perseverance and hard work."

Well, okay, there was that, too.

Grant led them to a small study that was executed in pale yellow and paler turquoise and furnished with overstuffed moiré chairs, a frilly desk and paintings of gorgeous landscapes. The room reeked of Marie Antoinette—the Versailles version, not the Bastille version—so Clara was pretty sure this wasn't a sanctuary for him.

As if cued by the thought, a woman entered from a door on the other side of the room. This had to be Grant's mother, Francesca. She looked to be in her midfifties, with short, dark hair liberally streaked with silver and eyes as rich a blue as her sons'. She was nearly as tall as Clara, but slimmer, dressed in flowing palazzo pants and tunic the color of a twilit sky. Diamond studs winked in each earlobe, and both wrists were wrapped in silver bracelets. She halted when she saw her guests, her gaze and smile alighting for only a second on Clara before falling to Hank…whereupon her eyes filled with tears.

But her smile brightened as she hurried forward, arms outstretched in the universal body language for *Gimme a big ol' hug.* She halted midstride, however, when Hank stepped backward, pressing himself into Clara with enough force to make her stumble backward herself. Until Grant halted her, wrapping sure fingers around her upper arms. For the scantest of moments, her brain tricked her into thinking it was Brent catching her, and she came *this close* to spinning around to plant a grateful kiss on Grant's mouth, so instinctive was her response.

Was it going to be like this the whole time she was here? Was the younger version of herself that still obviously lived inside her going to keep thinking it was Brent, not Grant, she was interacting with? If so, it was going to be a long week.

"Thanks," she murmured over her shoulder, hoping he didn't hear her breathlessness.

When he didn't release her immediately, she turned around to look at him, an action that caused him to release one shoulder, but not the other. For a moment, they only gazed at each other, and Clara was again overcome by how much he resembled Brent, and how that resemblance roused all kinds of feelings in her she really didn't need to be feeling. Then, suddenly, Grant smiled. But damned if his smile wasn't just like Brent's, too.

"Where are my manners?" he asked, his hand still curved over her arm. "I should have taken your coat the minute you walked in."

Automatically, Clara began to unbutton her coat... then suddenly halted. Because it didn't feel as if she was unbuttoning her coat for a man who had politely asked for it. It felt as if she was unbuttoning her shirt—or dress or skirt or pants or whatever else she might have on—so she could make love with Brent.

Wow. It really was going to be a long week. Maybe she and Hank should just head home tomorrow. Or even before dinner. Or lunch.

She went back to her buttons before her hesitation seemed weird—though, judging by Grant's expression, he already thought it was weird. Beneath her coat, she wore a short black dress and red-and-black polka dot tights that had felt whimsical and Christmassy when she put them on but felt out of place now amid the elegance of the Dunbarton home.

She and Hank should *definitely* leave before lunch.

Her plan was dashed, however, when Francesca, who had stopped a slight distance from Hank but still looked like the happiest woman in the world, said, "It is so lovely to have you both here. I am so glad we found you. Thank you so much for staying with us. I've asked Timmerman to bring up your bags." Obviously not wanting to overwhelm her grandson, she focused on Clara when she spoke again. "You must be Clara," she said as she extended her right hand.

Clara accepted it automatically. "I'm so sorry about Brent, Mrs. Dunbarton. He was a wonderful person."

Francesca's smile dimmed some, but didn't go away. "Yes, he was. And please, call me Francesca." She clasped her hands together when she looked at Hank, as if still not trusting herself to not reach for him. "And you, of course, must be Henry. Hello there, young man."

Hank said nothing for a moment, only continued to lean against Clara as he gave his grandmother wary consideration. Finally, politely, he said, "Hello. My name is Henry. But everybody calls me Hank."

Francesca positively beamed. "Well, then I will, too. And what should we have you call me, Hank?"

This time Hank looked up at Clara, and she could see he had no idea how to respond. They had talked before coming to New York about his father's death and his newly discovered grandmother and uncle, but conveying all the ins and outs of those things to a three-year-old hadn't been easy, and she still wasn't sure how much Hank understood. But when he'd asked if this meant he and Clara would be spending holidays like Thanksgiving and Christmas with his new family, and whether they could come to Tybee Island for his birthday parties, it had finally struck Clara just how big a life change this was going to be for her son.

And for her, too. It had been just the two of them for more than three years. She'd figured it would stay just the two of them for a couple of decades, at least, until Hank found a partner and started a family—and a life—of his own. Clara hadn't expected to have to share him so soon. Or to have to share him with strangers.

Who wouldn't be strangers for long, since they were family—Hank's family, anyway. But that was something else Clara had been forced to accept. Now her son had a family other than her. But she still just had—and would always just have—him.

She tried not to stumble over the words when she said, "Hank, sweetie, this is your grandmother. You two need to figure out what y'all want to call her."

Francesca looked at Hank again, her hands still clasped before her, still giving him the space he needed. Clara was grateful the older woman realized that a child his age needed longer to get used to a situation like this than an adult did. Clara understood well the enormity and exuberance of a mother's love. It was the only kind of love she did understand. It was the only kind she'd ever known. She knew how difficult it was to rein it in. She appreciated Francesca's doing so for her grandson.

"Do you know what your father and Uncle Grant called their grandmother?" Francesca asked Hank.

He shook his head. "No, ma'am. What?"

Francesca smiled at the *No, ma'am*. Clara supposed it wasn't something a lot of children said anymore. But she had been brought up to say *no, ma'am* and *no, sir* when speaking to adults—it was still the Southern way in a lot of places—so it was only natural to teach Hank to say it, too. One small step for courtesy. One giant step for the human race.

"They called her Grammy," Francesca told Hank. "What do you think about calling me Grammy?"

Clara felt Hank relax. "I guess I could call you Grammy, if you think it's okay."

Francesca's eyes went damp again, and she smiled. "I think it would be awesome."

Now Clara smiled, too. The woman had clearly done her homework and remembered how to talk to a child. A grandmother's love must be as enormous and exuberant as a mother's love. Hank could do a lot worse than Francesca Dunbarton for a grandmother.

"Now, then," Francesca said. "Would you like to see your father's old room? It looks just like it did when he wasn't much older than you."

Hank looked at Clara for approval.

"Go ahead, sweetie," she told him. "I'd like to see your dad's room, too." To Francesca, she added, "If you don't mind me tagging along."

"Of course not. Maybe your uncle Grant will come with us. You can, too, Mr. Fiver, if you want to."

Clara turned to the two men, expecting them to excuse themselves due to other obligations, and was surprised to find Grant looking not at his mother, but at her, intently enough that she got the impression he'd been looking at her for some time. A ball of heat somersaulted through her midsection a few times and came to rest in a place just below her heart. Because the way he was looking at her was the same way Brent had looked at her, whenever he was thinking about…well… Whenever he was feeling frisky. And, wow, suddenly, out of nowhere, Clara started feeling a little frisky, too.

He isn't Brent, she reminded herself firmly. He might

look like Brent and sound like Brent and move like Brent, but Grant Dunbarton wasn't the sexy charmer who had taught her to laugh and play and frolic one summer, then given her the greatest gift she would ever receive, in the form of his son. As nice as Grant was trying to be, he would never, could never, be his brother. Of that, Clara was certain. That didn't make him bad. It just made him someone else. Someone who should not—would not, could not, she told herself sternly— make her feel frisky. Even a little.

"Thank you, Mrs. Dunbarton," Gus said, pulling her thoughts back to the matter at hand—and not a moment too soon. "But I should get back to the office. Unless Clara needs me for anything else."

She shook her head. He'd only come this morning to be a buffer between her and the Dunbartons, should one be necessary. But Francesca was being so warm and welcoming, and Grant was *trying* to be warm and welcoming, so… No, Grant *was* warm and welcoming, she told herself. He just wasn't quite as good at it as his mother was. As his brother had been, once upon a time.

"Go ahead, Gus, it's fine," she said. "Thank you for everything you've done. We appreciate it."

He said his goodbyes and told the Dunbartons he could find his own way out. Clara waited for Grant to leave, too, but he only continued to gaze at her in that heated way, looking as if he didn't intend to go anywhere. Not unless she was going with him.

He's not Brent, she told herself again. *He's not.*

Now if only she could convince herself he wouldn't be the temptation his brother had been, too.

Two

Unfortunately, as Francesca led them back the way they'd all come, Grant matched his stride to Clara's and stayed close enough that she could fairly feel the heat of his body mingling with hers and inhale the faint scent of him—something spicy and masculine and nothing like Brent's, which had been a mix of sun and surf and salt. It was just too bad that Grant's fragrance was a lot more appealing. Thankfully, their walk didn't last long. Francesca turned almost immediately down a hallway that ended in a spiral staircase, something that enchanted Hank, because he'd never seen anything like it.

"Are we going up or down?" he asked Francesca.

"Down," she said. "But it can be kind of tricky, and sometimes I get a little wonky. Do you mind if I hold your hand, so I don't fall?"

Hank took his grandmother's hand and promised to keep her safe.

"Oh, thank you, Hank," she gushed. "I can already tell you're going to be a big help around here."

Something in the comment and Francesca's tone gave Clara pause. Both sounded just a tad…proprietary. As if Francesca planned for Hank to be *around here* for a long time. She told herself Francesca was just trying to make things more comfortable between herself and her grandson. And, anyway, what grandmother wouldn't want her grandson to be around? Clara had made clear through Gus that she and Hank would only be in New York for a week. Everything was fine.

Francesca halted by the first closed door Clara had seen in the penthouse. When the other woman curled her fingers over the doorknob, Clara felt like Dorothy Gale, about to go from her black-and-white farmhouse to a Technicolor Oz. And what lay on the other side was nearly as fantastic: a bedroom that was easily five times the size of Hank's at home and crammed with boyish things. Brent must have been clinging to his childhood with both fists when he left home.

One entire wall was nothing but shelves, half of them blanketed by books, the other half teeming with toys. From the ceiling in one corner hung a papier-mâché solar system, low enough that a child could reach up and, with a flick of his wrist, send its planets into orbit. On the far side of the room was a triple bunk bed with both a ladder and a sliding board for access. The walls were covered with maps of far-off places and photos of exotic beasts. The room was full of everything a little boy's heart could ever desire—building blocks, musical instruments, game systems, stuffed animals… They might as well have been in a toy store, so limitless were the choices.

Hank seemed to think so, too. Although he entered

behind Francesca, the minute he got a glimpse of his surroundings, he bulleted past his grandmother in a blur. He spun around in a circle in the middle of the room, taking it all in, then fairly dove headfirst into a bin full of Legos. It could be days before he came up for air.

Clara thought of his bedroom back home. She'd bought his bed at a yard sale and repainted it herself. His toy box was a plastic storage bin—not even the biggest size available—and she'd built his shelves out of wood salvaged from a demolished pier. At home, he had enough train track to make a figure eight. Here, he could re-create the Trans-Siberian Railway. At home, he had enough stuffed animals for Old McDonald's farm. Here, he could repopulate the Earth after the Great Flood.

This was not going to end well when Clara told him it was time for the two of them to go home.

Francesca knelt beside the Lego bin with Hank, plucking out bricks and snapping them together with a joy that gave his own a run for its money. She must have done the same thing with Brent when he was Hank's age. Clara's heart hurt seeing them. She couldn't imagine what it would be like to lose a child. This meeting with her grandson had to be both comforting and heartbreaking for Francesca.

Clara sensed more than saw Grant move to stand beside her. He, too, was watching the scene play out, but Clara could no more guess his thoughts than she could stop the sun from rising. She couldn't imagine losing a sibling, either. Although she'd had "brothers" and "sisters" in a couple of her foster homes, sometimes sharing a situation with them for years, all of them had maintained a distance. No one ever knew when they would be jerked up and moved someplace new, so it was always best not to get too attached to anyone. And none of the kids ever shared the same memories or histories as the others. Everyone came with his or her own—and left with them, too. Sometimes that was all a kid left with. There was certainly never anything like this.

"I can't believe y'all still have this much of Brent's stuff," she said.

Grant shrugged. "My mother was always sure Brent would eventually get tired of his wandering and come home, and she didn't want to get rid of anything he might want to keep. And Brent never threw away anything. Well, no material possessions, anyway," he hastened to clarify.

When his gaze met hers, Clara knew he was backtracking in an effort to not hurt her feelings by suggesting that Brent had thrown away whatever he shared with her.

"It's okay," she said. "Brent and I were never... I mean, there was nothing between us that was..." She stopped, gathered her thoughts and tried again, lowering her voice this time so that Francesca and Hank couldn't hear. "Neither of us wanted or expected anything permanent. There was an immediate attraction, and we could talk for hours, right off the bat, about anything and everything—as long as it didn't go any deeper than the surface. It was one of those things that happens sometimes, where two people just feel comfortable around each other as soon as they meet. Like they were old friends in a previous life or something, picking up where they left off, you know?"

He studied her in silence for a moment, and then shook his head. "No. Nothing like that has ever happened to me."

Clara sobered. "Oh. Well. It was like that for me and Brent. He really was a wonderful person when I knew him. We had a lot of fun together for a few weeks. But neither of us wanted anything more than that. It could have just as easily been me who walked away. He just finished first."

She tried not to chuckle at her wording. Brent finishing first was pretty much par for the course. Not just with their time together, but with their meals together. With their walks together. With their sex together. Yes, that part had been great, too. But he was never able to quite…satisfy her.

"He was always in a hurry," Grant said.

Clara smiled. "Yes, he was."

"He was like a hummingbird when we were kids. The minute his feet hit the ground in the morning, he was unstoppable. There were so many things he wanted to do. Every day, there were so many things. And he never knew where to start, so he just…went. Everywhere. Constantly."

Brent hadn't been as hyper as that when she met him, but he'd never quite seemed satisfied with anything, either, as if there was something else, something better, somewhere else. He told her he left home at eighteen and had been tracing the coastline of North America ever since, starting in Nome, Alaska, heading south, and then skipping from San Diego to Corpus Christi for the Gulf of Mexico. When she asked him where he would go next, he said he figured he'd keep going as far north into Newfoundland as he could, and then hop over to Scandinavia and start following Europe's shoreline. Then he'd do Asia's. Then Africa's. Then South America's. Then, who knew?

"He was still restless when I met him," she told Grant. "But I always thought his restlessness was like mine."

He eyed her curiously, and her heart very nearly stopped beating. His expression was again identical to Brent's, whenever he puzzled over something. She wondered if she would ever be able to look at Grant and *not* see Hank's father. Then again, it wasn't as if she'd be looking at him forever. Yes, she was sure to see Grant again after she and Hank left New York, since Francesca would want regular visits, but Clara's interaction with him would be minimal. Still, she hoped at some point her heart would stop skipping a beat whenever she looked at him. Odd, since she couldn't remember it skipping this much when she looked at Brent.

"What do you mean?" he asked.

"I thought his restlessness was because he came from the same kind of situation I did, where he never stayed in one place for very long so couldn't get rooted for any length of time. Like maybe he was an army brat or his parents were itinerant farmers or something."

Now Grant's expression turned to one of surprise. And damned if it didn't look just like Brent's would have, too. "He never told you anything about his past? About his family?"

"Neither of us talked about anything like that. There was some unspoken rule where we both recognized that it was off-limits to talk about anything too personal. I knew why I didn't want to talk about my past. I figured his reasons must have been the same."

"Because of the foster homes and children's institutions," Grant said. "That couldn't have been a happy experience for you."

She told herself she shouldn't be surprised he knew about that, too. Of course his background check would have been thorough. In spite of that, she said, "You really did do your homework."

He said nothing, only treated her to an unapologetic shrug.

"What else did you find out?" she asked.

He started to say something, then hesitated. But somehow, the look on his face told Clara he knew a lot more than she wanted him to know. And since he had the finances and, doubtless, contacts to uncover everything he could, he'd probably uncovered the one thing she'd never told anyone about herself.

Still keeping her voice low, so that Francesca and Hank couldn't hear, she asked, "You know where I was born, don't you? And the circumstances of why I was born in that particular location."

He nodded. "Yeah. I do."

Which meant he knew she was born in the Bibb County jail to a nineteen-year-old girl who was awaiting trial for her involvement in an armed robbery she had committed with Clara's father. He might even know—

"Do you know the part about who chose my name?" she asked further, still in the low tone that ensured only Grant would hear her.

He nodded. "One of the guards named you after the warden's mother because your own mother didn't name you at all." Wow. She'd had no idea he would dig that deep. All he'd had to do was make sure she was gainfully employed, reasonably well educated and didn't have a criminal record herself. He hadn't needed to bring her— She stopped herself before thinking the word *family*, since the people who had donated her genetic material might be related to her, but they would never be family. Anyway, he hadn't needed to learn about them, too. They'd had nothing to do with her life after generating it.

"And I know that after she and your father were convicted," he continued in a low tone of his own, "there was no one else in the family able to care for you."

Thankfully, he left out the part about how that was because the rest of her relatives were either addicted, incarcerated or missing. Though she didn't doubt he knew all that, too. She listened for traces of contempt or revulsion in his voice but heard neither. He was as matter-of-fact about the unpleasant circumstances of her birth and parentage as he would have been were he reading a how-to manual for replacing a carburetor. As matter-of-fact about those things as she was herself, really. She should probably give him kudos for that. It bothered Clara, though—a lot—that he knew so many details about her origins.

Which was something else to add to the That's Weird list, because she had never really cared about anyone knowing those details before. She would have even told Brent, if he'd asked. She knew it wasn't her fault that her parents weren't the cream of society. And she didn't ask to be born, especially into a situation like that. She'd done her best to not let any of it hold her back, and she thought she'd done a pretty good job.

Evidently, Grant didn't hold her background against her, either, because when he spoke again, it was in that same even tone. "You spent your childhood mostly in foster care, but in some group homes and state homes, too. When they cut you loose at eighteen, where a lot of kids would have hit the streets and gotten into trouble, you got those three jobs and that college degree. Last year, you bought the bakery where you were working when its owner retired, and you've already made it more profitable. Just barely, but profit is an admirable accomplishment. Especially in this economic climate. So bravo, Clara Easton."

His praise made her feel as if she was suddenly the cream of society. More weirdness. "Thanks," she said.

He met her gaze longer than was necessary for acknowledgment, and the jumble of feelings inside her got jumbled up even more. "You're welcome," he said softly.

Their gazes remained locked for another telling moment—at least, it was telling for Clara, but what it mostly told her was that it had been way too long since she'd been out on a date—then she made herself look back at the scene in the bedroom. By now, Francesca was seated on the floor alongside Hank, holding the base of a freeform creation that he was building out in a new direction—sideways.

"He'll never be an engineer at this rate," Clara said. "That structure is in no way sound."

"What do you think he will be?" Grant asked.

"I have no clue," she replied. "He'll be whatever he decides he wants to be."

When she looked at Grant again, he was still studying her with great interest. But there was something in his eyes that hadn't been there before. Clara had no idea how she knew it, but in that moment, she did: Grant Dunbarton wasn't a happy guy. Even with all the money, beauty and privilege he had in his life.

She opened her mouth to say something—though, honestly, she wasn't really sure what—when Hank called out, "Mama! I need you to hold this part that Grammy can't!"

Francesca smiled. "Hank's vision is much too magnificent for a mere four hands. My grandson is brilliant, obviously."

Clara smiled back. Hank was still fine-tuning his small motor skills and probably would be for some time. But she appreciated Francesca's bias.

She looked at Grant. "C'mon. You should help, too. If I know Hank, this thing is going to get even bigger."

For the first time since she'd met him, Grant Dunbarton looked rattled. He took a step backward, as if in retreat, even though all she'd done was invite him to join in playtime. She might as well have just asked him to drink hemlock, so clear was his aversion.

"Ah, thanks, but, no," he stammered. He took another step backward, into the hallway. "I... I have a lot of, uh, work. That I need to do. Important work. For work."

"Oh," she said, still surprised by the swiftness with which he lost his composure. Even more surprising was the depth of her disappointment that he was leaving. "Okay. Well. I guess I'll see you later, then. I mean... Hank and I will see you later."

He nodded once—or maybe it was a twitch—then took another step that moved him well and truly out of the bedroom and into the hallway. Clara went the other way, taking her seat on the other side of Hank. When she looked back at the door, though, Grant still hadn't left to do all the important work that he needed to do. Instead, he stood in the hallway gazing at her and Hank and Francesca.

And, somehow, Clara couldn't help thinking he looked less like a high-powered executive who needed to get back to work than he did a little boy who hadn't been invited to the party.

Grant hadn't felt like a child since... Well, he couldn't remember feeling like a child even when he *was* a child. And he certainly hadn't since his father's death shortly after his tenth birthday. But damned if he didn't feel like one now, watching Clara and her son play on the floor with his mother. It was the way a child felt when he was picked last in gym or ate alone at lunch. Which was nuts, because he'd excelled at sports, and he'd had plenty of friends in school. The fact that they were sports he hadn't really cared about excelling at—but that looked good on a college application—and the fact that he'd never felt all that close to his friends was beside the point.

So why did he suddenly feel so dejected? And so rejected by Clara? Hell, she'd invited him to join them. And how could she be rejecting him when he hadn't even asked her for anything?

Oh, for God's sake. This really was nuts. He should be working. He should have been working the entire time he was standing here revisiting a past it was pointless to revisit. He'd become the CEO of Dunbarton Industries the minute the ink on his MBA dried and hadn't stopped for so much as a coffee break since. Staying home today to meet Clara and Hank with his mother was the first nonholiday weekday he'd spent away from the office in years.

He glanced at his watch. It wasn't even noon. He'd lost less than half a day. He could still go in to the office and get way more done than he would trying to work here. He'd only stayed home in case Clara turned out to be less, ah, stable than her résumé let on and created a problem. But the woman was a perfectly acceptable candidate for mothering a Dunbarton. Well, as an individual, she was. Her family background, on the other hand...

Grant wasn't a snob. At least, he didn't think he was. But when he'd discovered Clara was born in a county jail, and that her parents were currently doing time for other crimes they'd committed... Well, suffice it to say felony convictions weren't exactly pluses on the social

register. Nor were they the kind of thing he wanted associated with the Dunbarton name. Not that Hank went
by Dunbarton. Well, not yet, anyway. Grant was sure
his mother would get around to broaching the topic of
changing his last name to theirs eventually. And he
was sure Clara would capitulate. What mother wouldn't
want her child to bear one of the most respected names
in the country?

Having met Clara, however, he was surprised to have
another reaction about her family history. He didn't
want that sort of thing attached to her name, either.
She seemed like too decent a person to have come from
that kind of environment. She really had done well for
herself, considering her origins. In fact, a lot of people
who'd had better breeding and greater fortune than she
hadn't gone nearly as far.

He lingered at the bedroom door a minute more,
watching the scene before him. No, not watching the
scene, he realized. Watching Clara. She was laughing
at something his mother had said, while keeping a close
eye on Hank who, without warning, suddenly bent and
brushed a kiss on his mother's cheek—for absolutely
no reason Grant could see. He was stunned by the gesture, but Clara only laughed some more, indicating that
this was something her son did often. Then, when in
spite of their best efforts, the structure he'd been building toppled to the floor, she wrapped her arms around
him, pulled him into her lap and kissed him loudly on
the side of his neck. He giggled ferociously, but reached
behind himself to hug her close. Then he scrambled out
of her clutches and hurried across the room to try his
hand at something else.

The entire affectionate exchange lasted maybe ten
seconds and was in no way extraordinary. Except that it

was extraordinary, because Grant had never shared that kind of affection with his own mother, even before his father's death changed all of them. He'd never shared that kind of affection with anyone. Affection that was so spontaneous, so uninhibited, so lacking in contrivance and conceit. So...so natural. As if it were as vital to them both as breathing.

That, finally, made him walk down the hall to his office. Work. That was what he needed. Something that was as vital to him as breathing. Though maybe he wouldn't go in to the offices of Dunbarton Industries today. Maybe he should stay closer to home. Just in case... Just in case Clara really wasn't all that stable. Just in case she did create a problem. Well, one bigger than the one she'd already created just by being so spontaneous, so uninhibited, so lacking in contrivance and conceit, and so natural. He should still stay home today. Just in case.

You never knew when something extraordinary might happen.

Three

Actually, something extraordinary did happen. On Clara and Hank's second day in New York, the Dunbartons had dinner in the formal dining room. Maybe that didn't sound all that extraordinary—and wouldn't have been a couple of decades ago, because the Dunbartons had always had dinner in the formal dining room before his father's death—but it was now. Because now, the formal dining room was only used for special occasions. Christmas Day, Easter, Thanksgiving, or those few instances when Brent had deigned to make time for a visit home during his hectic schedule of bumming around on the world's best beaches.

Then again, Grant supposed the arrival of a new family member was a special occasion, too. But it was otherwise a regular day, at least for him. He'd spent it at work while his mother had taken Clara and Hank to every New York City icon they could see in a day, from the Staten Island Ferry to the Statue of Liberty to the Empire State Building to whatever else his mother had conjured up.

Grant had always liked the formal dining room a lot better than the smaller one by the kitchen, in spite of its formality. Or maybe because of it. The walls were painted a deep, regal gold, perfectly complementing the long table, chairs and buffet, which were all overblown Louis Quatorze.

But the ceiling was really the centerpiece, with its sweeping painting of the night sky, where the solar system played only one small part in the center, with highlights of the Milky Way fanning out over the rest—constellations and nebulae, with the occasional comet and meteor shower thrown in for good measure. When he was a kid, Grant loved to sneak in here and lie on his back on the rug, looking up at the stars and pretending—

Never mind. It wasn't important what he loved to pretend when he was a kid. He did still love the room, though. And something inside him still made him want to lie on his back on the rug and look up at the stars and pretend—

"It's pretty cool, isn't it?" he asked Hank, who was seated directly across from him, his neck craned back so he could scan the ceiling from one end to the other.

"It's awesome," the little boy said without taking his eyes off it. "Look, Mama, there's Saturn," he added, pointing up with one hand and reaching blindly with the other toward the place beside him to pat his mother's arm…and hitting the flatware instead.

Clara mimicked his posture, tipping her head back to look up. The position left her creamy neck exposed, something Grant tried not to notice. He also tried not to notice how the V-neck of her sweater was low enough to barely hint at the upper swells of her breasts, or how its color—pale blue—brought out a new dimension to her uniquely colored eyes, making them seem even greener somehow. Or how the light from the chandelier set iridescent bits of blue dancing in her black curls. Or how much he wanted to reach over and wind one around his finger to see if it was as soft as it looked.

"Yes, it is," she said in response to Hank's remark. "And what's that big one beside it?"

"Jupiter," he said.

"Very good," Grant told him, unable to hide his surprise and thankful for something else to claim his attention that didn't involve Clara. Or her creamy skin. Or her incredible eyes. Or her soft curls. "You're quite the astronomer, Hank."

"Well, he's working on it," Clara said with a smile. "Those are the only two planets he knows so far."

Grant's mother smiled, too, from her seat at the head of the table. "I have the smartest grandson in the universe. Not that I'm surprised, mind you, considering his paternity." Hastily, she looked at Clara and added, "And his maternity, too, of course!"

Clara smiled and murmured her thanks for the acknowledgment, but his mother continued to beam at her only grandchild. *Only* in more ways than one, Grant thought, since Hank was also likely the only grandchild she would ever have. No way was he suited to the role of father himself. Or husband, for that matter. And neither role appealed. He was, for lack of a better cliché, married to his business. His only offspring would be the bottom line.

"I also know Earth," Hank said, sounding insulted that his mother would overlook that.

Clara laughed. "So you do," she agreed.

Frankly, Grant couldn't believe a three-year-old would know any of the things Hank knew. Then again, when Grant was three, he knew the genus and species of the chambered nautilus—*Nautilus pompilius*. He'd loved learning all about marine life when he was a kid, but the nautilus was a particular favorite from the start, thanks to an early visit to the New York Aquarium where he'd been mesmerized by the animal. If a child discovered his passion early in life, there was no way to prevent him from absorbing facts like a sponge, even at three. Evidently, for Hank, astronomy would be such a passion.

"Do you have a telescope?" Grant asked Clara.

She shook her head. "If he stays interested in astronomy, we can invest in one. He can save his allowance and contribute. For now, binoculars are fine."

Hank nodded, seeming in no way bothered by the delay. So not expecting instant gratification was something else he'd inherited from his mother. Brent's life had been nothing *but* a demand for instant gratification.

Yet Clara could afford to give him instant gratification now. She could afford to buy her son a telescope with his newfound wealth, whether he stayed interested in astronomy or not. But she wasn't. Grant supposed she was trying to ensure that Hank didn't fall into the trap his father had. She didn't want him to think that just because he had money, he no longer had to work to earn something, that he could take advantage and have whatever he wanted, wherever and whenever he wanted it. Grant's estimation of her rose. Again.

As if he'd said the words out loud, she looked at him and smiled. Or maybe she did that because she was grateful he hadn't told her son that if he wanted a telescope, then, by God, he should have one, cost be damned. That was what Brent would have done. Then he would have scooped up Hank after dinner and taken him straight to Telescopes "R" Us to buy him the biggest, shiniest, most expensive one they had, without even bothering to see if it was the best.

As Hank and Francesca fell into conversation about the other planets on the ceiling, Grant turned to Clara. And realized he had no idea what to say to her. So he fell back on the obvious.

"Brent had an interest in astronomy when he was Hank's age, too," he told her. "It was one of the reasons my mother had this room decorated the way she did."

"I actually knew that," Clara said. "About the astronomy, not the room. He took me to Skidaway Island a few times to look at the stars. I've taken Hank, too. It's what started his interest in all this."

Grant nodded. Of course Brent would have taken her to a romantic rendezvous to dazzle her with his knowledge of the stars. And of course she would carry that memory with her and share it with their son.

"Hank is now about the same age I was when I started getting interested in baking," she said. "My foster mother at that time baked a lot, and she let me help her in the kitchen. I remember being amazed at how you could mix stuff together to make a gooey mess only to have it come out of the oven as cake. Or cookies. Or banana bread. Or whatever. And I loved how pretty everything was after the frosting went on. And how you could use the frosting to make it even prettier, with roses or latticework or ribbons. It was like making art. Only you could eat it afterward."

As she spoke about learning to bake, her demeanor changed again. Her eyes went dreamy, her cheeks grew rosy, and she seemed to go…softer somehow. All over. And she gestured as she spoke—something she didn't even seem aware of doing—stirring an imaginary bowl when she talked about the gooey mess, and opening an imaginary oven door when she talked about the final product and tracing a flower pattern on the tablecloth as she spoke of using frosting as an art medium. He was so caught up in the play of her hands and her storytelling, that he was completely unprepared when she turned the tables on him.

"What were you interested in when you were that age?"

The question hung in the air between them for a moment as Grant tried to form a response. Then he realized he didn't know how to respond. For one thing, he didn't think it was a question anyone had ever asked him before. For another, it had been so long since he'd thought about his childhood, he honestly couldn't remember.

Except he *had* remembered. A few minutes ago, when he'd been thinking about how fascinated he'd been by the chambered nautilus. About how much he'd loved all things related to marine life when he was a kid. Which was something he hadn't thought about in years.

Despite that, he said, "I don't know. The usual stuff, I guess."

His childhood love was so long ago, and he'd never pursued it beyond the superficial. Even though, he supposed, knowing the biological classification of the entire nautilus family—in Latin—by the time he started first grade went a little beyond superficial. That was different. Because that was…

Well, it was just different, that was all.

"Nothing in particular," he finally concluded. Even if that didn't feel like a conclusion at all.

Clara didn't seem to think so, either, because she insisted, "Oh, come on. There must have been something. All of Hank's friends have some kind of passion. With Brianna, it's seashells. With Tyler, it's rocks. With Megan, it's fairies. It's amazing the single-minded devotion a kid that age can have for something."

For some reason, Grant wanted very much to change the subject. So he turned the tables back on Clara. "So, owning a bakery. That must be gratifying, taking your childhood passion and making a living out of it as an adult."

For a moment, he didn't think Clara was going to let him get away with changing the subject. She eyed him narrowly, with clear speculation, nibbling her lower lip—that ripe, generous, delectable lower lip—in thought.

Just when Grant thought he might climb over the table to nibble it, too, she stopped and said, "It is gratifying."

He'd just bet it was. Oh, wait. She meant the bakery thing, not the lip-nibbling thing.

"Except that when your passion becomes your job," she went on, "it can sort of rob it of the fun, you know? I mean, it's still fun, but some of the magic is gone."

Magic, he repeated to himself. *Fun*. When was the last time he had a conversation with a woman—or, hell, anyone—that included either of those words? Yet here was Clara Easton, using them both in one breath.

"Don't get me wrong," she hastened to clarify. "I do love it. I just…"

She sighed with something akin to wistfulness. Damn. *Wistfulness*. There was another word Grant could never recall coming up in a conversation before—even in his head.

"Sometimes," she continued, "I just look at all the stuff in the bakery kitchen and at all the pastries out in the shop, and, after work, I go upstairs to the apartment with Hank, and I wonder… Is that it? Have I already peaked? I have this great kid, and we have a roof over our heads and food in the pantry, and I'm doing for a living what I always said I wanted to do, and yet sometimes… Sometimes—"

"—It's not enough," Grant said at the same time she did.

Her eyes widened in surprise at his completion of her thoughts, but she nodded. "Yeah. So you do understand."

He started to deny it. Was she crazy? Of course he had enough. He was a Dunbarton. He'd been born with more than enough. Loving parents. A brother who, had life worked the way it was supposed to, would have been a lifelong friend. Piles of money. All the best toys. All the best schools. Not to mention every possible opportunity life could offer waiting for him around every corner. And yet… And yet.

"Yeah, I do understand," he told her.

"So you must be doing something you love, too," she said.

Damn. She had turned the tables again. But his response was automatic. "Of course I love it. It's what I was brought up to do. It's the family business. Dunbartons have loved it for generations. Why wouldn't I love it?"

Belatedly, he realized how defensive he sounded. Clara obviously thought so, too, because her dreamy expression became considerably less dreamy. He searched for words that would make the dreaminess return—

since he'd really liked that look, probably more than he should—but he couldn't think of a single one. They'd already used up *magic*, *fun* and *wistfulness*. Grant wasn't sure he knew any other words like that.

Then he considered Clara again and was flooded with them. Words like *delightful*. And *luscious*. And *enchanting*. They were words he never used. But somehow, they and more like them all rushed to the fore, until his brain felt as if it was turning into a thesaurus. A purple thesaurus, at that.

Fortunately, their cook, Mrs. Bentley, arrived with the first course, and Clara was complimenting the dish and thanking Mrs. Bentley for her trouble. Grant started to point out that it wasn't any trouble, since that was Mrs. Bentley's job and had been for years, and she was being paid well for it. Then he remembered that Clara prepared food for a living, so expressing gratitude for it was probably some kind of professional courtesy. It also occurred to him that he was suddenly in a really irritable mood. But the subject of childhood passions evaporated after that, something for which he was grateful.

Now if only he could get rid of his troubling thoughts as easily.

Clara didn't think she'd ever been happier to see a salad than she was when the Dunbartons' cook placed one in front of her. Of course, the woman could have placed a live scorpion in front of her, and Clara would have been happy to see it. Anything to break her gaze away from Grant's. Because never had she seen anyone look more desolate than he did when he was talking about what he did for a living.

And he couldn't remember what he loved most as a child. Who didn't remember that? Everyone had loved something more than anything else when they were a kid. Everyone had wanted to be something more than anything else when they grew up. For Clara, it had been a baker. For Hank, at the moment, it was an astronomer. For Brent, it had been an astronaut. Even if it was something as unlikely as zookeeper or movie star, every child had some dream of becoming something. Of becoming someone. Every child, evidently, except Grant Dunbarton.

Then again, when a family had owned a business for generations, like the Dunbartons had, maybe it was just a given that their children's professional destiny lay in that business. Except that Brent hadn't gone to work for Dunbarton Industries. He'd been a professional vagabond, which was about as far removed from corporate kismet as a person could get. And he and Grant were the same age, so it wasn't as if taking over the business was a firstborn offspring responsibility for which Grant specifically had been groomed since birth. Nor did Francesca strike Clara as the kind of parent who would insist that her children pursue a preplanned agenda for the sake of the family. If Grant had shouldered the mantle of CEO for Dunbarton Industries, he must have done so because he wanted to.

Even if he didn't look or sound as if he'd wanted to.

The moment was now gone, however. Which was good for another reason, since it kept Clara from wondering if that was what the Dunbartons might have in mind for Hank. He was as much a Dunbarton as Grant and Francesca were. So he was as much a part of the family heritage—and family business—as they were. Surely they didn't have expectations like that for him, though. Although their blood ran in his veins, their society didn't. Nor would it ever, since there was no way

Clara would uproot her son from Georgia and move him to New York.

Even in Georgia, she planned to shield him from this world as much as she could. She didn't have anything against rich people—at least not the ones who earned their wealth and paid their employees a decent wage and gave something back to the community that had helped them build their empire. But the world those people lived in wasn't the real world or real life any more than Clara's upbringing had been.

And she wanted Hank to have a real life. One that involved both hard work and fun play, both discipline and reward. One where he would experience at least some anguish and heartache, because that was the only way to experience serenity and joy. It was impossible to appreciate the latter without knowing the former. And a person couldn't know the former if he was handed everything he wanted on a silver platter.

Maybe that was Grant's problem, she thought, sneaking another look at him. He was blandly forking around his salad, looking way more somber than a person should look when blandly forking around a salad. Maybe by having everything he'd ever wanted all his life, he was incapable of really *knowing* what he wanted. Except that he hadn't had everything he wanted, she thought. He'd lost his father when he was a child, and had lost his twin brother less than a year ago. He'd just told her how he understood what it was to not have enough, and she had a feeling there was more to it than just his personal losses.

She told herself to stop trying to figure him out. Grant Dunbarton's unhappiness and lack of fulfillment were none of her business, and they weren't her responsibility. She reminded herself again—why did she have to keep doing that?—that her life and his were only intersecting temporarily for now and would only be intersecting sporadically in the future. He wasn't her concern.

So why couldn't she stop feeling so concerned about him?

Four

*B*eware the Park Avenue doyenne with a platinum credit card. That was the only thought circling through Clara's head at the end of her third day in New York, probably because she was so exhausted at that point that it was the only thought that *could* circle through her brain. Francesca Dunbarton was a dynamo when it came to spending money.

As Clara lay beside a sleeping Hank in Brent's old bedroom, she did her best to not nod off herself. No easy feat, that, since the three of them had hit every place Francesca insisted they needed to hit so her only grandchild would have all the essentials of other Park Avenue grandchildren: Boomerang Toys and Books of Wonder, Bit'z Kids and Sweet William, the Disney Store, the Lego Store...pretty much anything a three-year-old would love with the word *store* attached to it.

Then Francesca had insisted they *must* do the

Children's Tea at the Russian Tea Room, because Hank would find it enchanting. They just had *so* much catching up to do!

Hank had finally succumbed to fatigue on the cab ride home and hadn't stirred since. Not when the elevator dinged their arrival on the top floor, not when Clara laid him on the bed, not when Francesca brushed a kiss on his cheek, not when the doorman arrived to deliver all the bags containing his grandmother's purchases for him. And those bags had rattled *a lot*. And there were *a lot* of bags to rattle.

Now Clara lay beside Hank, her elbow braced on the mattress, her head cradled in her hand, and as she watched the hypnotic rise and fall of her son's chest, her eyelids began to flutter. Until she heard the jangle of something metallic and the fall of footsteps in the hallway beyond the open door. Grant, arriving home from work. He appeared in the doorway wearing an impeccable dark suit, tie and dress shirt, the uniform of the upper-crust environment in which he thrived. It was Clara, in her olive drab cargo pants and oatmeal-colored sweater, not to mention her stocking feet, who was out of place here.

When he saw her, Grant lifted a hand in greeting and was about to say something out loud, but halted when he saw Hank sleeping so soundly. Clara lifted her finger in a silent *Hang on a sec*, then carefully maneuvered herself around Hank until she could slide to the floor and tiptoe toward the door and into the hall.

"You didn't have to get up," he said softly by way of a greeting.

"That's okay," she told him. "I needed to get up. I was about to doze off myself."

"Go ahead. Dinner won't be ready for another few hours, at least."

She shook her head. "If I sleep now, I won't sleep tonight. And I'm already a terrible insomniac as it is. I have been since I was a kid."

Because growing up, there had just been something about sharing a room with other kids she didn't know well that lent itself to lousy sleep habits. Clara's experiences in foster care and group homes hadn't been horrible, but most of them hadn't been especially great, either. She'd been the victim of theft and bullying and rivalry like many children—even those who weren't wards of the state—all things that could create stress and wariness in a kid and contribute to insomnia. Sure, none of those things was a part of her life now, but it was hard to undo decades' worth of conditioning.

She and Grant studied each other for a moment in strained silence. It was just so difficult to take her eyes off him, just so strange, seeing the mirror image of Brent dressed in the antithesis of Brent's wardrobe. And the close-cropped hair, in addition to being nothing like Brent's nearly shoulder-length tresses, was peppered with premature silver. She wondered if Brent had started to go gray, too, in the years since she had seen him, or if Grant's gray was simply the result of a more stressful life than his brother had led.

Then the gist of his words struck her, and she smiled. "A few hours till dinner? You must be home earlier than usual, then."

She meant for the comment to be teasing. Evidently, Grant wasn't the workaholic she'd assumed if he ended his office hours early enough to have some relaxation time before dinner. The realization heartened her. Maybe he did have something in common with his twin.

But Grant seemed to take the comment at face value. "Yeah, I am, actually," he said matter-of-factly. "But I could bring the work home with me, and I thought maybe you—and Hank, too, for that matter—I thought both of you, actually, might…um…"

Somehow, she knew he'd intended to end the sentence with the words *need me*, but decided at the last minute to say something else instead. No other words came out of his mouth, though.

Clara had trouble figuring out what to say next, too, mostly because she was too busy drowning in the deep blue depths of his eyes. Looking into Grant's eyes somehow felt different from looking into Brent's eyes, even though their eyes were identical. There was more intensity, more perception, more comprehension, more, well, depth. She'd never felt as if Brent was looking into her soul, even though the two of them were intimately involved for weeks. But having spent only a short time in Grant's presence, she felt as if he were peering past her surface—or at least trying to—to figure out what lay in her deepest inner self. It was…disconcerting. But not entirely unpleasant.

"Um," she said, struggling to find anything that would break the odd spell. But the only thing that came to mind was something about how beautiful his eyes were, and how very different from his brother's, and how she honestly wasn't sure she ever wanted to stop looking into his eyes, and…well…that probably wasn't something she should say to him right now. Or ever.

Thankfully, he broke eye contact and glanced beyond her into Hank's room—or, rather, Brent's old room, she hastily corrected herself—and said, "Looks like my mother did her share to bump up the gross domestic income today."

Clara turned around to follow his gaze. The pile of bags on the floor seemed to have multiplied in the few minutes since she'd last looked at it. Once again, she was reminded of how much more the Dunbartons could offer her son than she could. Materially, anyway. They'd never be able to love him more than she did. But when one was three years old, it wasn't difficult to let the material render the emotional less valuable. Especially when the material included a toy fire truck with motion-activated lights and sound effects.

"I cannot believe how much stuff she bought for Hank," Clara said. She looked at Grant again. "She really shouldn't have done that. I mean, Hank is extremely grateful—and I am, too," she hastened to add. "But…" She couldn't help the sigh that escaped her, nor could she prevent it from sounding melancholy. "I don't know how we're going to get everything home."

"Leave most of it here," Grant said. "Hank can take home his favorites and play with the rest of it when he comes back to visit." He smiled. "That was probably Mom's intention in the first place."

The thought had crossed Clara's mind, too. More than once. As many times as she'd tried to excuse Francesca's excessive purchasing by telling herself Hank's grandmother was just trying to make up for lost time, Clara hadn't been able to keep herself from wondering if all the gifts were bribes of a sort, to ensure that Hank would badger his mother to bring him back to New York ASAP. Having Grant pretty much confirm her suspicions did nothing to make Clara feel better.

Hank stirred on the bed, murmuring a sleepy complaint, and then turned from one side to the other and settled into slumber again. So Clara pulled the door closed to keep him from being awakened by her conversation with Grant.

"We can talk in my room," he said.

Clara scrambled for an excuse as to why she wouldn't be able to do that, but couldn't come up with a single one. Then she wondered why she was trying, since there had been nothing untoward in his invitation. Brain exhaustion, she told herself. She was too tired to follow him, but too tired to find a reason not to follow him. It had nothing to do with the fact that she just maybe kind of wanted to follow him, for a reason that might possibly be slightly untoward on her part.

So follow him she did, to the room next to Brent's. Even though it was next door, it seemed to take forever to get there; this place was enormous. Grant's room was the same size as Brent's, with the same two arched, floor-to-ceiling windows looking down on the same view of Park Avenue and, beyond it, Central Park.

The similarities ended there, however. Where Brent's room was painted a boyish bright blue, Grant's was the color of café mocha. And where Brent's curtains where patterned in whimsical moons and stars, Grant's were a luxe fabric that shimmered with dozens of earth tones. The furniture was sturdy mahogany—a massive sleigh bed, dressers and nightstands, as well as the bare essentials of manhood: alarm clock, lamps, dish for spare change and keys.

The only bit of color in the room was an aquarium opposite the bed. It was far bigger than anything Clara had ever seen in a pet store, and it was populated by fish in all sizes and colors, darting about as if oblivious to the glass walls that enclosed them.

Clara was drawn to it immediately. Even living so close to the water, she'd never seen so many fish in one place, and the brilliant colors and dynamic motion captivated her. Vaguely, she noted that Grant entered the room behind her, tossed his briefcase onto the bed and approached a wooden valet in the far corner of the room. Vaguely, she noted how he began to loosen his tie and unbutton his shirt, and—

Whoa. Whoa, whoa, whoa, *whoa.* No, she didn't note that vaguely. She noted that *very clearly.* Grant undressing caught Clara's attention in much the same way a tornado swirling toward her front door would catch her attention, and she spun around nearly as quickly. Even if—she was pretty sure—he wouldn't go any further than unfastening his shirt a couple of buttons below the collar or rolling up his sleeves, he was still undressing. And that tended to have an effect on a woman who hadn't seen a man undress for a while. A long while. A *really* long while. Especially a woman who had always enjoyed watching a man undress. A lot. A *whole* lot.

Although his movements were in no way provocative, heat flared in her belly at the sight of him. With an elegant shrug, he slipped off his jacket, then freed the buttons of his shirt cuffs and rolled each up to midforearm, exposing muscles that bunched and relaxed with every gesture. As he slung his jacket over the valet, she noted the breadth of his shoulders, too, and, couldn't help remembering the last time she had seen shoulders and arms like his. Except those shoulders and arms had been naked, and they had been hot and damp with perspiration beneath her fingertips. They had belonged to Grant's brother, who had been lying on top of her, gasping.

She remembered, too well, how that had felt—too good—and her face grew warm as her blood rushed faster through her veins. The heat multiplied when

Grant lifted a hand to his necktie and freed it, and then slowly, slowly...oh, so slowly...dragged the length of silk from beneath his collar to drape it over the jacket. But it was when his hands moved to his shirt buttons, loosening first one, then two, then three, that Clara felt as if her entire body would burst into flame. Because she couldn't stop watching those hands, those big, skillful, seductive hands, and remembering how they had felt on—and in—her body.

No, not those hands, she reminded herself. It had been Brent's hands that made her feel that way. Even if, on some level, she suspected Grant was every bit as skilled as his brother when it came to making a woman feel aroused and sexy and shameless and wanton and...and...and...

Um, where was she? Oh, yeah. Fish.

Except she wasn't thinking about fish. Because she was too busy wondering if sex with Grant would be as fierce and incendiary as it had been with Brent, and if it would leave her wanting more—

"...and firemouth."

It took Clara a minute to realize it was Grant who had spoken, and not Brent, so lost had she been in her memories of making love to the latter. Apparently he'd been speaking for some time, too, and might have even called her something that sounded a lot like *firemouth*. But how could he have known what she was thinking?

She gazed at him in silence, hoping her expression revealed nothing of the graphic images that had been tumbling through her brain. But when his gaze finally connected with hers, his smile fell and his eyes went wide, and she was pretty sure he could tell down to the last hot, sweaty detail *exactly* what she had been thinking since she started watching him undress, which meant that whole firemouth thing wasn't too far off the mark. So she did the only thing she could.

She spun quickly away from him, focused on the aquarium, and asked, "What kind of fish are these?" In an effort to look as if she was truly fascinated by the little swimmers, she even bent over and brought her face to within an inch of the glass.

Belatedly, she realized the idiocy of the question. Not only because thanks to her, *both* of them were now doubtless thinking about sex, not fish, but also because asking it caused him to move closer to her. He did so slowly and uncertainly, as if he were approaching a barracuda, which wasn't that far off the mark, really, since, at the moment, she was feeling more than a little predatory.

Breathe, Clara, breathe, she instructed herself. *And calm down.*

Unfortunately, it was impossible for her to do either, because, by then, Grant had moved behind her, his pelvis situated within inches of her, well, behind. If he'd wanted, he could have tugged the drawstring at her waist and pulled down her pants right there. Then he could have tugged down her panties, too, to expose her in the most intimate, most vulnerable way. Then he could have unfastened his belt, unzipped his fly and freed himself. He could have gripped her naked flesh and pulled her toward himself, and then buried himself inside her, slowly, deeply, possessively. Over and over and over again.

If he wanted.

Because in that moment, Clara wouldn't have stopped him, since she suddenly wanted him, too.

Oh, no. Oh, God. Oh, Grant.

Instead, he stepped to her left and bent forward, his

face scant inches from hers, to gaze into the aquarium with her.

She told herself that had been his intention all along. He couldn't possibly have been thinking about doing all the things she had been thinking about him doing. Her brain was just a muddle of memories about her time with Brent—most of which had been spent in sexual pursuits, she had to admit—and was transferring those desires to Grant. She'd known the man a matter of days. Then again, she'd been steaming up the sheets with Brent within hours of meeting him…

"I was just telling you the names of the fish," he said. She could tell he was struggling to keep his voice even and quiet.

"The one in front," he continued, "well, the one that was in front a minute ago, when you were, ah, looking at him, is a firemouth."

Ah. So he hadn't been calling Clara that. At least she didn't think he had. Probably best to not ask for clarification. "This one," he said, pointing to a spotted one that had swum to the front, "is a Texas cichlid. *Herichthys cyanoguttatus*, if you want to get technical. From the family Cichlidae. Actually, all the fish in this tank are cichlids, but there are more than a thousand different species, and new ones are turning up all the time, so I only put a handful of my favorites in here. That one," he continued as another fish, this one speckled with purple, blue and green, darted by, "is a Jack Dempsey."

"Like the boxer?" Clara asked.

"Yep. That's who the species is named after. Because they have kind of a boxer's face, and they can be pretty aggressive in small groups. They're native to Central America—Mexico and Honduras specifically—so they get along well with the Texas cichlid."

The tension between the two of them was ebbing now, allowing Clara to breathe again. She smiled at the image of two fish from opposite sides of the border interacting without incident. Nice to know someone in this room could get along swimmingly. So to speak.

"And that one is called a convict," Grant said, indicating a fish that was black-and-white striped. "For obvious reasons."

"I'm sure he was framed," Clara said, doing her best to lighten the mood further. "He looks too sweet to be a criminal."

Grant identified a half dozen more species as they swam by, offering up snippets about the habits or personalities of each. The more he talked, Clara noted, the more he smiled. And the more he smiled, the more he relaxed. She gradually relaxed, too, until all traces of sexual awareness eased, and she was confident the charged moment they'd shared was only an aberration, never to be repeated.

At least, she was *pretty* confident of that.

As Grant wound down his dissertation on the fish, Clara waited for him to add something that would explain how he came by all his knowledge. But he never did. He only gazed into the aquarium, watching the parade of color. She caught her breath as she watched him, because in that moment, he looked exactly like Hank. Not just the physical resemblance, thanks to the identical genes, but the childlike fascination, too. He looked the same way Hank did when he found a particularly interesting bit of jetsam on the beach. Grown-ups—especially super serious, workaholic grown-ups like Grant—weren't supposed to be distracted by things like colorful fish. Grown-ups were supposed to be worried about stuff like whether or not they were getting enough vitamin D or how they were going to make rent this month.

Well, okay, that was why *some* grown-ups—like, say, Clara—couldn't be distracted by something like colorful fish. Grant hadn't had to worry about making rent his entire life.

"You know, for a guy who sits behind a desk all day," she said, "you sure know a lot about fish. I live just a couple of blocks away from the ocean, and the only thing I know about marine life is which ones are my favorite on any given menu."

He laughed lightly as the two of them straightened, the sound of his voice rippling through Clara like a warm breeze. "Well, that's important to know, too. And these are all freshwater fish. My saltwater aquarium is in my office. It's twice the size of this one, and you'd probably recognize a lot of the guys in there. Clownfish, damselfish, sea horses, grouper…"

"I love grouper," she said. "Grilled, with dill butter on the side."

He chuckled again, and Clara realized the reason she liked the sound of his laughter so much was because she hadn't heard it until now. Frankly, she'd begun to wonder if he was even able to laugh. But the knowledge that he could was actually kind of sobering. If he was able to laugh, why didn't he do it more often?

"You probably love more of them than you realize," he told her. "*Grouper* is a word that applies to fish from several different genera in the *Serranidae* family. There's some sea bass and perch in there, too."

"Wow, you really do know a lot about fish."

For some reason, that made him suddenly look uncomfortable. "It's kind of a hobby," he told her. "Left over from when I was a kid. Back then, I wanted to be a marine biologist and live in the Caribbean when I grew up. Maybe the South Pacific. I even picked out the colleges I wanted to attend. I had this crazy idea as a kid that I could start a nonprofit for research and conservation. My dad even helped me set up a business plan for the thing." He grinned. "I remember I wanted to call it Keep Our Oceans Klean. With a *K*. That way, I could say I worked for a KOOK."

Clara grinned, too. Ah-hah. So, as a child, he *had* wanted to be something specific when he grew up. He *had* had a passion like any normal kid. She was glad for it, even if she wasn't sure why he was sharing that so readily today when, just last night, he'd claimed no memory of such. And she could see him being the kind of kid who would prepare for his college future and make out business plans when most kids were trying to figure out where to go to camp.

"What colleges?" she asked.

He hesitated, and for a minute, she thought he would try to backtrack and tell her he couldn't remember again. Instead, quietly, he said, "College of the Atlantic in Maine for a BS in marine science, then on to Duke for my master's in marine biology. After that, it was a toss-up between University of California Santa Barbara and University of Miami for any postgrad work."

"Why didn't you go?" she asked. "Why didn't you start KOOK? It sounds like a lifelong dream if you're still keeping fish and know so much about them."

Now he looked at her as if she should already know the answer to that question. "There was no way I could do that after my father died."

Clara still didn't understand. For a lot of people, the unexpected death of a loved one made them even more determined to follow their dreams. "Why not?"

Once more, he hesitated. When he finally did speak again, it was in halting sentences, as if the information were being pulled from him unwillingly. "Well... I mean... After my father died, we all... And Brent..."

He halted abruptly, and then tried again. But he was obviously choosing his words carefully. "Brent was actually the one who was supposed to follow in my father's footsteps and run the business after he retired. He was the firstborn, technically, and he seemed to genuinely love the idea of going to work for Dunbarton Industries after he graduated from college. Even when we were little, he used to go in to the office with Dad sometimes, and it wasn't unusual for the two of them to hole up in the office at home in an unofficial Junior Achievement meeting. But after Dad died, Brent..."

He sighed heavily. "Brent reacted to our father's death by regressing. He started shirking responsibility, never did his homework, locked himself up in his room to play for hours on end. Instead of maturing as he aged, he only got more childlike. Even in high school. There was no way he could have gotten into a decent business school with his grades, which was just as well, since he made clear after our father's death that there was no way he was going to take over the company. And Mom wasn't much better. She retreated, too, after Dad died, from just about everything. And she let Brent do whatever he wanted."

It didn't escape Clara's notice that Grant had left himself out of the equation when describing how his family reacted to the death of the Dunbarton patriarch. She could almost see Grant as a child, feeling the same emptiness his mother and brother felt, but not wanting anyone to see him that way.

Before she could stop herself, she asked, "And how

did little Grant react after his father's death? You must have been heartbroken, too."

"I was," he said. "But with my mother retreating and Brent regressing... Someone had to be an adult. Someone had to make sure things got done around here. Mom wouldn't even pay the bills or our employees. The company almost went into receivership at one point. Some of my dad's colleagues stepped in and took over until I could graduate from college and step into the CEO position. So I majored in business and did just that. If I hadn't, the company would have been cut up into little pieces and sold off bit by bit. And then where would the Dunbarton legacy be?"

Clara wanted to reply that the Dunbartons would have made a boatload of money, so their legacy wouldn't be much different from what it was now, and Grant could have followed his dream. But she didn't think he would see it that way. He'd obviously started feeling responsible for his family and the family business when he was still a child himself. Clara got that. She'd assumed responsibility for herself as soon as she understood what responsibility was, and had done the same for Hank as soon as she realized she was pregnant. As a mother, she understood well what it was to put someone else's wants and needs ahead of her own. But she had still pursued her dream of doing something she loved for a living. And if she'd had hundreds of millions of dollars like the Dunbartons did, she'd now have a whole chain of Bread & Buttercream bakeries, and her home office would be in Paris.

"I guess legacies are important," she conceded half-heartedly—mostly because she knew Grant would think that, even if she wasn't quite on board with it herself. "Y'all have had your company for generations and everything. And you want to have something to pass on to your kids someday."

"Oh, I'm not having kids," he told her with conviction.

Too much conviction, really. Grant was only thirty-two. How could he be so sure of something like that? He still had plenty of time.

"Why not?" Clara asked.

Again, he looked at her as if the answer to her question should be obvious. "Because I don't want kids. Or marriage. I don't have time to be a father or husband."

Fair enough, she thought. But… "Then why do you need a legacy? If you're going to be the end of the line, that's even more reason for you to go after your dreams. You could sell the business now, go back to school to major in marine biology and study every ocean on the planet."

Of all the questions she'd asked and observations she'd made, that one seemed to upset him most. "That's not the point," he told her tersely.

"Then what is?"

He waved a hand in the general direction of the aquarium. "The point is that being an aquarist is a hobby. Not a career."

Clara was going to argue with him, since hobbies rarely included knowledge of Latin, never mind use of the word *aquarist*, which she'd sure never used in her life. But he truly did look kind of angry—and not a little distressed—and she didn't want to prolong an exchange that was threatening to become adversarial. So she tried to lighten the mood.

Smiling, she said, "Well. I don't know about you, but I suddenly hope we're having fish for supper."

At first, her attempt at levity seemed to confuse him.

Then it seemed to make him relax. Then he looked kind of grateful that she had relinquished the matter. He even smiled, but it wasn't like the smiles when he was watching his fish, and it never quite reached his eyes. In fact, his eyes were pretty much the opposite of smiling.

"I think it's going to be kebabs," he said. "But we can certainly put in a request for grouper at some point this week. Or next, if you and Hank want to stay a little longer."

Was that an invitation? Clara wondered. Because it kind of sounded like one.

"We can't," she told him. "I don't want Hank to miss too much school, and the bakery will be super busy the closer it gets to Christmas. I just can't afford to stay away any longer," she added when it looked as if he would take exception. "I'm the only full-time baker I have."

But instead of taking exception, he said, "No one would object if you needed to withdraw funds from Hank's trust to help you out with the business. It's there for his needs, but until he's an adult, his needs are joined to yours. If expanding your business and hiring more people would make you more money and increase the quality of Hank's life, then it would be a perfectly acceptable use of the trust."

Clara was shaking her head before he even finished talking. "That's Hank's money," she insisted. "He'll need it for college and for starting his life afterward, whether that's on his own or with someone he loves. Or he'll have it in case of emergency."

"But—"

"I've been taking care of myself and him for a long time, Grant. I've managed fine so far, and I'll continue to manage fine."

"But—"

"You and your mom have been great to both of us, but we'll be heading back to Georgia as scheduled. Thanks, anyway. Now, if you'll excuse me," she continued when he opened his mouth to object again, "there are a couple of things I need to do before supper."

And without waiting for a reply, Clara headed for the door. She assured herself she hadn't lied when she told Grant there were a couple of things she needed to do before dinner. The first was to make sure Hank didn't sleep too long, or he'd be even more insomniac tonight than she was. The second was to remind herself—as many times as it took—that Grant Dunbarton wasn't his brother, and that she needed to stop responding to him as if he were. Because although it hadn't broken her heart when she parted ways with Brent, if she got involved with Grant and then parted ways with him...

She thought again about the happy, childlike look on his face when he was talking about his fish, and the way his expression sobered and grew withdrawn when it came to talking about his work. Well. Something told Clara that if she got involved with Grant and then they parted ways, her heart might never be the same.

As Grant watched Clara leave, he did his best— really, he did—to not stare at her ass. Unfortunately, that was like trying to not breathe. Because the minute his gaze lit on her departing form, his eyes went right to the sway of her hips. And then all he could do was mentally relive that beyond-bizarre moment when he'd been standing behind her by the aquarium, wondering what she'd do if he pulled down her pants, tugged down her panties, freed himself from his trousers and buried himself inside her as deep as he could. Hell, he'd been hard enough to do it, thanks to the expression on her face when he'd looked up from unbuttoning his shirt to find her gazing at him as if she wanted to devour him in one big bite. There was just something about a woman with hungry eyes that made a man's body go straight to sex mode.

Besides, she had a really nice ass.

This was not good. It had been a long time since Grant had been this attracted to a woman this quickly. In fact, he wasn't sure he'd ever been this attracted to a woman this quickly. And the fact that the woman in question was Clara Easton made things more than complicated. He couldn't just have sex with her and then move on. She was going to be a part of his life, however indirectly, for, well, the rest of his life. She would be accompanying Hank to New York whenever he came to visit until the boy was old enough to travel on his own. Hell, she'd be coming to New York with Hank even after he was old enough to travel by himself, because his mother would insist that Clara come, too. She'd also insist Clara and Hank be included in all future holiday gatherings. Hell, knowing his mother, Grant wouldn't be surprised if she convinced Clara and Hank to move into the penthouse at some point. She might even ask Clara to change her name to Dunbarton, too.

Even if none of that did happen, Grant couldn't do the "Yeah, I'll call you" thing with Clara that had always worked well for him in the past, since he was excellent at avoiding women who wanted more than sex and even better at avoiding the ones who wanted a family. After having sex with Clara—who came ready-made with a family—he wouldn't be able to escape seeing her again with some regularity. And *seeing a woman again,* never mind *with some regularity,* was something that wouldn't fit Grant's social calendar.

He wasn't good at relationships. Not family ones, not social ones, not romantic ones. And Clara was threatening to be all three. He couldn't afford responsibilities like that. He had too many other responsibilities. And none of them included other people. Even people who had a great ass. So no more thinking about Clara in any way other than the mundane. Which should be no problem.

All he had to do was make sure he didn't think about her at all.

Five

Grant wasn't surprised when he woke up in the middle of the night. It had taken him forever to get to sleep, thanks to his inability to banish thoughts of Clara from his brain, and he'd slept lightly. Nor was he surprised that when he awoke, it was from a dream about Clara, since he'd still been thinking about her when he finally did go to sleep. He likewise wasn't surprised that the dream had been a damned erotic one, since his last thoughts of her before going to sleep had mostly revolved around her ass. What did surprise him was that he awoke to the smell of cake. Probably chocolate cake. Possibly devil's food cake. Which was easily his favorite.

He glanced at the clock on his nightstand. Three twenty-two. He didn't doubt that there were a number of bakers already up and plying their trade this early in the morning in New York City. However, none of them should have been plying it in the Dunbarton kitchen.

Either someone got seriously lost on their way to work, or Clara was awake, too.

He told himself to go back to sleep. She had said she was an insomniac, so her reasons for being up were probably totally normal and had nothing to do with damned erotic dreams like his. But was it normal for her to be baking at three in the morning? Didn't insomniacs usually just read or watch TV until they fell back asleep?

With a resigned sigh, Grant rose from bed and pulled a white V-neck T-shirt on over his striped pajama bottoms. Then he padded barefoot down the hall toward the kitchen, the smell of cake—oh, yeah, that had to be devil's food—growing stronger with every step. When he finally arrived at his destination, though, he saw not cake, but *cup*cakes, dozens of them, littering the countertops, all with red or green icing. He also saw Christmas cookies and gingerbread men bedecked with everything from gumdrops to crushed peppermint. There were bags of flour and sugar—both granular and powdered—strewn about untidily, as well as broken eggshells and torn butter wrappers, whisks, spoons, spatulas and other things he hadn't even realized they had in the kitchen.

In the middle of it all was Clara, dressed in red flannel pajama pants decorated with snowflakes and an oversize T-shirt bearing the logo for something called the Savannah Sand Gnats. It also bore generous spatters of chocolate and frosting. On her feet were thick socks. Grant had never known a woman who slept in socks. Or flannel. Or something emblazoned with the words *Sand Gnats*. Of course, whenever he was sleeping with a woman, she wasn't wearing anything at all. In spite of that, strangely, there was something about

Clara's socks and frumpy pajamas that was even sexier than no clothes at all.

Her mass of blue-black curls was contained—barely—by a rubber band, but a number of the coils had broken free to dance around her face. Another streak of chocolate decorated one cheek from temple to chin, and when his gaze fell to the ceramic bowl she cradled in the crook of her arm, he saw that it was filled with really rich, really dark chocolate batter, something that meant—*Who's the man?*—the cupcakes in the oven were indeed devil's food.

"Um, Clara?" he said softly.

When she glanced up, she looked as panicked and guilty as she would have had he just caught her helping herself to his mother's jewelry. "Uh, hi," she replied. "What are you doing here?"

"I live here," he reminded her.

"Right," she said, still looking panicked and guilty. "Did I wake you? I'm sorry. I was trying not to make any noise."

"It wasn't the noise. It was the smell. Devil's food, right?"

She nodded. "My favorite."

Of course it was. Because that just made him like her even more. "Were the pecan tarts we had for dessert tonight not to your liking?"

Instead of replying, Clara chuckled.

"What?" he asked.

"Pecan," she repeated, pronouncing it the way he had—the way he always had—*pee*-can. "The way you Northerners say that always makes me laugh."

"Why?"

"Well, first off, because it's wrong."

"No, it isn't."

"Yeah, it is." Before he could object again, she continued, "Look, we Southerners claimed that nut as our own a long time ago, and we say 'pi-*cahn*.' Therefore, that's the correct pronunciation. Also, in case you were wondering, *praline* is pronounced '*prah*-leen,' not '*pray*-leen.' That's another one that really toasts my melbas."

"But—"

"And second of all, I laugh because it always seemed to me like it should be the other way around. Saying 'pi-*cahn*' sounds so hoity-toity, like you Northerners, and saying '*pee*-can' sounds so folksy, like us Southerners." Instead of taking issue with the whole pecan thing—everyone knew the correct pronunciation was "*pee*-can"—he repeated, "So you didn't care for the tarts?"

She started spooning batter into the cupcake pan, an action that delineated the gentle swell of muscles in her upper arms and forearms. Grant wouldn't have thought muscles could be sexy on a woman. But on Clara, muscles were *very* sexy. Then again, on Clara, lederhosen and waders would have been sexy.

"They were delicious," she said. "But I couldn't sleep. And when I get anxious, I bake."

He wanted to ask her what she had to be anxious about. Her son was worth a hundred and forty-two million dollars. She'd never have to be anxious about him— or herself—again. Instead, he asked, "How long have you been up?"

She looked around for a clock. Or maybe she was just gauging the piles of cupcakes and cookies and trying to calculate how long it took to produce that many. "I don't know. What time is it?"

"About three-thirty?"

Now she looked shocked. "Seriously? Wow. I guess I've been up a few hours, then."

She'd been in here for a few hours? Dressed like that? Baking devil's food cupcakes? And he hadn't known it? He was slipping.

In an effort to keep his mind where it needed to be, he focused his attention on the bowl of batter still folded in her arm. Unfortunately, it was way too close to where her T-shirt strained over her torso, offering a tantalizing outline of her breasts and—

"So, what's a Savannah Sand Gnat?" he asked, driving his gaze up to her face again.

"It's our baseball team," she told him as she went back to scooping batter into the cupcake pans.

"Savannah's baseball team is called the Sand Gnats? Seriously?"

She looked up again, narrowing her eyes menacingly. "You got a problem with that?"

"No," he quickly assured her. "But sand gnats aren't exactly endearing, are they? I mean, they might as well have named the team the Savannah Clumps of Kelp."

She shook a chocolate-laden spoon at him. "Don't be dissing my team, mister. I love those guys. So does Hank."

He lifted his hands in surrender. "I apologize. Let me make amends. Dunbarton Industries has a suite at Citi Field. I can take you and Hank to a game someday. Maybe when the Mets play the Atlanta Braves."

And holy crap, did he just invite her to something that was months away and would bring her back to New York for a specific reason to do something with him and not because his mother wanted to see Hank? What the hell was wrong with him?

She dropped the spoon back into the bowl. "See the

Braves play? From a suite? Are you kidding me? Hank would love that."

Grant wanted to ask her if she'd love it, too. Instead he said, "It's a date, then." Crap. Putting it that way was even worse than asking her out in the first place. Quickly, before she could think he meant a *date* date—which he absolutely did not—he added, "For the three of us. Maybe four. Mom doesn't care for baseball, but if Hank is coming, she'll probably want to be there, too."

The comment made Clara's expression go from elated to deflated in a nanosecond. But she said nothing, only went back to furiously spooning the last of the batter into the last cups in the pan, as if wanting to put too fine a point on the whole baking-when-anxious thing.

"Clara?" he asked as she scoured the last bit of chocolate from the bowl. "Is something wrong?"

She didn't look up, only continued wiping the bowl clean, even though she had already scraped it within an inch of its life. Softly, she muttered, "What could possibly be wrong? My three-year-old just became a tycoon. That's every mother's dream, right?"

"I don't know," Grant said. "I'm not a mother. But I would venture a guess that, yes, it would be every mother's dream. You won't have to worry about his future anymore."

At that, Clara did look up. But she no longer looked anxious. Now she looked combative. "I wasn't worried about his future before," she said tersely. "Why would I be?"

Clearly, Grant had hit a nerve, though he had no idea how or why. Clara, however, was quick to enlighten him.

"Look, maybe I've been struggling financially since he was born. Maybe I was struggling financially before he was born. I still manage. I always have. I started a college fund for him as soon as I found out I was pregnant, and I make a deposit into it every month. He's never missed an annual checkup at the pediatrician or twice-yearly trips to the dentist. He gets three nutritious meals a day, clothes and shoes when he needs them, and although Santa may be at the bottom of his toy sack by the time he gets to our apartment, Hank has never had a Christmas morning where he wasn't delighted by his take. No, I can't lay down my platinum card whenever I feel like it and buy him anything he wants, but I give him more love and more time than anyone else ever has, and I will always give him more love and more time than anyone else, and that's way more important than anything a platinum card could buy."

The longer Clara spoke, the more her voice rose in volume and the more vehement she became. By the time she finished, she was nearly shouting. Her eyes were wide, her cheeks were flushed, and her entire body was shaking. When Grant only gazed at her silently in response—since he had no idea how else to respond—she seemed to realize how much she had overreacted, and she slumped forward wearily.

"I'm sorry," she said. She turned around and set the now-empty bowl on the countertop. But instead of turning around again to say more, she only gripped the marble fiercely, as if letting go of it would hurl her into another dimension.

Grant tried to understand—he really did. But the truth was, he had never loved or feared for anyone as much as Clara obviously loved and feared for her son. Grant got how she felt obligated to be the one to provide for Hank. But he didn't understand how she could not be overjoyed about the windfall he had received.

Especially since it could ease significantly all those obligations that could sometimes feel so overwhelming.

As if she'd heard the thought in his head, Clara finally turned slowly to face him. Thankfully, she no longer looked combative. Nor did she look anxious. Now she only looked exhausted.

"I've always been the center of Hank's world," she said quietly, "the same way he's always been the center of mine. Now, suddenly, he has family besides me. He has people to love him and provide for him besides me. And even if they can't love him more than I do, they can provide for him better. There's no way I can deny that. At some point, he's going to realize that, too. If he hasn't already." Her eyes grew damp, but she swiped them dry with the backs of her clenched fists. "There's already a part of me that's afraid he'll want to stay here instead of go home when the time comes for us to go back to Georgia."

Ah. Okay. Now Grant understood. She was afraid of losing her son to his grandmother, because his grandmother was, at this point, pretty much the equivalent of Santa Claus. Actually better than Santa Claus, since Santa evidently arrived at the Easton home having to scrape the bottom of his bag. Grant wished he knew what to say to ease her fears. But the fact was, his mother *could* give Hank anything he wanted, and Clara couldn't. Not that he would ever say that to Clara.

He just wished he did know what to say to her.

He was spared from having to figure it out, however, because the timer went off on the oven, and Clara sprang to grab two oven mitts and remove the pans of cupcakes from inside. Just as deftly, she inserted two more and closed the door, setting the timer again. When she spun back around to face him, she still looked troubled. So much for baking alleviating her anxiety.

"This money from Brent is just going to be so life changing for Hank," she said.

"But it will change his life for the better," Grant told her.

"Will it, though?" she asked. "With so much money comes so much responsibility. And people treat you differently when you have that much money. You treat yourself differently when you have that much money. And I don't want Hank to change."

"Everyone changes, Clara. Change is inevitable."

Without removing the oven mitts—and damned if there wasn't even something about those on her that was sexy—she wrapped her arms around herself, as if physically trying to hold herself together.

"But change should come gradually and naturally," she said. "I don't want Hank to be robbed of a normal childhood or adolescence. I want him to have a childhood where he can go barefoot all summer and catch lightning bugs and put them in a jar with holes punched in the lid and have a lemonade stand on the sidewalk and eat peaches picked right from the tree. I want him to have an adolescence where he works a crappy part-time job and drives a crappy car but loves both because they give him his first taste of freedom. The kind of childhood and adolescence I always wished I had when I was a kid. Hell, I just want Hank to *be* a child and adolescent. I don't want him to grow up too soon. Kids who get thrust into adult positions too early in life…"

When her gaze lit on his, Grant was knocked off-kilter again by just how huge and haunting and bewitching her eyes were. They were even more so when she was so impassioned. He found himself wanting to reach out to her physically, to curl his fingers around her nape and pull her close, and—

"Kids like that," she continued before he could act on his impulse, "kids who are cheated out of a normal childhood, they never grow up to be truly happy, you know? They don't learn how to play as kids, so they never relax or feel joy as adults. They don't make friends as kids, so they never trust or love other people as adults. They just never become the kind of person they might have become if they'd had the same upbringing and chances that regular kids have, and they never stop wondering what kind of person they might have—should have—been, if they'd just been able to grow up at a normal pace. They never stop feeling like, no matter what they have, it's not..." She shrugged, but the gesture was more hopeless than it was careless. "It's not enough."

Grant knew she was talking about herself. He knew everything she said was based on her own experiences growing up, and on her own reality as an adult. He knew she was worried Hank would end up like her. There had been nothing in her monologue that was directed at him, not one thing he should take personally.

For some reason, though, he did take it personally. He took everything she'd said personally. Her comments just struck a chord inside him, too. Discordantly at that. Because although Clara's reasons for being denied a normal childhood were nothing like the reasons he had been denied one, they had both ended up in the same place. That had been made clear at dinner the night before, when both had chorused the same sentiment.

But his life *was* enough, he told himself. Even if, sometimes, it felt as if it wasn't. He wouldn't change a thing about the way he'd grown up, because *his* experiences had made him who and what he was today. And he liked who and what he was. He didn't want to relax—relaxing wasn't in his nature. And he didn't want to love other people—love only complicated otherwise satisfactory relationships. He didn't care if he hadn't grown up to be the person he might have—should have—been, if he'd been allowed to grow up at a normal pace. He liked the person he was just fine. No, not just fine. A lot. He liked the person he was a lot.

But in spite of all his self-assurances, he still sounded defensive when he said, "There's nothing wrong with growing up too soon." Because he said it a little too quickly. A little too tersely. And he couldn't rein it in when he added, "What? Would you rather Hank be like his father and never grow up at all? Spend his life running from one hedonistic adventure to another, leaving before he's done any good, never making a difference anywhere?"

"Of course not," Clara said. "But—"

"At least now Hank has a future," Grant interrupted her. "He can even work in the family business if he wants to. *He* could be the Dunbarton legacy. He could become CEO of Dunbarton Industries after I retire."

Instead of looking pleased, or even intrigued, by the suggestion, Clara looked horrified. "Oh, God, no," she said. "The thought of sweet, happy-go-lucky Hank becoming a joyless, relentless, workaholic CEO who only cares about money is just so…so…"

She shook her head without finishing, obviously unable to find a word abhorrent enough to convey her disgust at the prospect of Hank following in his uncle's footsteps.

She seemed to realize exactly what she'd just said because she immediately told him, "That came out wrong.

I didn't mean *you're* a joyless, relentless, workaholic CEO who only thinks about money. I only meant…"

"Actually, Clara, I think you did mean that," he said.

For some reason, though, Grant couldn't stay angry about the comment. Which could only mean that, on some level, he agreed with it. Not so much that he was joyless. He knew how to enjoy himself. The opportunity for enjoyment just didn't present itself all that often. Nor was he relentless. He could relent under the right circumstances. The need for it just rarely materialized. And he thought about a lot more than money. But money was what kept business in business, and it was as essential to maintaining a quality of life as food and drink were.

So it must be the workaholic part of Clara's accusation that hit home. And, okay, maybe that part was true. Maybe he did work more than the average person did. He had an important job, and it was one no one else in the company could do, because, in spite of its huge size and profits, Dunbarton Industries was still a family business. His position didn't afford time for slacking off. Or, okay, being particularly yielding. Or finding a lot of enjoyment. And it meant he spent a lot of time thinking about the bottom line.

But Clara must understand those things. She was, in effect, the CEO of her own company. Hers was an important job, too, that no one else could do. She must put in longer than usual hours and take work home with her in the form of books to keep and orders to place. She was the last person to be pointing a finger at someone who worked too much at a joyless, relentless job and kept his eye on profitability. She must be as joyless and relentless and profit minded as he was.

But she was doing the thing she had always wanted

to do, he reminded himself, noting the streak of chocolate on her face again…and battling the urge to draw nearer and wipe it—no, lick it—off. She had followed her childhood dream. And she made time for her son. She'd taken off work to bring him to New York to meet the family they hadn't realized he had. Grant thought back on how she'd sat on the floor in Brent's room to play with Hank, and laugh with him, and share an affectionate embrace.

Maybe Clara thought she'd grown up to be unhappy and unfulfilled as a result of being denied a "normal" childhood, but she hadn't. She had learned how to play and to love. Hank had made that possible for her.

So there was really only one joyless, relentless, workaholic CEO who only thought about money in the room. And it wasn't Clara Easton.

She opened her mouth to say something else, but Grant held up a hand to halt her. Nothing she said at this point would ring true. She thought all he did and cared about was work. Which shouldn't have bothered him, since work was pretty much all he did or cared about. It hadn't bothered him when that was his own opinion of himself. But knowing Clara felt that way about him, too…

"Um. Well," he said. "I'll leave you to it."

She hesitated, and then said, "I promise I'll clean up my mess before I go back to bed."

He nodded. "Mrs. Bentley will appreciate that."

"And I'll put some cupcakes and cookies in the freezer, since there are so many. Maybe that will get you and Francesca through Christmas after Hank and I go back to Georgia."

"Mom will appreciate that."

"And you?" she asked.

He looked at her again. "What about me?"

"Will you appreciate them, too?"

He found the question odd. "Of course."

This time Clara was the one to nod. But there was something disingenuous about the gesture. As if she were trying to make him think she believed him, but she really didn't.

"Good night, Clara," he said before turning toward the door again. "I hope you get some sleep."

"Good night, Grant," she replied. Then she said something else he didn't understand. "I hope you get some, too."

Six

The good news was that Clara would have no trouble avoiding Grant the day after calling him a joyless, relentless, workaholic CEO who didn't think about anything but money. The bad news was the reason: as soon as she and Hank had woken up, Francesca announced that the three of them would be spending the day together again, this time at the Bronx Zoo, because Hank loved *Madagascar* so much when he and Francesca watched it together. They might also go to the New York Aquarium if they had time because it had been one of Brent and Grant's favorite places when they were Hank's age.

Although Clara would be able to avoid Grant for the day, she wouldn't be able to avoid him for the morning, since, as she and Hank and Francesca sat in the smaller dining room near the kitchen eating breakfast, Grant joined them.

It quickly became clear that he wasn't exactly happy to see her, either, and wanted to bolt from the house as soon as he could. He was dressed for work in another one of his pinstripe power suits and had his briefcase in hand and a trench coat thrown over one arm. And he barely acknowledged Clara and Hank with a quick "Good morning" before turning to his mother.

"Don't forget you need to look over and okay next year's revised budget before you go out," he told her. "The board is voting on it tomorrow."

Francesca waved a hand airily at her son. "Oh, I'm sure it will be fine. Hank and Clara and I are spending the day together again."

Grant looked surprised by his mother's lack of interest in the corporate budget. "You need to read it, Mom. And you need to be at the meeting to vote on it. We need a quorum, and some of the other board members are—"

"All right, all right," Francesca interrupted him. "I'll read it tonight, I promise. And yes, I'll be at the meeting. Nine o'clock," she said quickly when he opened his mouth, presumably to remind her. Then she looked at Hank and Clara again. "I'll arrange for you and Hank to tour the company while I'm in the meeting tomorrow. It's never too early for a child to learn the ropes of the family business. You could come and work for us someday," she said directly to Hank. "Wouldn't that be fun?"

Clara couldn't help the way her back went up—literally—at Francesca's suggestion. And she could tell that Grant had noticed. Francesca, however, seemed oblivious. As did Hank. At least, he was oblivious to what exactly *coming to work for the Dunbartons* meant, because he jumped on the opportunity faster than a person could say *corporate drone*.

"Okay," he agreed around a mouthful of waffles. "Do you work there, too, Grammy?"

Francesca smiled. "No, but I used to. I was the vice president in charge of public relations before your father and Uncle Grant were born. After that, I helped their father when he was the boss and needed my advice on something. Nowadays, I help the company make money by sitting on the board of directors."

"Are you the boss now?" Hank asked.

"No, sweetheart, your uncle Grant is the boss."

"But you're his mom," Hank objected. "That makes you his boss."

Francesca smiled again and looked at Grant. "Well, in some things, maybe," she said. "But even moms stop being the boss of most things at some point. Uncle Grant is the one who runs Dunbarton Industries." She winked at Grant, and then looked at Hank again. "For now, anyway. But maybe you'll be the boss there someday, Hank. Wouldn't you like that? With your own office and a big desk and lots of people calling you *Mr. Easton*?"

And migraines and chest pains and high blood pressure? Clara thought before she could stop herself. *And no life outside the office whatsoever?*

Grant seemed to know what she was thinking, because although he addressed his next comment to his mother, it was clearly intended for Clara. "Don't push him, Mom. Hank might not want to grow up to be a joyless, relentless, workaholic CEO who only thinks about money. He might want to be a professional beach bum like his father."

Now Francesca threw her son a puzzled look. "What on earth are you talking about? Brent wasn't a beach bum." But she didn't repudiate the first part of Grant's statement.

"Right," Grant said. "Well, then. I'll just head to work to be joyless, relentless and profit obsessed. Have a fun day seeing the sights."

The remark had the desired effect. Clara felt like a complete jerk. She scrambled for something to say or do that might make for a reasonable olive branch. "Grant," she said before he could make his escape. "Don't you want to come with us today? I bet you haven't been to the aquarium in a long time."

He had started to turn away, but halted when she said his name. It was only when he heard the word *aquarium*, though, that he finally turned around.

"It has been a long time," he said. He thought for a minute. "Before my father passed away, in fact."

Clara had figured it had been a while, but even she was surprised to hear it had been decades since he visited a place that must have been a utopia for him when he was a child.

"Then you should take the day off and come with us," she said.

Francesca looked surprised when Clara extended the invitation, but said, "Oh, do come with us, Grant. You loved the aquarium when you were a little boy." Now she looked at Clara. "He would have gone there every day if he could have. I remember there was this one thing he loved more than anything else. We could never pull him away from it. Brent and I could see the entire aquarium in the time Grant took to look at that one thing. What was it called, dear?"

"The chambered nautilus," Grant said in the same tone of voice people used when talking about deities or superheroes. Clara half expected the skies to open and a chorus of angels to break into song.

"That was it," Francesca said to Clara. "I always

thought it was kind of creepy and macabre myself, but Grant was enchanted by it."

"It's a living fossil," he said. "It hasn't changed in four hundred million years. And it lives almost two thousand feet deep and can use jet propulsion to move more than sixty meters per minute. What child wouldn't be enchanted?"

Or what adult? Clara wanted to ask. Since Grant was still obviously enchanted.

"Then you should come with us," Clara said. "You two have been apart for too long."

For one brief, telling moment, Grant's expression changed to the same one that came over Hank whenever Clara took a pan of baklava—his absolute most favorite thing in the world—out of the oven. Then, just as quickly, Grant changed back into businessman mode.

"There's no way I can take today off for that," he said. Though there was something in the way he said it that indicated he really wished he could.

"We could go another day," Clara said. "One you *could* take off."

For a moment, Grant only looked at her in an almost anguished way that seemed to say, *Don't. Just... don't.* But all he said was, "There are no days I could take off for that."

For some reason, Clara just couldn't let it go. "How about Saturday?" she asked. "You don't have to work Saturday, do you?"

His *don't* expression didn't change. "Not at the office, but I'll have plenty to do here."

She opened her mouth again, but he cut her off.

"I can't take time away from work. For anything," he said tersely. Adamantly. Finally.

"Okay," she said. "I just thought maybe—"

"Now if you'll excuse me," he interrupted her, "I have to get to the office. Enjoy the zoo." Almost as an afterthought, he added, "And the aquarium."

And then he was gone, before any of them could say another word. Like "Goodbye," for instance. Or "Have a nice day." Or even "Don't work too hard. Or too relentlessly. Or too joylessly." Though it was clear that Grant Dunbarton didn't have a problem with any of those things.

It was dark when Grant got home from work that night. As it always was this time of year. As it was some days in summer, come to think of it, when he worked especially late. But always, in winter, it was dark. There was a part of him that liked the shorter days. It was quicker to get through them. In summer, when the sun didn't set until eight or nine o'clock, it just felt as if that much more time was wasted somehow. Dark was good. Dark meant night. And night meant the day was almost over.

As he headed through the penthouse toward the stairs, he heard voices coming from the direction of the living room and turned in that direction instead. The room was lit up like, well, a Christmas tree, even though the Christmas tree twinkling in the corner offered the least amount of light. The main illumination came from the two lamps on the tables bookending the sofa, where his mother was sitting reading next year's budget, as she'd promised to do. Although the glass of wine she held and the pajamas and slippers she was wearing seemed incongruous with her reading material, seeing her there reminded Grant of occasions in the past when she'd been more involved with Dunbarton Industries.

She'd always enjoyed working, he remembered, even if she had left the day-to-day operations of the business behind years ago. She still seemed perfectly comfortable now, going over the budget for next year.

On the floor not far from where she sat, Clara and Hank lay on their stomachs with coloring books open before them and crayons littered about. Hank was in his pajamas, too, but Clara was still dressed as she'd been that morning, in khaki cargo pants and a black sweater, her shoes discarded now to reveal socks patterned with images of Santa Claus. Grant smiled at seeing them.

Mother and son were chattering about their individual coloring book creations, Clara saying something about how the jungle animals on her page were conspiring to escape from the zoo, and Hank telling her his had already done that and gone to Madagascar, like in the movie. Clara replied that her animals weren't going to Madagascar. They were going to open a vegetarian café on Fordham Avenue, and that way, they'd be close enough to still visit their animal friends who stayed behind. Hank deemed the plan a solid one, then went back to coloring his own pages, which seemed to consist mostly of jagged lines of, if Grant's Crayola memories served, Electric Lime, Hot Magenta and Laser Lemon. They'd been some of his favorite colors, too, when he was a kid. He was surprised he was able to remember their names so easily. Funny, the things the brain stored that then returned to a person out of nowhere like a surprise birthday present.

"You all look busy," he said as he strode into the room—and wondered when he had decided to do so. His original plan had been to retreat to his office before anyone saw him, the way any self-respecting workaholic CEO would. Not that he was still bothered by Clara's comment or anything. So why was he wading into this patently domestic scene where the only work getting done was by his mother—who tempered her work with wine and did it in her pajamas.

"Hello, dear," his mother said without looking up from the budget. "How was your day?"

He figured he'd played the relentless, joyless workaholic card as much as he could, so he only said, "Fine. Yours?"

"It was lovely," she told him. Finally, she looked up from the budget. "Until I started reading this. There are some huge problems here, you know."

"I know," he said. "That's why I wanted you to look it over before the meeting tomorrow. Have any ideas for where to make improvements?"

"Dozens," she told him. She pointed to the tablet sitting next to her on the sofa. "I'm making notes. Lots of them."

"Good. I've made some, too. We can compare later."

"Uncle Grant!" Hank piped up before Francesca had a chance to reply. "We saw that thing you like so much. At the aquarium. It was awesome!"

Grant smiled. "The chambered nautilus?" he asked. "What did you think of him?"

"I think he winked at me."

Grant chuckled. He'd thought the same thing the first time he saw it, even though that was impossible for the animal. Even so, he told Hank, "That means he likes you. They don't wink for just anyone, you know."

"Really?" Hank asked, sounding genuinely delighted that he had left such an impression.

"Really," Grant assured him. "I bet he's telling all the other cephalopods about you right now, and they're all hoping you'll come back soon to see them." Which was what Grant had always imagined them doing when he was little. He'd completely forgotten about that until Hank mentioned the winking thing. Huh.

Hank looked at Clara. "Can we go back tomorrow, Mama?"

Grant looked at Clara, too, only to find she was already looking at him. And even though her son had asked her a question, she continued to look at Grant. She was smiling at him, too. Smiling in a way that made his heart rate quicken and his blood warm. Not in a sexual way, as usually happened when he looked at her. But in a way that was…something else. Something he wasn't sure he'd ever felt before. Something that almost felt better than sex.

"We can't go back tomorrow, sweetie," Clara told her son. Though she was still looking at Grant and smiling in that…interesting…way. "Grammy wants to show us the place where Uncle Grant works. Where your grandfather used to work. But maybe the next time we come to New York, we can go back."

The next time we come to New York, Grant echoed to himself. How could Clara be talking about leaving already? They'd just gotten here.

Then he remembered they were on day four of their visit. Halfway through the week and a day Clara had said she and Hank could stay in New York. When Gus Fiver had told him and his mother that, Grant had been thinking a week and a day would be more than enough time for an introductory visit. He'd figured all of them would need to take things slowly, that there would have to be a number of such short visits to gradually welcome and include Hank and Clara into the family. But only four days in, Hank and Clara already felt like part of the family. They seemed to be right where they belonged. Their leaving in four days felt wrong somehow.

But they'd be leaving next Monday evening. And who knew when they would make it back?

"Okay," Hank said glumly in response to Clara's promise that they would visit the aquarium on their— admittedly nebulous—return. He went back to his coloring, but his crayon strokes were slower and less enthusiastic than they'd been before.

"Want to join us?" Clara asked.

When she tilted her head toward an assortment of coloring books on the floor that had yet to be opened, it took a moment for Grant to realize her invitation was to lie down beside her and Hank and start filling one in. Yet she had extended the invitation in all seriousness, as if this was the sort of thing people their age did all the time. And, okay, maybe it was something Clara did all the time, being the mother of a three-year-old. It wasn't something Grant did all the time. Or ever. Even if there was something about the idea that sounded kind of fun at the moment.

"Um, thanks," he said. "But I'll pass." Then he couldn't help adding, "It isn't something CEOs do."

"Oh, sure they do," Clara said. She smiled that interesting smile again. "They just color everything the color it's supposed to be and never go outside the lines."

"Very funny," Grant replied dryly. Though, actually, he did kind of find the remark funny.

Ha. He'd show her. He'd lie right down beside her and grab a coloring book and a handful of crayons— Atomic Tangerine, Sunglow and Purple Pizzazz had been other favorites, he recalled—and color all over the damned page, going out of the lines whenever he felt like it, and—

Or, rather, he would do that if he could. If he didn't have so many other things he needed to do. Like go over the budget again so he and his mother could compare notes. Even if he had gone over it twice already. The meeting was tomorrow. He should refresh his memory. Even if he did remember everything pretty well.

"Thanks," he told Clara. "But I have some other things I need to get done before tomorrow."

Because tomorrow was always another day. Another day of things he needed to get done before the next day. Because that day would have things that needed to get done before the day after that. Such was life for a high-powered CEO who didn't have time for things like going to aquariums and coloring zoo animals and having a life outside the office.

"You two have fun," he said to Clara and Hank. To his mother, he added, "I'll be in my office whenever you're ready to go over your proposed changes."

His mother nodded. "Give me another hour or so."

"That's fine," Grant told her. Because that would mean they were an hour closer to the end of the day. An hour closer to bringing on tomorrow. An hour closer to getting done all the important things that needed to get done before other important things took their places.

An hour closer to when Clara Easton would leave New York to return to Georgia.

For the first time in a very long time, Grant was suddenly much less eager to see the day draw to a close.

Seven

By Friday evening, day five of her "vacation," Clara was more exhausted than she was after a full week at her physically demanding, labor-intensive, stress-provoking work, even after sleeping a full five hours later than she normally did on Friday morning. Because the moment she swallowed the last bite of her bagel and the final sip of her coffee, Francesca had hustled her and Hank out of the house to tour Dunbarton Industries' headquarters while she and Grant attended their meeting. Clara had to admit, the tour had been eye-opening and surprisingly interesting. But upon the meeting's conclusion, Francesca had swept the two of them off again, this time to zigzag across Central Park, from the zoo to the carousel to the castle to the Swedish Cottage and its marionettes. Though Clara might just as well have stayed at the penthouse the whole day for all the attention Francesca and Hank had paid her. The majority of her day had been spent catching up with the two of them.

Clara understood. Really, she did. Hank was Francesca's only grandchild, and he was all she had left of Brent. She had a lot of lost time to make up for with him and was trying to squeeze the three and a half years of Hank's life she'd missed into a week's worth of shared experiences that could tide her over until she saw him again. And it was the first time Hank had been the center of someone's universe who never said the word *no*. Yes, he and Clara had plenty of fun together, but there were a lot of times Clara had to tell him no, either because of time or money constraints. Francesca had neither of those, so she was completely at Hank's disposal. And, boy, was he learning that fast.

By the time they returned to the penthouse—after, oh, yeah, dinner at Tavern on the Green—Grant had shut himself up in his office.

Clara grimaced as she thought back on when she'd accused him of being a corporate drone the other night. She hadn't meant to insult him. The words had just popped out. She could hardly be held responsible, because she'd been A) anxious, B) exhausted, C) in the middle of baking enough cookies and cupcakes to feed the United Nations—and their respective nations—and D) trying not to notice how sexy Grant Dunbarton was in a V-neck T-shirt and striped pajama bottoms.

Seriously, when that guy dressed like an ordinary person, he was extraordinarily hot. She was still thinking about just how hot as she sat in the spectacular Dunbarton library to which she had escaped for a little peace and quiet, sipping a glass of luscious pinot noir she hoped would help her forget how hot Grant Dunbarton was. *No!* she immediately corrected herself. The wine would help her relax after yet another day of worrying that her son would abandon her in favor of his grandmother. *No! Not that either!* She was just having a glass of wine to—

Oh, bugger it.

She was having a glass of wine because she really needed a glass of wine—thanks to her growing anxiety over Hank's allegiances *and* her growing attraction to Grant. But where she could pretty much convince herself that Hank would never abandon her, she was less successful convincing herself that her attraction to Grant would go away. Because she was definitely attracted to Grant. Very attracted to him. And the attraction had nothing to do with any misplaced affection for Brent that might still be lingering somewhere inside her. What Clara was feeling for Grant wasn't the breathless infatuation a girl had for a cute guy who was funny and charming and a great kisser. It was… something else. Something she wasn't sure she even wanted to identify, because that could make things even more complicated.

Maybe Clara was only four years older now than she was when she met Brent, but they'd been years filled with mothering and working and trying to build a life for herself and her son. Years of taking on responsibilities and obligations she would have for the rest of her life. The easy, breezy girl who'd fallen for Brent was gone, as were the fast, fun feelings she'd had for him. But the woman who was coming to know and care about Grant? She was another story.

And the last thing Clara needed was to fall for Grant Dunbarton. She shouldn't even find him hot. Sex with him wouldn't be like sex with a guy with whom she'd had no future—precisely because, with Grant, she did have a future. Even if it wasn't a future together, he'd still be in and out of her life thanks to Hank's ties to the family. It was already awkward enough between them. Throwing sex into the mix would only make it more so. Wouldn't it? Of course it would. So she had to keep her distance from the other Dunbarton brother.

"I'm sorry. I didn't know anyone was in here."

As if conjured by her thoughts, Grant spoke from behind her. Clara was so jumpy from both the day and her thoughts that she simultaneously leapt up from the settee and dropped her wine, which crashed into the spectacular Dunbarton coffee table before shattering and sending shards of glass and seemingly gallons of wine—red, of course—falling onto the spectacular Dunbarton Oriental rug.

She cried out at the mess she'd made, then, "Quick!" she shouted at Grant. "I need a towel and some club soda!"

Without questioning the order, he hurried to a bar in the corner of the room and collected the requested items. When he returned, he was already pouring club soda onto the towel and looked even more panicked than Clara was. Damn. The rug must be worth more than she thought.

"Should I call nine-one-one?" he asked.

Well, she didn't think it was worth *that* much.

She grabbed the towel from him, dropping to her knees beside the stain. Grant dropped with her. He wrapped one arm around her shoulders as he withdrew his phone from his pocket. "My God. Are you okay? I'm calling nine-one-one."

"Don't be silly. It's just wine," she said, trying to ignore the heat that seeped through her at the feel of his arm around her shoulder. Why was he doing that? "I can get the stain out, I promise. Or I'll pay to have it professionally cleaned."

He had pressed the nine and the first one, but halted. "You're not bleeding?" he asked. "You didn't fall because you're lightheaded due to blood loss?"

Only then did Clara realize he thought she'd cut herself badly on the broken glass. Meaning his concern wasn't for the rug—it was for her. Which was saying something, because the carpet was massive, stretching from one side of the library to the other, and it could very well have been here since the penthouse was built. It had to be worth a fortune. But he hadn't given it a thought. Some joyless, relentless, workaholic CEO who only thought about money he was.

"I'm fine," she said. She held up her hand for inspection, and realized it was covered with red wine. Hastily, she wiped it off with the towel. "See?" she said, wiggling her fingers to prove it. "Not hurt. Just clumsy."

He took her hand in his and turned it first one way, then the other, just to make sure. Heat shot through Clara from her fingertips to her heart, then seeped outward, into her chest and belly. If she didn't remove her hand from his soon, that heat was going to spread even farther, right down to her—

Oops. Too late.

She tugged her hand free and went back to work on the stain. But Grant circled her wrist with sure fingers again and drew her hand away. Once more, Clara was flooded with sensations she hadn't felt for a long time. Too long. She'd honestly forgotten how nice it could be, just the simple touch of a man's bare skin against her own.

"There could be broken glass in there," he said from what sounded like a very great distance. "I'll call someone tomorrow to have the rug cleaned professionally. Until then, we can close off the room to make sure Hank doesn't wander in here."

"But—"

"It's okay. Really. We don't use this room that often anyway."

"You were about to use it tonight," Clara pointed out.

"No, I wasn't. I just came in to fix a drink." He smiled. "The good bourbon is in the library."

She smiled back. "Right. All that stuff in the kitchen pantry must be complete rotgut."

His smile grew, reaching all the way to his eyes, and the bubbling heat in Clara's torso bubbled higher. "We only keep that for the servants, so they'll have something for when we drive them to drink."

So much for his being humorless, Clara thought. When he put his mind to it, Grant could be every bit as funny and charming as his brother. Though he was being a bit relentless about not letting go of her wrist. Not that she really minded, even though she should.

"But club soda is amazing," she objected halfheartedly, trying to focus on something other than the gentle feel of his warm fingers around her wrist. "It'll work. I swear."

He didn't reply, but didn't let go of her hand, either. In fact, he ran his thumb lightly over the tender flesh on the inside of her wrist, making her pulse leap wildly. Something he probably felt, since his thumb stilled on her skin right about where her pulse would be. He continued to watch her intently, his lips parted, his eyes dark. For one tiny moment, Clara thought he might actually lean in to kiss her. For one tiny moment, she really wished he would. Then, suddenly, he freed her wrist and reached for the towel in her other hand, pressing it carefully into the stain.

"Club soda is good for stains, is it?" he asked as he worked. He picked up pieces of glass where he found them, setting them on the coffee table.

Clara nodded. Then, realizing he couldn't see the gesture, because he was still dabbing at the rug and picking up glass, she said, "Uh-uh." Mostly because that was the only sound she could manage.

"Spill wine a lot, do you?" he asked, smiling again, more softly this time. But he still didn't look at her as he continued to work on the stain.

"Well, not as often as juice," she said, "which club soda also works great on. But I am a harried mother of a toddler, so there are days when wine is one of the four basic food groups."

"They don't use the four basic food groups anymore," he said. Still cleaning up her mess. Still smiling. "It's the food pyramid now."

"Actually, that's been replaced, too," she told him. "By something called MyPlate. Which is pretty much the four basic food groups again, except they separated fruits and vegetables, and they put dairy in a cup."

Having evidently decided he'd done as much as he could to control the damage, Grant looked at Clara again. But his eyes were still dark, and his mouth was still much too sexy for her well-being. "So what are the four basic food groups of the harried toddler mother?" he asked.

Clara was tempted to say merlot, Chardonnay, pinot grigio and Cabernet, but stopped herself. She almost never drank pinot grigio. So she said, "Smoothies, whatever's left on the toddler's plate when he's done eating, Lärabars and wine."

Grant nodded. And still looked as though he might kiss her.

So she said, "Really, just give me ten minutes and I can have this rug looking good as new."

"You'll have your work cut out for you," he told her. "It's more than a hundred years old."

Clara closed her eyes. "Wow. That so doesn't make me feel better."

He chuckled at that. "It should. Can you imagine how much stuff has been spilled on this rug in that length of time? In my lifetime alone? Brent and I weren't exactly clean kids."

His expression cleared some at the mention of his brother, and Clara was grateful for the change. He picked up a few more pieces of glass and gave the rug a few more perfunctory pats, then left the towel over the stain to alert any unsuspecting library visitor of its presence. Then he rose from the floor and held out a hand to help up Clara. But she pretended she didn't see it and stood on her own.

"'Clean kids' is an oxymoron," she said when they were both vertical again. "I can't imagine having two of them underfoot at the same time. Francesca must have had her hands full with the two of you."

Grant smiled again. "Yeah, well, I think the fact that she and my father never had any more kids after the two of us speaks volumes."

Clara waited for his expression to cloud over again at the realization that he was the only Dunbarton child left. Instead, he still seemed to be steeped in fond nostalgia for their childhood. He looked past Clara, gesturing at a chair near the fireplace.

"I remember once, my dad was sitting over there reading an annual report when Brent and I came tearing through here. I don't remember which one of us was chasing the other. Maybe we were racing or something. Anyway, my dad was also enjoying what was probably some ridiculously expensive brandy—he did love his Armagnac—and Brent knocked it off the table and onto the hearth. Broke the snifter into bits, which probably added another couple hundred bucks to the damage. Then he tried to pass himself off as me, so I'd have to take the blame."

"You don't sound too mad about that."

Grant shrugged. "It was only fair. I'd passed myself off as him at school the week before when I got caught in the halls during class without a hall pass. Problem was the teachers really did have a tough time telling us apart. But Mom and Dad never did. Brent had to pay for that snifter out of his allowance. But I paid for half. Least I could do."

Now Clara chuckled. "Did you guys do that often? Pretend to be each other?"

Grant smiled again. "Only when we were absolutely sure we could get away with it."

She could believe that about Brent, mischievous guy that he was. But she was having a hard time imagining Grant as the naughty child.

"Come on," he said, tilting his head toward the bar. "I'll pour you another glass of wine. There's a really nice Harlan Estate in the rack. So much better than that rotgut from the pantry."

She was about to tell him the rotgut in their pantry cost about five times what she had in her own pantry, but halted. Who was she to turn up her nose at a really nice Harlan Estate?

He opened a bottle and poured them each a generous serving of dark red wine. He handed one glass to

Clara and then, almost as an afterthought, picked up the bottle to take it with them.

"Is Mom with Hank?"

Clara nodded, her stomach knotting with anxiety again. This was the first time Hank had spent more of his day with someone else than with Clara. For his first two years, he'd stayed in the bakery with her, playing in a part of the kitchen the then-owner had childproofed for him. Everyone who worked there had looked after him. When he'd started preschool at two, he'd still spent the bulk of his day with Clara at the bakery. Since coming to New York, though, Francesca had clocked more time with him than Clara had. And Clara still wasn't quite okay with that. But she couldn't bring herself to deny Francesca all the time with Hank she wanted, knowing it would be months before they could come back to New York for a visit.

"The marionette show was 'Jack and the Beanstalk,'" Clara said. "Francesca told Hank it was his father's favorite book when y'all were kids, and promised to read it to him when we got ho— Ah, back to the penthouse."

After mentioning his brother, Clara waited to see if Grant would revisit memories of his childhood again, but he only said, "The living room, then. It will be quiet in there." He hesitated for a moment before adding, "You look like you could use some quiet."

Was it that obvious? But all she said was, "Thanks. Some quiet would be good."

The Dunbarton living room was even more spectacular than the Dunbarton library, with its veritable wall of windows on one side looking out on the nighttime skyline and a dazzling blue spruce trimmed with glittering decorations and seemingly thousands of twinkling lights. The furnishings were elegant and tailored, the color of luscious gemstones, and the walls were painted a deep, rich ruby. The only other illumination in the room came from a fire someone had set in the fireplace, warmly crackling in invitation, and a half dozen candles in a candelabrum placed on the center of the mantelpiece amid pine boughs and holly berries.

Grant must have seen how her gaze lingered there, because he told her, "Mrs. Weston always lights the place up before she retires for the day. And then we just let the fire burn itself out."

Clara marveled again at the lifestyle the Dunbartons enjoyed. The lifestyle Hank might enjoy someday, if he wanted. She just couldn't jibe the life he'd led so far with the one that awaited him. Every year it was going to be harder to tear him away from this and get him to return to their modest life in Georgia. Living here was like living in a Hallmark Christmas card, Clara thought. Until she sat down on the sofa and noticed there wasn't a single present under the tree.

"Someone needs to start shopping," she said. "There are only twenty-two shopping days left until Christmas."

Grant smiled as he placed the bottle of wine on the end table beside him. "No worries. We stopped exchanging gifts years ago. Bonuses for the servants, doormen and concierge, but that's about it."

"You and Francesca don't exchange gifts?"

He seemed to find the question odd. "No."

Maybe when people reached a certain income bracket where they didn't really need anything anymore, they stopped buying Christmas presents for each other. Clara supposed it was possible. But it seemed unlikely. There was more to Christmas than getting stuff, and there was more to gift giving than simply supplying someone with an essential item—or even a luxury.

Gifts under a Christmas tree weren't meant to replace love and attention. They were meant to symbolize it. That was why even the poorest families struggled to put *some*thing under the tree. To show the other members that they were important and cherished. To find an empty Christmas tree in a home like the Dunbartons', who should find gift giving effortless and enjoyable, was just... Well, it was kind of heartbreaking, truth be told.

"Why not?" she asked. She told herself she should just let it go. It was none of her business why Grant and Francesca didn't exchange gifts. For some reason, it just bothered her that they didn't. A lot.

But he didn't seem bothered at all. He just shrugged and said, "I don't know. We just don't. We haven't since..." He thought for a minute, clearly not able to even remember when the tradition came to a halt. "I guess since Brent left home. He always bought gifts for me and Mom, so we always got him something. After he left, we just...didn't do it anymore."

Meaning that, if it hadn't been for Brent, they would have stopped even before then.

"But there should always be gifts under a Christmas tree," Clara objected. "Even if there are only a few. It's naked without them."

Grant didn't seem to take offense. "Okay. I'll tell the service who decorates for us that next year, they should wrap some boxes and put them under the tree when they finishing decorating it to add to the holiday mood."

Clara gaped at that. "You don't even put up your own Christmas tree?"

He shook his head. "Mom hires a service to do that every year."

Clara gaped wider. "There are people who get paid to put up other people's Christmas trees?"

"Sure. And the wreaths and the garlands and everything else." When he finally realized how appalled she was by the concept of a Christmas-for-hire, he added, "I mean, they do use our stuff. We're not renting from them the way a lot of people do."

"People *rent* their Christmas?" Clara asked, outraged. Why bother decorating at all if you weren't going to do it yourself?

Instead of being offended by her tone, Grant just shrugged again. "Welcome to the twenty-first century, Clara. And to New York City. A lot of people like to have their houses decorated because they entertain friends or clients. But they don't want the hassle of doing it themselves."

"But putting up the tree is the best part of Christmas. Well, after opening presents, at least." Then she thought about that some more. "No, it is the best part. It still feels Christmassy before and after the presents are opened. But it can't feel Christmassy without a tree."

"I bet Hank's favorite part is the presents."

Clara shook her head. "Oh, don't get me wrong. He loves the loot. But that part only lasts one day. The tree stays up for a month. And decorating it is easily the funnest thing of all. Don't you miss that part?"

"What part?"

"How every year, when you take out the ornaments, you remember some of them you forgot you had, and then you remember where you got them and what you were doing then and how much has changed. Putting up a Christmas tree is like revisiting your whole life every year."

Grant looked dubious. "Correct me if I'm wrong, but you and Hank have only had…what? Four Christmases together?"

"But even before Hank," she said, "I always put up a tree, starting with my freshman year in college. My dorm mates and I pooled our funds and bought a tree, and we found ornaments at thrift shops and discount stores. We split them up after we graduated. I still have mine," she added. "And when I put them on our tree every year, I remember those dorm mates and being in college, and that first breath of freedom where I could do anything I wanted without permission." She smiled. "Like put up a Christmas tree in my own place, with my own stuff, and if I fell in love with one of the ornaments, no one could say it didn't belong to me so I couldn't take it with me when I went to live somewhere else."

Grant had been smiling while she talked, but he sobered at that. "Did that happen to you?"

She hesitated, wondering why she had even brought the incident up. Wondering, too, why it still hurt nearly twenty years after the fact. "Yeah," she said softly. "When I was eight. Looking back, the ornament wasn't all that great, really. A little plastic Rudolph with a broken leg whose red nose had been rubbed white over the years. I painted him a new one with some red nail polish, and I glued his leg back on with way more glue than was necessary, so it left a gigantic lump. Then I put him back on the tree and admired him every day. I don't know why I loved him so much. I guess I felt kind of responsible for him or something. I was moved to a new place the week before Christmas that year, and

I wanted so badly to take him with me. But my foster mother said no."

"Why?"

This time Clara was the one to shrug. "I don't know. She didn't say. A lot of questions I asked back then never got answered, though. It wasn't unusual."

He looked as if he wanted to say something else, but instead, he only gazed at her in silence. Long enough that the air around them began to grow warm. Long enough that she thought again he might kiss her. Long enough that she wished he would.

"Um, I should go check on Hank and Francesca," she said. "If he likes a story enough, he wants it read over and over again, and it can get kind of annoying."

She stood before Grant had a chance to say anything and hurried out of the living room. Only after she was heading down the hall toward Hank's room—she meant Brent's old room—did she realize she hadn't even tasted the glass of wine Grant had poured for her.

Eight

Grant went into the office the day after his and Clara's heart-to-heart by the Christmas tree, even though it was a Saturday. Not because he had a lot of things to do he hadn't finished during the week. On the contrary, things slowed down a lot between Thanksgiving and New Year's. He just figured he would take advantage of the weekend to catch up on some email and other things. It had nothing to do with how he wanted to avoid Clara, because she might still look the way she had last night. Not just when she'd shown her distress that the Dunbartons didn't do Christmas the traditional way. But when she told him about the Rudolph ornament at her old foster home. She might as well have been eight years old again, being shuttled to a new, strange place, so lost and lonely had she seemed in that moment.

Once he arrived home, Grant still wanted to avoid her, and for the same reasons. He sighed as he tossed his briefcase onto his bed and then went about the motions of undressing. After slipping into a pair of dark wash jeans and a coffee-colored sweater, he headed to the library for a bourbon. The rug cleaners had already come and gone, and the carpet looked good as new again. Well, okay, good as a hundred years old again. He poured a couple of fingers of Woodford Reserve into a cut crystal tumbler and headed out to the living room. It, too, looked exactly as it had the night before, minus Clara, a glaring absence that made the whole room seem off somehow. He was about to turn and make his way somewhere else, somewhere that wasn't so quiet, when his gaze lit on something that hadn't been in the room the night before—four gifts under the Christmas tree, each wrapped in a different color of foil paper, topped with curly ribbon.

Although he was sure he knew who had left them there, he couldn't help moving to the tree for a closer look. When he stooped, he saw that each bore a tag and that two were for him and two were for his mother. The larger ones were from Clara, the smaller ones were from Hank. Not that Grant thought for a moment that Hank had shopped and paid for them. But he wouldn't be surprised if Clara had asked the boy for final approval.

He set his drink on the floor and reached for the gift that was addressed to him from Clara. It was cube-shaped, large enough to hold a basketball and heavy. Unable to help himself, he gave it a gentle shake. Nothing. Whatever was in there, she'd packed it well enough to keep it from moving. He replaced it and lifted the one to him from Hank. It was square and flat and much lighter. But it, too, was silent when he gave it a shake. He set it next to the other one, palmed his drink and stood.

Damn. Should he give gifts to them in return? Not that Grant minded giving gifts. He just didn't want to brave the crowds to shop for them. Especially since he had no idea what to get a three-year-old boy. Or Clara, for that matter. The only time he'd bought gifts for women, they were to make up for some oversight. A date he'd forgotten, a wrong word at the wrong time, taking too long to return a call, something like that. He generally bought jewelry, because that was always a safe bet with women. At least, it was for the women he dated. Clara, though... For one thing, she didn't seem to wear much jewelry. For another, jewelry seemed like the kind of thing you gave a woman when you didn't know what else to get her. It was his go-to gift because he'd never wanted to work that hard to figure a woman out. Clara, though...

Clara. For some reason, he did want to figure her out. He just had no idea how to go about it. And he couldn't help thinking it would be a bad idea to try. Because the more he'd learned about her over the past few days, the more he'd liked her. And the more he'd wanted to learn. And he just couldn't risk getting involved with her, not when he wouldn't be able to make a clean break after whatever happened between them came to an end.

Because it would come to an end. It always came to an end. Grant wasn't the kind of man to make a long-term commitment to a woman. Not when he already had a long-term commitment to his work. Besides, in spite of the undeniable attraction he and Clara felt for each other, they weren't well suited. She'd made clear she wanted what she considered a "real" life for her son, one in her small town, surrounded by simple pleasures. She wanted to temper her work with play and her reality with dreams and her sense with sensibility. And that just wasn't Grant's way. At all.

Sure, they could potentially engage in a sexual liaison. Sure, it could potentially be incredible. But it wouldn't last. He was sure of that, too. He and Clara were too different from each other, and they both wanted entirely different things from life. Getting involved with each other would only make life more difficult for them both when their paths inevitably—and regularly—crossed in the future.

The living room, like the library, was too quiet. The whole house was too quiet. Where was everybody?

He wandered into the kitchen to find it empty, though there were signs someone had been snacking in here not long ago. There were cookie crumbs on the counter, and an empty milk glass in the sink. Suddenly, he heard laughter that sounded as if it was coming from the dining room. He headed in that direction and found Clara and Hank lying on the floor on the other side of the expansive table, gazing up at the planets on the ceiling. Clara was pointing at one of them, and Hank was still laughing at something one of them must have said.

Neither of them had seen or heard him come in, so Grant stood still and silent in the doorway, watching them. Hank was already in his pajamas, blue ones dotted with some cartoon character Grant had never seen, and Clara was in a pale green sweater and blue jeans. But the sweater was cropped at the waist, and riding higher because of the position of her arm, revealing a tantalizing bit of naked torso between its hem and the waistband of her jeans. Grant did his best not to notice how— Oh, hell, no he didn't. He zoomed right in on the milky skin and wondered if it felt as soft as it looked.

"No, not Plu-*toad*," Clara said, sending Hank into

another fit of giggles. "Plu-*toh*." But she was laughing, too, by the time she finished.

"I think it should be Plu-toad," Hank said. "And only frogs should live there."

"You know, Hank" Grant said, "frogs and toads aren't the same thing."

Both Hank and Clara scrambled up off the floor as if it had caught fire, looking guiltily at each other before turning to Grant.

"Don't worry," he hurried to tell them. "I used to lie in here looking at that ceiling all the time. Go back to what you were doing."

"That's okay," Clara said. "We were finished."

"Anyway," Grant said to Hank, "If you want frogs to live there, you should call it Plu-frog."

That made the boy giggle again, which gave Grant an odd sense of satisfaction. He didn't recall having put *Make a child laugh* on his bucket list, but now that he'd accomplished the feat, it seemed like something everyone should attempt at least once. It felt kind of good, having done it.

When it seemed as if none of them was going to ever speak again, Grant said, "So I noticed someone left some presents under the Christmas tree today."

"We did!" Hank cried. "Mama and me went out this morning and—"

Clara clamped a gentle hand over her son's mouth and shot him a meaningful look. "And got coffee," she finished for him. "Right, sweetie?"

Hank hesitated, and then nodded vigorously, so she removed her hand. "Right," he agreed. "Mama got coffee, and I got hot chocolate. And then we didn't—"

Clara clamped her hand over his mouth again. "We have no idea how those gifts got under the tree."

"Funny," Grant said, "the tags said they were from you and Hank."

Clara and her son exchanged another look, this one full of comical wide-eyed innocence. Then they both shook their heads in exactly the same way and stretched out their arms in identical comical shrugs. Then they looked at Grant again.

"No clue," Clara said.

"No clue," Hank echoed.

"Then I guess it would be okay if I open mine now?" Grant asked.

Clara shook her head. "No, that would not be okay. You have to wait until Christmas morning, just like everyone else."

"I can't even open it Christmas Eve?" he asked.

"Don't worry, Uncle Grant," Hank said. "Mama never lets me open my presents till Christmas morning, either." He threw his mother a chastising look as he added, "Even though *all* my friends get to open one on Christmas Eve."

"Oh, and if all your friends jumped off a bridge, would you do that, too?" Clara asked him.

"Maybe," Hank told her. "If it was on Plu-toad!" He punctuated the statement with a childish laugh. Clearly this was high humor for three-year-olds.

Actually, Grant wanted to laugh, too, but Clara gave her son a stern look that silenced them both...until she groaned and started laughing, too. Then the three of them made a few more jokes about Plu-toad, until the humor just became so weird, only a three-year-old—or a couple of especially silly adults—could understand it.

"Enough," Clara finally said to her son with one last breathless chuckle. "You're never going to get to sleep tonight. Go brush your teeth and tell Grammy good-night. If she doesn't have time to read you a story, I can. But bedtime is in thirty minutes!" she called after him as he scampered off. "I mean it, Hank!"

She looked exhausted when she turned back to Grant. "He's been sneaking out of his room...I mean, Brent's room...after bedtime to watch TV with your mother. He's fallen in love with *Oliver and Company*, which is probably one of the movies Disney just stuck back in the vault, so I won't be able to find it on Tybee Island, or it will cost a fortune on eBay, so I won't be able to afford it, which is just one more way your mother will lure us back here. I don't know which one of them I want to ground more."

Grant smiled. "Take away her Bergdorf's card for a week. That'll teach her."

Instead of laughing, Clara sat down on the floor and lay back again to gaze up at the ceiling. Not sure what made him do it—maybe it was the way her sweater rode up again—Grant lay down beside her.

And looked up at the star- and planet-studded ceiling from that vantage point for the first time in twenty years. Wow. He'd forgotten how much cooler it was from this angle. He really could almost pretend he was lying in a field out in the middle of nowhere, the way he had done when he was a child.

"We have to go home in two days," Clara said abruptly.

The comment surprised him, even though she wasn't telling him anything he didn't already know. Somehow, it just felt as if she and Hank had been here for months. It felt as if they should be here for more months. Surprising, too, was how melancholy she sounded about going home. She'd made no secret of her fear that Hank wouldn't want to leave after spending time with his grandmother. Grant would have thought Clara would be relieved to be going home in a few days. Of course, he thought he'd be relieved about that, too, since it meant he would stop entertaining such ridiculous ideas about the two of them. But he didn't feel any more relieved than she sounded.

"Maybe you can come back after the holidays," he said, intending the comment to be casual and perfunctory. Realizing after he said it that it was actually serious and hopeful.

She said nothing at first, just looked up at the stars. Then she turned her head to look at him full on. She was so close. And her eyes were so green. Her black curls were piled on the floor, scant inches away, close enough for him to reach over and wind one around his finger. Would it be as silky as it looked? It was all Grant could do not to find out for himself.

"It's going to break Hank's heart to leave," she said. "He's fallen in love with your mother, and she's been so wonderful with him. And between his school and my work, it's going to be summer before we can get back for a visit."

"What about spring break?"

She shook her head. "Too close to Easter. It's super busy at the bakery then. No way could I take the time off. Especially after taking this week at Christmastime."

"Then Mom can come visit Hank in Georgia."

Clara looked fairly panicked at that.

"Is that a problem?" he asked.

"Well, our apartment is just so small. There's only the two bedrooms. And only one bathroom. No way would Francesca be comfortable staying with us."

Grant smiled. Of course Clara would assume that family would want to stay with, well, family. "She'd stay in a hotel, Clara. They do have hotels on Tybee Island, I assume?"

Clara nodded earnestly, thinking he was serious about asking if there were hotels in a popular seaside destination.

"She'd probably prefer that, anyway," he said. "She does like her room service."

For some reason, that made Clara look even more panicked. "Hank might want to stay with her at the hotel. He loves hotels. We hardly ever get to stay in one. Especially the kind that have room service. He'd be thrilled."

"Then his staying with Mom would give you some time to yourself. Surely, it would be nice to have a break."

She sighed and looked at the ceiling again. "Yeah."

Funny, she didn't sound as if she thought it would be nice.

She was still worried about losing Hank to the Dunbarton lifestyle. Still worried his mother would take her place in Hank's heart. Which was crazy because, number one, no child who had a relationship like Hank clearly did with Clara would put anyone else before his mother. And number two—

Number two, Grant really, really wanted to tangle his fingers in her hair and trace the elegant line of her jaw with his fingertip, and then, when she looked at him again, roll toward her and cover her mouth with his, and then cover her body with his, and then—

"Breaks are good, right?" she said softly. She was still gazing at the stars overhead, but she seemed to be seeing something else entirely.

It took him a minute to rewind to the point in the conversation when they'd been talking about his mother visiting her and Hank in Georgia. But even when he remembered, the thought fell by the wayside, because he was still too focused on one strand of hair that had stayed pressed against her cheek when she turned her head to look back up at the ceiling.

Without thinking about what he was doing, he reached across the few inches separating them and tucked a finger beneath the sable curl. He told himself it was just to free it from her skin—her luscious, glorious skin—since hair stuck in place like that could be pretty damned annoying. But his gesture left the back of his knuckle pressed against her cheek—her luscious, glorious cheek—and the moment he realized her skin was indeed as soft as it looked, he couldn't quite pull his hand away again. Instead, he grazed his finger lightly along the elegant line of her jaw, once, twice, three times, four, even after the strand of hair had fallen away.

At first, he thought he must be touching her so lightly that Clara didn't even notice he was doing it. Then he glimpsed a hint of pink blooming on her cheek and noted how the pulse at the base of her neck leaped higher. Her lips parted softly, and her chest rose and fell with her more rapid respiration. Grant noted then how his own breathing had hitched higher, how his own heart was racing and how heat was percolating beneath his own skin, too. When she turned her head again to look at him, her pupils were expanded, her cheeks were ruddy and her lips parted wider, as if she would absolutely welcome whatever he wanted to do. And what Grant wanted to do in that moment, what he wanted more than anything in the world, what he wanted more than he'd ever wanted anything in his life was to…

Slowly, he pulled his hand away from her face and settled it on his chest. "Your hair," he said, having to push the words out of his mouth as if they were two-ton boulders. "It…it was caught on your, um…your cheek."

Clara continued to gaze at him in silence, looking as if she couldn't remember any better than he did where they were or what they were supposed to be doing.

He tried again. "I just wanted to, um… I know how damned annoying that can be."

She nodded slowly, but said nothing for another charged moment. Then, softly, she told him, "Thanks. Yeah. I hate when that happens."

But she didn't stop staring at him. And she didn't stop looking sensuous and desirable and hot as hell. And he didn't stop wanting to…

He had to stop thinking about her this way. It really was ridiculous, his pointless preoccupation with Clara. He should be happy she was leaving in a few days. After she was gone, he could go back to being preoccupied with other things. Things that were actually important. Like work. And also work. And then there was work. And he couldn't forget about work. All of which were really important, something he wished Clara could understand. Maybe if she realized just how important his work was, she wouldn't be so quick to dismiss a position at Dunbarton Industries, working toward CEO, as a possible future for Hank. Who knew? Maybe the boy would end up being more like his mother than his father and actually enjoy running a business. Just because it might not be the business he originally wanted to run… Just because it wasn't, say, Keep Our Oceans Klean… Hank could adapt.

"It's good that you're here now, though," Grant told her. "And you know, it just occurred to me that the company holiday party is tomorrow night."

Which actually hadn't just occurred to him. He'd

known it was on his schedule for some time. And he'd thought about asking Clara if she wanted to come, but had decided she wouldn't want to because of her less than warm and fuzzy feelings about the corporate world. Suddenly, though, for some reason, inviting her seemed like a really good idea. For Hank's sake. Not for Grant's.

"It's a family friendly event," he added. "We encourage all of our employees to bring their spouses and kids. I'm sorry I didn't invite you before now. I wasn't sure you'd be interested. Mom and I go every year. Kind of necessary for us, me being the boss and her being on the board of directors. But you and Hank should come this year, too. You can see what Dunbarton Industries is really all about."

"You mean I can see what Hank's legacy could be," she amended.

"Okay, that, too," he admitted. "Maybe you'll see that it's not as joyless and relentless as you think."

She sighed softly, meeting his gaze earnestly now, something that somehow made her seem even more accessible than her heated looks had a moment ago. Something that somehow doubled his desire to reach for her.

He really, really had to stop thinking stuff like that.

"I truly am sorry about saying that, Grant. I didn't mean I thought you were like that."

Yeah, she did. But maybe her coming to the party would change her mind. Instead of saying that, though, he only said, "Apology accepted." Then, because she still hadn't accepted—or declined—his invitation, he asked, "So do you and Hank want to come to the holiday party with me and Mom?"

She hesitated only a moment—but it was still a moment, which was telling in itself—then replied, "Sure.

Why not? It's probably the only holiday party I'll get to attend this year. With grown-ups, anyway. I'm going to be swamped at the bakery after we get back." Then she smiled, and her distress seemed to evaporate. "Thanks for inviting us, Grant."

She was thanking him? For what? He was the one who had just received a gift in the form of her acceptance. And it was the nicest gift he'd received in years.

"It'll be fun," he told her. Which was something he always automatically said about the Dunbarton holiday party, even though he never meant it. This year, he did mean it. And for that, he was grateful to Clara Easton, too.

Okay, so the corporate headquarters of Dunbarton Industries wasn't as sterile and soul-sucking as Clara had assumed it would be before her first visit here with Francesca. So the main offices looked as if they'd been designed by Frank Lloyd Wright, with open spaces, organic lines, satiny woodwork and sleek Prairie School furnishings. So Grant made sure that a sizeable chunk of the company's profits went toward making its employees more comfortable and happier in their work environment. She still couldn't see Hank working here someday.

But then, she couldn't really see Grant working here today. As nice as the place was, and as upright, forthright and do-right as he was, he still seemed out of place here, even after having helmed the corporation for nearly a decade, and even though his employees clearly liked him. Francesca, yes, Clara thought. She was totally at home here, not just amid the polished, sophisticated surroundings, but also in flitting from one person to another, saying hello and chattering about their work and their families and ensuring that everyone was happy at their jobs in general and having a good time this evening. But Grant?

Although he, too, had spent much of the evening moving from one person to another to speak to them all, there had been no flitting or chattering on his part. He'd seemed reserved without being standoffish, serious without being stodgy and businesslike without being self-important. Which, okay, were all good traits for a boss to have.

He still seemed out of place here.

And Clara felt out of place, too, even having been here twice now. She just wasn't used to being in a workplace that was so…clean. Her professional environment was always scattered with utensils and dusted with flour and sugar. Stains in a rainbow of colors were an integral part of any shift. By the end of her workday, there was confectionary chaos to clean up, and she was a sticky mess. And she liked it that way. All of it.

She would never go into her workplace dressed as she had for the party tonight, in a formfitting, claret-colored, off-the-shoulder velvet cocktail dress and pearl necklace and earrings—even if they were faux. And black stilettos? Uh-uh. Not unless she wanted to break her neck on some spilled pastilles or frosting.

Grant, however, wore another one of his dark power suits and looked perfectly normal—if not quite comfortable—in it. His only nods to festivity were in his necktie—one that was dark red and spattered with tiny bits of holly—and a small boutonniere of evergreen and berries that his mother had affixed to his lapel before they left the penthouse.

He'd been much less restrained with the office decorations—or, at least, whomever he'd put in charge of decorating had been, but they'd obviously met with his approval. Everywhere Clara looked, she saw signs of the season. A giant Christmas tree in the corner was lit up like, well, a Christmas tree. A shiny silver menorah was ready for lighting when Hanukkah began. Not far from it was set up an mkeka for Kwanzaa, along with a kinara set to be lit the day after Christmas. She'd learned a lot about Kwanzaa as the room mom planning the holiday party for Hank's class last year and through orders at the bakery. And the oversize ice bucket with the magnum of champagne had to be for New Year's. Someone had even installed a plain metal pole for the observers of Festivus. The only decorations Clara hadn't been able to figure out yet were the—

"Pentacles?" she asked Grant, who had affixed himself to her side since concluding his rounds of guest-mongering. He was lifting for a sip from the tumbler of bourbon he'd been nursing all night before lowering it again to look at Clara with confusion.

"What pentacles?" he asked.

She gestured toward the display on the other side of the room near the rest of the holiday icons.

"Oh, those pentacles," he said. "For Solstice. The incense, too. Don't want to leave out the Wiccans."

"I wondered what that was I smelled."

"Mostly frankincense and myrrh, I think," he said.

"Which brings it all full circle," Clara replied with a smile.

She was about to say something more about how there really were a lot of December holidays when Hank ran up, clutching a misshapen paper star that was painted bright purple, sprinkled with neon pink glitter and tied with a chartreuse ribbon. He thrust it up toward her.

"Mama, look! Another ordament for our Christmas tree!"

"Or-*na*-ment," Clara corrected him automatically as she took the star from him, knowing she'd probably be correcting him another dozen times before Christmas actually arrived. "And it's beautiful, sweetie. I like the colors you picked."

"The or-*na*-ment lady helping us said we could pick whatever colors we want. I made another one that's orange and blue, but it's still drying."

Clara held up the ornament for Grant to see. "Now every year when we hang this on the tree, I'll think back on this moment and remember I was standing here with you when we got it."

It was true. Every year, when she or Hank hung it on the tree, she would be thinking fondly about the time she had spent with Grant this year, even if nothing ever came of it. She also knew she would be thinking about how she wished something *had* come of it, something that went beyond fondness, because that way, she would have another memory to carry with her.

Hank fairly beamed. "I made the other one for Grammy. Now she can think about me every year when she hangs it on her tree."

Without awaiting a reply, he spun around and ran back toward the room where the party organizers had set up the children's crafts. Which was just as well, since Clara had no idea how to tell him that his grandmother hired out their tree decorating, so she wasn't sure his star would even make it onto the Dunbarton tree. Though maybe now that Francesca had an original work of art from her grandson, she'd go back to doing their trimming the old-fashioned way.

"I guarantee you that Hank's star will be on our

tree every year," Grant said, clearly knowing what she was thinking. "And it will probably hang somewhere in Mom's office or bedroom the rest of the time."

Clara smiled. "Thanks. I kind of figured that, but it's nice to hear reassurance." She looked at the star again, then at the tiny cocktail purse she'd brought with her. "Now if I could just figure out what to do with it till we go home, so it doesn't get wrinkled. Well, any more wrinkled," she amended with a sigh.

"Here, let me have it," Grant said.

He took it from her hand and draped the loop of ribbon around his boutonniere, so that the garishly painted paper star—larger than his hand—dangled on his chest against his expensive suit for all the world to see. And if Clara hadn't already been halfway in lo— Uh, if Clara hadn't already been halfway enamored of him, that gesture would have finally put her there.

"There," he said. "That should keep it safe for the rest of the evening."

Yes, it should, she thought. Now if only Grant would do the same thing for her heart.

Nine

It was nearly midnight by the time the partygoers left for home. Hank was sacked before the car pulled away from the curb, so when they arrived back at the penthouse, Clara handed him over to Grant to carry upstairs. Hank murmured sleepily at the transfer, then looped his arms around his uncle's neck, nestled against his shoulder and fell asleep again. Clara tried not to notice how easily Hank curled into Grant or marvel at how much trust he had placed in him in such a short time. Instead, she battled another wave of affection for the man who had won that trust and showed such tenderness for her son.

Grant carried him effortlessly up to the penthouse and, after Francesca murmured her good-night to her grandson and gave him a kiss on the cheek, continued the journey back to Hank's...or rather, his father's—why did Clara keep making that mistake?—old bedroom and laid him carefully on the bed. Then she removed Hank's shoes and the little clip-on necktie decorated with snowmen that his grandmother had bought for him—she'd also bought his little man suit that was a miniature version of Grant's—and tucked him in. It was no problem to let him sleep in his clothes. Hank wouldn't be wearing them again before they went home. Tomorrow, she thought further. No, today, she realized when she noted the time on the little rocket ship clock sitting on the nightstand. Which had arrived much too quickly.

In fact, she might as well just leave Hank's new outfit here, since she couldn't see him having an opportunity on Tybee Island to dress like a tiny businessman—unless it was for Halloween. But she could see Francesca finding lots of reasons for Hank to dress like his uncle here in New York.

Clara swallowed against a lump in her throat, brushed back his dark curls and pressed a light kiss to his forehead. She whispered, "Good night, Peanut," which was the nickname she'd given him when he appeared on her first ultrasound looking like one, but which she hadn't used since she'd decided on a name for him, before he was even born. Then she turned toward the bedroom door to leave.

She was surprised to see Grant leaning in the doorway, waiting for her, but was happy that he had stayed. As exhausted as she was from the evening and the hectic week before it, she was entirely too wound up to sleep. Or maybe it was something else that had put her in that state. Some churning eddy of emotions that wouldn't stay still long enough for her to identify any of them, but which were pounding against her brain and heart with the ferocity of a tsunami.

"Nightcap?" Grant asked when she was within whispering distance.

"Oh, yes. Please."

She followed him to the library and waited while he fixed their drinks. He poured a bourbon for himself, then reached into the wine rack for what was sure to be another very nice red for her. But Clara halted him. A very nice red wasn't going to cut it for her tonight.

"I'll have what you're having," she told him when the bottle was barely halfway out of its slot.

He looked surprised, but tucked the wine back into its resting place and tugged free the cork from the bourbon again instead. She watched as he splashed a few swallows of the amber liquor into a cut crystal tumbler like his—at home, Clara would have poured a drink like that into a juice glass decorated with daisies whose paint was beginning to fleck—and looked at her for approval. She shook her head.

"I'll have what you're having," she repeated. "Same generous two-and-a-half fingers."

"Okay," he said, pouring in a bit more. "Funny, but I didn't take you for a bourbon drinker."

"Normally, I'm not," she said. "But nothing in my life has been normal since August Fiver showed up at the bakery."

And nothing in her life would ever be normal again. That, really, was the reason Clara needed something a little more bracing tonight. She didn't know if it had been seeing Hank dressed like a little millionaire, or how out of place she'd felt in Dunbarton Industries' offices, or how out of place she still felt here in the penthouse, or a combination of all of those things and a million more to boot. But tonight, more than ever before, Clara felt the need for something to dull a reality that was too fast closing in. Her son had become part of a world that wasn't her own, and he would be spending much of his future living a life that had nothing in common with hers. And it would be that way forever.

When Grant turned around holding both their drinks, looking as much a resident of this alien world as her son was now, Clara realized he was part of the problem, too. Because over the past week, especially the past few days, it had become clear that Grant didn't belong in this world, either. Not really. He may have been born to it, and he may be reasonably comfortable in it, but he wasn't truly, genuinely happy here. As a child, he'd had much different plans for himself, and passions that had nothing to do with the existence he was plodding through now. He was living his life out of obligation, not because it was the one he had chosen for himself. With each new day, that had become more clear.

But what was also clear was that he had no intention of leaving it.

Clara thought back to the way he'd been when he answered the front door upon her and Hank's arrival. Had that been only seven days ago? It felt like a lifetime had passed since she had stepped over the Dunbarton threshold. Grant's reception that day had been formal and awkward, and he'd seemed to have no idea how to react to Clara *or* Hank. Since then, he'd taught her about aquarium fish, had made jokes about Plu-toad and had lain on the floor, gazing up at the stars with her. And tonight, he'd hung a gaudy child's creation from his lapel as if it were the Congressional Medal of Honor. That first day, he hadn't seemed capable of laughter or whimsy. That first day, he hadn't seemed capable of happiness. But tonight…

She looked at the star, still dangling from his lapel,

then at the careless smile on his face. Tonight, he seemed very happy indeed. And Clara would bet everything she had in the world that it wasn't because the office holiday party had gone off without a hitch. It was because, at some point over the past few days, Grant had gotten in touch with something in himself that had reminded him what his life could have been like if he hadn't turned his back on his childhood to dive headfirst into adulthood decades before he should have. Maybe it was having Hank around that had done that. Or maybe it was something else. Clara just hoped Grant kept in touch with that part of himself after she and Hank were gone.

They made their way into the living room in time to see Francesca in front of the Christmas tree, admiring the star from Hank that she had hung on it front and center. She turned when she heard them approach, and she was smiling, too.

"You know," she said, "maybe next year we should put up the tree and decorate the house ourselves instead of hiring the service."

"I think that's an excellent idea," Grant told her.

He unlooped the star from his boutonniere and placed it beside the one Francesca had hung. "Just for now," he told Clara. "You can take it home with you tomorrow. But they do look good there together."

"Yes, they do," Clara had to admit. She was going to hate breaking the two of them up.

Francesca looked at Clara. "Maybe you and Hank could come for Thanksgiving next year," she said. "And we could all decorate the day after. That's when the service usually comes."

Clara started to decline, since it had been tough enough to swing a trip during the holidays this year. But the hopeful look on Francesca's face made her hesitate. The bakery was closed on Thanksgiving—and on Mondays, too, for that matter—and it wasn't especially busy the day after, since most people had so many left-overs and were out raiding the shopping malls. She could maybe close that weekend, too, without taking too big a financial hit. Things didn't really start hopping until a few weeks before Christmas. Her employees would probably like having the extra time off after Thanksgiving, too. It might be possible.

"Let me crunch some numbers," she told Francesca. "And look at the calendar for next year. I'll see what I can do."

Francesca smiled. "It would be lovely to have you both here. Grant and I usually go out for Thanksgiving dinner, since Mrs. Bentley has the day off. But we could have her prepare something the day before and put it all in the fridge. Then we'd just have to heat it up."

Clara shook her head. "I'll do the cooking on Thanksgiving." Hastily, she amended, "I mean, I *would* do the cooking on Thanksgiving. If we're able to come. Which I'll see if we can."

Francesca looked both delighted and a little appalled. "But that's so much to do! And you don't want to have to work on a holiday."

"It wouldn't be work for me," Clara said, knowing that was true. "I enjoy it. I always cook for Hank and me and some of our friends who spend Thanksgiving with us."

Funny, but she suspected that, as much fun as it was to cook for friends, she'd enjoy it even more cooking for family. Even if the Dunbartons weren't, technically, her family. They were Hank's family. So, in a way, that made them her family, too. Extended family. But still family. Kind of. In a way. More than anyone else had ever been family to her.

Francesca smiled again. "That really would be lovely," she said.

She told them both good-night and cautioned them not to stay up too late, because she had plans for Clara and Hank tomorrow before they headed to the airport in the late afternoon. Clara waited for the internal cringing that usually came with the prospect of enduring more of Francesca's gadabout tourism, but it never materialized. Interesting. Or maybe not. In spite of not belonging here in the Dunbarton world, Clara was beginning to kind of like it. New York had turned out to be not such a scary place, after all. And Central Park, right across the street, was as lush and bucolic as anything she'd ever found in Georgia. Hank could still climb trees here, even if he couldn't pick fresh peaches from them. And he could still go barefoot from time to time. And who knew? Maybe there were even fireflies in the summer that he could catch in a jar.

As she and Grant moved to sit on the sofa, he loosened his tie and unbuttoned the top two buttons of his shirt, then shrugged off his jacket and tossed it over the arm. Clara toed off first one high heel, then the other, immediately after sitting down. It was then that she noticed the additional gifts under the tree. The last time she'd been in here, there had been only the four she and Hank secretly placed there. Now there seemed to be dozens.

"Wow. Francesca's been busy," she said.

Then she noted that the tag on the gift nearest her was addressed to Hank from "Uncle Grant."

"She even did some shopping for you," she added.

Grant looked mildly offended. "Hey, I'll have you know I did my own shopping."

Clara was even more surprised. He hadn't asked her for suggestions as to what Hank would like. That first day, he hadn't even seemed to know how to talk to a three-year-old. Now he was Christmas shopping for one? He really had come a long way over the past week.

"I'm sure he'll love whatever you got him," she said.

"Yes, he will," Grant replied with complete confidence.

"It was nice of you to think of him," Clara said. Then she looked at the pile of gifts again. "It was nice of Francesca, too."

She didn't add that Francesca shouldn't have overdone it the way she had. Somehow Clara knew Hank's grandmother would always overdo it where he was concerned. Funny, though, how that didn't bother her quite as much as it would have a week ago.

"Hank won't know what to think when he sees that all those gifts are for him," Clara said.

"Well, not *all* of them are for him," Grant told her.

Right. There were the ones from Hank and Clara to Grant and Francesca under there, too. Somewhere.

"I just hope you and Francesca like yours from us as much as I'm sure Hank will like his from y'all."

Grant said nothing in response to that, only gazed at her looking… Hmm. Actually, he was looking kind of smug. Happily smug. Maybe he'd had more to drink at the party than she'd thought.

Clara lifted her own drink to her lips and sipped carefully, letting the bourbon warm her mouth before swallowing, relishing the heat of the liquor as it passed through her throat and into her stomach, spreading warmth throughout her chest. "Oh, yeah," she mur-

mured. "That's what I needed. It has been such a—"
She stopped before saying that it had been such a long
week. Because, suddenly, the week hadn't seemed long
at all. She and Hank really were leaving much too soon.
Finally, she finished, "Such a busy week."

"I guess you'll be happy to get back home," Grant
said softly. "Back to your routine."

Clara wanted to agree with him. And she did agree
with him. To a point. Yes, she would be happy to get
back to Tybee Island. She'd be happy for her and Hank's
lives to go back to normal. She'd be glad to get back
to work at the bakery. She'd even be glad to return to
their tiny apartment. Regardless of where or what it
was, there really was no place like home.

She should have been glad to be leaving New York.
But she actually kind of liked New York. Even more,
she kind of liked what New York had to offer. The parks
and museums and fun stuff, sure. And the lions at the
library and the pear blinis at the Russian Tea Room.
But more than any of those, Clara liked the Dunbartons.
Especially Grant Dunbarton. And even having only
been here for a short time, it was going to be strange
returning to the place where she had lived her entire
life. Because now she had experienced life away from
home. And strangely, life away from home, as weird
and foreign as it was, was starting to feel a little like,
well, home.

"Yes, it'll be nice to get back to Tybee Island," she
said. "But it'll also be..."

"What?" he asked when she didn't finish.

She sighed. "I don't know," she said honestly. "It
kind of feels like we'll be returning to a different place
from the one we left."

She was about to say more—though, honestly, she

still wasn't sure what she was thinking or feeling at the moment—when something over Grant's shoulder caught her eye. Beyond the windows, fat, frilly flakes of white were tumbling from the night sky.

"Oh, look, Grant! It's snowing!"

She set her drink on the end table and rose from the sofa, crossing to the window as if drawn there by a magic spell. Snow was magic. At least, in her part of Georgia it was. As rare a sighting as Santa Claus himself. The flurry of white seemed to pick up speed as she gazed through the glass, blowing first left, then right, then spinning in circles. Beyond the snow, the lights of New York sparkled merrily, making the scene even more entrancing.

She sensed more than saw Grant move alongside her at the window, but she couldn't quite tear her gaze away from the falling snow. Or maybe there was another reason she didn't want to do that, a fear that if she looked at him in that moment, she might very well succumb to the enchantment of the snow, of New York, of the Dunbarton world and of Grant himself. And Clara couldn't afford to be enchanted. Not by any of it. Because enchantments were only as good as their magic. And as bewitching as it was, at some point, magic always failed.

"It doesn't snow down in Georgia?" he asked softly.

She shook her head. And focused on the snow. Because it kept her from focusing on the soft velvet of his voice that was as magical as everything else.

"Not where I've lived," she told him, keeping her voice quiet, too. "Not much, anyway. For sure, it never did like this. I kind of hoped it would snow while we were here—for Hank, I mean," she quickly amended, even though it was only a half-truth, "but the weather was so mild when we got here, and then I didn't check again to see if it was going to stay that way or get colder." Not that it seemed to have gotten colder. On the contrary, it was getting warmer all the time...

But then, Clara hadn't checked a lot of things this week, she realized now. Not the weather, not the time, not—

She looked at Grant again. Not her heart. And now it seemed as if it might be too late for all those things. Unless...

Not sure why she did it, just knowing she had to, Clara cupped her hand over his cheek, pushed herself up on tiptoe and pressed her mouth to his. She had thought he would be surprised by the kiss. She certainly was, and she was the one who instigated it. But he returned it as swiftly and intimately as if it was something the two of them did all the time. Then he wrapped his arms around her waist and pulled her against him, seizing control of the embrace completely. And for the first time in her entire life, Clara knew what it was to feel as if she was home. Really home. In the place she belonged more than anywhere else in the world. Grant kissed her as if she were a part of him, a part he'd lost a long time ago and only just regained. He kissed her as if she was as essential to life as the air he breathed. He kissed her as if he couldn't not kiss her. So she looped her arms around his neck and kissed him deeper still.

She didn't know how long they stood there embracing in front of the window—maybe seconds, maybe centuries. She only knew she never wanted to move away from him again. He kissed her mouth, her temple, her cheek, her jaw, her neck. And when Clara tilted her head back to give him better access, he drew his mouth lower, along her bare shoulder and back again, over her collarbone and down her breastbone, skimming his lips over the top of one breast where it was revealed by her dress and then the other. She tangled her fingers in his hair and relished the feel of his warm breath against her sensitive flesh. Then she gasped when he cupped a hand over her breast.

He turned to move them out of the window, pressing her against the wall as he pushed his body into hers and kissed her more deeply still, covering her breast again, scrambling her thoughts and heating every part of her. When he raked his thumb over her nipple through the fabric, she tore her mouth from his and cried out. So he buried his head in the curve where her neck joined her shoulder and dragged open-mouthed kisses over both. Clara was so lost in sensation that she barely noticed when he dropped a hand to the hem of her dress. But when he tugged it up over her thigh, then her hip, and bunched it at her waist, she gripped the back of his shirt in both fists, holding on for dear life. Her legs nearly buckled beneath her, though, when he cupped a hand on her fanny over the lace of her panties.

"Oh, God, stop," she gasped. "Grant, we have to stop."

He lifted his head to look at her, and for a moment, it was as if he'd never seen her before and couldn't imagine how they had become so passionately entwined. Then realization must have come crashing down on him. Hastily, he removed his hand from her bottom and pulled her dress back down over her legs. But he didn't move away from her.

"Right," he whispered. His breathing was ragged and labored. "I guess it's not a good idea."

Clara smiled at that. "Oh, it's a very good idea," she assured him.

At least, it was right now. And *right now* was all she

wanted to think about. Because it was the only thing she could be absolutely sure of. And right now, she wanted Grant absolutely.

His gaze locked with hers. "You're sure?"

"Yes," she said. "This just isn't a good place for it. Let's go to your room." When he still didn't move, and only continued to study her face as if he couldn't quite believe she was real, she added softly, "Now, Grant. I want you now."

He nodded, then, with clear reluctance, pushed himself away from her. He took her hand in his and led her out of the living room and down the hall to the spiral staircase that led to the bedrooms below. Clara had no idea how she was able to make it without stumbling, so shaky was her entire body, but finally, finally, they made it to his bedroom. It was dark, save the soft blue light of the aquarium that threw wavy white lines on the wall behind it, giving the place an otherworldly aura that was strangely fitting. Clara felt as if she was in another world at the moment. One she never wanted to leave.

He closed the door behind them—locking it, she noted gratefully, clearly thinking about Hank sleeping so close by—then turned to her again. Before she could say a word, he pulled her back into his arms and kissed her, taking up exactly where they left off. Except this time, when he moved his head down to trail soft, butterfly kisses along her neck and shoulder, he tucked his fingers into the top of her dress and nudged it down to bare her breasts. As he covered one with a big hand, he dropped his other hand to her hem again, drawing the garment up over her thighs and hips once more. Blindly, Clara jerked his shirttail from his trousers and freed the buttons one by one, pushing it open so she could rake her fingertips over the warm skin beneath.

Grant Dunbarton may have been a workaholic, she thought as she touched him, but he clearly worked out, too. She traced the elegant cant of his biceps and triceps, then ran her fingers along the bumps of muscle on his shoulders, chest and torso until she reached the buckle of his belt. Instead of unfastening it, though, she drove her hand lower, over the swell of his erection beneath his trousers. He was already hard and ready for her. She need only unfasten his fly to enjoy him flesh on flesh. But she waited on that, pressing her hand against him to palm him through his clothing, marveling at how he grew harder still.

He pulled his mouth from hers and sucked in his breath at her caress, but didn't stop her. He only stroked her breast with sure fingers, thumbing the nipple and tracing the curve. Every time Clara moved her hand on him, he drew his thumb over her, until they were both panting with desire. Finally—quickly—she unbuckled and unzipped him, dipping her hand into his trousers and through the opening in his boxers to wrap her fingers around him. He was…oh. So hard. So stiff. So big. She drove her hand down the solid length of him, then pulled it back up again, loving the way his entire body reacted to the stroke. So she did it again. And again. And again.

Until he wrapped his fingers tight around her wrist and halted her motions. Until he told her, "Your turn."

Before she could object, he cupped his hands over both her shoulders and spun her around so she was facing away from him. Then he gripped the top of her zipper and lowered it until he could push her dress down over her hips and legs to puddle around her ankles. Her bra went just as quickly—a simple flick of his fingers did it—then he pulled her against him, back to chest, and looped an arm around her waist to anchor her there. Good thing, too, since the heavy weight of him pressing into her fanny through her underwear made her legs go weak.

He dipped his head to her neck again, skimming his lips lightly along her shoulder, then moved his free hand back to her breast. For long moments, he only held her close and caressed her, then he moved his hand lower...and lower...and lower still, easing his fingers into the juncture of her thighs. Then he was touching her there, through her panties, fingering the damp fabric and folds of flesh beneath, pushing and pulling to create a delicious friction she never wanted to end. As she grew wetter, he ducked his hand under the lacy garment and rubbed her more insistently, until his fingers were sliding against her and in and out of her with an easy rhythm. Clara matched it with her hips, pushing back against him when he entered her and levering forward when he withdrew, her bottom rubbing his erection with every motion.

As they moved that way, his breathing became as ragged as hers. Then he was pulling her panties down along with his trousers, rolling on a condom and sliding himself between her legs. Finally, he pushed himself into her as easily as he had done with his fingers. Only this time, he filled her deeply. She sighed at the sensation of him inside her. So full. So thorough. So complete. She had forgotten how good it felt to be joined to another human being in the most intimate way possible. Oh...so good. She picked up the rhythm, once more, taking all of him. He opened his hand over her back, splaying his fingers wide, and pushed her forward, bending her at the waist so he could enter her more deeply still. All Clara could do was go along for the ride.

He pumped her that way for long moments. Then, just when she thought they would both go over the edge, he slowly—and with clear reluctance—withdrew. They shed what little clothing remained and made their way silently to the bed. He shoved back enough covers to make room for them, then sat on the side of the bed and pulled Clara toward him. When she was sitting in his lap, straddling him, he pulled her breast to his mouth and tongued its sensitive peak. Then he moved to the other. Then back to the first, sucking her deep into his mouth and raking her with his teeth. As he did, he traced the delicate line bisecting her bottom, up, then down, then up again.

Just when she thought she would explode with wanting him, he pulled his mouth away from her breast to look at her face. She threaded her fingers through his hair and gazed into those blue, blue eyes, nearly drowning. She wanted desperately to say something. Something he needed to know. Something she needed to tell him. But she couldn't find a single word to tell him how she felt. So she kissed him, long and hard and deep, and hoped it would be enough.

He cupped her face in his palms and kissed her back, with a gentleness and tenderness that was at odds with their steamy passion and the carnality of their position. Sex had never been like this for Clara, a balance of hot and sweet, of need and generosity, of take and give. It had always been too much of those first things and too little of those last. Until now. And now...

Grant moved his hand between her legs and began the sweet torture of his fingers again. Oh, *now*. She never wanted to leave this bed. This room. This place. She never wanted to be with another man again.

Just as that thought formed, he lifted her up and over his heavy length again, entering her more deeply than ever. As he curved his palms gently over her bottom, she twined her fingers possessively around his nape and her legs around his waist. Their bodies merged as one a second time, each complementing the other perfectly, each completing the other irrevocably. He was hers. She was his. At least, for now.

In one last, fluid motion, Grant turned their bodies so that Clara was lying beneath him. He braced his elbows on the bed by each of her shoulders and dropped his thumbs to her jaw. Then, as he caressed her face and gazed into her eyes, he buried himself as deeply in her as he could go. She wrapped her legs around his waist again and lifted her hips to meet him, sliding her hands down his slick back to hold him there. Over and over, he thrust into her. Over and over, she opened to him. Then, as one, they came, each crying out in their climax before slowly descending again.

Grant rolled his body to lie on his side next to her. He smiled as he looped a damp curl around his finger, and kissed her one more time. Sweetly this time. Chastely. As if the whole world hadn't just shattered beneath them.

And it occurred to Clara in that moment that *right now* with Grant would never be enough.

Ten

Grant awoke the way he did every morning—alone in his bed during the dark hours just before dawn, to the beeping of his alarm clock. No, wait—that wasn't actually true. Yes, he was alone in his bed, and yes, it was still dark, and yes, he had to slap his hand down on the alarm to shut it off. But usually he woke up rested and clearheaded and ready to rise from bed, then immediately launched into a mental rehearsal of all the things he had to do once he arrived at work. Today, he was anything but rested and clearheaded, and the last thing he wanted to think about was work. The first thing he wanted to do was make love to Clara again. Then he wanted to spend the rest of the day thinking about her. And work? No way. He'd much rather spend the day with Clara. Doing whatever they felt like doing. Even if that was nothing at all. And then he wanted to go to bed with her at day's end and make love with her again. Then he wanted to do the same thing the next day. And then the one after that. For weeks and months and years on end.

Oh, this wasn't good. Grant needed to wake up the way he always did. Because that was the way he lived his life. Every day. All day. Day in. Day out. One day at a time. If he ever strayed from his routine…

Well. He just might not make it through the day.

He rolled onto his side and stared at his aquarium, its pale blue night-light a soft counterpoint to the tumble of thoughts bouncing around in his brain. Normally, the sight of his fish gliding about in blissful ignorance of the world and its constant pressures made Grant feel calm. Normally, watching the slow parade of myriad colors and elegant motion put him in touch with a part of himself where lived all the merriment, fancy and simplicity he'd stowed away decades ago and never allowed to roam free. Normally, that was enough to keep him going for another day. But this morning, watching the dappled, indolent to-and-fro, he knew that a momentary reconnection with what he'd left behind wouldn't be enough. Because he'd awoken alone. And in the dark. And where those two things had never bothered him before, this morning, they bothered him a lot.

He rolled over again, to the other side of his bed, where Clara had slept for an hour or so, before waking up and telling Grant she needed to finish the night in her own bed. Before Hank awoke and went looking for her, she'd said. Before his mother awoke and saw the door to the guest bedroom open and the bed still made. Clara had kissed him one last time on the mouth, and smiled in a way that could have meant anything. Then she'd slipped back into her dress and stolen away like a thief in the night. Which was appropriate. She was a thief. She'd stolen something from Grant he might never get back. Especially if she took it with her when she returned to Georgia.

He lay his head on the pillow where hers had been only hours ago and inhaled deeply. Yeah, there it was. The faintest hint of cinnamon. The merest suggestion of ginger. And something else, too, something that was inherently Clara Easton. Something that could never be bottled the way spices were and opened whenever he wanted to enjoy it. Something he would never find anywhere else, no matter how hard he tried. And now she was going home, and she would be taking that with her, too.

He looked at the clock on the nightstand. 6:17 a.m. Seventeen minutes later than he always got up. Usually, by now, he was in the shower, readying himself for another day of running the family business that he'd never really wanted to run, but which had to be run by someone in the family because...

Because. He was sure there was a reason for that. He was sure there had been one when he shouldered the responsibility so many years ago. But he couldn't quite remember now what that reason was. There was one, though. There must be. He was sure of it.

He couldn't take the day off, as much as he might want to. Even being the boss had its limits. Grant had a meeting this morning that had been on his agenda for weeks, a meeting that had been nearly impossible to organize in the first place, thanks to the schedules of everyone involved. He couldn't miss it. He was the one who had called for it. Clara's plane didn't leave until this evening. He could head home after the meeting and be back in time to take her to the airport himself. It shouldn't go past noon. One at the latest. Two at the outside. Even that would give him a two-hour window to get her and Hank to LaGuardia. But he wouldn't make the meeting at all if he didn't get a move on and get into the shower now.

He rose and shrugged on his robe, then headed for the bedroom door to make the short trip up the hall to the bathroom. Instead of heading left, however, he turned right. He strode past the closed door to Hank's room and paused at the one opposite. He started to knock quietly, then figured he probably shouldn't wake Clara. Just because he wanted to see her before he went to work. Just because he was having trouble thinking about anything but her. Just because it would be nice to have a smile from her to carry with him for the rest of the day.

He should leave her a note, he thought. To tell her he would be home in time to take her to the airport for her flight. No, to tell her how much he'd enjoyed last night, and that he would be home in time to take her to the airport for her flight. There was just one problem. How could he possibly convey how much he'd enjoyed last night in a note?

He'd call her before the meeting. There would be just enough time after he got to work. It would be good to hear her voice, anyway. It had been hours since he'd heard her voice. Eons. Just hearing her say "Good morning" would be enough to get him through the day. At least until he saw her again this afternoon.

For a moment, Grant only stood with his open palm against the bedroom door. He really wished he didn't have to go to work today. He couldn't remember a time when he'd ever felt that way. But he did today. Then he reminded himself that the sooner he got to work, the sooner he could call Clara. So, morning planned, he headed down the hallway again.

So he wasn't going to call or anything.

Clara looked at the pile of bags by the Dunbartons' front door—the two she and Hank had arrived with and two additional, newer and bigger ones for him, thanks to his and Francesca's negotiations about what he would be taking back to Georgia with him right away because he just couldn't live another minute without it. Would that Clara was able to do the same. But Grant probably would have objected to being packed up in such a way. Then she looked at Hank, who was giving his grandmother one final hug before they left. Then she looked at Renny Twigg, who had arranged for a car from Tarrant, Fiver & Twigg to take Clara and Hank to the airport, the way Gus Fiver had arranged for one to pick them up there…had it only been a week ago? Funny, Clara felt as if it had been a lifetime since she and Hank showed up at the Dunbartons' front door like a couple of secondhand relations.

"We should get going," Renny said gently. "Traffic and all."

Clara nodded. "Hank, sweetie," she said, "it's time to go."

Francesca had wanted to come to the airport with them, but Clara had told her it was okay, that if she did, it would be hours before she got back home, and that it would be easier for all of them if Renny had the driver just drop her and Hank off. A long goodbye wouldn't be good for any of them.

Of course, if Grant had been there—or if he had, oh, Clara didn't know…maybe offered to drive her and Hank to the airport himself, say—it would have been a different story. She would have taken the longest goodbye she could get from him. Evidently, though, he wasn't going to give her a goodbye at all. He'd already left for work by the time she woke up, and she hadn't heard a word from him all day. No text. No call. No email he could have fired off from his desk. She hadn't expected sonnets from him. Or even a haiku. But she would have liked to hear *some*thing. A few words or emojis to let her know he was thinking about her and that last night had meant more to him than...

What? she asked herself. The way she was thinking, it almost seemed as if it had meant something more to her than...well, whatever it had meant. A physical reaction to a sexual attraction they'd both been feeling all week. Her attempt to exorcise a bundle of turbulent emotions that had been bouncing around in her head and heart demanding release. An effort to make sense of something that defied sensibility. She still wasn't sure what last night had been, so how could she expect Grant to think it was more than any of those things? Still, it would have been nice if he had at least acknowledged that it happened, if he had let her know he'd thought about her once or twice today.

Because she sure hadn't been able to stop thinking about him.

She'd hated leaving his bed to return to her own last night. But she had been afraid Hank might wake up fretful, which he sometimes did after going to bed so late following a highly stimulating event like the party. And if he'd come looking for her in the guest room and seen she wasn't there, or that her bed hadn't been slept in...

Well, she just hadn't wanted to make him think she wasn't there for him when he needed her, that was all. And at the other end of the spectrum, if Francesca had seen that Clara never went to her own bed, she might have thought something was going on between her and Grant that would…

Well, she just hadn't wanted to make Francesca think there was a chance Clara was falling in love with her other son, thereby ensuring her grandson would be linked to her more decisively than before. Even if Clara was kind of falling in love with Francesca's other son.

That was obviously a pipe dream. Grant hadn't even waited around long enough to tell her good morning. How could she have expected him to be here to say goodbye?

"You've been wonderful, Francesca," Clara said as she and Hank finally ended their hug. "I can't thank you and Grant enough for making us feel so welcome here."

"But you *are* welcome here," Francesca told her, sounding vaguely alarmed that Clara might not think so. "Any time, under any circumstances. I'm already making plans for your next visit. Can you believe we never made it to a show?" she added, sounding scandalized. "How can anyone come to New York and not see a show? You must come back as soon as it's convenient."

Clara forced a smile. "We'd like that."

She looked down at her son, who had moved away from Francesca to affix himself to Clara's side the same way he had that first morning. Except this time, any apprehension he might be feeling was because he didn't want to leave. Neither did Clara. But there was no way she could take any more time from the bakery, and Hank needed to get back to his routine before he forgot what it was.

"Maybe you could come visit us on Tybee Island," she told Francesca. That way, there wouldn't be the risk of running into Grant. "Hank's preschool has spring break in April. Come down for Easter. I'll bake a giant ham and a sweet potato casserole, and we can have bacon-braised green beans and cheese grits for sides and banana pudding for dessert. How does that sound?"

"It sounds like my cholesterol will go through the roof," she said with a smile. "But I'd like that very much. Maybe I can convince Grant to take time away from work to come with me."

Clara started to object, then decided it wouldn't be necessary. There was little chance Grant would take time away from work for anything. So Clara said nothing at all.

"I'll miss you, Grammy," Hank said.

His eyes grew moist, but he swiped at them with one fist. It was all the encouragement Francesca needed. Her eyes went misty, too. Not that Clara could blame either of them. She felt like crying herself. Though maybe for a slightly different reason...

Hank broke away for one more hug, then Renny Twigg echoed their need to leave. At the same time, the doorbell rang, heralding the arrival of their driver and a doorman with a luggage cart to carry down the bags. Francesca promised again to pack up the gifts under the tree and ship them to Tybee Island tomorrow, though Hank had opened one this morning after she had insisted. Inside had been a plush, squishy planet Jupiter, complete with arms, legs and smiling face, that Hank hadn't put down since. He'd also kicked science to the curb by naming it Plu-toad.

The flurry of bag-gathering and final goodbyes dried whatever tears were left, and then Hank, Clara and Renny were in the elevator with the driver and doorman, heading down to the lobby. Clara surreptitiously checked her phone as they descended, to see if there were any new texts. There weren't. Then she checked to see if she'd missed a call. She hadn't. Email? Nope.

Then the elevator doors were opening, and she and Hank and Renny were following their driver and luggage toward the door. Once through it, Clara looked up and down Park Avenue. But there was no handsome, dark-haired, blue-eyed man in a power suit running toward them shouting, "Clara! Wait!" the way there would have been if this were the Hollywood version of the story. So once she and Renny were settled inside the car with Hank fastened into his car seat, there was no reason for her to look back.

This wasn't Hollywood, Clara reminded herself as the car pulled away from the curb. And, like Hollywood, it wasn't real life, either. The Dunbarton family lived in a way few people were able to manage, in a world few people ever entered. Hank may have been her ticket into it, but she would always be here temporarily, and always as a fringe dweller. She would never be a permanent resident, and she would never really belong. It was time she started accepting that and went back to the life she knew. The life to which she'd been born. The life where she belonged. The life she—usually—loved.

The life that would never be the same again.

Grant sat at the head of the giant table bisecting the boardroom of Dunbarton Industries, glaring at the man seated halfway down the left side. Not just because he was the reason this meeting had gone on hours too long—so long that Clara and Hank must, by now, be on their way to LaGuardia without him—but because he had spent the majority of those hours contributing to the very problems Grant had called this meeting to avoid. He hadn't even had a chance to slip out and call

Clara to tell her goodbye, because the meeting had become so contentious he hadn't wanted to risk making it worse by breaking for anything. He'd even arranged for lunch to be brought in, because by that point, he'd been worried everyone might leave and not come back.

It had been that way since the moment Grant arrived at work. He'd exited the elevator to hear voices raised in controversy and had entered the reception area to see that two members of the meeting had already arrived and were engaged in not-so-civil debate over the only item on the agenda—Dunbarton Industries' acquisition of an abandoned wharfside property in an area a group of historians had halfheartedly slated for revitalization once upon a time. But the Waterfront Historical Society had been forced to scrap the project when the economy tanked, and the massive warehouse complex had been sitting vacant and decaying for years. Grant wanted to buy and revamp all of it to make it a safe, environmentally friendly work and living space, the centerpiece of what could potentially become an industrial-retail-entertainment-residential complex. He'd invited a handful of the city's leading developers to attend today, knowing a number of them would be interested. All he should have had to do was iron out a few minor problems that might arise with Dunbarton Industries and some of the other involved parties, and they'd be set. He'd figured that part of the meeting would take, at most, a couple of hours. Then it would just come down to a matter of which developer could offer the most attractive package to all involved, which should have taken no time at all.

Unfortunately, the developer he had considered the best fit for the enterprise had, unbeknownst to him, already had a number of run-ins with the Waterfront

Historical Society that had either ended very badly or hadn't ended at all. Both sides had used the first part of the meeting to try to iron out those problems instead of the ones they were supposed to be talking about. It hadn't taken long for everything to escalate to the point where now *everyone* at the table was bickering about past wrongs. Every time Grant thought he had things back on track, someone—usually the man half-way down the table on the left side—drove everything over a cliff again. Try as he might to point out how well his proposal could benefit most of the people present, most of the people present preferred to talk about—or argue about—something else instead.

Sometimes Grant felt like the world of big business was populated by nothing but three-year-olds. No, wait. That wasn't true. Hank Easton was three, and he behaved better than anyone currently seated in the Dunbarton Industries boardroom. At this point, it was beginning to look as if Grant would never see Hank or his mother again.

Then again, whose fault was that? Grant was the boss here. He was the one who called the meeting. He could have also called an end to it any time he wanted today and then tried to reconvene at some point when everyone was more amenable to making progress. But he hadn't. Instead, he'd done everything he could to en-sure it *didn't* end. At least not until he achieved the out-come from it he hoped—no, needed—to achieve. The acquisition of that property could ultimately be worth billions in company revenue. It could be the biggest success Dunbarton Industries ever had. They weren't the only company interested in it. Waiting even a week could mean another company swooped in and grabbed all that potential for itself. Grant needed to act quickly if he wanted this thing to succeed for them. And, hey, wasn't success the whole point to life? Wasn't that why he worked as hard as he did? So that the family business would thrive?

Yes, yes and yes. At least, all of that had been true before. Before Clara Easton and her son showed up at his front door.

He looked at the group of people surrounding the table again. There were eight of them. At least four of them besides him would be affected positively by this arrangement if he could pull it off. Those four represented dozens more who would become involved further down the road and benefit. From those dozens, hundreds more. In the long run, if this project worked out the way Grant envisioned it, it would create thousands of jobs, most of them permanent. A dangerous public eyesore would become a safe, walkable area with green space. Property values would rise. Investors would reap rewards. From a business standpoint, it could be a massive success.

From a business standpoint.

But what about other standpoints? What about other successes? Clara was on her way home to Georgia, and Grant hadn't even told her goodbye. And who knew when he would see her again? She had a business to run eight hundred miles away from the one he had to run here. They both had commitments to their work that were equally demanding. And hell, it wasn't as if they'd made any commitments beyond those. It wasn't as if they'd made a commitment to each other. On the contrary, Clara had told him last night she wanted him "now." Maybe that meant she wanted him in the heat of that moment. Maybe it meant she only wanted him that once. She had left his bed to return to her own afterward. Sure, she'd had a good reason for it. But she had left his bed to return to her own.

And he hadn't stopped her.

No commitment. From either of them. No promises. No plans. No talk of the future at all. But that was good, right? It meant neither of them had expected anything more from last night than one night. Yes, they would see each other again eventually. They would have to, since Hank was a part of the Dunbarton family now. But Clara...

Clara had offered no indication that she wanted to be part of the family, too. At least in any capacity beyond the one that included her son. She'd had to get back to Georgia for her work. She couldn't come visit New York over Hank's spring break because of her work. Grant couldn't visit her in Georgia for the same reason. Both of them had put their work first. Both had made that their priority.

He could still end this meeting now. If he hurried, he might even make it to LaGuardia before her plane left. If nothing else, he could call for a ten-minute break that would allow him to retreat to his office long enough to call Clara and tell her goodbye.

He glanced at his phone, sitting on the table to his right. It had gone off a number of times during the meeting, but always with notifications he knew he could attend to later. Not once had it gone off with a notification from Clara. She was leaving without telling him goodbye, too.

And maybe that, really, told Grant everything he needed to know. About himself and Clara both.

"All right," he said to the group seated around the table. "Let's start from the top. Again."

* * *

"Did you have a good time in New York?"

It took a moment for Clara to realize Renny Twigg was speaking to her. Hank had been chattering at the other woman ever since the car pulled away from the curb, recapping everything he'd done with his grandmother over the past week. And Renny, bless her heart, had hung on every word. Funny, but Clara wouldn't have pegged her as someone who would respond as well as she did to a toddler. Not that the high-powered lawyer life seemed especially fitting for her, either. Renny definitely gave off a vibe that made her seem as if she was more suited to a life away from suits. Clara had no idea why, but somehow, she pictured her being the kind of woman who would be happier in a job where she could corral livestock.

"I did," Clara said in response to her question. Because she had mostly had a good time in New York. The fact that her heart had been broken there at the end didn't change that.

"Was it your first time?" Renny asked.

Once again, it took a moment for Clara to reply. Because for a moment, she thought Renny was referring to something that really wasn't any of her business and frankly should have been obvious with Hank, the fruit of Clara's loins, sitting right there. Then she thought maybe Renny meant something else that still wasn't any of her business—jeez, Clara was just realizing herself that it was hard to recognize the first time you fell in love with someone. But of course, Renny was talking about coming to New York.

"Yes," she said. "It was my first time." In New York *and* in love.

"What did you think?" Renny asked.

"It's not what I expected at all," Clara told her. Not New York. And not love, either.

"It always surprises people," Renny said.

Well, Clara could certainly understand why.

"They expect it to be this huge, overwhelming thing where they'll never feel comfortable or safe."

Yep, that was pretty much the way Clara had always thought about love.

"They're scared they'll get robbed or end up so lost they'll never be able to find their way."

Exactly, Clara thought.

"But after a while, they realize it's not so scary. And it can be...*so* wonderful. And then people can't believe they waited so long."

Well, Clara didn't know about that. New York, sure. She agreed with everything Renny said. But love? Not so much. Because Clara had indeed been robbed while she was here—Grant had stolen her heart. And she was certain she'd never be able to find her way back to the place where she was before she came here. And she definitely didn't know if she'd ever feel comfortable or safe again. Not the way she'd felt comfortable and safe with Grant. So for now, the score was New York, one, Clara nil, and Grant...

Well, Grant had certainly scored, she couldn't help thinking. Unfortunately, it was looking as if, now that he had, he wanted to drop out of the game completely.

Gee, he had a lot more in common with his brother than she'd thought.

Their arrival at the Delta terminal of LaGuardia airport came way too quickly for Clara's comfort. So much for New York City's notorious rush hour traffic. Then again, when she glanced down at her watch, it was to see the trip had taken them more than forty-five minutes. She'd just been so lost in her thoughts, she hadn't even noticed the passage of time.

With any luck, it would continue to pass quickly once she and Hank were back on Tybee Island. She'd just have to make sure she threw herself into her work once they were home. Work was good for passing time and keeping her focused on the things she should be focusing on. And it was good for making her forget the things she should be forgetting about.

Things like the pale blue eyes of a man who refused to let himself be happy.

Eleven

Clara did her best to take a page from the Grant Dunbarton workaholic playbook when she got back to Tybee Island, throwing herself into the ebb and flow of the bakery to the point where she thought about nothing else—save Hank, of course. But now that Hank was inextricably tied to the Dunbartons, thinking about him—and talking to him and being with him—meant she would always be thinking about them, too. And thinking about them meant thinking about Grant, which then made her all the more determined to throw herself into her work and think about nothing else save Hank.

Which only started the cycle all over again.

It was exhausting, frankly, trying to focus on nothing but work, from the moment she rose in the morning until she switched off the light at night. She didn't see how Grant lived this way. No wonder he'd been so joyless.

No, she told herself. That wasn't right. He wasn't joyless. At least, he hadn't been at the end of her time in New York. But more than a week had passed since she and Hank had left, and Clara hadn't heard a word from Grant *or* Francesca, save a quick call to the latter immediately after their arrival back in Georgia to let her know they'd arrived home safely. Silence from Grant hadn't surprised her. Well, okay, it had. Part of her had thought he was starting to break away from the relentless CEO who had usurped his childhood and get back in touch with the little boy who'd wanted to head up a nonprofit called KOOK. But silence from Francesca? The mother of all grandmothers? That had surprised Clara a lot. She would have thought Francesca would be calling every day.

But it was Christmas, she reminded herself, and people got busy over the holidays. She knew that, because she felt as if she was single-handedly catering every holiday party on the island. Francesca was probably just so bogged down in entertaining and being entertained that she didn't have a minute to spare for anything else.

The timer on the big oven went off, pulling Clara's thoughts back to the matter at hand—snowman cookies. Two dozen of them. For starters. They were destined for the holiday party at Hank's preschool tomorrow—the last day of class before Christmas, which was scarcely a week away—along with dozens more. Clara had baked Christmas tree cookies, too, along with dreidel cookies and kinara cookies and New Year's baby cookies and pentacle cookies.

Well, who knew? She didn't want to leave out the Wiccans. Or maybe she'd just been thinking too much about the last night she'd spent in New York. And not just the party at Dunbarton Industries. About making love with Grant, too.

But she wasn't going to think about him, she reminded herself. Again. She was going to think about work. Unfortunately, going back to work meant looking at two dozen Rudolph cookies she'd frosted earlier that were set enough now to go into one of the cases in front. And seeing those just reminded Clara of Grant all over again, and how she'd told him the story of the Rudolph ornament in her former foster home that she'd nurtured and repaired and hadn't been allowed to take with her when she'd been reassigned. What had possessed her to tell him that story? She'd never told that story to anyone.

Stop. Thinking. About. Grant. She really did need to focus on work. Which, naturally, made her think of Grant. Gah.

Hastily, she picked up the tray with all the Rudolphs staring at her and carried them out to the shop. The bell over the door was ringing to announce yet another customer—gee, she hoped they could fit another customer in here, since the shop was already full to the gills—so Clara threaded her way through her three busy salesclerks, toward the cookie case, to tuck the tray into an empty spot. And wow, there were a lot of empty spots. At this point, she was going to be baking until midnight Christmas Eve if she wanted to have something for Hank to leave out for Santa.

She slid the Rudolphs into the case and was heading back to the kitchen to retrieve more cookie dough from the walk-in when Tilly cupped a hand over her shoulder to halt her.

"Is it too late for someone to place a special order?" she asked.

Well, it was, Clara thought. Christmas was only eight days away, and she'd taken on about as many special orders as she could manage for what was left of the holidays. But depending on what the customer wanted, she might be able to squeeze in one more.

"Maybe," she told Tilly. "What does she need?"

"It's not a she," Tilly said. "It's a he."

The comment immediately carried Clara back to the day Gus Fiver entered the bakery and turned her world upside down. She pushed the thought away. Her world would get back to normal, she told herself. Eventually. Someday. Okay, it would get back to a new kind of normal. She just had to figure out what it was going to be.

"All right, what does *he* need?" she asked Tilly.

Before the salesclerk could respond, a voice—much too deep to be Tilly's, but infinitely more familiar—replied loudly enough to be heard over the buzz of the customers, "You, Clara. He needs you."

The crowd went silent at the announcement, every head turning to see who had spoken. When Clara followed their gazes, she saw Grant on the other side of the counter, standing head and shoulders above and behind the group of women who had been waiting to be served. Though they now seemed much more interested in waiting to see what happened next. They parted like the Red Sea to reveal him from head to toe, then, as one, looked back at her, to see how she would respond.

"Uh, hi," was all she could manage.

The heads turned toward Grant.

When he realized they had an audience, he grinned. With absolute, unadulterated joy and genuine, unbridled playfulness. Which, Clara couldn't help thinking, wasn't exactly the reaction she might have expected from a joyless, relentless, workaholic CEO. He wasn't dressed like one, either. He wasn't even dressed like a CEO on vacation. No, Grant Dunbarton looked like any other island local, in knee-length surf jams, a Savannah Sand Gnats sweatshirt and Reef Rover shoes.

"Hi yourself," he greeted her in return.

If Clara didn't know better, she could almost believe it was Brent Dunbarton, not Grant, who had ambled into her bakery. Except for one noticeable difference. She'd never come close to being in love with Brent. But the man standing in her bakery now?

Well, there was a time when she had thought she might love him. Before he'd chosen his work over his own happiness. Before he'd chosen his work over her and her happiness, too.

The heads had turned again, to get Clara's reaction. But she wasn't as comfortable being the center of attention as Grant obviously was, so she tilted her head toward the door that connected the shop to the kitchen in a silent invitation for him to follow her. The disappointment of the crowd was palpable—a couple of women even *Aww*ed or muttered *C'mon, Clara*, but she didn't care. She was happy to provide them fodder for their holiday parties. Not so much to provide fodder for the coconut telegraph.

She trusted Grant to follow, because she wasn't about to turn around and look at all those speculative faces. The only speculation she was interested in the moment was her own. What was he doing here? Dressed the way he was? Why hadn't he called first? Or texted? Or, jeez, sent up a flare? He could have at least given her some small notice, so she wouldn't have to be greeting him in her once-white-now-rainbow-hued baker duds of formerly white pajama pants, T-shirt and head scarf. And— *Oh, no*, she thought when she saw her wavy reflection in the silver door of the walk-in—her now rainbow-hued face, too.

She grabbed a towel from the counter and did her best to scrub the remnants of frosting and chocolate from her face. Then she spun around to face Grant... who had somehow become even more handsome and sweet looking in the handful of seconds it had taken them to escape the crowd.

But she wouldn't succumb to a sweet and a handsome face. Especially one that couldn't even be bothered to call her. Still, he had come here for something. She couldn't imagine what, but the least she could do was hear him out.

"Okay, let's try this again," she said. "Hi."

He grinned again. "Hi yourself," he repeated.

An unwieldy silence ensued. Mostly because Clara had no idea what to say. Seriously, why was he here? And how could a man who had rejected her in favor of a corporate conglomerate still stir so many feelings inside her she didn't want to feel? She needed to get back to work. *Best wind this up ASAP.*

In spite of that, she asked lamely, "So... How's things?"

He chuckled. Honestly, she could just smack him for looking so—

Happy. Oh, God, he looked *happy*! How could he be so happy when he'd made her feel so lousy?

"Um, different," he said.

She gave his outfit an obvious once-over. "So I see."

He sobered a little at that. "Yeah, I guess I look a lot like Brent, don't I? I didn't mean to—"

"No," she interrupted him. "You don't. I could easily tell the two of you apart. You look nothing like Brent. You *are* nothing like Brent. But you know, for all his

faults, at least your brother followed his heart and fulfilled his dreams and lived his life in a way that made
him happy. But you… You'd rather…"

When she trailed off without finishing—mostly because she was afraid she wouldn't be able to do that
without revealing just how hurt she was—he asked,
"I'd rather what?"

She shook her head, still not trusting her voice or
herself to answer.

He took a step closer. She took one in retreat. He
frowned at her withdrawal.

"C'mon, Clara," he said softly. "I'd rather what?"

She inhaled a deep breath, crossed her arms over her
midsection, arrowed down her brows and tried again.
"You've buried your dreams, Grant. Your life is nothing
but your work. It means more to you than anything—
anyone—else ever will. And your heart? Jeez, there's
a part of me that sometimes wonders if you really have
one."

He winced at that last, closing his eyes and turning his head as if she really had smacked him. Then he
opened his eyes and looked at her again, his gaze un-
flinching this time.

"Why didn't you call me to tell me goodbye before
you left New York?" he asked.

It wasn't exactly what Clara had expected him to say.
Nor was it a question she knew how to answer. So she
only said, "What?"

He shrugged. "Why didn't you call me to tell me
goodbye before you left New York?"

She studied him a moment longer before answering.
Finally, truthfully, she said, "I don't know."

He was right. She could have called him to say
goodbye. Or she could have texted him. Or sent him

an email. She just…hadn't. She'd been too focused that day on getting herself and Hank packed and ready for their flight back to Georgia. Because she had needed to get Hank back into his routine here, and because she had needed to get herself back to...

Work. She hadn't been able to spend any more time in New York, because it had been too important for her to get back to the bakery, which would be incredibly busy before Christmas. There was no way she'd have any time for things like…

But she had a business to run, she reminded herself. And she had employees who depended on her for their weekly paycheck. It wasn't that she had chosen her work over Grant. It was that…

She sighed again. It was that she had chosen her work over Grant. Because her work was important. Because she had obligations. Because people were relying on her.

"Wow," she said softly. "I guess we're both a couple of workaholics, aren't we?"

He nodded slowly.

"And I guess we've both sort of lost sight of what's really important."

He took another step toward her. This time, Clara didn't take one in retreat. "So what are we going to do about that?" he asked.

She shook her head and replied honestly again. "I don't know."

He studied her again. But he didn't say anything.

So Clara did the only thing she could. She nodded toward his shirt and said, "I thought you were a fan of the Savannah Clumps of Kelp."

He expelled a single chuckle—it was a start. To what? She still wasn't sure. But something inside her that had been wound too tight gradually began to unknot. "What, those losers?" he asked. "Nah. The Sand Gnats are where it's at."

She braved a smile. "I'm glad you've seen the light."

Now he sobered again. "Yeah, I have. And not just there. A whole lot of things have come clear to me in the last couple of weeks." He took a step closer. "Thanks to you."

Clara took a step closer, too. He was trying to meet her halfway. That was a little better than a start. The least she could do was help him get there. "Oh?" she asked.

He moved closer. "Yeah."

She did likewise. "In what way?"

By now, they were nearly toe-to-toe and almost eye to eye thanks to Clara's height in her work clogs. There was still an inch or two separating them—both distance-wise and stature-wise—but it wouldn't take much work for either of them to close that distance. Should either of them want to. Grant seemed to be trying to do that. Clara wished she knew how to help him.

"I resigned from Dunbarton Industries," he told her. "Effective immediately."

Her mouth dropped open at that. She couldn't help it. He might as well have just told her there was a giant squid dancing the merengue behind her, so astonishing and fantastic was the announcement.

But all she managed for a response was, "You did?"

He nodded. "I did. But it's taken some time to get the kinks ironed out of the arrangement, and I didn't want to say anything to anybody until we knew it would all work out the way we wanted it to."

"We?" Clara asked.

He nodded again. "Mom and I. She's taking over as CEO." He smiled again. "Effective immediately."

Clara's mouth almost dropped open again. Almost.

But somehow that news wasn't quite as astonishing or fantastic as the other had been. She'd seen for herself how at home Francesca was at the Dunbarton Industries holiday party, and how much the employees liked her. And she'd seemed to really know what she was doing when she went over the budget. From what Clara had seen, Francesca had been passionate about her ideas for keeping the company running. She'd been one of its vice presidents once upon a time. And she was a Dunbarton. Why shouldn't she run the family business if she wanted to? As long as she wanted to.

"And Francesca is okay with that?" Clara asked. Even with all the other considerations, Francesca hadn't exactly been Ms. Corporate America while Clara and Hank were in New York. She'd been much more Ms. Grandmother America.

"Yeah, she is," Grant said. "The minute you and Hank left, she started feeling aimless. She wanted to call you two the day after you left but was afraid you'd think she was being intrusive and trying to insinuate herself into your life down here or trying to bribe Hank to tell you to bring him back to New York."

"I would never think that about Francesca," Clara protested.

When Grant raised a single brow in response, she relented. "Okay, maybe I thought that about Francesca at first," she admitted. "But that was just the leftover foster kid in me being insecure and fearful."

"Anyway," Grant continued, "When I told her I wanted to step down from the company—hell, not just step down, but leave it completely—she just kind of smiled and told me it was about time. She'd always known following in my father's footsteps hadn't made me happy, but that it had seemed so important to me, she didn't question it. She said she'd always known I would finally figure out what I really wanted and pursue that instead, and wondered what took me so long. She'd always planned to take over for me when that happened, and that was why she stayed on the board and kept a finger in what was going on in the business. Now she'll have something to keep herself occupied so she won't miss Hank as much." His grin returned as he added, "And, unlike *some* CEOs, she'll be the kind of boss to give herself time off for the things she really wants to do. Like be with her grandson when he comes to visit."

Clara grinned back. "So you finally figured out what you want?"

"Yeah," he said. "And I wonder what took me so long, too. Then I remembered what I want didn't come into my life until recently, so there was really no way I could know that. Not until…"

"Until?" Clara asked.

"Until I met you."

She smiled.

"And Hank, too," he added. "But mostly you. The day you left New York was just…" He blew out an exasperated breath. "Actually, the day at work was like every other day. Except that by the end of the day, I knew there was something besides work I could be doing. Something I *wanted* to be doing. A lot more than I wanted to be working, that's for damned sure. Before you, Clara, I could pretend my work gave my life purpose, that it was important …" He made that exasperated sound again. "Before you, I could pretend I was happy," he finally said. "Or, at least, happy enough."

"'Happy enough' doesn't sound like happy," Clara told him.

"It's not. I know that now. I could never go back to

being the workaholic CEO after that night you and I…"
He halted, and there was something in his eyes that
made her heart turn over. "I couldn't be that again after
that night, Clara. Hell, I could barely maintain that ve-
neer the whole time you were in New York. The minute
you stepped through the door, you started reminding
me of too many things I'd made myself forget. Things
that made me happy when I was a kid. Things that made
me want to be happy as an adult. But I felt like I could
only go after those things if I turned my back on what
I thought was my duty to my family. I'd completely forgotten about my duty to myself."

Wow, did that sound familiar. Not the part about being
reminded of a happy childhood, since Clara's hadn't exactly been that. But the part about wanting to be happy
as an adult. She, too, had convinced herself she was
"happy enough." She had Hank and a reasonably solid
business, and she kept a roof over both. But she'd been
pretty driven to ensure things stayed that way. She put
nearly every hour of her day into something else—being
a mom or being a businesswoman, thinking she could
only do those things by not thinking about herself. When
was the last time she had been just Clara? Really, had
she *ever* been just Clara?

"So what will it take to make you happy as an adult?"
she asked him.

"I think you already know that," he said.

"I'd still like to hear you say—"

"You," he told her without hesitation.

"—it."

Wow, this was going to work out so well. Because
the only other thing she needed to be happy—happy
for just Clara—was Grant.

She took a final step forward that literally brought

her toe-to-toe with him. And then she tipped herself up on her toes and pressed her mouth to his. It was a glorious kiss, even better than the first one they'd shared. Because this time, there was no doubt. This time, there was only...

Joy. Complete, unmitigated, take-no-prisoners joy. And if there was one thing the world needed more of at Christmas—and one thing Clara and Grant needed more of forever—it was joy. Lucky for both of them, it could be found just about anywhere. All you had to do was look for it. Or, if you were very lucky, joy came looking for you. Clara was just glad it had found her and Grant both.

It was snowing in New York City, Clara saw as she sipped her coffee and looked out the window of the Dunbarton living room onto a Central Park that was completely cloaked in white. Which was the way it should always be on Christmas morning. The way it would be every morning, if she had her way, since she would forever associate snow with the first time she and Grant made love. Of course, she'd also think about him whenever she saw stars in the sky. And whenever she saw Christmas cupcakes. And fish. And chambered nautiluses...nautili...those macabre floaty things. And—

Well, suffice it to say she'd think about Grant a lot. Pretty much all the time. Since they would have so much time now that they had *both* abandoned their workaholic ways. Clara had even closed the bakery for the week between Christmas Eve and New Year's Day—with full pay for everyone—so that she and Hank could spend the holiday here in New York with family. It was the least she could do in light of Grant's giving up his position at Dunbarton Industries to ensure his own happiness. Learning how to let herself be happy was, hands down, the nicest gift she'd ever received for Christmas.

She turned to look at the pile of unopened packages under the tree behind the dozens of toys Santa had left for Hank. She didn't care what was in any of those boxes. Nothing could be better than what she'd already been given this year. Even so, she couldn't wait to open them. Just looking at them made her feel like... Well, like a kid at Christmas. Grant wasn't the only one who'd needed to get in touch with his inner child. Clara had needed to do more of that, too. Because she wanted to give that child the kind of Christmas she'd never had as a kid. And from here on out, she would.

True to her baker's hours, Clara had woken before everyone else. So the coffee was made, cinnamon buns and gingerbread were warming in the oven and a fire was crackling in the fireplace. She was still in her pajamas—the red flannel ones with snowflakes, identical to Hank's, which was a Christmas tradition for the two of them—and planned to stay in them all day. That was a Christmas tradition she and Hank had created, too, one she would introduce to the Dunbartons along with the handful of others she and her son had forged. They'd go nicely with the Dunbarton traditions, especially now that Grant and Francesca were planning to return to the ones they'd embraced when Grant was a child. Hence the cinnamon buns and gingerbread warming in the oven, something Grant had told her they'd always had for breakfast on Christmas morning when he was young.

As if conjured by her thoughts of him, he strode into the living room with a cup of coffee in one hand and a hunk of gingerbread in the other. He was still disheveled from sleep in dark green-and-gray-striped pajama bottoms and a gray T-shirt. Next year, he and Francesca would be in red flannel with snowflakes, too. This family was going to be so obnoxiously sweet in their Christmas clichés that they would gag a cotton candy factory. Because they all had a lot of time to make up for.

Grant smiled when he saw her, then held up the gingerbread. "I couldn't wait for breakfast. It smelled so good. Just like Christmas."

Clara smiled, too. "The best Christmas ever."

"How do you know?" he asked. "It's barely started."

"Doesn't matter," she told him. "I'm with you. That makes it the best Christmas ever."

He seemed to suddenly remember something, because he hurried to the end table and placed his coffee and gingerbread there, then headed for the tree and began sorting through the gifts.

"While it's just you and me," he said, "I want you to open your present. Well, one of them," he amended. "This one," he added when he located a small square box wrapped in shiny green paper.

"Okay, but you have to open one from me, too," she told him as she moved toward the tree to look for the one she wanted. She found it quickly, flat and rectangular and wrapped in bright blue. Like the ocean, she'd thought when she saw the paper. The perfect color.

For a moment, each of them knelt on the floor by the tree, clutching the packages they'd picked out for the other, knowing this first official sharing of Christmas gifts was a precedent for them both. She and Grant were family now. Not just through their ties to Hank. But through their ties to each other. Family ties didn't have to be blood ties. They didn't even have to be matrimonial ties. They just had to be love ties. And even if neither of them had said the actual words yet, she and Grant definitely had those.

As if decided upon in their mutual silence, they each thrust their present at the other. Then, as excited as children, they began to tear the paper to shreds.

Grant finished first, opening the box to reveal a trio of coloring books Clara had bought him at the New York Aquarium, along with a box of twenty-four crayons. At first she feared he was disappointed, because he just looked at them without touching them, not even to see what other books were under the one on top, which was called *Under the Sea* and was the most generic of them. She really wanted him to see the one on the bottom, called *I Am a Cephalopod*, because that was the one she knew he'd love most.

"Are there not enough crayons?" she asked. "I mean, I almost got the sixty-four count, but that just seemed so ostentatious, and I—"

"It's perfect, Clara," he said. When he looked up, his expression was absolutely sublime. "The twenty-four pack has Blue Green, which is what I always colored the ocean. And there's Red Orange for the firemouth cichlid. And Brown for the nautilus. You've given me everything I could ever need. Everything I could ever want."

She smiled at that. It was all she could ask a gift to do.

"Now finish opening yours," he told her.

She looked at the box in her lap, now completely freed of its wrappings. It was plain white, with no logo to give her a hint as to what it might be. Carefully, she pulled off the top. Beneath it was a crush of glittery tissue paper. She withdrew that, then caught her breath at what lay under it. A Christmas ornament. Rudolph the Red-Nosed Reindeer. Plastic with chipped paint and a red nail polish nose and a gigantic lump of dried glue on one leg. Her eyes filled with tears as she lifted it from its tissue paper bed, as carefully and reverently as she would have held the Hope Diamond.

"I can't believe you found this," she said. "Where...? How...?"

He grinned. "Would you believe...the magic of Christmas?"

She grinned back. "Gee, I don't know. Something like this would take an awful lot of magic."

"Then how about a friend who's a high-ranking member of the NYPD and married to a social worker who knew who to call to ask about your file in Georgia and find out who you were living with when you were about eight years old?"

Clara shook her head in astonishment. "I can't believe you went to all that trouble."

"It was no trouble," he said. "Anything to make you as happy as you've made me."

"It doesn't take a Christmas ornament to do that," Clara told him.

"Maybe not," he said. "But if it makes you happy..."

"Very happy," she assured him.

"Then I'm happy, too."

Clara was leaning in to give him a kiss when she heard the patter of Hank's feet slapping down the hall toward them, followed by an admonishment from Francesca to *Wait for me!* Hah. Not likely. No kid could wait on Christmas morning. Not for anything.

"You started without me!" Hank exclaimed when he saw the evidence of opened presents littering the floor between her and Grant.

But he was quickly sidetracked when he saw the toys from Santa scattered about and headed immediately for those. Francesca dove in right behind him, her merriment rivaling his.

Clara and Grant looked at each other. And she knew in that moment that they were both thinking exactly the same thing. Yes, they had started without Hank this morning. But that was just the point. They had *started*. Finally. They had started living. They had started loving. They had started feeling happy. Really happy. The kind of happy that only came in knowing they were exactly where they wanted and needed to be. Exactly where they belonged.

"Merry Christmas, Clara," Grant said softly. "I love you."

Had she just been thinking that learning how to let herself be happy was the nicest Christmas present she'd ever received? Gee, she'd been mistaken. That was the second best. The first was sitting right across from her, telling her he loved her.

"Merry Christmas, Grant," she replied just as quietly. "I love you, too."

And amid the ringing of laughter and the aroma of evergreen and gingerbread, closing their fingers over remnants of their childhood that now brought joy instead of sadness, Clara and Grant shared another kiss. The first of many they would share that day, Clara was certain. The first of many they would share in life. Because that was what life was. Sharing. Living. Loving. From one Christmas morning to the next.

Epilogue

Clara was dabbing a smile on the last of two dozen dolphin cookies when the bell over the entrance to Cairns, Australia's Bread & Buttercream rang for what she hoped was the last time that day. Not that she didn't love every customer who came into her new digs in Clifton Beach, but with the grand opening just over and Christmas only a few weeks away, the bakery had been super busy. Not to mention she had to pick up Hank from Camp Australia for first graders—um, she meant year one students—in… She glanced at the clock. Yikes! Less than an hour! Where had the day gone?

She placed the dolphin on a rack with the rest of his pod to let the glaze dry, setting aside a basket of papayas that she and Hank had picked fresh from a tree in their backyard yesterday evening, before they'd stopped to catch fireflies in a jar. Then she wiped her powdered sugar–dusted hands on her white apron, which was easier now with the soft curve of her baby bump rising up to greet them.

She let her hands linger over the slight swell. She was barely four months along, but had already outgrown some of the maternity clothes that were supposed to last till her third trimester. Her ob-gyn had said they were going to do an ultrasound next visit to check for twins, something that still made Clara a little woozy. Still, Hank was already jazzed about the prospect of having one little brother or sister. Two might very well make him Big Brother of the Year.

She heard her salesclerk Merindah greet someone out in the shop with a happy hello, then Grant's voice replying. Clara smiled. He always took off from work early on Friday to meet her at the bakery so they could pick up their son together and get an early start on the weekend. He'd been busy, too, the past few months, getting his nonprofit, A Drop in the Ocean, off the ground. Okay, so it wasn't as catchy as KOOK, but it still had a certain whimsy. And already, it was making a difference. The organization employed more than two dozen people here and would be helping to preserve ecosystems from the Great Barrier Reef to Nauru and the Cook Islands. For starters. Although Grant had chosen Cairns for the main headquarters, he wanted to open satellite sites for A Drop in the Ocean all over the world. He'd funded much of its endowment with his own money, but thanks to his contacts in the business world, he had regular—and substantial—donors from some pretty major sources. Yes, he was the organization's CEO. But he wasn't relentless. He wasn't joyless. He wasn't a workaholic. He'd taken his dream and run with it. The same way Clara had. But they both made sure those dreams included time for each other.

After ensuring that Merindah and Clara's part-timer, Susan, didn't need anything before the bakery's close, she kissed her husband and asked him about his day.

"It was busy," he said.

But it was a good busy, Clara could tell. In the three years she'd known him, she'd never seen Grant look happier than he had since their move here. His skin was burnished from his time outdoors, and his hair was longer and less tidy than it had been when she first met him. He lived in Hawaiian shirts and cargo shorts these days, and he drove an old, army-green Range Rover—the kind he'd said he always wanted to have when he was a kid. They lived in a big house on the beach, surrounded by palm and mango trees, where they were occasionally visited by dolphins and goannas. The night sky was amazing, completely different from the one Hank had learned when he was little. And there were a million things to explore. It was a better life than Clara could have ever imagined for her son. Or for Grant. Or for herself.

She'd never been happier, either.

Grant helped her into the Ranger Rover, and after she was buckled in, he placed his hand gently over her swollen abdomen. "Think there are two in there?" he asked.

"Could be," Clara told him. She suspected there were, and her doctor had all but said she thought there were, too, but they wouldn't know for sure until after the ultrasound. "Would you be okay with that?"

He grinned. "Totally. And Mom would be beside herself. She's sure if we just have enough kids, one of them is bound to inherit the CEO gene, and then she can train them to follow in their grandmother's footsteps."

Clara grinned, too. "So she's coming next week, right?"

He nodded. "She gave herself the rest of December off, flying back to New York the day after New Year's."

Clara looked up at the sun and swiped at a trickle of perspiration on her neck. "Guess we can forget about white Christmases here." Funny, though, how that didn't bother her as much as she might have thought it would.

Grant closed the door of the Range Rover and, through the open window, told her, "We don't need snow to make it Christmas."

And that was certainly true. They could make it Christmas anywhere. And everywhere. And not just at Christmastime, either. All it took was knowing they were together. Exactly where they wanted to be. Exactly where they needed to be. Exactly where they belonged.

* * * * *

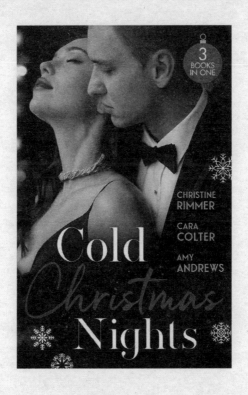

LET'S TALK
Romance

For exclusive extracts, competitions and special offers, find us online:

f MillsandBoon

🐦 @MillsandBoon

📷 @MillsandBoonUK

♪ @MillsandBoonUK

Get in touch on 01413 063 232